TATTOO OF THE
BLACK ANGEL

A E KIRK

Published by Three Acre Books

Copyright © A E Kirk, 2015

Layout by Guido Henkel

This book is dedicated to Tim for his bravery, Anna for her enthusiasm, Cris for her never-ending hopefulness to see this book published and Ness for her fearless tenacity.
You have all been my inspiration.

CHAPTER ONE

"That's the thing with magic. You've got to know it's still here, all around us, or it just stays invisible for you."

— *Charles de Lint*

WHEN I LOOK BACK ON IT ALL, I THINK, 'HOW DID THIS all take place?' and 'What would've happened if I'd never gone into the tattoo parlour?' Naturally all the events that happened after that now feel like a dream or a fading memory. Did I really train in a secret base? Did I really fight with mythical creatures? And did I really fly? I try to imagine life without magic, but find it dull and boring. Of course, magic is real, but only to those who believe.

So I suppose you could say that my new life began when I was invited to May Cup's Café one blustery October afternoon by some university friends. The café was quaint and bright and was usually quite busy during the weekend. Nestled down a little narrow lane between some small miners' cottages, in the heart of rural West Wales, the café sat opposite the only tattoo parlour in town called Needle and Ink.

Approaching the café, I saw my friend Amanda heading in the same direction. She glanced at the tattoo parlour as we went past it. Her friends Beth and Heather tagged along.

'Amanda, don't be such a baby,' Beth snapped at her. Amanda sighed heavily, looking forlornly at the window. It was ridiculous. There was nothing to see in the window apart from local advertisements. Two stood out in bright yellow flyers: "Wanted, Solo Singer for new and upcoming Punk Rock Band, the Shazmo's", or "Snake's for Sale, £130 O.N.O". It was a weird parlour run by a very heavily tattooed bald man.

Pulling my coat tightly around me to ward against the cold, I followed the girls into the warm aromatic-smelling café and saw a small clean table by the window.

'Oh hey, Tara,' Beth called waving at me. 'Come and sit with us!' Amanda and Heather turned around; they gave me a small smile and beckoned me over. Taking my coat off, I sat opposite Amanda, she seemed sulky but I didn't ask why.

'Have a look,' Beth smiled, passing me the menu. 'We already know what we want; we come in here a lot.'

I had a quick flick through and decided on something chocolaty. 'Special hot chocolate it is.'

Sitting directly in front of a still pouting Amanda, I tried to infiltrate their conversation about the upcoming Halloween Dance at the University. I wasn't planning on going, but I found their conversation interesting.

'I was thinking of like a partly decapitated witch,' Beth said indicating her neck. 'I could have a deep fake wound on the side of my neck with blood oozing from it, ooh that would be so cool.'

Heather smiled. 'Defo! And what about the witch costume you are going in?' she asked her. 'Are you going for bare legs or those weird stripy leggings?'

'They aren't leggings, they are very long socks,' Beth told her. 'And maybe, I don't know, depends on how cold it is. But I will be taking my black and purple dress.'

'Ooh, it sounds so pretty,' I said butting in.

Beth and Heather turned to look at me and comically blinked in shock. 'Oh, it's so fantastic!' They said together, happy that I was joining in.

Amanda caught Beth's attention. 'Isn't there a costume competition?' Finally contributing to the conversation.

Happy that Amanda was talking, Beth nodded, 'Yup and I hope I win it.'

Laughing, I shook my head.

'So what are you going as?' Amanda asked me as a waitress came round and took our orders, scribbling them down, she took the menu and left. The conversation continued, uninterrupted.

I shrugged, 'I don't know. I didn't really want to go if truth be told.'

'Please do, it'll be fun.' Heather smiled.

'Well... I won't be going as a witch.' I laughed. Beth winked at me again. 'I've never been good with costumes,' I told them truthfully. 'All of the formal dances I had at school were stuffy and boring. I didn't take much interest in them.'

Heather cocked her head and stared into space. 'A mummy would be interesting... Oh, I have it!' she practically screeched, 'you could go as an Egyptian goddess! It's perfect, plus you have the long raven black hair too, so no need for hair dyes. Also, I have the perfect costume for you. I have this gold slip,' she said in a whisper so that other customers around us wouldn't hear. 'And I have a load of gold jewellery you could borrow and Beth is great with makeup, oh this is coming together nicely.'

'I do like that idea, Heather.' Beth nodded in approval.

As I thought of a way to get out of this disastrous party, I noticed the girls went quiet, their attention turning quickly to someone seemingly much more important than a dance. 'Oh my god, its Henry Simmons,' Heather whispered as she and I looked over towards the door.

Amanda and Beth remained facing forwards as Henry Simmons, the most gorgeous guy in the entire second year, and probably the university, walked into the café. My eyes flicked up to look at him carefully and, strangely enough, his eyes found me. I had seen him quite often around the campus. Sometimes I'd see him alone in the sports hall where he'd come to practise squash. Though most of the time, he'd seem uncomfortable to be near me. And yet other times he'd be accompanied by his girlfriend at the Student Union. But whenever he was close, I couldn't help but feel those weird butterflies in my stomach. And when he didn't notice, I'd steal a glance at his eyes; they were like a deep pool of water, endless and mystifying. He was the epitome of tall dark and handsome.

I snapped back to reality and found that I'd been staring at him. He frowned at me a little, and then after a quick glance at the girls around me, walked past our table and sat down at the back of the room, not saying a single word.

'One day, he shall be mine,' Beth said, her eyes watching him constantly.

Snorting, I said, 'Yes when pigs fly and he dumps Jennifer, then he can be yours.'

Beth and Amanda were leaning so far to the right to get a peek at Henry that they nearly smacked into one of the waitresses who was carrying a tray full of drinks. The door then opened again and there was Jennifer Ladle, a very petit mousey brown haired girl with soft hazel eyes. I'd heard she was a pleasant girl but was possessive.

'Move in, move in!' Heather told Beth and Amanda quickly but, it was too late. Jennifer saw exactly who the girls were staring at and came in for the kill.

'Can I help you two with anything?' Jennifer asked in a sweet manner as she waltzed right up to our table. I felt my face blush and I tried to find something other to stare at than her leering, cold eyes, but there was nothing on our table that was interesting enough.

Amanda and Beth immediately turned bright pink in embarrassment.

'No, we're fine thank you,' Heather told her smiling.

'Uh huh, well if I catch you lot looking at my boyfriend there will be trouble,' she spat then walked over to Henry.

'Well, it could have been worse,' I said letting out a huge sigh.

The waitress came to our table carrying our drinks and the conversation about Henry was instantly dropped for fear of Jennifer eavesdropping. So the next topic was university courses, and instantly the girls were intrigued by me.

'What is it you do?' Amanda asked me, drinking her drink slowly while trying to catch Henry and Jennifer's reflection in the napkin dispenser. I didn't really want to get onto the topic of my course. Not that there was anything wrong with it, but sometimes I found myself placed in a situation where people thought I was too stupid to apply for a "real" course.

I drained my special hot chocolate, giving me a perfect excuse to leave if necessary and clearing my throat, I replied, 'It's a BA in Sport and Exercise Science.'

The girls were clueless. I hadn't really known them very well, so they were curious about me. They were really acquaintances, meeting them in town now and again and also at our Student Union.

'Wow, well as long as you're getting good exercise.' Beth smiled. Unable to extend the conversation about me, I decided to let them off the hook and leave them to finish their drinks.

'Well hey, pop round some time for a chat when you're free,' Amanda suggested.

'Yeah, we live on Cedar Road, Flat 4D, it's the blue door, can't miss it,' Heather added.

'Sure, that sounds fun.' I bobbed my head like some demented pigeon and taking the empty cup back, I paid then left the café in a hurry. However, as I walked down the street, I had barely taken ten steps when I heard the café door open behind me and a voice call out, 'Hey.' But as I turned round to see Henry looking at me, the café door opened once more, and Jennifer appeared angry. Without waiting for her, Henry instantly began to walk off.

'I know you fancy her!' Jennifer began to follow an ill-tempered Henry, who had his hands in his pockets with his shoulders hunched. I moved out of the way and hid by the doorstep of the tattoo parlour so they wouldn't see me. 'I saw her looking at you just now, and I've seen you stare at her from across the room. Since you spotted her a fortnight ago you always seem to be there when she's there. It makes me sick!'

'I'm not stalking her,' he said bitterly. 'And it doesn't make you sick, it makes you jealous.'

'I can't be around you anymore. If you can't devote your attention to me then I've had enough! I want you to leave me alone!' She stomped past him and began to walk up the lane towards where I was standing.

I didn't want her to see that I had been eavesdropping on her argument, but where to go? I saw the door handle to the tattoo parlour. A bell rang above me as I opened the door and darted inside. The door closed just in time to watch Jennifer walk by. She was crying. I felt sorry for her, but I didn't have time to ponder on her and Henry's break-up then, as suddenly I heard a loud bang behind me. Jumping a mile in the air, I spun around and saw two men in front of me. One was a bald man who was nearly completely covered in tattoos. He was standing behind a counter that was laden with books that were about mythological creatures. The second man wore a smart brown suit and a bolo tie. I had never seen them before.

'How prophetic,' the bald man laughed gruffly.

The second man gave him a short nod and came towards me. I had a bad feeling about this and backed away, pressing myself up against the door, fumbling for the handle.

'I ain't gonna hurt ya little lady,' he said in a South American accent. He stopped short and looked at me, his eyes lit up. 'I didn't take ya for a girl who wants tattoos, so the logical question is what brings ya in here?'

I wasn't going to tell him the truth. I mean, who runs into a shop that they wouldn't normally go in just to escape being seen by a crying girl? It doesn't make sense, so I lied. 'Er, I was cold.'

'Ah,' the American nodded. 'Well, I suppose it is a little cold outside.'

'I'm sorry; I'll go.' I found the door handle.

'Actually,' the Texan man began, 'Tara, I'd like you to stay.'

I stopped; my hand was about to pull the door open. Turning around, I stared at him curiously. 'You know me? Are you from the university?' My mind tried to come up with reasons on how he knew me. I had never seen him before but maybe he knew one of my lecturers? They both chortled. I guess he didn't know me from the university.

'I know your parents,' he said with a small smile. 'I had a chat with them a while ago, you see, I actually came up here to have a word with you.'

'You talked to my parents?' That confused me. My parents were out of the country, had been for several months on business, they weren't back for weeks. 'Oh, well my parents didn't tell me you were coming.'

The American turned to look at the bald man and with a small nod to him, the man left us alone.

'My name is Mr Maynard.' He smiled. 'Your parents and I are old acquaintances. They believe, as well as I, that you have the potential to be part of a special group of people with very interesting abilities.'

'Abilities?' I frowned, thinking that they had shown him my exam results from school.

'Indeed, however time is running out and I need an answer now.' He shrugged and turned away from me, leaving me hanging.

'Well, what would I be doing? Is this like MI5 or MI6 or something with computers and spying? I don't think I'd be good at anything like that. I'm really not that intelligent and-.'

'This is nothing like it.' He cut me off, glancing at the mythological creatures books on the counter. 'It is a secret, but I need you to be part of the group. Without you, it's useless.'

That was putting a lot of pressure on me. I was in the second year of university; I hadn't finished my course yet. I couldn't just drop everything without first thinking it through thoroughly.

I watched him move to the counter and pick up a thick silver ring and place it on his right index finger. His eyes then turned and looked past me to see Henry Simmons peer into the shop. Henry and Mr Maynard locked eyes and nodding, Henry headed off. It looked very odd.

Shaking my head I pulled the door open, a cold breeze wrapped around me in seconds. It was a very weird offer, and the guy was giving me the creeps. 'I'm sorry but I can't give you a decision now.'

He sighed. 'I'm sorry t'hear that.' He came towards me and offered me a card. 'Please call me though when you have changed your mind.'

Hesitating, I accepted it and placed it in my pocket. There was no way I was going to call him, and I suspected he knew the same thing.

'It has been nice meetin' ya, Tara,' he said, moving towards me to pull the door wider. Peering out of the shop, I saw Henry at the end of the lane. With his hands in his pockets, he stared at me, unmoving. 'I do hope I'll see ya again,' Mr Maynard offered his hand.

I shook it and suddenly yelped. Withdrawing my hand, I noticed a small pinprick of blood that formed on my palm. 'What the he…' I barely managed to say as the room turned to liquid before my eyes. The last thing I remembered was seeing Henry run towards me and the melted ground fly towards my face. Just before I fell to the floor, all the lights went out.

★ ★ ★

When I woke up, I was in a dimly lit room that resembled a hospital room from the cold war. There were bland grey concrete walls and ceiling, no windows and one heavy metal grey door with a small hatched glass pane.

My back was killing me; it felt as though I was being stung by hornets over and over again. The pain was making it difficult to breathe. I was also extremely thirsty and hungry. I didn't know what the time was, where I was, what day it was, and I was so scared that thinking about my current situation made me cry. What the hell was happening to me?

One thing I knew for a fact was that for some unknown reason, I'd been kidnapped. But to make this scenario strange was that I wasn't being held down and shackled to the bed. There really was no need. I was unable to move because of the intense pain that was relentlessly pulsating in my back. I was already rendered useless. Whoever had kidnapped me, they were sure that I wasn't going to make a run for it.

Moving slightly, I felt some wrapping around my back and chest. It seemed as though they were taking care of me, but what had they done to me? I hadn't experienced pain like this before. Sure, I'd pulled a back muscle once or twice and that was painful enough. But if I had to guess, it felt like my back was sliced open and poorly stitched back together.

Not wanting to provoke my sore back, I turned my head gently to the left. I saw an old grey plastic chair in the corner next to the closed metal door but saw no small table with a jug of water, which most hospitals are meant to provide. I needed to talk to someone; I needed help.

'Hello,' I managed to croak, my voice was barely audible. Gently placing my hands beneath me, I pushed myself up. Though the pain in my back flared up, it was manageable. After a few minutes of panting through the pain, I was on all fours on the bed though my head still felt quite woozy.

'Please don't move. You'll damage yourself.' A woman's voice sounded from somewhere above me. She had a slight American accent and didn't sound nasty, but then again she was a kidnapper. Could she and the Texan, Maynard, be in league with each other?

I closed my eyes and tried to focus and clear my head. I wanted answers. 'Who are you? Where am I? What have you done to me? Please let me go!'

'You are safe,' she replied, giving me no additional information.

From fearing the unknown of what they were going to do with me, I began to cry again. I didn't ask for this, I didn't even agree to be part of Maynard's stupid group. I hadn't even given him my decision. He didn't even bother to wait! My back twanged again, and I yelled out in pain. 'Why does my back hurt?' I asked through gritted teeth, hoping that she could tell me that much.

There was a pause before the woman spoke softly again. 'You have undergone a procedure.'

'A procedure for what?' I snapped. My eyes flung open and inhaling deeply, I turned round to search where the voice was coming from, and then found it! Up in the corner on the far right-hand side was a small camera and a speaker next to it. They had been watching me.

'I cannot answer that question,' she said softly. 'Please lie down; you are only prolonging the healing process.'

Gingerly I let myself lay on the bed and remained still. Any sudden movement caused my back a great deal of pain, and I was never one for pain. The woman became quiet and I tried desperately to get some sleep but whatever drug they had given me had quickly disappeared from my system and now I was wide awake and wanted nothing more than to run away and call the police.

Sometime later and having the unbearable sensation of dehydration I asked, 'Could I have some water please?' I called out to whoever was still monitoring me but there was no reply. Waiting patiently, sure enough some time later a mechanism unlocked and the heavy door swung open. I saw a petite, dark brown haired lady in a white lab coat holding a jug of cold water and a cup. 'Thank you,' I said as I tried to move but she shook her head.

'Don't move, please,' she said with an American accent. I guessed it was her over the speaker from earlier.

Placing the jug and cup down on the floor, she grabbed the chair from the corner and brought it towards me.

'Who are you?' I asked her as she poured the delicious looking water into the cup and pushed it towards my dry mouth.

'I can't tell you.' She nervously looked in the direction of the camera. 'But you are safe here.'

As I drank the water, I found that it wasn't delicious at all, in fact it tasted bitter.

Oh no. Not again.

★ ★ ★

'Tara, oh my freaking God you're awake.' Amanda's voice pummelled into my left ear.

My eyes fluttered open to bright sunshine hitting my eyes from a lovely scene outside a window to my right. In front of me on a stand in the corner of the ceiling was a TV and below, sitting on chairs were Beth, Amanda and Heather, all looking tired with bags under their eyes.

'What…what happened?' I asked as I got flashes of the windowless room, the large metal door and the petite brown haired woman.

'There was an incident,' Amanda told me looking horrified. 'The doctor's said you had a major allergic reaction to something in that grubby tattoo parlour.'

'What?' To my right, I saw that I had been hooked up to an intravenous drip of saline. 'But my back…' Sitting up, I rubbed it but felt no pain.

'You nearly died.' Heather burst into tears onto Beth's shoulder.

'She's so overdramatic,' Beth tutted, disgusted as Heather sniffed her runny nose. 'We heard that you were absent from your housemates and checked with the university. They told us where you'd be.'

I nodded, confused at what they had said and the memories that were still replaying in my head. Taking a deep breath, I closed my eyes.

'You look tired,' Amanda said as she stood up, giving me an encouraging smile.

'I'm more confused than tired. But thank you so much for being here. It's very touching,' I told them truthfully.

'We'll be back soon, sweetie.' Beth kissed me on my forehead.

'Do you want me to contact your family?' Amanda asked.

'No, it's best not to bother them. It'll only worry them. I'll send them an e-mail when I get the chance.' I smiled at them, but it seemed to make Heather worse. She gave me another round of sobs before Beth took her out of the room, followed quickly by Amanda.

A minute or two later a nurse, wearing a white uniform and black Crocs, walked over to the window and closed the curtains. She leaned over my bed towards me, our noses almost touching and whispered threateningly. 'Do not tell anyone about what happened to you. We are letting you out because it would draw attention to the tattoo parlour, and we cannot allow that to happen.'

It took me a while to realise that I had heard that voice before; it came from a speaker in the strange windowless room. It wasn't a dream; the whole ordeal was real. 'Okay stop,' I said a little too loudly as I began to freak out. My mind was racing as pangs of rear rushed at me as though a tidal wave of memories engulfed me, drowning out the released faces of my friends. The windowless room, the excoriating back pain and being drugged *was* all real. And so was Maynard, the git who did this to me. Then why go to such lengths to cover up my back operation? What had they done that was so bad, they had to lie to doctors and nurses at a hospital?

I sat up in bed, the nurse pulled away from me, putting her hands on her hips like my mother used to do. She was quite pretty, with a slender face that framed her short brown 1930's style hair. 'Who the hell are you and what did you do to me?'

Folding her arms she sighed and motioned to the en-suite bathroom. 'Go and see for yourself.'

I gingerly got out of bed. My back was tender as I stood upright, like the feeling of sunburn that's beginning to heal. It wasn't so bad that I couldn't walk properly. Pushing the door open, a waft of lemon passed my nose. I flicked on the bathroom light; it gave a small hum from the extractor fan. I pulled back my hideous plain blue hospital gown; I turned around to see my bare back in the mirror and gasped in horror... 'WHAT THE HELL HAVE YOU DONE TO MY BACK?'

Chapter Two

A SENSATION OF NAUSEA CREPT UP TOWARDS MY THROAT AS I saw my freckled white skin tarnished in a hideous inky, permanent splodge. As there, in the dead centre of my back was a tattoo of black wings; etched delicately on my back and folded with some feathers crossing at the bottom. It served as a horrid reminder that I had been drugged and kidnapped. I couldn't understand it. Why would someone go to such lengths to give me a tattoo?

'You need to calm down, don't get all upset,' the nurse said soothingly as she came into the bathroom. I hurriedly covered myself up, but she scoffed. 'Who do you think undressed you? Don't worry I am a nurse or was a nurse,' she added as she walked back towards the bed and sat down on it.

'Who are you?' I demanded. 'What's your name?'

She looked like she was going to shake her head.

'You can at least tell me that since you've seen my bare arse!'

Smiling, she replied, 'its Lynn. Now, will you calm down, you're T.A.T can't take the stress of you yelling or shouting like that, hence why it's showing on your back.'

'Oh for crying out loud,' I snapped at her. 'Aren't you a little old to be calling it a tat?'

Looking affronted she dug into her uniform pocket and brought out a shiny card. 'T.A.T stands for Tattoo of Arcane Technology. And I am not old,' she glowered.

'What on earth does Tattoo of Arcane Technology mean?' I asked, but she quickly pocketed the card and turned away from me.

'If you stress out too much the tattoo will appear and if you get angry, which I suggest you don't…it…will happen.'

'It? What's it?' Frustrated and upset from the lack of information, it was beginning to make me angry and, strange as it was, my back began to hurt. 'Look, you drug me, kidnap me, and give me a tattoo that hurts like hell and you're not even going to fill in the blanks? Please tell me what is going on!'

'Please, don't get angry. You'll be in a lot of pain if you get too angry... *They* will come out and then it's back to the bunker for you.'

'Bunker? What bunker? For God's sake! Give me answers!' My back twanged painfully, and I recoiled. 'What have you done to me? Why can't I get angry? Cos I'm telling ya now, I ain't a happy bunny!' Unable to say anything else, I felt this cold yet white hot pain stab at my spine which made me involuntarily arch my back. It was as though something had dug into the skin trying to rip my shoulder blades out.

'Please, calm down.' Lynn begged. She looked scared as she approached me. 'Take deep breaths through your nose.'

I fell to the floor in agony, tears strolling down my face like a waterfall... 'What is happening to me?' I gasped through gritted teeth.

'I can't say anything here. The place isn't secure. Listen to me and take deep calming breaths,' she repeated. 'The pain will subside, just do as I ask.'

I began to breathe deeply and soon, like she said, the pain receded to a dull throbbing. I was still on all fours and unwilling to move. Coming to my side, Lynn lifted up my gown and examined my back. With cool hands, she placed them where the pain was; I felt instant relief.

'There, do you feel better?' she asked softly.

'Yes,' I mumbled and rolled over and sat on the floor still breathing.

'Good.' Lynn sat down on the floor next to me. 'You need to keep your temper and I can understand how difficult it is for you.' Her eyes were sad and sympathetic.

'Why have you done this to me... whatever it is you've done?' I asked, not stopping the tears of both pain and hurt.

'I can promise you that things will be explained soon. But here isn't a good place to tell you.' She glanced at the door next to me. 'Just promise me one thing... do not tell anyone about this, you will put everyone in danger, including yourself. You must keep quiet.'

'Yeah, sure okay,' I said nonchalantly trying to get up, but Lynn grabbed my hand to stop me.

'I mean it Tara.' She stared right at me with dead set eyes. 'Keep your head down and wait for instructions.'

Lynn helped me to bed, checked my back again then when she was satisfied went to the bathroom and checked her make-up and hair. 'I'm going to get your discharge papers. You will be able to return university, but as I said, do not breathe a word of this to anyone, do you understand me?' She went to the end of the bed and picked up my chart.

Studying at her hardened face, I knew she meant business and nodded. 'I promise I won't say anything.'

'Good,' she sighed, 'I'll keep in touch.'

With that, Lynn left the room, closing the door behind her with a dull click. Alone in the antiseptic smelling hospital room with nothing but confusing thoughts and feelings about what had happened... all I could think of: could this get any worse?

★ ★ ★

Feeling absolutely delighted that I was released from the hospital a day later; I joined the girls for a "Welcome Back from the Hospital" celebration in the Student Union. The girls also invited a few other people who I was briefly acquainted with. One of them was Henry Simmons, and the best thing about it was-

'Jennifer broke up with him!' Heather squealed in my ear when he turned up to the party in blue baggy jeans, a black Metallica t-shirt and a beanie cap. His black messy hair flicked out of his cap near his ears and all I thought was, damn he looks good.

'I heard they had a massive argument,' Beth told me, giggling in my ear, 'so she broke up with him. So watch out girls you are in the presence of the future Mrs Simmons.' The four of us began chatting about the break up when-

'Um excuse me,' said a sweet, sultry voice. Snapping our heads around Beth, Heather and I were face to face with Henry Simmons, our mouths instantly fell open as he towered over us. 'Who's the girl who came out of the hospital,' he said looking between the three of us.

'That would be Tara,' Beth said, shutting her slacked mouth, pointing to me.

'Er hi, I'm me, um Tara.' Way to go at being articulate, I thought mentally hitting myself.

'Well, it's nice to see that you're all better.' He smiled; my knees went weak. God, he was gorgeous. I felt like a fan-girl with a crush on one of those famous boy bands or something. My insides squirmed whenever I saw him and I became quite hot under the collar when I was close to him. It was ridiculous. 'I don't think we've met before. I'm Henry.'

'Yeah, I know,' I said in a goofy manner. I made a quick mental note to slap myself again at sounding like an idiot in front of such a cute guy. 'So, did you come for the party to welcome me back from a trip to the hospital?' I asked confidently, hoping that he would say yes and that he was going to get me a drink which would end up the two of us talking and getting to know each other... But that's not what I got.

Henry's face fell a little. 'Er no, I didn't know there was a party. I came to see some friends and saw the banner outside in the window.'

'Oh,' I said crestfallen.

'But, anyway I'm glad to see that you're better, excuse me.' He gave me a brief smile and walked on through the crowd.

I turned to the girls and each of us was confused at what had just happened. It felt as though I got slapped in the face. 'Damn it I'm such an idiot for asking that. I thought he would at least have offered to get me a drink,' I said to Beth and Heather a little loudly than intentioned.

'Sorry again,' Henry said as he came back. 'Um, would you like me to get you a drink for getting out of the hospital?'

Crap did he just hear me. I felt my face blush in embarrassment and tried to pass it off as the room being too warm.

'Er,' I looked down at my half-empty glass, 'please.' I passed it onto Beth and headed off with Henry to the bar.

'So what are you studying?' he asked me as we squeezed our way to the front of the bar.

'Sports Technology,' I told him. I could feel myself grinning from ear to ear at how lucky I was that Henry was talking to me. I needed some normality in my life. Something to ground me, to keep me from screaming out at how insane my life had suddenly become. I wanted to forget Lynn and that horrid tattoo on my back. Wanted to forget about the hospital, the bunker, the acrid taste of that drugged water. It was a god awful experience and one I didn't want to remember. 'What about you?' I asked, finally taking the leap to force all those memories out of my mind.

'English Literature, but I specialise in poetry.' He smiled at me and I swore my heart stopped. How romantic.

'I bet you're a great romantic then,' I laughed but Henry seemed confused. 'You know being a poet and all that, it comes with the romance or something...' I said stupidly, but Henry still seemed confused.

Laughing like an arse, I shrugged my shoulders. But there was nothing I could do to hide my blushing face.

'I understand,' he said to me, briefly touching my arm to get my attention, 'but my poetry is more to do with nature, not love.'

'Oh,' I said turning back to look at him, but he appeared to be searching for someone.

'Are you waiting for your friends still?' I asked him, feeling annoyed that he was ignoring me.

'Um, sort of,' he said and then I realised why his attention wasn't fully on me. Just at that moment Jennifer had walked into the bar, along with three of her friends, all dressed up to the nines, commanding attention from the entire union.

Jennifer's eyes quickly searched the room and saw instantly that Henry was watching her. Scowling she linked arms with her friends and went in a different direction.

Henry turned away from her and called attention to one of the bartenders, a girl with blonde hair and big boobs. He ordered our drinks and we became silent until they arrived.

'Do you want to grab a table?' I asked him, glancing around the room.

'Um... ' he began, unsure of what to say.

'Sorry, yeah you'd better go and find your friends, thanks for the drink,' I said sadly and walked off back to the girls who had been watching me from the very start.

'No, um we can get a table.' I inwardly screamed as Henry picked the "Lovers Booth." It was a small little alcove in the bar that had minimal light and was completely secluded from the rest of the room; perfect for having an uninterrupted snog.

'So Tara, tell me about what happened to you?' He leant back against the 1970's brown leather seats, appearing calm and relaxed.

'About what happened to me?' I asked him, a sense of fear rising in my cheeks making me flush hot.

'You ending up in the hospital,' he said looking curious.

'Oh... I had a major allergic reaction to something in the tattoo parlour.' I stopped and realised that he frowned as I explained and remembered he saw me go in there. 'You saw me go inside; you peered in through the window.'

He took a sip of his drink and shook his head. 'No, I didn't,' he said awkwardly. 'But it's really lucky that you are all right now.'

'What are you dressing up as for Halloween?' I quickly changed the subject as it was becoming apparent that he wanted to wrap our conversation up.

'Ah, I'm not going this year,' he replied. 'I've got something to take care of.'

'Were you going to go with Jennifer?' I asked him without thinking, instantly horrified at what I said and shook my head. 'I'm sorry; I shouldn't have pried like that.'

'No, it's okay, and yes I was but now...' He looked forlorn, 'I've got something to do so...'

'I'm going,' I piped up, trying to make him smile. 'I've never really been good at costumes but my friends have decided to dress me up as an Egyptian Goddess,' I laughed.

'Oh, which one?' he asked me enthusiastically.

I didn't have an answer. I wasn't particularly good with pre-history. My face felt hot again as I was put under pressure. 'I'm not sure.'

'Well, you have Hathor, Bastet, Nephthys or Isis.' He counted them on his fingers. 'I think you should go as Nephthys. She was a very responsible Goddess, kind of like a leader. You could be a leader,' he said with a twinkle in his eye.

'Oh yeah...? Wow, you know your mythology.'

He shrugged. 'I have to, part of my training...' He gave me an awkward smile. 'You know for English literature, the old um... classical works.'

I laughed at him and he smiled back. It was nice getting to know Henry. He seemed very mysterious to me, but kind and caring. There was a lot I wanted to find out about him, but I got the feeling that he didn't like opening up. However, before I even managed to utter another word, Amanda came strutting up towards us and sat down opposite Henry.

'Hi, I'm Amanda.' She offered her hand.

'Hi.' Henry frowned slightly, and then suddenly got up out of his seat. 'I've just seen a friend of mine. I'll talk to you later Tara,' and with that, he walked off, leaving me staring after him feeling as giddy as a schoolgirl and with Amanda, seething in a silent jealous rage.

★ ★ ★

The following day was Halloween, well the afternoon of it anyway. I had a nice lazy lie-in until well past noon, made myself a late breakfast of egg and toast and sat down in my bedroom and watched DVDs.

I glanced over at my Egyptian Goddess costume that was unceremoniously thrown over an old rocking chair in the corner. It was so stupidly flimsy I swear I would catch my death come this evening.

As I got halfway through my all time favourite comedy, there was a knock on my door.

'Hey Tara, can I come in?' asked my landlord slash housemate Kevin.

'Sure,' I said, pausing just as one of the actresses was about to climb into a rocket car.

Kevin came in with a strange expression on his face, 'There's a man at the door who's delivered a parcel. He won't let me sign for it; he said it's got to be you.'

'Oh okay.' I glanced down at my attire, a scruffy white-ish robe. Not really caring to get dressed, I went to the front door to see the... delivery man? Not your normal delivery man. Usually they wore a uniform, but this guy was wearing a black suit.

'Going to a funeral or wedding?' I asked him as I opened the door wider.

'Tara Young?' he asked me, raising a suspicious eyebrow.

'Yes...?'

'Could you sign here please?' He handed me a small digital terminal with a pen. Scrawling my signature at the bottom, he snatched it back and gave me a black box. 'Read the letter carefully and follow the instructions,' he said frowning at me.

'Okay...' I said confused. 'Are you from the-.'

'Post Office, yes,' he said. 'Read the instructions carefully.' He muttered under his breath. I heard movement from behind me. 'I'm on my way to a wedding,' the "post-man" laughed, giving himself a cover, 'just like you said.'

'Oh, that's great.' Kevin's voice came from behind me. 'Who's the lucky couple?'

The man raised his eyebrow again and smiled robotically, 'Have a good day Miss Young,' and with that walked off.

I closed the door and looked at the plain black box.

'He was unfriendly.' Kevin peered over my shoulder. 'Maybe it's from your parents as a Halloween present.'

'Yes, it is,' I said turning to face him and smiling politely. 'I asked them to send me some things, just to brighten up my costume.'

'Excellent, it's going to be a fun night.' He slapped his hands together. 'Got loads of chocolaty goodness for the children and their parents,' he laughed. 'What are you dressing up as?'

'Egyptian Goddess,' I told him as I shook the box lightly but felt nothing move.

'Oh, wow. I'm going as Merlin, or maybe Gandalf, I haven't decided yet, but both are equally as cool as the other. Well, I'd best be off to the library, got some books to get out for an essay.'

I headed back to my room and closed the door firmly behind me. After prising the box lid open, I saw a white envelope on top of some black cloth and next to that was a smaller black box.

Tearing at the envelope, I unfurled the letter which read:

Dear Informant,

Included in this parcel is your uniform which must be on your person at all times as it will be needed once we call for you.

The T.A.T. is based in London. It is part of an operation which specialises in the recruitment of individuals such as yourself as well as helping with investigations.

Be warned that you must keep this information to yourself otherwise you will endanger all of those who are in this organisation.

Put in your earpiece and destroy this letter.

Re-reading the letter a good few times, I was satisfied that I had indeed gone mad. I had forced myself to believe that everything I had experienced in the tattoo parlour and the windowless hospital and Lynn was just one freaky stupid dream. Also, I had refused to look into a mirror since I was released from the hospital and I didn't even want to go into town and pass by the alley which led to the parlour itself. Staring at the letter I sighed and ripped it up a few times and putting it in the bin, I pulled out the smaller box and opened it.

'Wow, cool,' I exclaimed as I saw a natural colour earpiece. Fitting it into my right ear I instantly got Lynn shouting at me.

'Bloody took you long enough, what the hell were you doing? The parcel was delivered to you exactly fifteen minutes and thirty-seven seconds ago.'

'I'm sorry?' I said loudly to the room.

'Ah, you don't have to shout, just talk normally. I can even hear you whisper you know. So, before I give you the details, as I am on a safe line, have you destroyed the letter?'

'A safe line?' I repeated, but I heard her sigh in annoyance. 'Yeah, I ripped it up and threw it in the bin.'

'Stupid cow!' Lynn shouted at me. 'Burn it, do not leave any scrap of evidence of that letter, do you understand?'

'God, yes stop yelling at me,' I shouted back, getting a slight twinge in my spine. Taking a deep breath, I said, 'So, now what?'

I heard some tapping on a keyboard then she said, 'There are a few things to tell you. Firstly, Maynard is our boss. You met him the day you got the tattoo.'

Thinking of the parlour, I remembered two men. I doubted that the man with the tattoos was Maynard so I asked, 'Maynard? Is that the Texan bloke?'

'Yes, that's him. Now, secondly, you will be picked up and taken to London in the near future. Don't ask, we'll tell you when. Thirdly, when you arrive in London you will undergo training; you will also be given all the details about missions, what to do, where to go. Understand?'

Sitting on my bed, I stared at the paused screen of my film. I found it surreal. I was talking to a lady through an earpiece, being told I am now part of this weird T.A.T. team in London where I get to go on missions. Nothing computed, it sounded like a big joke. 'Yes,' I said eventually, understanding what she said but not fully comprehending. 'Um, can I ask any questions?'

'No. Your house isn't secure. I can give you as much information as possible, but the rest you'll have to wait until you get here. Now, the T.A.T or Tattoo of Arcane Technology is a secret group based in London. It recruits special people from around Britain who have unique talents and abilities. You have been given a special tattoo that reacts to your anger, to your emotions. If you get upset and angry, your tattoo will become real.'

'The wings, they'll become real?' I whispered, hearing Kevin walking outside of my door.

'Yes. You can keep them under control if you don't get angry or agitated.'

'I have been trying but it's difficult. I have you in my head as well as the twenty million questions all swimming around in there,' I snapped and my back itched uncomfortably, coupled with a wave of uneasy adrenalin.

'That then brings me to something which is the most important for you.' She spoke in such a way that it scared me. It was as though I was waiting for the worst news I could possibly hear that would probably ruin an entire life. 'Tara, if you get too angry, real black wings will burst out of your back.' She took a deep breath. 'It's not a joke; it's not something that you should take lightly. It's an enormous responsibility. And when they do, when you lose control of your emotions, they'll cause you excruciating pain.'

For ten minutes, I lay on my bed, closing my eyes and trying not to be sick. My body had been violated without my consent. I could never be angry again without feeling that horrible pain that made every single nerve ending in my back scream out in protest. Why had I been chosen? Were my parents involved? After all Maynard said that he knew them, or was he just lying?

'Lynn,' I said quietly as I glanced over at the paused television screen, turned it off. I wasn't in the mood for a comedy. 'You can't undo this can you?'

Lynn was silent for a while before she softly said, 'No... we can't. If it helps, you are meant to have the tattoo. You were picked because of who you are.'

I scoffed. 'And who is that?'

'An intelligent and thoughtful girl. We know you'll be able to tackle this. Your life won't be normal again but you're not alone Tara,' she said gently. 'We are here to help you. All you have to do is listen to us. We know what we're doing.'

Chapter Three

With my costume, jewellery, stupidly high-heeled shoes, my makeup bag, and Lynn in my ear, I left the house at five that afternoon and headed to the girls' apartment. I was invited to go to their place so that they could help me put my costume together.

It was quite a cold day as autumn had fully taken over the Welsh countryside. Walking along the roads where red, yellow, orange and brown leaves collected at the side of the paths, I deeply inhaled the scent of pine trees and tried to think of the fun night ahead. Halloween was a special time. It wasn't that I celebrated it, I don't believe in ghosts. But it was the only time when my family were at home watching scary movies. And if truth be told, it was the only time that we were all together under the same roof at the same time. My parents were away on business so much, it was pointless that they had a house. They hardly lived it in. Yet at the end of October, that was always a time when we were all together. Of course, that changed when I went to university. October was a studying month, not a holiday. If it was any other time throughout the year, I was alone in the house with my older brother who I hated with a passion. But as far as I knew, he was off gallivanting in New York as a banker or some such nonsense.

Approaching the door to their apartment, I knocked hard as I heard Halloween themed music blasting from the inside. Beth answered the door with wet hair and a face mask.

'Oh, hey come in!' She smiled. Following her up the stairs, I kicked off my shoes and was lead into their lounge. 'Just put your bag there.' She pointed to an old raggedy settee where Heather was sitting, staring at a medium-sized mirror with a pair of hair tongs.

'Hey Tara.' Heather turned awkwardly holding a clump of her hair in the tongs. 'You want me to do your hair?'

I shrugged. 'I thought I would just have it loose. My hair is black already.'

'Well then, let me do your makeup?' she suggested, turning back to the mirror.

Hearing thunderous footsteps behind me, Amanda came in with a towel wrapped around her head with black fishnet tights and a short mini-skirt. 'No, hang on Heather; I wanted to do her make-up.'

'Can't I do my own?' I asked them, but Amanda shook her head and looked at Heather.

'Why must you do this?' she shouted at her. 'I said I'd be doing her make-up. You can help Beth with her costume.'

Heather sighed, 'Fine, whatever.'

'Good,' Amanda smiled. 'But don't spend too long on her; you need to help me look pretty for Henry.' Amanda left the room and I heard Heather tut and continue with her hair. I felt a stab of anger towards Amanda and felt the familiar pang of pain in my back. Shrugging it off, I smiled as Beth came in to give me a drink of a Bacardi breezer. As I drank, I remembered that Henry wasn't going to attend the party. Something that Amanda didn't know.

A few minutes later, Amanda called me into her room, the first door on the left. She did my makeup in less than ten minutes. And giving me a mirror to look at, I tensed up as I had a flashback of seeing the tattoo on my back in the hospital bathroom. Glancing at my face for the briefest moment, I was irritated with the sloppy, almost childish appliance of the mascara. 'Wow, hey that's great,' I said with a fake smile. 'Thanks.'

Snatching the mirror from me, she smiled sweetly. 'You are very welcome, Tara.'

The clock showed half-past six, which gave us less than an hour to get ready. 'Can I use your bathroom to get changed?' I asked Heather and Beth as they had both finished their hair and make-up and were now ready to put on their costumes.

'Sure,' Heather smiled. 'It's next to Amanda's bedroom.'

Closing the door, I took out my make-up bag and re-applied my own. 'She's done such a poor job,' I whispered to myself, but Lynn, of course, was listening.

'What does it look like?'

I sighed. 'Looks like a bird has shat on my eyes.'

Lynn laughed, but I didn't find it funny and began to get angry. Gasping in pain, Lynn suddenly went quiet. Taking a moment to breathe, I shook my head. 'It's not like I have never been mad before, but it's too easy to get upset and angry. You know?'

Lynn replied sadly, 'I understand.'

Finishing my make-up and putting on my costume of a short white dress with a gold belt and thick gold jewellery, I left the bathroom to find Amanda right in front of me.

'Who were you talking to?' She eyed me curiously and folded her arms as though expecting me to tell her everything. I gathered that she usually got her way and, if she didn't, she'd do anything in her power to get it.

'Myself?' I said with a small smile then walked past her. Heather and Beth were nice people, but there was something about Amanda that put me on edge. She was bossy and brash for starters, but also she was easily jealous and that never bodes well. 'Okay guys, this is my costume, how does it look?' I did a twirl and their eyes grew wide.

'It looks great,' they said together but didn't comment further. Instead, Heather lent me a pair of her gold dangly earrings and gold lipstick.

Ten minutes later, we were all dressed, but the make-up wasn't to perfection, not in Amanda's eyes anyway. She checked and re-checked the mirror to see if it would go with her costume of a fallen Angel. With black tear drops running down her eyes and her nails painted in a blood colour, Amanda did actually look the part.

Heather was what I could only describe as, a ghost but when I asked her she gave me an exasperated sigh and said, 'Banshee.'

'Ahh.'

The four of us then left the warmth of the house, heading into the Halloween night where the weirdos come out to play.

★ ★ ★

Paying the £3.50 entrance fee, the four of us pushed our way into the very packed student union. It was festooned with black streamers, black and orange balloons, fake candles and candelabras. From the ceiling, there were dangling plastic spiders and ripped cotton to look like old draping spiderwebs. And on the tops of the bar sat lit pumpkins. Each had an eerie carved face staring eerily at the student customers.

'Yay they're playing Shewolf!' Amanda yelled as she jumped up and down. We dropped off our coats, for an extra £1, and then headed inside. Amanda ran straight to the dance floor. The music pumped loudly into my ear drums and vibrated in my chest. It was so loud I was thankful I couldn't hear Lynn.

'Chav,' Beth and Heather mouthed as they stared at Amanda.

'I'm going to get some drinks,' I said as Beth and Heather tried to find somewhere to sit amongst the witches, wizards, vampires, mummies and God knows what else. Heather had spotted a space and grabbing Beth, took off.

Making a mental note of the direction they went, I made my way to the crowded bar. I laughed at some of the people who turned up in their costumes. Some of them were either extremely good or very poor. One even dressed up like a cotton wool ball in which they were tied to what I could only guess was a "Naughty" Nurse who wore white PVC everything, holding a horse whip!

Behind me, two girls started to giggle and as I turned round they abruptly stopped and looked the other way. Shrugging it off, I moved about two centimetres in the queue.

'That music is terrible,' I heard Lynn yell in my ear. 'You do listen to some crap.'

'Oh shush,' I said as I tried to mask it as a sneeze.

'She's such a slut,' I heard one of the girls saying behind me. 'Look what she's wearing for God's sake. It makes me sick!'

'What is she anyway?' the other asked.

'An Egyptian slut?' the girl laughed.

My face suddenly felt hot. Were they talking about me?

Trying to ignore their hurtful comments, I managed to make my way to the bar by squeezing in between two werewolves who decided to lick my arm.

'Alright back off,' I shouted at them, but they laughed and howled in my face. 'Arses,' I said under my breath.

'What's going on?' Lynn asked me, but I was in no position to reply to her.

After being served, I grabbed the chilled bottles and passed the girls who were behind me, both giving me evil looks. I began to feel paranoid and started to notice people around me point and stare. I didn't like this type of attention, I felt like I was back in primary school again.

After ten minutes of searching for Heather and Beth and being pushed and shoved by a gang of zombies, I had just spotted them in the corner laughing with a couple of people, when strangely enough Jennifer came waltzing up to me.

'Hey,' she began awkwardly, and then looked over her shoulder in a nervous manner.

'Um, hi.'

She leant closer so that I could hear her. 'So you slept with Henry?'

'Oh what?' Lynn said into my ear, not helping me.

'Pardon?' I asked, frowning at what she said.

'You heard me.' Jennifer looked over her shoulder again and I saw Amanda talking to two girls who were behind me while I was getting drinks.

'No, of course, I haven't.' I frowned, feeling a flush of anger and a pinch of pain in my upper back. 'Last time I saw him was at a party the girls threw for me when I came out of the hospital.'

'I broke up with Henry because of you,' she said angrily. 'He's been following you, looking at you.' Angry tears spilt from her eyes and she quickly wiped them away. 'I want the truth, Tara.'

'I'm telling you the truth Jennifer. I have barely spoken to him. I'm sorry I was responsible for you two breaking up, but I haven't seen him at all. Amanda is the one who's been after him, she really likes him.'

Jennifer pursed her lips and huffed angrily. 'She's going around telling everyone about you and him. My friends told me what you had done but…
'

The cold bottles were making my hands numb and I was starting to feel sick as I heard about Amanda and her bitchy lies. Jealousy obviously made her do very stupid things and all for a guy.

'Look, Jennifer, I'm sorry alright, but I haven't done anything with Henry. Anyway, why are you telling *me* this, why not Henry?'

'Because Henry is a decent guy,' she said sadly. 'And I know that he's been upset since we broke up.'

'Jennifer, Amanda is lying. I wouldn't do something like that. Yeah, Henry is cute, but she's been trying to make the moves on him, not me.'

Nodding, she turned and walked away, moving away from her friends, who saw her and followed like sheep. Standing there, staring, was Amanda, who caught my eye from across the room. She gave me a sickly sweet smile and moved to sit next to Heather and Beth. She whispered in their ears and both turned to face me with a look of horror on their faces. I realised that this was Amanda's true self, a jealous cow who wanted Henry for herself and wanted to purposefully hurt me. But what was I going to do? I couldn't yell at her, not anymore.

Trying to keep my temper, I threaded my way towards the girls and slammed their drinks on the table. My hands shook, I felt sick at the thought of the upcoming argument with Amanda and with it, my back began to ache, but I ignored it. At this moment in time, I didn't care how angry I got.

'Thanks for the drinks,' Beth said as she and Heather stopped talking and realised that I placed their drinks right in front of them. 'Hey, what's wrong?' she asked me.

Shrugging my shoulders, I didn't reply as I glared at Amanda, who picked up her drink and turned her back on me. Another bout of anger flared then suddenly my back seared in pain. The ache that I had felt not seconds before became overpowering and I cried out.

'Whoa Tara, are you okay?' Heather sounded worried.

Amanda turned around and stared at me strangely; just looking at her and her tarty dress made it worse. I doubled over, my fists banging down on the table, unbalancing one of the bottles. It fell off the table and onto the floor with glass and drink pooling all around my feet. Instantly people cleared the area around me and I heard people laugh and clap and yet, in the slight commotion I had caused, I closed my eyes and heard Lynn in my ear.

'What's going on? You had better not be getting angry, Tara! We can't afford you to mess-up now!'

'I KNOW!' I snapped at her, not caring what Heather and Beth were thinking of me as they tried to scoop up the glass from the floor. I stood up straight, which thankfully relieved some of my pain and with a quick reaction, I grabbed Amanda's arm and spun her around to face me. 'I need to have a word with you.'

I heard Beth say, 'Uh oh this is going to get ugly,' from behind me, but I focussed totally on Amanda.

'What's this about you spreading stuff behind my back, Amanda?' I demanded, while taking calm steadying breaths as the pain in my back was now making me cry.

'What are you talking about?' She gave me a stupid smile.

I moved closer to her, ensuring that she understood everything I told her. 'I just had Jennifer ask me if I slept with Henry. She told me you started the rumour. I want to know why?'

'Don't go down this road Tara, it's not gonna be pleasant,' Lynn said in my ear but I ignored her.

Amanda put her hands on her hips and made a fake light laugh. 'Tara, you are not a pretty person or even remotely popular and, to be quite frank with you, Henry cannot be seen in public with someone like you. He needs to have someone who'll look just as good as he does. I have been doing you a favour. If you are out of the picture, then Henry can be happy with some-one as beautiful as me. Do you understand sweetheart? You are too un-popular and too plain for someone like Henry.'

My mouth dropped open in shock. I couldn't believe what I had just heard.

'Tara, don't get angry.' Lynn instantly said in my ear, panic clearly in her voice, but I didn't want to hear it. Amanda had crossed the line and without realising it, my hands instantly became fists and my rage boiled over. I glared at Amanda and the pain started to sear in my back again. I left her gaping after me as I ran off, heading to the toilets.

Barging my way in, I was glad that there was no one in there. I locked myself in a cubicle and screamed out in agony as it felt like my back was about to explode.

'Tara, calm down please.' Lynn sounded worried. 'Screaming is just go-ing to make it worse.'

'It hurts,' I cried as mascara-filled tears started to pour from my eyes and splash onto my white costume.

'I know it does, just take deep breaths and calm down.'

'Damn!' I kicked the cubicle door. I fell to the floor, gasping in agony, trying to breathe and concentrate on things that weren't making me angry. But all I could think about was Amanda's smug face. Her words. Her lies. What did I ever do to deserve that?

After a few moments, the pain seared again. 'This isn't working!' I yelled and pressed my back against the cubicle door, willing the pain to stop. 'They are going to come out, I can feel them!'

'Tara, you cannot expose yourself, you are not in a secluded place. You need to calm down.'

'I think I have surpassed being calm,' I said through gritted teeth. 'Please do something!'

Lynn went quiet. I tried to breathe through the pain; I felt the coolness of the October night air flow in through a cracked window behind the toilet. I glanced up but only saw a strange white blur of the moon through frosted glass. How I longed to be anywhere but here. Suddenly the door to the toilets banged open. I heard two people come in sounding drunk as they laughed copiously.

'She needs to chill out,' said a familiar voice who was shuffling her high-heeled shoes towards the sinks.

'Why is she so weird?' asked another familiar voice.

'Beth, give me your eyeliner!'

Crap, it was Beth and Amanda.

There was the sound of an unclasped purse and then...

'She hasn't got any friends apart from us,' Amanda said. 'I mean, come on? Look at her. Plus she talks to herself. Like earlier on, back at ours, she was in the bathroom talking like she was having a conversation with herself. Crazy or what?'

'And the way she was talking to Henry at the party we threw for her,' Amanda continued, 'I'm sorry but she was a total slut. She stole Henry from me.'

'IS THAT IT?' I screeched. Standing up I yanked open the door. 'YOU HORRIBLE NASTY COW!'

'TARA, NO! ' Lynn suddenly yelled in my ear, but it was too late.

Pain like I had never felt before shot through my back like a million white-hot knives cutting deep and jagged into my spine. The girls were silent as my eyes nearly popped out of their sockets from the shock of the pain. Then, as nature intended, I screamed.

The sound ripped through my throat, making me go hoarse in seconds. It was the type of scream that pierces people's souls, making them cringe away from your agony. I'd never screamed like this before. I was loud, I was crying and I was sprouting wings.

Falling to the floor, I was screeching continuously, catching breath whenever I could. Beth and Amanda had backed away from me towards the sinks looking horrified. They didn't know what to do and neither did I.

Trying to get to grips with what was going on around me, I had to at least try and ensure that the girls didn't see what I could feel rip and tear the white fabric of my costume. Slithering back into the cubicle, I pushed against the door so they couldn't get in. Attempting to lock it, my arms wouldn't let me reach up to the door handle; my entire body was in torture.

Beth or Amanda began to bang on the door calling out to me, but all I could do, was scream and cry. No coherent words would come out.

'Oh my God, I'm getting a steward,' I heard Beth yell over the top of my own screams.

'LYNN, IT'S NOT STOPPING!' I yelled until my voice extremely sore from screaming so much.

'What's wrong?' I heard someone bang on my door. It wasn't Amanda or Beth, it was the steward.

My back began to pulsate in pain, like contractions. Then with one large pulsation coupled with extreme pain I yelled out one last time as huge oily looking black wings burst from my back splattering a strange black liquid all over the cubicle. The force of them pushed me, face forward, towards the toilet. It was a good decision as I then promptly threw up.

'I'm calling an ambulance,' I heard the steward say.

Gulping for air and wiping away my black stained tears, the pain was subsiding exceedingly quickly. 'Lynn,' my voice quivered as I spoke softly. 'Help me.'

'Tara, don't move from where you are. We're going to intercept the ambulance and send one of our own to pick you up,' Lynn told me, but that wasn't worrying me. What I heard next chilled my soul.

'There's a river of black blood coming out from the cubicle.' Amanda gasped. 'Oh my God, what is she?'

CHAPTER FOUR

SHAKING FROM THE TRAUMA AND THE SHOCK THAT I HAD just experienced, I stifled a sob that was threatening to escape. I lay there in the black horrid smelling liquid that was strangely starting to dry up and disappear like dust. Lynn was still yelling in my ear, but I didn't want to hear her. Taking the earpiece out, I placed it in my bra and took a deep shuddering breath and glanced up towards the window. There was no way I was going to go out and face Amanda and Beth. I couldn't let them see me like this.

The moon was now casting a shining ray of its brilliant white light in my direction and for some reason it made me feel calm. I felt I could get out of this situation, albeit in a stupid fashion.

The window in front of me was small, in fact it was so small even without these freaky things that just sprouted from my back, I would find it difficult getting out. But I had to try.

Closing the lid of the toilet seat, I stood on top of it and pushed the window open as wide as it would go, which wasn't much. Turning around, I locked the door.

'Tara?' I heard Beth bang on the door, 'let us in.'

Ignoring her, I put my right leg out of the window and pushed myself through, the wings giving me more grief as I strained the muscles in my back. Breathing in, I managed to get half of my body out before I heard another bang on the door.

'Tara, what the hell is going on? Come out!' Amanda yelled at me.

I turned around in time just to see hands on the tiled floor as she was trying to peer under the door. Struggling to get out of the cubicle quickly, I pushed down hard on the windowpane and with a small grunt of pain I fell out and landed onto the cold gravel floor below.

'Ow,' I whined as I saw my grazed knee which I had caught as I fell out of the window. Picking myself up, gingerly I closed the window and bolted from the toilet block, trying to find somewhere, anywhere, that would conceal me and these wings.

The music from the student union blasted out all around me, which was confusing because I tried to run away from it, not toward. Dodging left and right, avoiding being seen by people, I saw a large hydrangea bush by a wall and did a running leap head first into it.

'OW,' I yelped out loud again as I felt something warm run down my hands. Holding them up to the dim orange light that was cast from a nearby lamppost, I saw that I had cut my hands. 'God damn it!' I groaned, rubbing the mud and blood off onto my already ruined costume.

With my stinging knee and hands, the only thing that wasn't causing me any pain anymore was my back. I was about to open my mouth to talk to Lynn when suddenly I heard footsteps from my far left-hand side. I ducked back as far as I could and remained silent. The only thing I heard was my panicked heart that was racing so fast, it felt like I had run a mile.

The person walked by me and turned towards the Student Union. I waited in the bush for a couple of minutes, hearing nothing and thinking it may be a good idea to make a run for it back to my house. I made a snap decision and crawled through the bush on my hands and knees. My stupid wings got caught in the branches and I managed to rip some feathers out, which didn't hurt me as much as I thought it would. As I stood up, I ran without turning back and headed towards the tennis courts on the right-hand side. I needed to get over the river that ran right through the university campus as it was the quickest way to my house.

I breathed heavily as I ducked behind a low wall waiting for the right time to run the last leg of my escape. It hid me from view of the Halloween party that still raved in the Student Union. I waited patiently for a minute or two and I ran as fast as I could go. But oddly enough, I seemed a bit slower than usual. I guessed it was either due to my painful knee or these blasted wings!

Suddenly, I heard movement behind me and while running, I glanced back to make sure I wasn't being followed then THUMP! My body collided with someone's hard muscle-packed chest forcing me to fall over.

'I'm sorry!' I squealed, as now my head and shoulders hurt from hitting the person who I hadn't noticed.

The reply I got wasn't what I had imagined. Also, the person I ran into wasn't who I thought it would be.

'Tara, what the hell?'

Oh my God. It was Henry Simmons, on the ground, frowning at me. I scrambled to get up, but Henry caught my arm and stopped me. I looked right at him. Was this it for me now? Was this it for Lynn as well? This moment now was the epitome of exposure.

Henry stared at those hideous things that were right there on display, these jet black and oily wings. But suddenly he burst out laughing. I snatched my arm away from him and standing up, took a couple of paces away from him, confused.

He continued to laugh, shaking his head in disbelief. 'I'm sorry, but they look so ridiculous.'

I frowned and felt a pang of annoyance erupt from me, and then BANG, the wings unfurled, shooting out on either side of me. I gasped as I saw the wingspan. It was huge!

Henry took a step back from the shock and then doubled over in a fit of laughter.

'What the hell is so funny?' It wasn't a question I should have been asking him, but I was completely confused. Why wasn't he calling for the police? Or running away from me in fright? Why was he just standing there, feet from me, bent over laughing as though it was the most comical thing he'd ever seen?

Henry moved closer to me and pointed out large cat tattoos on each side of his neck. 'See?' I stared at him blankly and didn't understand why he showed me. 'What? You didn't think you were the only one did you?' He let me stare at them a while longer before covering them back up with his collar. 'I don't sprout wings mind, but my ability is quite cool.'

It finally clicked. He was like me! 'So you were kidnapped and drugged too?' I asked, gasping in horror.

'Er, something similar.' He guided me away in the shadow of a building. 'That was a couple of years ago,' he said staring at my wings.

'Will you stop,' I snapped at him. 'Little bit self-conscious over here.'

'Sorry yeah um, they weren't what I expected, but then we all differ from one another I guess.' With my confused face Henry continued. 'My tattoos are for defensive purposes. My nails become the claws of a large cat like a lion or tiger, I can scratch through titanium.' H smiled proudly. 'I was placed here at the university, to watch out for you.'

'Oh.' Piecing things together. 'Makes sense now: the following me to the café, the tattoo parlour and meeting up at the Student Union.' I inwardly sighed and felt really pathetic. He didn't like me; it was just part of this T.A.T thing. 'Jennifer told me I was the reason you two broke up because you were following me.'

'Yeah.'

'So, Jennifer was a cover-up then?'

I seemed to touch a nerve as he turned away from me. He sighed heavily with furrowed brows. Perhaps it was a mistake and he was trying to forget about it. 'No. I wasn't supposed to get close to anyone, that wasn't my mission. But yes she broke up with me because of you. She caught me staring at you that day in the café, before you went into the tattoo parlour,' he said ruffling his hair, making it messier. 'My mission was to keep an eye on you and she thought that I fancied you,' he laughed.

'Oh,' I said sadly.

Henry continued, trying to veer off the topic. 'But I've been told by the T.A.T to keep away from her, she became a bit suspicious of me, especially when she saw my uniform. Are you wearing it?'

I shook my head then jumped as my back hurt again.

'What's wrong?' Henry asked sounding concerned.

'My back.' I nodded to the outstretched wings. 'These are starting to hurt.'

'Ah, it's because you've got new muscles which you haven't used yet,' he said in a matter-of-fact way. 'And you aren't wearing your uniform, which also helps,' he added with a small smile. 'Just relax and they'll fold back.' Henry then put a finger to his ear and moved away from me, talking in whispers to himself. It was probably to Lynn or to someone else from the T.A.T. So I sat down on the cold, hard floor and remained there for only a couple of minutes before he turned up with some thermal silver foil. I wondered where he'd got it from, but I guess it didn't matter. He placed it around me and suddenly I felt the heaviness of the wings slowly disappear.

'What's happening?' I asked, taking the foil away to see the wings turn to ash then blow away in a slight autumnal wind.

He knelt beside me. 'You've calmed down. They'll do that.'

'Oh. And if I get angry again?'

'They'll come out again,' he said then helped me up. 'Anyway, you don't have to worry, we're leaving now.' Silently guiding me back towards the Student Union, we passed a lot of people who were hanging around an ambulance, curious, worried or just drunkenly wanting a ride.

As we approached, I was met by a very stern looking woman with chocolate brown hair styled in a 1930's haircut. It was Lynn. She was wearing a green paramedic outfit with a silver pen and a watch attached to her right breast pocket and a security badge clipped to her hip. She was folding her arms and tapping her right foot.

'Talk much?' she snapped as she glanced at my ears.

'Sorry,' I mumbled but Henry laughed.

Moving towards me, she pointed at me warningly. 'You're just lucky I heard everything and managed to get here on time. You could have been exposed and screwed up big time and you've not even been inducted yet!'

Henry frowned. 'Give her a break Lynn she's been through a lot tonight.' He put his arm around me protectively and rubbed my back. 'She's had a big shock and I mean big.'

Lynn raised her right eyebrow in a mild surprise. In an exasperated tone she said, 'Forget it, just get in.' She pointed to the ambulance. Henry opened the doors and helped me in. I peered ahead and saw a bald man in the driver's seat. He barely moved an inch when I got in and only glanced at the mirror once. He was wearing sunglasses, which I thought was odd as it was night-time. Henry got into the back with me and Lynn slammed the doors closed.

'Okay,' Henry called to the driver as Lynn got into the passenger's side.

'Where are we going?' I asked sadly as I glanced at him in the bright lights of the ambulance that trundled out of the union car park and onto the main road. Henry rubbed his face. He appeared a little worse for wear and for the first time that night, I noticed he had heavy grey bags under his eyes.

'We are taking you to a safe-house in London, but I won't be going with you. I have to remain at the university and try and smooth over your departure. They'll drop me off outside my house.'

Nodding, I remained quiet as the ambulance sped along the road for a few minutes then slowing down, pulled over with a small squeak of the breaks. Henry got out and bade me good night.

'Will I see you again?' I asked hurriedly as he opened the back doors. A wave of fresh cold air blew into the ambulance, making me shiver.

Jumping onto the dewy tarmac road, he turned and nodded. 'You will but not for a while yet. I still have another mission in Liverpool. I hope to be in London within the upcoming week.'

'Oh,' I said simply, understanding that he had other things to do and I wasn't all that important. 'Well, I'm sorry I ruined your night.'

He laughed and closed the first door. 'You made it interesting. You'll be an exciting addition to the team. Night Tara and get some sleep.' He closed the second door and the ambulance took off once again, rolling along the road. Lynn remained quiet and seemed to have left me alone with my thoughts. It quickly dawned on me that I had blown it. I had ruined my chance of even having a semi-normal life at university. Everything was happening so fast that I hadn't even had time to adjust. I was so preoccupied in forcing myself to believe that it was all some stupid dream. But it was real, the entire wing-sprouting ordeal. I would never see my 'friends' again and I would never go back to university. As lame as it sounded, it was the end of my life as Tara Young, the student who attended the small university in the middle of nowhere.

Bumping along in the back of the ambulance, and not hearing the driver or Lynn utter a single word to each other, I felt myself starting to fall asleep. It had been a very trying and tiring night. Laying down on one of the hard leather gurneys, I turned over and closed my eyes.

★ ★ ★

Before I knew it, I was being roused by Lynn's sharp voice. 'Hey Tara, we're here.' The ambulance had stopped and I heard two doors being slammed. Moments later the back doors were open letting in a cold blast of very early morning air, coupled with a strange smell of rotting leaves and exhaust fumes. A bald man in a black suit came around the back and helped me out. I think he was the driver, but I wasn't so sure.

Still wrapped in the foil, I was glad that it was still considerably early in the morning and not many people could see my ripped and ruined costume.

'This is going to be your new home for a few days,' Lynn told me as she pointed over to the large Edwardian house behind her.

Stretching in both directions, there were a long row of Edwardian houses. Some were bed and breakfasts and others were private houses. It looked like something out of Oliver Twist.

The door that Lynn pointed to was as red as strawberries with a large brass knocker on the front and above that, the number 81 in gold.

'Where are we?' I asked her as the bald man closed the ambulance doors with a sharp bang making me jump.

'You're on Southampton Row, close to Russell Square Gardens.' My knowledge of London was extremely limited. I once visited the Millennium Dome some time ago, but that wasn't particularly memorable. 'Okay you, put your earpiece in,' Lynn snapped at me and marched up the steps towards the red door. Fiddling in my bra, I picked it out and put it in my ear. 'This is a hotel essentially, but only for new members such as you,' Lynn told me as she opened the large door for me.

I entered the warm, potpourri smelling building and instantly, I was in awe. The foyer was unbelievably stunning in every way possible. A large black shiny grand piano was set up in the far left-hand corner, on top of which sat a crystal vase and a bunch of red roses. There was a medium sized water fountain, with a mermaid on the top combing her hair that was right in the centre of the room. It was both strange to see one in such a small foyer and yet, it was extremely extravagant for such an apparent modest hotel. The walls were intricately decorated with silver filigree ivy vines that crept around the border between the walls. And the beautifully painted ceiling of what appeared to be Noah's Ark, which I thought, even though brilliantly painted, seemed odd with the rest of the décor.

'Ah Lynn, it's good to see you again,' said a small Indian woman at the reception desk, which was highly polished black marble, on the far right-hand side of the foyer. 'And I see you've brought a friend.'

'Ah, Amjee, I can't stay long, I have to get back, but yes this is Tara Young. Have you got a room for her?'

Laughing she said, 'Oh you and your short notices.' She bent down and brought out a fawn coloured book and after flicking through the pages, came to a stop. 'Yup, we've got her; she's on the third floor in room fifteen.'

'Fantastic.' Lynn smiled at her.

Closing the book with a snap, Amjee turned around and headed towards a grey metal box that was fixed on the back wall. When she had prised it open, I saw a load of keys with smart, polished brass key-rings on it, each with a different number.

'Yup, here you go.' Amjee grabbed a key with the numbers 3-15 on it. 'Now there are some rules you need to know while staying here,' Amjee said to me before giving me the key. 'Rule number one, you are not to leave this building under any circumstance. Rule number two, please keep your voice down, there are other people in this building and they are busy people who do not wish to be disturbed. And rule number three, if your tattoo shows,' she said giving me a meaningful look, 'you must contact me at once. I can be reached on eight-two-eight and I shall quickly come to your aid. Do you understand all of this?'

'Yes I do,' I told her, trying to sound alert.

'Good,' Amjee smiled and handed me the key.

'Right kid this is where I leave you,' Lynn said as she turned to me. 'Keep your bloody earpiece in alright? I can't pass on information to you if only your boobs can hear me.'

Blushing, I nodded.

'Good, now we are trying to sort out your papers and other nonsense that comes with you being a new member. For Christ sake stay here, keep low and do NOT get angry. Do I make myself clear?'

'Yes.' I tried to stifle a yawn but it didn't work. Lynn's eyes became soft with understanding.

She shook her head. 'You're tired, I get it. Go rest and just take some time to chill out. Have a decent meal inside you and see how you feel. When I hear anything, I shall tell you and come and pick you up, but don't bother Amjee if you can't get hold of me. When we're ready for you, we'll tell you.'

'Okay fine, I understand.'

'Good.' She gave me a brief pat on the back. 'Amjee, if you could fill her in for me? I'm a bit busy,' she said, walking out of the door.

'Sure.' She said begrudgingly. 'Night, Lynn.'

Lynn was out of the door in a flash without a backwards glance and I was left standing there in the beautiful foyer hearing her footsteps fade away into the busy London streets of a very early November morning.

I glanced at Amjee and she folded her arms and stared at me. 'Um, maybe I can ask you stuff tomorrow.'

'Smart girl,' she said and inclined her head towards my left where the bottom of the stairs began next to an archway that led off to an unknown green carpeted corridor. I hastily left the foyer and promptly ran up the pale-green carpeted stairs. Arriving on the third floor, I found my room a few doors down on the right. Upon closing my door and locking it, I threw the soft duvet back, slipping my shoes off and throwing the foil that Henry had given me earlier, onto the floor. I collapsed onto the bouncy mattress and pulled the duvet right over my head, shrouding my entire being into darkness and waiting blissfully for my unconscious to black out my nightmarish Halloween experience.

★ ★ ★

I woke up the following morning with new fresh November sunlight hitting my eyes and finally I took a good look at my room. I didn't know how long I would be staying here, but it didn't bother me, it was gorgeous and everything seemed so pristine. There was a chest of polished English oak drawers with a matching wardrobe by the back wall facing the bed. Beside it was a rich oak bedside table with a phone, a pad of paper and a pen next to a small vase of luscious red roses.

The double bed I was still laying on was soft with goose feathered pillows. As I pulled my still sore hand from underneath me, I found that, apart from that it was still bloodied and scratched; it was also now covered in mint chocolate.

'Ah bugger,' I said as I rolled over and found that my arse had a big brown and minty smelling stain on it. 'Nice job for the cleaners,' I moaned.

Climbing out of the bed and feeling sore all over, I glanced around to take in the rest of the room. The carpet was beige, very fluffy and I guessed it was also expensive. There was an Indian-style patterned rug by the dresser drawer and I smiled as it reminded me of the rug I had back in my house at University. Then as the shock of the realisation that I would never go back quickly sank in again and the tears began to fall.

My already smudged make-up from the previous night began rolling down my cheeks again. I wiped away the fresh tears with my grimy hand and decided to take a well-deserved shower, but finding new clothes seemed to prove a problem. Careful, not to sit down on the bed with my mint chocolate arse, I picked up the phone and scanning the small list of numbers, dialled down for the reception.

'Hello?' came Amjee's crisp voice.

'Um, hi it's Tara. I wondered if there were any clean clothes around. My costume is um, ruined and I can't-.'

'Have you looked in the wardrobe and drawers?' Amjee interrupted me.

Frowning I replied, 'No.' I thought it was a stupid thing for her to tell me. Why would I look in an empty wardrobe or drawers? Last night, Amjee said that I was short notice. Did she stock up my room before I arrived? And if so, when did they do it? The day I got my tattoo? It wouldn't have been last night. No shop would be open late on Halloween.

'Well then do look inside them. Have a nice, quiet day. I plan to,' she said before putting the phone down on me.

'Thanks for your hospitality,' I said into the dead phone, then headed for the wardrobe and opened it up. 'Holy cow!' I stared at the different clothes that were in there. Dresses, t-shirts and jeans all neatly hung up, with various assortments of shoes at the bottom.

Leaving the wardrobe doors open, I headed to the dresser drawers and hurriedly pulled them open. 'Ah, knickers, bra's and socks, awesome!' I took what I needed from the drawers and wardrobe and headed to the bathroom, which was situated by the door and had a nice, long, refreshingly warm shower. Once I'd finished, I glanced into the mirror and saw the black wing tattoo's on my back. In a new light, they appeared pretty, but for them actually coming out of my back, that was something I wasn't looking forward to and hoped it wouldn't be a common occurrence.

Getting changed into nice, clean clothes, I stripped the chocolate stained duvet covers and placed them on the floor, then headed towards the window to take in my view of London, which wasn't much. Being on the top floor the window seemed slightly slanted so I didn't get a full view of the street below me, but in truth it didn't matter. I heard everything. Cars beeping, bicycle bells ringing, buses revving, police sirens wailing, the whole enchilada.

I stayed in the room for most of the morning before deciding it was a good idea to get some food in me. Taking my key from the bedside table and putting my earpiece in, I made the first step out of the door and SMACK! I head-butted something and with a blinding pain stabbing me in the head, I squinted and saw a small mousey haired girl in front of me, who was rubbing a hand over her forehead.

'Oh, I'm so sorry,' I said rubbing my head. 'I didn't see you.'

The girl bowed her head and hid behind her hair, but she gave me a small nod.

'I really am sorry.'

She glanced up at me and sweeping her hair away, I noticed that she had a small tattoo of a bird's eye by her right eye. And by her left eye, there was another one, exactly the same. She was the same as me!

'Hi, I'm Tara,' I said offering her my hand.

'Macie,' she said quietly, shaking it. 'Um, I wasn't stalking you or anything.' She sounded scared.

'Er okay,' I replied, not sure how to answer her, so I decided to change the subject. 'I see you have tattoos?'

Suddenly Macie grabbed her hair and brought it forward, covering them. I didn't blame her. If I had weird, freakish tattoos on the side of my face I would do the same. So being polite, I changed the subject again. 'I'm off to get something to eat, do you want to come?'

Shaking her head she mumbled a 'No thank you,' and began to walk away.

'No, please, don't go,' I called to her.

Stopping, she turned around to face me, her soft hazel eyes curiously staring at me.

'I just, I only arrived last night and well...' I sighed. I had to face the facts and come clean about my dilemma. I was pathetically friendless and wanted company from anyone, even if it was a timid girl who despised her tattoos. 'I don't have any friends anymore,' I said feeling my face turn hot with embarrassment. 'And, I don't know where to go to get food,' I added lamely.

The faintest smile formed in the corners of her mouth and nodding, she quietly beckoned me to follow her. Leading me down the stairs to the very bottom of the foyer, she took a left through the arch. I glanced at the reception desk and saw Amjee lean over to look at me. There was something odd about her, but I had no time to think about it. I was starving, and all I wanted was a nice hearty meal.

Macie led me down the green corridor which I saw last night, and nearing the end, I smelt an array of delicious foods. She then abruptly stopped and pointed to her right. Written in curly writing on a brass label and tacked to a white door, were the words "Dining Room."

'Thank you, Macie,' I said smiling at her.

Returning the smile, Macie skipped off towards the end of the hallway and took a right at the bottom, heading off to some other place I had yet to explore. My stomach gave me an impatient grumble and, deciding to calm its hunger, I opened the double doors.

'Wow,' I gasped as I saw the room. A huge crystal chandelier hung down from the high white plastered ceiling. I started to get the impression that the T.A.T spared no expense. There were dozens of white linen covered circular tables, all set out with two sets of knives and forks and spoons, along with a napkin rolled up in a silver ring.

'Good morning Miss.'

'GARH!' I yelped and quickly turned to see a smartly dressed waiter in a white shirt and black trousers standing by a small podium.

'Sorry to have scared you,' he said smiling slightly. 'Are you dining alone?' He peeked over my shoulder. I turned around and was surprised to see Macie hovering behind me.

'Um, no, a table for two please,' I said to him.

'Very good, please follow me.' He inclined his head.

As I began to follow him, I turned to see that Macie wasn't following me. 'Come on Macie, I'm not going to bite,' I laughed.

Macie tagged along with a small bounce in her step.

Although there were only three other patrons in the dining room, the waiter led us to a window table that looked out into a little garden behind the hotel. I then discovered where the roses came from. The garden was full of trellises of red roses that covered a long archway that curved round to the left and out of sight. I must go outside and visit that garden if I was allowed.

Macie and I sat down facing each other as the waiter brought lunch menus. 'As breakfast is over, we are now serving lunch. We have a variety of food and drinks.'

I glanced at the menu but saw no prices.

'The food is free…. for us,' Macie whispered.

The waiter smiled and nodded slightly.

We ordered tomato soup with soft crusty white rolls and then the waiter turned around and left, bowing slightly before he did.

'That's Jeff,' Macie told me. 'He's the nicest person here.'

'How long have you been here, Macie?' I asked her in a casual tone.

Shrugging as though it wasn't a big deal she replied, 'About a week. I spend most of my time in the library.'

'They have a library here?'

'Oh yes, but the books aren't what you'd find in a normal library,' she said frowning slightly. 'Most of them are transcripts.'

'Transcripts of what?'

'The missions the T.A.T have done,' she said in a matter-of-fact way. 'But you'll have to ask for a key to get in.'

Nodding, I asked about how she arrived here and how she got her tattoos but she clamped up and refused to make eye contact. Instead, she turned her attention to the garden. I had somehow upset her. Talking about her tattoos seemed a sore subject.

After a while of contemplation, out of the blue Macie said, 'They arrived about a month ago.' A tear rolled down her cheek. 'They came to my house in Radstock in Somerset and tried to persuade me to come on a trip with them.' Giving a fake laugh she turned to face me. 'I thought they were rapists or something like that and I called the police. But the police didn't turn up. I freaked out and then the next thing I knew I had a bandage around my head and I was unable to see anything for at least two weeks. My eyes and head burned all the time and I was constantly crying into bandages. Then when the bandages were taken off, I was in what I thought was a hospital but it wasn't. Hospitals have windows. This room had no windows. It was dull and lifeless and I was being watched closely by a camera in the corner. It was then that I met Matt. He told me what had happened to me. I cried for hours after I realised the implications that were involved. I would never see my parents again. Idiot evil people,' she said in a harsh tone. She angrily wiped away another tear.

At that moment, Jeff had zoomed around the tables and carefully placed the bowls of delicious smelling tomato soup and warm rolls in front of us.

'Enjoy,' he said as he gently placed a supporting hand on Macie's shoulder.

'Thank you, Jeff,' she said giving him a watery smile.

When we had finished, Jeff came around quickly to take our empty soup bowls away and told us that the main-course would arrive shortly.

'So, can I ask about your story since you know mine?' Macie asked me in a more relaxed way.

'Um, where to start,' I said to her in an exasperated tone. 'It wasn't that long ago, a few days before Halloween. I accidently walked into a tattoo parlour then I was drugged and kidnapped. I woke up in agony at the hospital you described, no windows and a camera. My memory is fuzzy after that, but I woke up in an actual hospital and I met Lynn. She's a little harsh, but okay,' I said hoping that Lynn would say something in my ear but it was silent. 'She told me about my tattoo and what would happen if I got angry. Well, last night I got annoyed and the tattoo kicked in, painful as hell, but this guy called Henry Simmons helped me out.'

'Oh my God, you've met Henry Simmons?' Macie asked with wide eyes.

Startled, I replied with, 'How do you know Henry?'

She laughed. 'The transcripts. He's completed some really interesting missions, usually difficult ones. Were you one of his missions?'

'Er yes actually, I was,' I muttered bashfully.

'Oh my gosh! That means you've got a cool tattoo,' she said, her eyes brightening up for the first time since I had met her. 'I bet it's useful.'

'How so?'

'Well,' she began, shifting uncomfortably in her seat, 'can you see mine?' Leaning closer to me, she turned her head slightly so I could look at her tattoo closely. What initially I thought were bird's eyes was only half true, they were, in fact, two eagle's heads. 'When I get mad and my tattoo reacts, I have eagle sight. I can see for miles. It's really cool.'

'Wow, that is pretty cool,' I said smiling.

'So, what is your tattoo?'

'Er, wings, big freaky black wings.'

Macie's jaw dropped in awe and stared at me. 'That is so freaking cool! You can fly!'

'What?' I asked frowning at her, feeling a sense of vertigo already. 'No, I can't, and I don't want to. I'm terrified of heights.'

She cringed slightly, looking sympathetic. 'Wow, you're in for some rough training.'

I sighed heavily, it was my turn to peer out of the window and pause to think. The thought of training and flying made me feel sick. I gathered it wouldn't be training to run a marathon. I would imagine it would be army-type training and I didn't want to do things like that. I'd rather just sit out and watch other's do it. I didn't like that type of pain. They'd soon see that I was no good and hopefully let me go.

★ ★ ★

After a short few days had passed, Macie and I became fast friends. She showed me the library, thanks to Amjee and her keys, and when the weather was bearable, we went out into the rose garden.

'Oh wow!' In front was a little garden which seemed as though I had walked into feudal Japan. A rather large pond filled with various colours and sizes of Koi carp was built into the ground and was surrounded by large smooth multi-coloured rocks. In the middle of the pond, there was a small Japanese detailed wooden gazebo, with a pointy slanted dark grey roof. It was so idyllic, literally taking my breath away.

'This is unbelievable,' I said staring at the garden.

'We may get to go to Japan,' Macie told me looking happy. 'The transcripts talk about far-off places that we may get to visit.'

'What do you mean, like on holiday?'

Macie laughed and shook her head, 'No, on missions, actual missions to distant countries.'

I was a little confused and asked, 'But what will we do there?'

Shrugging, Macie began to step on the wooden planks, which were perched on top of the protruding rocks in the pond that crisscrossed their way towards the gazebo. 'Dunno.' She replied. 'The transcripts aren't really clear most of the time. But I think it depends on your ability from your tattoo. I have eagle eyes, what do you think I'm good for? Well, spying on the enemy, of course.'

A bolt of lightning passed through my stomach making me feel sick. Who was the enemy?

★ ★ ★

By the end of the week, Macie had finally come out of her shell. She showed her true colours and was such a fun person to be around, much nicer then Amanda ever was. The fourth day after I arrived at the hotel, I was to meet Macie for breakfast. Having a quick shower and changed and left my room and went and knocked on Macie's door, but there wasn't any answer, so I headed down for breakfast. As always, Jeff was there to meet me and I asked after Macie, but he hadn't seen her. Curious and a little worried, for the first time since being here, I finished breakfast alone. Once I finished, I headed back to Macie's room but was startled when I found it wide open and empty.

'Macie?' I called as I went into her room, but she wasn't there and nor was anything else belonging to her. I mean apart from the original furnishings, all the clothes and shoes were gone. It was as though she never existed. I hurried down to the foyer and after waiting for Amjee to get off the phone, I asked where Macie had gone.

'She got a call from Matt, and they came to collect her very early this morning,' Amjee told me simply. 'But don't worry you will see her soon.'

'How soon is soon?' I asked, but Amjee didn't reply to my question and decided to busy herself with paperwork.

Feeling dejected, I went upstairs to my room to lie on my bed; just staring at the ceiling feeling utterly bored and alone. For a brief moment in my life, I had someone with me, someone who was like me and who could understand me, and now I was friendless again and it hurt me a lot.

★ ★ ★

After a troubled afternoon kip, I woke up feeling restless. There had to be something useful I could be doing, but what? I didn't even want to bother having another walk in the gardens. The only place that could be mildly interesting was the library.

About half past three, I headed downstairs and back to the foyer. As I approached the desk, Amjee held up a set of keys.

'Library, right?'

'How did you know I wanted to use the library?' I asked her.

'Because Macie did the same thing when Darren left,' she told me and then returned to her work.

Macie never mentioned a Darren before. Was he a boyfriend, or maybe another member of the T.A.T.? Not wanting to bother Amjee as I hadn't done since I got here, I headed to the library.

The library wasn't huge, but it was jam-packed with books and tomes from floor to ceiling. With old leather chairs and small tables dotted around the place, it looked like I had gone back in time to the early 1900s'. Many of the books were leather-bound which I found interesting because I thought that the transcripts would have been relatively new.

Pulling out a book at random, I fell onto a nearby chair and opened it up.

'Um okay.' I saw that the book was about myths and legends, from manticores to mermaids, griffins to unicorns; practically every single myth imaginable on every continent from every era. Not particularly interested in it, I put it back and decided to actually look at the transcripts that Macie had told me about. Then as I edged past a large musty old bookshelf, I saw a metal bookshelf at the very end and went towards it.

'Bingo,' I smiled as I bent down to inspect the spine of one I had picked up. The front cover of the transcript had a date on it, "April 1943- Aug 1943". Looking at the others I saw that it wasn't the oldest and decided it was best to start from the very beginning. The oldest one was very tatty and tinted with age, giving it a deep musky smell to its yellowish covering. 'Holy cow, 1859,' I said gawping at it. Not bothering to sit on a chair I knelt on the floor placing it down in front of me and carefully opened it up:

"The O.M.C theory began approximately in 1825 when new discoveries by treasure hunters found what they thought to be a half-human half-fish skeleton in a small cove called Anstey's Cove in Devon. At the time, a young explorer named Father McEnry, who was living close-by, had written a brief account on this matter, which was quickly destroyed by the Bishop of Exeter under the Blasphemy Act 1698.

Then, years later in 1859 when Charles Darwin visited Devon, after re-searching for his Origins of Species book, he also had seen the skeleton and had stated that it was a hoax by local fishermen. As even then it contra-dicted his new and outlandish theory. But some months later after this half-human half-fish skeleton was dismissed by Mr Darwin, the remains were destroyed. (Dated September 1859 A.D Smith)"

"On Burray Island, part of the Orkney Islands North of Scotland, a fossil-ised skull was found of what appeared to be a strange animal which was part lion part bird. Upon further investigation, the locals had informed Mr Answorthy, of the University of St Andrews. This fellow was the Keeper of the Rare Books in the hidden University library, especially of the Alchemy Collection and a small compilation of the Whitman family. After Mr Answorthy had visited the site (X-71P12), he gathered intellectuals around the country. Thus, the O.M.C. had officially begun."

Flicking through the other pages there were sketches of fossils and bones and other documents of accounts people had discovered which soon be-longed to the O.M.C. Foundation, which Mr Answorthy had spearheaded during the end of 1859.

I did a double take of one of the sketches from Burray Island and was confused. Surely it wasn't real? It must be a fake? Believing that the 19th-century people were full of weird people, I put that particular transcript back and briefly glanced at others.

The one in 1943 was particularly interesting; it was based on explorations from Germany, in which the Nazi's went in search for the world's greatest treasures, but the O.M.C. Foundation managed to acquire some evidence of... I stared at the word for several minutes, waiting for it to sink in, but it couldn't; it just didn't make any sense.

'Dragons?' I said, my voice quivering with the word in my throat. 'There's no such thing. This is ridiculous!'

Snapping the book shut, I placed it back where it belonged and marched out of the fake library in a huff. 'Who do they take me for some gullible fool? I don't think so,' I muttered to myself as I crossed over to Amjee, who seemed puzzled as I walked right up to her.

Slamming the keys down, I said in a harsh whispered voice, 'I'm not some gullible idiot.'

Amjee took a step away from me, clutching her chest. Shocked at my outburst, she remained mute as I felt a painful twinge in my back and so, decided to go and chill out and eat something.

Jeff was sad that Macie had gone but was pleasant enough to talk to me. He was sitting opposite me watching me eat my bread and soup as he talked about all the things he wanted to do for the T.A.T.

'I was trained in combat, was meant to go out on missions and help, but I became a liability.'

'Why?' I asked quickly, afraid he would leave the interesting conversation.

Jeff looked at me and shrugged his shoulders. 'Sometimes things just aren't meant to happen and I ended up a waiter.'

'Hey, at least it's a job. I've been rejected for everything I tried. And after everything, this is how I have ended up.'

Jeff laughed and shook his head, 'I don't envy you. You guys are in far worse pain than I ever was. May I ask, what is your tattoo?'

'Wings, large black wings,' I said before finishing the rest of my soup drenched bread.

'Good lord, you got them?' Jeff asked looking shocked. 'The tattoo of the black angel? Wow, you must be special.'

There was a pang of panic that went through my stomach and after swallowing my bread quickly asked, 'Special? Why do you say that?'

'Tara, you're the leader.'

CHAPTER FIVE

'GOOD MORNING, TARA.' JEFF SMILED AT ME IN AN ANNOYingly perky way. I barely got any sleep the previous night and I woke up in an irritated mood. 'Table by the window again?'

'Sure.' He led me to it.

'The usual?' Jeff asked.

'Um, no actually can I have some melon and pancakes and maple syrup, please.'

'A healthy breakfast today? Why the change from your usual English fry-up that's swimming in fat?'

'Just want a change,' I told him, holding back a sigh. Jeff was too nice a bloke to start dumping all my fears and worries onto.

Within ten minutes, my breakfast had arrived and so did an unfamiliar face. I saw Jeff immediately brighten as he stopped to talk to the girl. She was about my height, with a blond bobbed haircut and was wearing dark blues jeans and a yellow long sleeved top. He briefly talked to her before leading her to my table.

'Tara, this is Saskia March, a new member,' he said giving me a wink. 'Saskia, this is Tara Young, also a new member, but she's been here a few days. Why don't I get you your breakfast and the two of you can have a talk?'

'Ta,' Saskia said in a harsh Liverpudlian accent. She casually sat down opposite me and gave me a small smile. 'So, what's ya tat?'

Still halfway through my melon, I held back a frown in puzzlement at her abruptness. It took Macie a long time being comfortable to talk to me about her tattoo and her past that went along with it. And now here was a new girl openly sharing, without any hesitation.

'Wings,' I said, not giving her any details.

'Oh, yeah? Same here,' she said in a nonchalant way.

'I beg your pardon?' I asked, melon juice dribbling down my chin.

'Ay, I've wings too. Big white things.'

'White?' I asked in amazement.

'Yeah, like from a swan or some bird like that. What colour ya got?'

'Black,' I said.

'Whoa, Gothic,' she laughed.

'So, did you get here last night?'

'Yeah, some guy called 'enry came to me house and collected me. He left after.'

Putting my melon down on the plate, I wiped my chin. 'Did Henry say where he went?' I asked her and immediately wished I hadn't as a broad smile appeared on her face.

'Fancy him do ya?' she laughed. 'He's custy alright, but didn't say anything t' me. He just dropped me off. I got me keys and told me to listen to the next instructions.'

'So, the tattoo, did they drug you and kidnap you?'

Saskia burst out laughing. 'Hell no. I already got me some tattoo's on me arse and shoulders. Tha' one on me back caned like hell, but it's worth it.'

I bit back a retort and smiled politely, continuing to eat my breakfast in silence. Instantly judging her I knew I didn't like this girl, but I didn't know why. I couldn't put my finger on it. Why was she so blasé about getting a tattoo that made you sprout wings? It scared me half to death. Even thinking about it made me feel queasy. Nope, there was definitely something wrong with her.

Her attention was caught by the other people in the room. Showing curiosity and awe, I got the impression she hadn't seen grandeur before. 'This is well boss. Like tha' feller in the penguin suit, the glass thingy in the ceil'n and tha' shiny jangler. Must have cost a pretty penny. The T.A.T must be brewsted. Mind if I have ya pancakes?' And without waiting for me to reply, she reached across and took my plate.

Cringing at her slang and vile manner, and her rudeness at stealing my food, I knew I made a good decision. I really didn't like this girl and as I watched her eating my food my hand twitched in annoyance. I wanted to slap her for sounding so injudicious about everything.

'I'm done for now, I'm goin' to have a nap, didn't get much sleep last night,' she said with a strange, mischievous grin and left me in the chair thinking. Not so long later, I found my way heading past the library door, which oddly enough was ajar. There was no one else in the hotel and Saskia was in bed. Making a snap decision, I decided to have a look.

'Hello, anyone in here?' I called, but there was nothing. No sound, not even a faint cough to confirm anyone's presence. I moved in closer and then suddenly BANG! Spinning around the door had closed and the lock was turning.

'Oy, let me out!' I shouted as I banged on the door.

I heard a loud evil laugh and then the running of feet, fading as they left.

'Let me out!' I yelled, banging on the door. 'Bloody brilliant. You COW!' I shouted, but it didn't do me any good as my anger suddenly turned into a burning pain, pitching me forwards on the floor. 'It's not hurting me, it's not hurting me. I am calm, I am calm,' I said over and over again. Sure enough, after a while, the pain eased off and I rolled onto my back, panting. Staring up at the polished wooden ceiling, there were painted scenes which I recognised as Minoan frescos from Crete. The pictures showed a large brown Minotaur in a maze. But what relevance did it have if not for decoration?

'Oh, I don't care,' I answered myself as I tentatively got up and went over to a red leather chair. Snatching its cushion, I threw it on the floor and flopped down in the chair. Lying back, I tried to get comfortable, but I couldn't, the chair felt oddly lumpy. I mumbled as I turned around to see the source of the lump in the chair and pushing my hand against the back-rest I felt what I could only describe as a book. How did it get in there and how could I get it out?

Crawling on the floor, I peered underneath it for some sort of hole, but there wasn't any; it was just old, untouched leather, with some weird patterns underneath. Checking the back I saw nothing, not even the slightest tear, only an undone brass stud that kept the leather in place.

How could someone get the book out?

'Holy cow.' It suddenly dawned on me. 'I may have actually found something interesting.' I laughed at myself at what I had just said. 'Yeah, because my life isn't interesting enough as it is.' If I were going to be stuck in here until someone wanted to use the library again, I would make-do with the privacy and limited time I had. There was no possible way I could rip the leather. For one, I didn't have anything sharp and secondly, anyone would notice if I did. So, there may be a way to get the book without ripping the chair apart. I sat down on the table opposite and scrutinized it, but I came up blank; my thoughts wandering from one thing to another. Putting my head in my hands, I stared at the floor. But my eyes couldn't focus on one single thing. My brain was a buzz of questions and annoying conundrums that I wanted to figure out.

'Come on, it can't be that difficult,' I scalded myself, as my eyes drifted onto the chair legs that had some sort of metal bit sticking out. After I had studied the legs for some time, it seemed like the chairs connected to one another by the legs... 'Oh, you've got to be joking me?'

Diving onto the floor, I inspected the chair's front legs and there, on both of them, were little metal rings that were big enough for a leg to slot into. I went to the other chairs, my heart beating madly; I saw the same thing on each of the front chair legs.

'Time for some heavy lifting Tara,' I told myself as I went to grab the nearest chair and dragged it along towards the first.

Up-tipping the weighty chair, I managed to slot the leg in half way but then the leg stopped and wouldn't slide any further. Squinting, I felt the legs and frowned; a small metal piece protruded out of the inside of the front chair leg. Depressing it, I heard the sound of a spring inside the chair leg. Slotting the leg fully into the metal ring, I noticed that when I finished, the chairs would end up in a circle. Seizing the other chair I did the same thing, and so with the others.

When all five chairs were linked together in a circle, I clicked in the final leg. The faintest click sounded from all the chairs, which was quickly followed by a small thud!

Nearly tripping over the chairs to get to the one that concealed the book, I looked underneath the seat but saw nothing. Quickly I felt the backrest and sure enough the book wasn't there anymore, but I heard a thud.

Sitting down in the middle of the circle of chairs, I was faced with another puzzle.

'There must be a box; the thud sounded wooden,' I told myself. But for the life of me, I couldn't seem to think of how to get at it. 'Okay, rule out the fact that it's not going to open from the bottom of the chair and also it's not going slide out or...' something occurred to me. Whoever made these chairs had obviously ensured that the person, who was going to uncover the truth, either had to be odd and strong, or was someone who thought outside-the-box. My eyes flicked to the tops of each chair where there were two decorative wooden grips on either side. I gently touched the top of one and then, it went down.

It was then what I knew what I had to do and it was going to be very taxing.

Unclipping all of the chairs, with great difficulty, I literally turned all of them upside-down and reattached them to each other. My heart thumped rapidly, both with exhilaration and tiredness. With each clip of the metal in the chair legs, there were extra clinks of something or other, which I didn't get, but I would find out soon.

Sweating and shedding my jumper, I hooked in the last chair leg. Each corner of the chairs was touching each other, making a perfect circuit. Then suddenly in the corner of my eye, the bottom of the first chair flipped open, revealing the book.

'Cool! I'm not stupid, after all,' I cheered feeling elated.

I pulled it out and closed the lid. Glancing at the other bases of the chairs, they seemed to make a pattern that ran around in a circle, as though continuously repeating.

'Damn, I can't take a picture.' I cursed myself. I searched the library hoping to find something I could use to copy it. Climbing over the circle of chairs, I went to a small bureau by the side of the locked doors and searched through the top drawers. 'Yes, scrap paper and is there a pen?' The top and middle drawers provided no pen, but the third one did. Racing back to the chairs, I climbed over them and marked out each pattern from each chair and then afterwards marked them out in a straight line, with more accuracy. They looked like the text of a strange cursive language, but I couldn't really be sure. The only thing I could make out was some lines which, if I hazarded a guess, could relate to the number 13, but I didn't know what it stood for.

Suddenly I heard movement outside the doors and I froze. Someone's footsteps walked by and continued on. 'Crap that was close,' I whispered. I had to put the chairs back; there was nothing they could offer me now.

It was three times more difficult unclipping the chairs as they seemed to be magnetised together and forcing them apart was challenging. But finally, after what felt like an hour, I fell down into one of the separated chairs, sweat dripping down my face. Reaching for the scrap paper and the book, I now had the time to look at it...

'Tara, ya still alive in there?'

It was that cow, Saskia. I remained silent. Then hearing the sound of the lock being turned I hastily placed the scrap paper inside the book, then wrapping my jumper around it, sat back in the chair just as the doors opened.

'You're not reading?' she asked as I heard her walk towards me.

'Oh is that why you locked me in here? You wanted me to read the whole library?' I snapped back feeling a pinch in my back.

'Oh, testy. I was only having a laugh,' she tittered.

'Well sometimes, both parties should be laughing and as you can probably tell by my tone, I am not amused.' I got up off the chair and went right up to her. 'I think you have just crossed the line, Saskia,' I said to her. 'First of all your pranks aren't funny, second of all I am not stupid,' I said with a small smile which she would never understand. 'And thirdly every tattoo is different and everyone has a different ability. We might have wings, but we are nothing alike and you shall figure that out if you even get inducted. Now, give me the keys,' I ordered.

Stunned at my outburst, Saskia handed me the keys and I marched out of the library, holding the door open for her. She passed by me, eyeing me carefully.

'You're not goin' to lock me in?' She asked as I slammed the doors behind her and locked the library firmly. I didn't want anyone going in there and figuring out the chairs as I had done. I didn't know why, but I felt a certain protection over the secret of the chairs. They held a mystery that led me to believe that I was the one to discover it.

I gave her a sharp look. She had been an idiot and though she didn't realise what she had done, I believed in karma. She'd get her comeuppance sooner or later. 'No, I'm not as spiteful as you,' I snapped and ignoring my back pain, stormed off to hand the keys into Amjee to tell her exactly what Saskia did. However, I'd keep the secrets of the chairs all to myself.

I headed up to my room and locked the door only to hear the noisy relentless traffic from outside. London was never a quiet city. I closed the curtains and stared at the little red leather bound book. It was rather old, probably somewhere in the region of a hundred to a hundred and fifty years. It had no title on the front cover or on the spine. If anything, it looked like a notebook. Intrigued by its appearance alone, I opened the cover and out fell an old yellow-tinged piece of paper.

Carefully unfolding it, I scanned the old scrawled writing and there on the top right of the piece of paper was the date.

March 7th, 1884

Dear Reader,

Congratulations upon discovering this book. No doubt you have already ascertained this little book has been a great burden in my life and unfortunately it is now up to you to finish the task I have been unable to complete.

This book contains my life's work on discovering how myths came to be as well as the inner workings of the Origins of Mythological Creatures Guild. Already a top secret foundation, it has hidden remarkable secrets on the myths and legends of our time. The O.M.C Guild is dangerous and one of its members, an immortal no less, has sought out one of the earth's most precious secrets, part of this secret I have already discovered. He is determined on finding this book and the secrets it holds. The Guild cannot find out the truth, if used unwisely, it would undo the world. The Golden Rule must be kept. For this reason, I leave you with the burden of protecting this book and destroying the evidence that is hidden around the world. I believe that you are the one to find the last piece of evidence and to learn the truth of the planet and all the magic it holds.

To get to the location, you must travel afar to a pitted bay. Seek out a natural sanctum where 'The dragon descends into the sea'. Find the shark that's out of water, keep a weather eye open and be prepared for some swimming. Reach its fin by a bamboo trail and X will not be the start but it will be the end of your beginning.

Keep the belief...

D.C Raleigh and Miss Ann Smith

Placing the letter beside me, I flicked through the book and laughed at what I was seeing. It was full of notes, scribbles, diagrams and pictures from years ago but they were all of dragons and fairies and other mythical creatures. On one piece of paper was the word, "Warning" and underneath was a small description that the O.M.C planned to capture bones and fossils of dragons, centaurs, and other magical creatures, to collect them. But it didn't explain why.

'Okay, this is beyond weird,' I said out loud.

'What is?' Lynn said in my ear.

Making me jump and yell in fright, I slipped off the bed and landed hard on the floor. 'Ah crap, that hurts. You could have given me some warning,' I moaned, rubbing my bum.

'Sorry. Anyway, pack your bags, missy. We're bringing you in.'

'What?' I gasped, sitting on the bed in shock.

'Are you deaf? I said we are bringing you in, so pack your bags.'

'I don't have any bags,' I frowned.

'It's a figure of speech. Just get ready. We'll pick you up in two hours.'

'Okay.' I looked at the book, 'gives me plenty of time to sort things out.'

I tidied the room as best I could and headed downstairs to say goodbye to Jeff, but as I passed the foyer, Amjee called me over.

'Yes, Amjee,' I said approaching the desk with a beaming smile. 'Can I help you with anything?'

'Come round here.' She said pointed to a small door by the desk.

I frowned in puzzlement and did what she asked and as soon as I went in, she grabbed my arm and pulled me close and put her fingers in my ears to take out my earpiece. She then shoved me down onto the floor and slammed the door shut.

Putting the earpiece into a heavy looking metal box, she slammed it shut and moved it aside.

'What?' I asked pretending to be dumb. 'Are you insane? Give that back please, I need it.'

'Don't play games.' She pointed a warning finger at me. 'I know you've got it. You were over two hours in the library and I just checked the chair and the book has gone.' Blinking at her angry face, I tried to get up but she wouldn't let me. 'You're not going anywhere until you tell me which side you're on!'

'Amjee, you're not making any sense,' I said to her in a frightened tone. 'I don't know what you are talking about.' Her looming figure scared me stiff. She had such a commanding air about her when she was angry. I was glad that she didn't have a tattoo.

'Tell me how you got the book from in the chair!' she hissed.

'Why should I tell you?' I said getting angry, feeling a twinge in my back. 'Why didn't you get it if you knew it was in there?'

'Tell me!' she shouted then peered over the desk to see if anyone had overheard her. She looked back at me, her eyes gleaming with anger and awe. She was surprised that I'd got it. Surprised I'd figured it out.

'It was a puzzle.' I explained. 'You had to line up the chairs, but turning them upside down. There was a mechanism. The chairs were magnetised or something like that. Then the bottom of the chair flipped open and the book was in the seat.'

Amjee smiled and nodded. She moved back and offering me her hand, helped me stand up. 'Clever girl.' She sighed with relief and shook her head. 'That's thinking outside-the-box.'

'You've tried to get the book?'

She nodded. 'I've tried for years to get it out. I discovered the book when my father and mother delivered the chairs from India many, many years ago. My family were in the same business that I'm in. I mean with the T.A.T,' she added.

'So the chairs, your parents placed the book inside one of them?'

She nodded. 'Yes, but of course I was never told how to open it. My father said if I were the right person, then I would be able to open it. But that was many years ago,' she said sadly. 'My parents, however, donated the chairs as a collection to this place and the chairs have been in the library ever since. And, of course, over the years I have had complaints from members saying there is something wrong with one of the chairs, but no one seemed to know its secret.'

'The book, where did your parents get it? And why was it placed in that chair in such an obscure manner?'

Amjee stopped smiling and looked at me. 'Tara you have discovered something beyond your years and understanding. Though I don't know the full extent of what the book is, I do know this. The T.A.T is dangerous. Whatever that book is, follow it and do what it says.'

'But-but we're part of the T.A.T,' I mumbled.

Amjee shook her head. 'Did Macie tell you about what she discovered on the T.A.T.?'

I was about to open my mouth to say no, but closed it again and thought about it. Macie had told me lots of things but then I recalled the time we were in the garden. "*I have eagle eyes,* she'd said. *What do you think I'm good for? Spying on the enemy, of course.*"

'You'll find out soon enough, Tara,' Amjee continued, 'but keep your mouth closed when you're wearing that.' She pointed to the box with my earpiece in. 'Whenever Lynn is talking to you, your conversations are being recorded and monitored. They spare no expense when it comes to detailed ops. I've managed this far without the T.A.T. knowing what I know about that little book you found, but if they know you have it, then both of us are in big trouble. Just keep your head down and do as they say.'

★ ★ ★

By half past six, I was waiting in the foyer. I had already said my goodbyes to Jeff and Amjee and sure enough, on the dot, the doors flew open and there was Lynn; completely drenched and looking cold.

'Dear God, I hate November weather, especially in London.' Lynn seemed angry as she approached Amjee. 'Evening Amjee, she wasn't any trouble, was she?'

Amjee looked over towards me and smiled, 'No she was a perfect angel.'

'Right, missy. Let's get you to the car.' Lynn nodded at me. 'Amjee, again thank you,' she said. 'And take care of Saskia.'

'Yes, I will do when she's not in trouble,' Amjee replied in a smarmy way. 'All the best,' she called, 'and take care, Tara!'

I waved goodbye as I hurriedly crossed the foyer, shadowing Lynn.

Outside the miserable cold November evening, a long sleek-looking black car was waiting. Its door opened for me as I got near to it.

'Get in,' Lynn shouted from inside.

Taking a steadying breath, I raced towards the car. Thick droplets of water splashed all over me within seconds then slamming the car door, the driver rolled off and I was taken away to the unknown place of the T.A.T.

Sometime later as the silent driver got through the congested city of London, where even in the rain there were too many people, he pulled up outside the back entrance to the British Museum where I saw a lion statue just outside my window. I had no clue why we were here, but I remained quiet. I had been to the museum before on a field trip in secondary school. It was to see Tutankhamen's treasure, though I didn't really appreciate it when I was fourteen; I just liked the fact that we had a day off from school.

'Wait here.' Lynn grabbed a black umbrella and got out the car. Watching her run through the back doors, she was in there for a few moments before I saw her run back outside beckoning me.

Opening the door to the pouring rain, I ran towards Lynn, who was waiting for me at the top of the steps, then guided me through the doors. Lynn shook off the droplets of water from her umbrella and handed it to a security guard who was posted by the door.

'Thanks,' she said shrugging off her coat and passing it to him. 'Come on you,' she said to me, as I tried to wipe the rain from my face.

Lynn directed me to what appeared to be a closet for coats on the left and I was instantly confused. 'I don't get it,' I began, but she shushed me and looked around to the security guard and nodded at him. He pressed a small red button on the wall which was marked for the Fire Bell. I gasped as the closet room revolved and a glass lift came into place.

'Quickly in you go,' she said to me.

As soon as I got in, Lynn followed behind me and closed the door. Waiting for a bit, the lift revolved back around and then going to the right-hand side, Lynn pressed the button that was marked 'Level 0'. Shuddering slightly, the lift began to descend.

'Tara, welcome to the T.A.T base,' Lynn said smiling; as I saw a large cathedral-sized room appear around me as we continued our way down.

'Oh my gosh!' The vastness of the room took my breath away, but that's not all it did. I noticed we were extremely high up. My vertigo kicked in and I pressed myself against the back wall and tried to breathe and not have a panic attack. I could feel my palms sweating and my heart rate go up, all the time peeking to see what I was getting myself into.

The room was sectioned into three parts. One part was concealed behind a red bricked wall; above it were glass offices that seemed to float in the air. The middle section was where two long desks were situated housing at least a dozen sleek black computers with people tapping away and talking into microphones behind them. On either side of the middle section were huge screens which had pictures of people showing their missions and whereabouts. The last section, where the lift was heading, looked like a security area.

As we got lower into the busy cathedral-sized room, I felt a little more relaxed and steadily, my heart rate began to beat at its normal pace. Lynn didn't see my moment of panic and I was unsure whether it was a good idea she should know I was afraid of heights.

'Up there is for the new recruits,' she told me simply, pointing at the glass offices. 'That's where you'll have lectures. Beyond the red bricked wall is the barracks or your bedrooms and beyond those are the combat and training rooms.'

The lift gently touched the ground and the glass door automatically opened to the hubbub of the T.A.T.

'Right, over here Tara,' Lynn said, guiding me to a small room to the left where another security guard was perched on a stool, looking utterly bored. 'Evening,' Lynn smiled at him. 'New recruit is called Tara Young.'

His eyes widened in surprise for the briefest second then, nodding, he turned around in his stool. Not even bothering to get up he bent down to retrieve something from a grey cabinet behind him.

'Standard uniform,' he said as he brought out a brown cardboard box and taking off the lid I saw the same black uniform that was delivered to me on Halloween.

'This time, please wear it,' Lynn said quickly as the guard brought out another object.

'Watch,' he said taking out a slim looking black watch. 'Tap the side and you can communicate with other members of your team. Also, there's a homing beacon in there should you ever get lost,' he told me. 'Now please relinquish any metal objects on your person.'

I gave him my own watch, a Christmas present from my brother several years ago, and my small peace-sign earrings.

'I think that's it,' I said as I felt the little box concealed inside my large jumper. Amjee had suggested I wear a baggy jumper to hide it.

'All clear, you can take her through now.'

Following Lynn out of the small room, she rambled on about what was in the middle section of the room.

'I was working in here when I was talking to you when you put in the earpiece for the first time,' she told me with a proud look. We passed men and women in drab-looking uniforms of white shirts and blue trousers who were tapping on their computers and speaking into their microphones. 'But for the time being, I shall be training you here. I am your operator.'

'What type of training? Because Macie told me that I would have to fly with those things and I have to tell you, I-um, I don't like flying.'

Lynn's face went from shock to utter amusement and burst out laughing. 'You cannot be serious?'

'Everyone has a fear,' I snapped at her. 'It's your own fault for not checking up on my background.'

Continuing to laugh, Lynn beckoned me forwards into the second chamber, leaving the hubbub and all its business alone. I had a feeling she didn't believe me.

Walking through the middle section, I noticed a few people look at me curiously. Some opened their mouths in surprise, others looked scared, but

Lynn didn't seem to notice and soldiered on towards the red bricked wall. It was completely covered in graffiti and had a small archway. In the centre of the archway was a large set of black shiny doors. I asked Lynn what the faded graffiti was and looking sad she pointed out one that seemed clearer than the others, "1940- Barry Henderson died here".

'Barry died, along with many people of the T.A.T, which was called the O.M.C back then, when the Duveen Gallery was destroyed by a bomb in the 1940 Blitz.'

I was stunned into silence. I had come across the O.M.C before; it was the Guild for the Origins of Mythological Creatures. Didn't that bloke, D.C Raleigh say that the O.M.C was a "dangerous guild"?

'I know how you feel,' Lynn said as she saw the look on my face. Then guiding me through the black doors which she opened with a passkey, we came to a long beige carpeted corridor where various doors were situated on either side. Then about one hundred yards down the corridor, I saw another set of doors. 'This is the barracks,' she explained. 'There are currently nine members of the T.A.T. You are the eighth. Saskia is the ninth and the last.' We walked down the corridor and stopped outside a door that had my name on it. 'This is your room. Breakfast is between seven and half past eight. The refectory is situated right at the very bottom of the hallway,' she said pointing ahead of me. 'All of your clothes and personal belongings from your room in the student house are in here.' She then pulled out a plastic card and swiped it through a small little door panel on the left-hand side which bleeped, flashed green then hearing a click, the door opened.

'Wow, spacious,' I laughed, as I saw that all of my stuff had been moved there. 'Um, so my university degree…'

'You quit,' she said simply with a sad face.

'And my family?'

She hesitated for a moment then said, 'We haven't been able to get hold of your mother or father. In fact, if you could let us know where they are, that might be helpful.'

I shrugged my shoulders. 'I don't really get along with my parents or my brother. Last I heard they were on a business trip in Europe. Haven't heard from them since.'

'I see.' Lynn's face changed from sad to irritated, but I didn't know why. Maybe it was her job to tie up loose ends with my family. But it would be a hard time trying to find them, when my parents were out of the country, they couldn't be reached. At all.

Giving me the card, she said in a stern voice, 'Well I shall see you tomorrow after breakfast. Good night.' Turning on her heel, she walked off and closed the doors behind her.

Leaving me alone in my new room, hidden beneath the priceless artefacts of the British Museum, I cried into my pillow that smelt of home. I wasn't angry, which was good because I couldn't stand another bout of feathers at this point in my life. I just wanted to cry, let every grief I had out of my bottle and cast the bottle into the sea, never to be seen again.

★ ★ ★

Many hours later, drifting in and out of a light sleep, I woke as I heard movement from outside of my door. Staring at the ceiling in my dark room, I waited with bated breath. Then sitting bolt up, I heard movement again. My alarm clock beside me read 00:33 pm and as strange as it seemed I was in no mood for sleep. I was restless. Throwing the duvet back and changing into a t-shirt and pyjama bottoms, I snatched my key card from the bedside table and decided to go for a wander.

Walking barefoot, my feet gently padded along the carpet as I quietly headed down the corridor. Now and again, I would stop and stare at the doors which had names on them. 'Darren Hay', 'Lottie Masters,' 'Hannah Smith', 'Samuel Paris', 'Lionel Stone,' and 'Macie Green.'

'Macie,' I whispered as I gently knocked on her door. 'It's me Tara, are you awake?' I waited for a reply, any type of reply, whether a snore or a yawn, but I got nothing.

Thinking that she was maybe in a deep sleep, I continued down the hallway towards the set of double doors that led towards the refectory. But as I opened the first set of double doors, I heard a large crash of what sounded like metal trays fall to the floor. Feeling a bit frightened, I crept towards the refectory doors and heard shouts and laughs. Pressing my ear against the wood, the voices continued and after a while, I gathered that they were not children. They sounded my age, especially when I heard one of them say, 'That got me right in the ass crack.'

Attentively, I opened one of the doors and peered inside. Everyone was in their nightclothes; it looked like some odd slumber party.

'TARA!' I heard Macie yell from across the chip-smelling room.

'Macie, shut up shouting,' a boy with messy, dirty blond hair chided her. I noticed instantly that he had fish tattoos by the side of his neck.

'I'm so happy you're here,' she said coming over to hug me as I went inside, closing the door behind me. 'Did you arrive today? Oh, it's been so much fun. Oh and guess what?'

'Um what?' I asked as the others stared at me, oddly. Some of them folded their arms in annoyance. They grouped together on three circular tables, sitting on the top and resting their feet on the chairs.

'It doesn't hurt anymore,' she said happily, drawing attention away from them, 'my tattoo. Isn't that brilliant?' she exclaimed. 'After my initiation or induction or whatever they call it, they gave me an injection in my eyes and voila, pain-free!'

The boy with the fish tattoos frowned at Macie's outburst. 'You're such a freak Macie.'

Sticking her tongue out in a childish way Macie said, 'This is Darren. He gets gills and breathes underwater but when he gets them, he can't breathe the air, so he ends up running around like an idiot trying to find water.' Macie laughed. 'The first day I got here I made him really angry and when he got gills, he ended up sticking his head in a bucket of water.'

I stifled a giggle as I saw Darren's mad-looking face, but he seemed to keep his temper. Looking at the others I gave a small smile, but they didn't return it.

Macie grabbed my hand, pulled me in their direction. 'Everyone, this is Tara, Tara this is Lottie, Hannah, Sam and Lionel.' She introduced them all in turn.

Glancing at them, I noticed their tattoos all too easily. Lottie, a pretty petite Asian girl childishly fingered her long dark hair. She tilted her head to show me her tattoo. It looked similar to Macie's eagle eyes, but they were smaller and darker. Lionel, a tall, muscular built guy had one jackal-looking head by his right ear. Hannah, a rather pretty full-figured girl who seemed to be the leader of the group, by how the others looked at her, had one tattoo on the back of her neck. Turning around and lifting her thick curly blond hair, I saw that it was in the shape of a triton. Then there was Sam, who had the most interesting tattoo, which was intricately decorated in such a way, it was almost as though it was its own species. He had a small black speckled Cobra just below his neck. The tail seemed to wrap around his neck, as though it could choke him.

'Each of us has unique abilities,' Hannah told me calmly. 'You must be aware now that our tattoos give us certain types of... powers.'

'For example, I can spit venom,' Sam said with an evil smile.

From behind me, Darren gargled in his throat. I cringed and felt instantly ill. 'Is it deadly?'

Sam looked at Darren and smiled. 'I haven't had the chance to test it, want to find out?'

Suddenly strong arms wrapped around my front, pinning my arms to my sides. Darren's voice then loudly rang in my ears. 'Do it, Sam.'

Macie shouted out, 'Stop!' but Lionel and Lottie suddenly grabbed her and held her back.

I looked pleadingly at Hannah, who was just giving me a vacant expression. 'Please stop this,' I begged her, but her face was impassive; completely emotionless.

As I continuously struggled against Darren's strong arms, he squeezed tighter, forcing me to breathe, in short, sharp gasps; just enough to keep myself conscious.

Sam's face suddenly contorted with rage and his eyes bulged out of their sockets, their hazel colour instantly changing to a hideous blood red. He then began to gargle what I could only think of was the venom in his mouth and was prepared to shower me with it.

Still struggling against my captor and begging for help, though no one seemed to bother apart from Macie, I said, 'Please don't annoy me... it hurts so much...' But my voice was barely audible as I tried to breathe in more oxygen.

'You idiot, we want to see these wings of yours,' Darren hissed in my ear.

I looked over at Macie; pain was etched on her face. 'I had to tell them,' she told me as she began to cry. 'They did the same to me. I'm so sorry Tara.'

'Please don't,' I said, as thick salty tears started to pour from my eyes. I could clearly feel the pain from the last time it happened and I didn't want it to happen again. 'It hurts more than you know, please don't!' But Darren began to laugh at me. I saw Sam's face and an evil grin appeared. Even though I tried to keep my temper, I did not like being held against my will and certainly not with the prospect of being spat at, with venom, so I began to feel angry.

Sam stopped gargling and took a step back.

'Sam's a crack shot,' Darren whispered in my ear. 'He never misses.'

The familiar pain rippled down my spine, feeling as though my back was going to explode. As my muscles tensed ready for the searing pain, I was about to scream out in frustration and agony when I felt a sharp prick in my arm.

Looking in front of me I saw Hannah; she had a strange smile on her face.

'Sam, swallow it, Darren get back,' she ordered them.

Darren did as he was told and backed off just as I felt a zap of white hot pain sear down my back. Unable to support myself, I collapsed to the floor. Then with a loud rip from the top of my t-shirt, the wings burst out of my back in spectacular fashion. The wingspan was well over fourteen feet.

'Holy kack.'

'Bloody hell.'

'Oh my god!'

'Cool!'

Confused as to what the hell was going on, I slowly stood up and the wings naturally folded back against my body. I made sure that my eyes didn't catch the black wings on either side of my body. The fact that I could sprout wings still freaked me out.

Hannah nodded and came towards me, then began to circle me, as though I was an object on exhibition.

'Do they open out when you are angry?' she asked me as she came to the front to face me.

I thought back to the first time this happened and remembered snapping at Henry. 'Yes,' I said hesitantly, taking a step back.

'So this is our new leader?' Hannah asked the others, smiling at me.

'I don't think so,' I heard Darren mumble to Sam.

Macie approached me but wasn't looking directly at me, she was looking behind me. 'Whoa Tara, they are so cool.'

'And so soft,' Lottie smiled as she joined Macie beside her.

'No, they are a pain in the arse,' I told them, 'and I don't think I'm your leader,' I added looking at Hannah. 'There is another girl with wings, same as me but hers are white.'

'What?' Hannah asked looking annoyed and stamped her foot. 'They can't do this! They told me, they said our leader would be the girl with the tattoo of the black angel, this is not right, something has to be done!'

After a while, the wings fell away, as I had no need for them. The black feathers fell to the floor like an odd rain and turned into fine ash, disappearing as though they never existed.

Macie told me that the injection Hannah had given me, albeit a stolen injection, was to relieve the pain of the transformation.

Hannah refused to say anything else and, as the small party dismissed themselves to bed, Macie walked back with me to my room.

'Oh, a few rules which you may need to know,' she said stifling a yawn. 'You are not allowed to leave here until expressly permitted by your operator, or for training or missions. The rest of the time, we spend in here learning, reading and studying martial arts for at least six weeks.'

'What?' I shouted in annoyance, but Macie flapped her hands at me, urging me to shush.

'I know but try and get some sleep and I'll see you in the morning.' She gave me a small hug and ran off towards her room.

★ ★ ★

The following morning as I went to the refectory for breakfast, I was amazed to see how many people were there. It wasn't just us tattooed people, but also other members gathered into groups around the tables. The chip smell from the night before had gone entirely and was now replaced by bacon, toast and coffee. My mouth began to water.

I didn't see Macie as I scanned the room, but I did see Lionel, Darren and Sam as the boys racked up a high mountain of food on their plates. They chatted away happily in the corner. The other workers seemed to give them a wide birth, though I didn't know why. I caught Darren's eye and gave him a small smile, but he ignored me so I headed over to get a tray.

'What'll it be?' the dinner lady asked, as I approached the counter.

She seemed pleasant enough, with a white apron and hairnet; she greeted me with a warm smile. I wish others would do that in the morning. 'Um, an egg and two slices of toast, oh and some bacon, please.'

'Right you are,' she said continuing to smile. She took a clean white plate from a pile in front of her and dished out the food.

'Where are the drinks?' I asked, looking hungrily at my breakfast.

'Just down there to your left.'

'Thank you.'

Finding an empty table near the wall, I sat down and began munching on my breakfast and sipping my tea, which perked me up. Sitting there alone, I watched the early birds laughing and talking amongst themselves and before

I knew it, I was being stared at by everyone. But also the noise level in the room had lowered to a general hush.

At first it was just a glance in my direction; their eyes flicking over towards me, or catching me out of the corner of their eyes. But after a while, I had people turning in their chairs to get a good look at me.

'Oh crap,' I muttered under my breath, as I tried to ignore them. I could feel myself going red. I was uncomfortable at being stared at. It was that feeling you got as a child, joining a new class and everyone is talking about you. I hated that feeling. I hated the limelight. It wasn't the fact that they were talking about me in a good or bad way. It was the fact that they knew something about me and I didn't know them. That was something I never liked. Being the centre of attention wasn't a good thing; it just attracted trouble.

'Hey Tara,' Macie's voice called out in the room.

Several people turned to state at her, briefly taking their eyes off me.

Macie came to my table after she got some food and sat next to me. 'Sleep well?' She asked cheerfully as she dug into her plate of various fruits. I hadn't seen Macie so upbeat and happy in the morning. Maybe Macie felt better surrounded by others who were similar to her, it made me feel slightly better at least.

I shrugged in response; I wasn't in the mood to talk much this morning. I wanted to get the hell out of there and go back to my room.

Looking around at people who were still staring at me, Macie saw how nervous I was.

'Don't worry about them,' she smiled. 'They just want to make you angry.'

'Erm why?' I asked, not fully paying attention to her.

'D'uh,' she laughed. 'They want to see your wings. Hannah was telling me last night, you need to be careful. Though these people are part of the T.A.T., they still freak out at the slightest thing.'

After breakfast, I headed back to my bedroom to get into my uniform. It was a one-piece that was both warm and waterproof, although to my horror, I found slits in the back and it took me a long time to figure out that they were for my wings. I shuddered as I stared into the mirror. The suit didn't look very attractive. The only upside was that it showed off my figure. But I wasn't in the showing off mood, so I thought it would be appropriate if I put on a baggy jumper. Searching through my clothes, I found the one I wore to the girl's house on Halloween. But thinking about that night and all the things that went wrong, about Amanda and her snide remarks, about and what Jennifer had told me I got angry. And before I knew it, I felt them in my back, as though they were itching to come out.

'Oh, please for the love of God NO!' I yelled. Just like last night there was no pain, only a slight discomfort and within seconds they blew out of my back, pushing black feathers all over the place. 'FOR THE LOVE OF GOD!' I yelled at the top of my voice. 'I do NOT need this right now. GARH!'

There was a small knock on my door. I heard Macie's voice. 'Tara, the operators have called for a meeting, are you ready to go?'

'No,' I snapped at her. 'Just go without me, please.'

There was a brief pause before asking softly, 'Tara, please let me in?'

Sighing, I went to the door and yanked it open. 'How the hell am I gonna go to a frigging class like this?'

Dressed in her one-piece uniform and looking totally relaxed, one of Macie's eyebrows rose up towards her forehead and shrugged her shoulders.

'GARH,' I yelled again as I kicked my wardrobe door, snapping it back and making a small dint in it.

'Why are you so angry?' Macie asked me in her small, meek voice, the same voice which gave Macie her lovely demeanour, quiet, humble and passive-aggressive.

I sat heavily on the bed and I told her about Amanda and the others and how they had upset me. Being a good friend, Macie had listened to everything of what Amanda and Beth had said and done to me, especially when it concerned Mr Hunky Henry Simmons.

'Ah,' she said a while later. 'Well, don't worry about them or them,' she said nodding towards my wings. 'It's tough getting used to your wings now that they won't hurt you. Anyway we'd better go to class or we'll get told off for being late.'

Feeling like a freak, I closed the door and followed Macie down the corridor towards the refectory and then took a right and up some marble steps. We came to two doors. A glass door on the right that led off to the floating offices, and a set of red doors in front. She took the glass door.

Opening it, I saw that everything was made of glass, even the floor. It felt odd and also very scary walking along it and I was determined not to look down or else I might faint. Instead, I looked at the rooms I passed and felt my face blush with pure and utter embarrassment. People stopped talking to their colleagues, or dropped papers or turned in their chairs to stare at my hideous large wings.

'They think your wings are cool, trust me,' Macie said with an encouraging wink, giving me a fleeting glance at my wings. But I wasn't convinced.

Hurrying past the on-lookers, Macie led me towards a room at the very end on the right which overlooked the middle section of the cathedral room.

'In here,' she said, as she opened the door.

Everyone was already there, including a few others I hadn't seen before. They all seemed particularly bored sitting in a chair staring at Lynn, who was at the front, until they noticed me and my big feathery problem.

'Are you determined to cause me trouble?' Lynn snapped at me, crossing her arms as Macie and I took a seat behind the others.

I sighed and shook my head. I wasn't in the mood to explain. 'Anyway, while you're finally here Tara, let's get something's straight. The T.A.T members are divided and led by an operator. Dave, here,' she pointed to a rather handsome late twenty-something man with dark ginger hair, 'is the operator for Henry and Sam.' He gave a small nod. 'Matt,' she continued, nodding to an extremely good-looking guy on her left with a half-moon scar around his right eye '–is the operator for Macie, Lionel and Lottie. And Roxy, who isn't here currently as she is overseas, is the operator for Darren and Hannah.' Lynn cleared her throat to get everyone's attention. 'Right, now I'm going to give you a brief overview of how the company started. So pay attention.'

Macie immediately sat up in her seat, attentive. Her eyes never wavered from Lynn as she paced back and forth, explaining how the T.A.T started. Within the space of seconds, I had zoned out and after a while, I felt my wings disappear. Lynn, Dave and Matt had noticed but said nothing on the subject and so, I continued to stare blankly into space. Then Lynn clapped her hands, getting everyone's attention. 'Alright listen up everyone. Please go with your operators for training. Hannah and Darren you can go back to your rooms, Roxy will reschedule some time for you when she gets back. Right you lot off you go, Tara, come with me.'

'See you later.' Macie smiled as I followed Lynn out of the classroom and turning left, we continued down the glass covered corridor. I was still ensuring I kept my eyes face forward; God how I wished I wasn't afraid of heights.

'Where are we going?' I asked her as I'd double backed towards the barracks section, but as we left the floating offices, Lynn took a right and went through the set of red doors.

'I want to see if you can fly.' Lynn continued walking, leaving me standing there, frozen in fear.

'Whoa! Wait, Lynn,' I called, catching up with her as she headed up a small set of red-bricked steps and stopped under an archway.

'Welcome to the training room,' she said dramatically as I reached the top.

'Wow.' I gasped. It was huge. Not as big as the cathedral room, but very close to it. Every wall was painted a very deep red colour and there were various exercise apparatus around, some that were old and careworn from the 1970's. There were also several brand new treadmills, weights and bars, exercise bikes, rowing machines and cross trainers, and even a handful of multi-gyms.

'Ignore those,' Lynn said as she walked past them all, with me following her like a lapdog.

'Can we use them?' I asked her as I passed a Body-Solid GLM84SM Lat Machine. In my head, I felt like a nerd and smiled to myself. I used one at my gym back home.

'In your free time yes, but I want you to use this,' she said as we headed towards the back of the red painted gym and came to yet another set of double doors.

'Gosh, how big is this place?'

'Big enough,' she replied. 'The British Museum doesn't know we're down here. This room is tattoo specific.'

'Okay, I take back the wow for the other room, holy cow!'

It was as tall as theatre and all of this hidden secretively under the British Museum. I was still amazed by it all.

There was a rectangular inbuilt swimming pool on the left-hand side, and Lynn noticed me look at it. 'That's for Roxy's charges, Darren and Hannah.' Nodding we walked past and I saw a thick metal wall on the other side that was completely covered in lion-like scratch marks, from Henry, I gathered. But what was the most stunning and purely terrifying thing in the room, was a circus-like catching-net suspended about three metres off the ground. The net was tied to the very top of the ceiling. It was at least fifteen metres off the ground and a small, narrow platform protruded over it, attached to some metal steps that led up to it.

'This is where you're going to learn how to fly.' Lynn looked at my horrified face.

'Um, Lynn I have a confession to make,' I felt sick. 'I'm afraid of heights.'

CHAPTER SIX

'I'M SORRY,' I SAID TO LYNN OVER AND OVER AGAIN AS SHE looked infuriated. 'I'm so sorry I thought you guys would have known that. I thought you would have picked up my flaw.'

'Flaw? Tara, sweetheart, that isn't a flaw. It's just I don't even think there's a big enough word for it. Dear God!' She yelled at me.

'I'm sorry,' I said to her again, a little more loudly than before. 'But I did tell you.'

Lynn took a couple of steps away from me as she began to think. Meanwhile, I was trying to think of new ways to apologise without saying the word 'sorry.'

'Look, if you want me to try I will but... '

Lynn put up her hand to stop me. 'Why are you afraid of heights? There's usually some logical explanation.'

'Not always,' I scoffed as one of my friends from secondary school was afraid of butterflies.

'Tell me, why are you afraid of heights?' Lynn asked me again.

I screwed up my face in thought as I tried to remember a good enough reason and then it came to me. The memory I had was when my brother dropped me when I was younger. He couldn't catch me, and I fell to the floor and ended up in A and E with a nice little cut on my head.' After I had explained this to Lynn, she let out a breath of relief.

'Ah okay, it's not heights,' she said with a reassured smile on her face. 'It's fear of falling which was why you connected it to heights. But this is good, we can work with this.'

'Oh yeah, how?' I asked, feeling slightly pessimistic.

Lynn laughed. 'Because you'll be entirely dependent on yourself. If you don't want to fall, open your wings and fly.'

'Well, in case you haven't noticed, I can't even flap. My wings feel like they've been glued on from a mean prank.'

'Then Tara, may I introduce you to your partner.' For a brief moment my heart sunk as I thought Saskia was going to appear but instead Lynn pressed a small button on the wall. To my amazement a panel in the wall turned around, like something you'd see in a spy movie, and revealed a large industrial sized circular fan. 'This is Mr Fan,' she said proudly.

'Oh, very funny, you're hilarious,' I said sarcastically.

'Now, get your wings out, climb that ladder and I'll turn on the fan when you reach the top,' she ordered.

Thinking of Amanda instantly made me angry and within seconds I had sprouted black wings again. Whimpering as I walked towards the flimsy-looking ladder, I ducked under the circus net and checked for holes. 'Are you sure this thing is safe?' I called to Lynn as I thought I saw part of it had frayed.

'Its nylon, you're fine,' Lynn called back, sounding a little annoyed. 'Just get up there.' Nodding but still worried, I went over to the ladder and grasped its cold metal sides and took a deep breath. 'Get on with it, we don't have all day,' Lynn snapped.

'You try and overcome your fear in a bloody minute why don't you!' I snapped back.

Lynn abruptly shut up, making me smile for just a millisecond before the realisation of what I was about to do. It hit me like a tonne of bricks. My heart palpitated; my hands sweated. Shaking the fogginess from my head, I tried to think of a song to distract me and wonderfully, as well as annoyingly, I had Funky Town in my head. Concentrating on the tune and the lyrics, I began to climb the narrow ladder.

'Have you got your eyes closed?' Lynn asked me in a curious tone, just as I was about to get into the second verse.

'Um yes. Why? Do you want me to up-chuck my breakfast over you?'

She paused and then said, 'Never mind, carry on.'

Sighing, I resumed the song and continued climbing, although I knew both the song and the ladder would end, soon.

'Tara, you'd better open your eyes now,' she called up to me, her voice echoing around the room.

'No, I don't want to, I don't want to, I don't want to,' I repeated over and over as I clutched onto the last part of the ladder. But then the ladder stopped and stretched out onto the platform.

'Are you listening to me?'

'Yes, but I don't want to,' I said under my breath. 'Yes, alright!' I shouted.

My right eye opened ever so slowly and through my eyelashes I saw the plank. It was narrow, looked slippery and I was stupidly high up.

I closed my eye shut and shook my head. 'Nope, I'm not doing it!'

Below me, I heard some swearing and then suddenly a whirring sound came from beneath me, and a blast of powerful air swooped upwards. I screamed out from the surprise of the cold wind circulating around me and clung to the ladder for dear life.

'I'm coming up!' Lynn shouted at me and, moments later, I heard her footfalls on the rungs and the vibrations becoming stronger as she got near me. 'Why do you make my life difficult?' Lynn barked as I heard her right behind me.

'I'm s-.'

'Don't say you're sorry,' she interrupted me. 'Now, I am not going to let you fall, alright. I have good reflexes, trust me. Now open your eyes and get up onto the platform.'

'I can't, I'm going to fall,' I whimpered.

'So what?' Lynn shouted over the noise of the whirring fan below. 'If you do, you'll land in the net, no harm done alright?'

'Ha, yeah right,' I mumbled, but I don't think she heard me.

'Please Tara,' she begged. 'Get onto the platform.'

Opening my eyes slowly and seeing it in front of me, I began to move onto it and reached out with sweaty palms to grab onto the narrow sides. Carefully, I inched forwards until I could feel Lynn standing right behind me.

'Okay, now give me your hand,' she ordered as she placed a hand on my left arm. 'I've got you no matter what, alright?'

Nodding, I let go and grabbed onto her hand and gently she helped me stand.

'Don't look down; it won't do you any favours. Now slowly turn and face me.'

Taking a steadying breath, I did as she asked, and suddenly she was right in front of me smiling with confidence. 'Right, open your wings,' she said.

I glimpsed at my wings curiously and tried to make them part of me. Denying them so long, I didn't have any control over them and only when I was angry did they fling out to the sides. Moving my new muscles that Henry had talked about, very slowly, I forced the feathery appendages open and felt relieved.

'Okay, brilliant,' she said still smiling at me. 'Now I am in a precarious position here, so I want you to move back a couple of steps to the edge, okay?'

Nodding stiffly and still holding onto her, I inched backwards in small shuffles.

'A bit more,' Lynn said as she wanted to plant both feet firmly on the platform. She looked at me and smiled, 'right now we are going to jump together alright?'

'You'd do that for me?' I asked in amazement.

'Of course I will. I'm your operator. So now, I want you to slowly turn around and face the end.'

'But-.'

'I'm still going to be right behind you, I promise,' she said.

Holding onto me, Lynn helped me turn around and face the plank of death, which I thought was a splendid name for it.

'Right, are you ready?' Lynn asked.

It felt like she had let go of me. 'Um, no not YET-'

I screamed as Lynn pushed me off the platform. My legs and arms flailed as I pitched forwards towards the ground, regardless of there being a net, that wasn't the point. The force of the wind was extremely strong as it pushed against me, and as though some strange instinct kicked in, my wings started to move on their own. Flapping up and down and making me glide on the air currents. Of course all the while this was happening I was screaming out in pure terror. Lynn on the other hand was shouting in joy, saying 'You can fly, you can fly!' I was not amused.

After a couple of seconds, I began to feel how the wings worked and for some strange reason my phobia had completely gone. It was as though I was meant to be in the air. I was born to be flying off the edge of cliffs or mountains and diving down towards the ground; taunting the earth as I swooped away from certain death. I was going against the very creation of man itself. I was flying. I was loving it.

The longer I was in the air, the more confident I felt in controlling my wings. To tilt them one way, to float off one direction or to fold them back to dive a little. I was getting the hang of it very easily. But then suddenly, Lynn turned the fans off, and that's when I realised that it was the wind that was keeping me airborne. I then had to work extremely hard to stay in the air.

'Keep at it, you're doing fine,' Lynn called up to me.

After a while, I was slowly starting to feel tired. My back was aching from the new muscles and my legs were numb from not being used. It was an odd feeling for my body, and soon I could not fly anymore and plummeted to the ground, being safely caught in the nylon net.

Lynn was laughing so hard she was bent over, clutching at her sides. 'That was brilliant,' she said. 'The look on your face when I pushed you, ah it was priceless.'

'Not funny,' I snapped at her, as I rolled off the net and jumped to the ground. 'Why did you do that?'

'I had a hunch that instincts would kick in if your wings were prepared to fly.'

Suddenly my wings crumbled into ash and disappeared.

'Ah, that's a weight off my back,' I said, stretching.

'Good. Now then, let's get you something to eat.'

Back in the refectory, I still noticed people watching me but also they were staring at Lynn.

'They are looking at you now, what have you done?' I asked as we sat down at a table together.

'Because I'm with you most likely.' She smiled.

'So, what does an operator do apart from making my life a living hell?' I smiled politely back.

'Hmm, well apart from getting you safely here, we are also in charge of your missions and training. And, to be honest, I wasn't prepared for that fear of heights thing.'

'Can I ask about the wings? How did I get them? How does a tattoo give you powers? You said that the T.A.T. stands for Tattoo of Arcane Technology... well what's the technology?'

'The technology can give you arcane abilities through your tattoo,' she said but didn't explain any further and instead changed the topic entirely. 'Oh and also you have your induction tonight, so wear something nice.'

'What do I have to do?' I asked her, feeling apprehensive as all thoughts flew out of my head.

'Just stand there and look pretty. It starts at six, but it won't last long as I have to get back to the hotel.'

'To pick Saskia up,' I said feeling a little irritated.

'Yes. I guess you didn't like her then?'

'Um no, I didn't. But that's another question. It was explained that I was to be the leader because I have wings. Well, how is that going to work out when there are two of us who have wings?'

'Well,' Lynn said as she relaxed back into her chair, 'after Saskia's induction we shall start the combat training and see how you fare in that. Being a leader, you need the strength to take command and do what's necessary to complete the mission. Of course, there's more to it, but I can't tell you. Just be yourself, you'll be fine. Besides, training is finished for this morning, so you can go and chill out in your room if you want?'

'Can I try the wind thing again?' I asked her but she shook her head.

'Not unless you are supervised by me no, sorry,' she added looking sad for me. 'Besides your wings have gone and I know how cumbersome they are for you.'

'Yeah, I guess.'

She suddenly got up, her chair scraping along the linoleum floor, and picked up her tray. 'Well, I'll see you tonight, six o'clock don't be late!'

'I won't.'

After I had finished my lunch alone, I headed back down to my room and closed the door.

I saw the edge of the little book by my pillow and went to it, flicking through the pages. I finally got the hint that this was the book that the T.A.T was after. It had all the evidence they needed on how to find myths and legends from across the world, but I still couldn't believe that this was real. Magic didn't exist; myths and legends weren't real… Or were they? Frustrated, I shoved the book back under my pillow and heading out of my room I went to see Macie. She was the only one who I knew who had read the transcripts. Walking up to her door, I rapped on it gently.

'I'm coming,' Macie door opened and smiled. 'Oh, hi Tara, what's up?'

'Can I come in?' I was nervous about what I was going to ask her.

'Oh sure,' she smiled and I closed the door after me. Macie's room was sparse with only a single bed, a desk, a small bedside table with a lamp and a notebook on top, a wardrobe and a set of drawers. There was no character to her room. No personality.

Leaning against the door, I gave Macie a smile but I knew it didn't reach my eyes, and she appeared automatically worried. 'Macie, I've come across something, and I need your opinion,' I told her hurriedly as she sat on her bed staring up at me.

'Oh, what's that?'

'Mythological creatures, legends and magic, do you believe that they are all real?'

Macie was stunned into silence then after a while asked, 'What do you know?'

Taking a deep breath, I explained to her about the things I read in the library and what I had just asked Lynn about my wings. 'She didn't go into much detail. It sounds as though she didn't want to tell me. But Macie there's something else.' I took my earpiece out and motioned for her to do the same. I held them in my hand, covering them entirely. 'The T.A.T. used to be called the O.M.C that stood for Origins of Mythological Creatures. They used to go out and collect evidence of myths and legends. I came across a book in the library, and there was a note inside it. It was from a Mr D.C. Raleigh. He said that there's someone within the O.M.C who is hell-bent on finding something that is dangerous to the world. The letter said that I'd have to find this thing before this person from the O.M.C. does.'

Macie stood up and began to walk around her room, flapping her hands and repeatedly saying, 'Okay, okay, okay.' Pacing the room a few times, she stopped and looked at me. 'I want to see the letter, please.'

Taking her back to my room, I wrapped the earpieces in a pair of jeans and then threw them at the back of my wardrobe. Macie was sitting on my bed with furrowed brows, staring at the floor, biting her nails. I pulled back the pillow and took out the note from the book.

'I found it in the library concealed in a chair,' I handed it over. 'Amjee said that the O.M.C, or rather the T.A.T., is a dangerous organisation. If that letter is correct, we have to find this thing in the pitted bay before the T.A.T. do.'

She read it carefully, then folding it, placed it back inside the book. 'Okay, so say this is real. Then what do we do?'

'We need the others on board; we need to know they are on our side. On Amjee's side.'

'Darren hates you,' she said apologetically.

'I'm not too fond of him either, but I don't see anyone else with abilities that can help, do you?'

'Tara, this is information overload.' She sighed heavily. I stared at her for a while; the silence grew between us as we thought out what I had just said. 'I think I'm going to go back to my room.' Nodding, I gave her back her earpiece and opened the door for her; she wandered down the corridor. Coming from the opposite direction, I saw Lottie and Hannah walk towards me with smiles on their faces. 'Lynn just told us you can fly, well congratulations,' Hannah smiled.

'Um thanks,' I said, forcing a smile.

'Want to join us in the entertainment room? The guys have got some weird programme on Youtube,' Lottie said pointing down the hall.

'Er, no I'm okay. I'm just going to chill out for a bit in my room and read.'

Hannah nodded. 'Alright then, see you at the induction.' She and Lottie linked arms and walked happily to the entertainment room. Closing my door, I put my earpiece in and getting out the little book, began to read.

Not realising the time flying by, I heard a knock on my door. Looking at the clock, I saw it was 5:15pm. 'Oh bugger. Hang on!' I called, tucking the book under my pillow and reaching out to open the door. 'Henry!'

'Hi Tara.' He appeared a bit bashful. 'I am here for your induction, but I need to tell you something.'

'Can it wait until afterwards? I haven't got dressed yet,' I asked breathlessly.

'Well-.'

'Great, thank you, see you in a bit!' Henry gave me a funny look then walked out of my room, forgetting to close the door. Closing it myself, I hurriedly got changed into my weird uniform with the slits in the back, which I had taken off earlier. Adding my personal taste of a smart matching black jacket, I grabbed my key for the door and ran out.

As I entered the cathedral room, as I was now nicknaming it, I was shocked to see all of the computers and desks had gone. To my amazement, they'd been replaced by a small metal stage, a podium in the centre of it and dozens of comfy red chairs; all neatly lined facing the stage.

'Tara Young?' asked an unfamiliar voice from my right.

Glancing over, I saw a woman with short red hair, flecked with blond highlights. She had a pair of very cool funky lime-coloured glasses which clashed with her hair, but abnormally enhanced her strange, almost violet coloured eyes.

She marched right up to me and stuck out her hand. 'I'm Roxy, Hannah and Darren's operator. I'm here to escort you to your seat.'

'Oh, thanks.' I shook her hand.

'This way please.' She gestured to the very right of the chairs. 'You know, I've heard a lot about you,' she said coyly. 'Lynn told me all about your flying and your penchant for it.'

I was about to sit down at the back, but Roxy kept going, heading towards the front row. I remained quiet as I was unsure what she wanted me to say. That I clearly had a reputation in the T.A.T. already? That I was terrified of flying? Or that I found the wings cumbersome?

'Your seat is here,' she said pointing to a chair in which on the back someone had written, "T.Young".

'Thanks.' I sat down, feeling very uncomfortable.

'When the President calls for you just go up, shake his hand, and say a few words, and then stand back, alright?' She looked at my jacket and frowned. 'And I suggest you take that off before you go on stage, you don't want to ruin it.' And abruptly she walked off, swishing her bum.

'Why, what's going to happen to it?' I called, but I didn't think she heard me. 'Hell, what do I even say?' I mumbled to myself as I looked around the room. More and more people were coming into the cathedral room to take their seats; their eyes glanced at me. 'Hi, I'm Tara, thanks for kidnapping me and giving me a tattoo that when I get angry, wings come out of my back.'

'You know, talking to yourself is one of the first stages of madness,' I heard Henry's voice behind, making me jump.

Turning around, I saw him take a seat behind me.

'Damn you scared me, don't do that again.'

Nodding, he then laid back in his chair with a strange expression appeared on his face. 'You're the boss.'

I frowned at his comment. 'Why are you sitting there?' I asked him changing the subject. 'Why don't you sit in the front with me?'

The same strange expression was suddenly slapped on his face and standing he replied, 'You're the boss.'

Still confused and unsure of how I managed to obtain Henry's free will, something just clicked in my head. 'Oh, you wanted to tell me something earlier?'

'I did?' He looked puzzled.

'Yes, when you came to my room. What was it?'

Henry gave me a vacant expression and shook his head. 'I'm sorry, I can't remember.'

'What is going on?' I asked loudly, attracting people's attention. 'You came into my room wanting to tell me something not half an hour ago.' I clicked my fingers in front of him. Blinking a few times, he slowly focussed on me, and ever so silently he said, 'Oh crap.'

'What, what is it?'

Shaking his head as though perplexed, he said, 'My last mission...' he gently touched his right arm. 'I must have been attacked. But I, I can't remember.'

'Attacked by what?'

But Henry didn't get the chance to reply as there was a squeal from behind me. Looking up, I saw Macie, Lottie and Hannah come into the cathedral room, followed by Darren, Lionel and Sam.

'Tara,' Macie said as I waved at her.

'Will you tell me?' I asked Henry hurriedly, as the group came over to us.

'You'll find out sooner or later,' he said pinching the bridge of his nose and sighing.

As soon as all the chairs were full, the Texan man, Mr Maynard, got up onto the metal stage by the podium.

'That's the President of the Company,' Macie whispered in my ear. 'I've only met him once during my induction. He seems like a nice man.'

I was about to turn around and tell her about my meeting with him, but I didn't get the opportunity. After a few short seconds the room became silent and clearing his throat he spoke into a small microphone before him. 'Ladies and gentlemen.' He opened his hands in a warm gesture. 'Thank you for coming this rather blustery evening. Tonight is a special night. Once again I want to welcome another member to the T.A.T. team.' He paused slightly and smiled like a toad as applause erupted around the room. He nodded in a happy way. 'Handpicked by our finest; she has the talent and skills to go far. And with the proper training from her operator, Lynn, she will be the perfect leader of the group.' He nodded at her. 'So, without further ado, I am pleased to welcome Miss Tara Young.' The room burst into applause again, and I felt my face blush in embarrassment.

Sitting there, all eyes on me, I tried to shrink back into my seat, but Macie suddenly pushed me out of the chair.

Nearly falling to the floor Macie quickly said, 'Get up there and take your jacket off.'

Doing what she said, I flung it over the back of the chair and got up on stage. The room suddenly began to cheer as I reached the podium. I gave them a nod and a weak smile, and suddenly realised my mouth was horribly dry. I swallowed, but my throat felt like I was eating sand.

Mr Maynard then turned to the room and said, 'And we shall welcome our lovely Lynn to the stage.'

Getting more whoops and jeers than me, Lynn trotted onto the stage and mouthed 'Thank you' at the crowd.

Mr Maynard took a step back for Lynn to approach the podium and address her adoring fans. 'Hello everyone.' She waved and shielded her eyes from the lights that shone on her like a small dazzling sun. 'I'm here to help introduce Tara Young to you and her great asset. A university student from Wales, she has already passed the personality test and aptitude test with flying colours this morning,' Lynn said giving me a sideways glance. 'And I say flying colours because, as you are probably already aware, Tara has been given a tattoo of black wings. Along with another new member Saskia, who has got white wings, we hope that this year, we can finally accomplish our goals. So without further ado, I give you, Tara...' she said clapping.

Lynn motioned me over to her and fiddled with something in her left hand, before thumping me on the back. I felt a small prick.

'Say something nice,' she whispered in my ear.

'Hi um,' I said weakly into the microphone. 'Before I came here I was afraid of flying.' The room suddenly erupted in laughter, and it took them a while to calm down. 'But today I overcame that fear and I... I hope to help the T.A.T. to the best of my ability.' The crowd clapped and cheered and having nothing else to say, Lynn placed her hands on my shoulders and brought me back while Mr Maynard stepped out of the way.

'Oh crap.' There was the familiar twinge in my back. 'Please, don't do this. It's so embarrassing,' I hissed at her.

'Let them rip, Tara,' Lynn called to me, clapping along with everyone else.

Having no choice as Lynn had obviously stabbed me with something, I tensed up as the massive black wings exploded from my back once again making the audience clap and cheer even louder.

'I give you Tara Young, the leader of the T.A.T,' Mr Maynard said clapping with everyone else.

My face flushed from embarrassment, and though I tried not to smile, I couldn't help it and grinned at my captive audience.

Everyone soon began to get up and head towards the back of the room. Macie beckoned me off the stage and together made our way towards the refectory.

I tried to find Henry in the sea of people, but he had slinked off.

'That was so freaking cool,' Macie laughed as we went into the refectory. 'Awesome timing on the wings.'

'Oh yeah, what a show I gave them.' I frowned in irritation as I watched Lynn and Maynard talking animatedly to the left of the stage. I then folded my wings back so I wouldn't hurt anyone. But as we approached the doors to the refectory, everyone had stopped moving. It looked like a queue for an important meeting, with everyone dressed up smartly.

'What's going on?' Macie asked as she tried to peer over people's heads but was too short to see barely over anyone's shoulder.

'Dunno.' Standing on my tiptoes, I saw that everyone was grouped together around something and then all of a sudden Dave went charging past us, pushing people out of the way.

'Move, MOVE!' he shouted.

A few people followed behind him, pushing everyone to get to the refectory. I heard a few murmurs from people and Henry's name came up. I was about to ask what was going on, but then the sea of people parted as Dave carried Henry, heading for the infirmary. A few other people in white lab coats came out of nowhere and followed Dave and Henry. Appearing as white as flour, Henry's limp body was taken back to the cathedral room, the doors closing quickly. A sense of shock spread through all of us like wildfire and more murmurs began as people moved away.

Macie and I continued to stare. Utterly dumbfounded.

'Macie, Tara!' Hannah called, as she Lottie and the others made their way back to join us.

'What happened?' Macie asked, but Hannah shook her head and looked around, watching people with suspicion.

Something about Hannah made me more concerned about Henry's situation and it was confirmed when she looked at me and said, 'We need a private chat.'

I understood and thought ahead. 'Quick, with me,' I motioned to them as I whipped out my key card and made them follow me to my room. Closing the door firmly behind me, I locked it and waited to see if anyone was outside. When I knew it was quiet, I turned my attention to the group that I was now in charge of commanding.

The boys stood around my bed, their arms folded, shocked and sullen. Lottie and Macie sat on my bed and bounced slightly. Hannah remained standing.

'Comfy bed,' Lottie smiled, trying to lighten the tense atmosphere.

'You have a bigger room than me,' Darren said crossly. 'Why is that I wonder?'

Sam rolled his eyes. 'Don't start. Everyone's got a bigger room than yours. Just deal with it.'

'Hannah?' I asked softly. 'What is it?' My wings suddenly melted into a fine ash. I stared at the small pile around my feet. Poor cleaners, I thought. I noticed that everyone turned to Hannah. She evidently seemed to know what was going on. But before Hannah opened her mouth to speak, I motioned for everyone to take out their earpieces. The boys were reluctant at first, but when they did, I explained to them that the T.A.T records everything what's said. They understood instantly.

When I finished placing the earpieces in the wardrobe, we all looked at Hannah for an explanation. 'Henry was attacked by Odin's Ravens the other day. Huginn and Munin,' she said quietly.

'What?' Everyone said together.

Nodding, she whispered, 'I overheard some of the operators talk about it. Whether they meant for me to hear them, I don't know.' She frowned, unsure.

'Not our operator's, right?' Darren said looking confused.

'Oh, they'll know. Believe me,' Lottie told him.

'Wait back up. Odin, the God of all Gods from the Norse myth?' I asked them.

Macie glanced at me in a confused way, but the others looked at each other as if they knew something we didn't.

'Tara, I have something to tell you,' Hannah said to me slowly. 'The T.A.T are liars. It may look like ink that they've put in our bodies, but it's not.'

A little shocked that Hannah was openly saying this, I gathered that possibly Amjee had something to do with it, or they were clever and figured it out for themselves. But it worried me that Hannah knew something about our tattoos because Lynn had neglected to tell me.

'Then what the hell is it?' I asked her, apprehensive.

Lionel stepped forward and put his hand up. 'Excuse me, but is she ready to know Hannah? She's only just been inducted. Can't we give her some time to figure it out?'

'It's mythical blood.' Hannah ignored Lionel's warnings. 'You can believe me or not, I don't care at this point,' she said looking at Lionel. 'Tara, you have been given the power of the Sirens and so as I understand, has Saskia.'

That took me back to one time when I was younger. I think I learnt about them when I was in secondary school. 'The Sirens, you mean those weird ladies who sing to sailors?' I asked as I remembered from Homer's Odyssey.

'The very same,' she nodded confidently.

The others didn't laugh or smirk or titter. Their faces were like stone, and it worried me that they weren't joking. The little book that I had found in the library, the warning that Mr Raleigh had given me, were all real. But then that meant that it was someone from the T.A.T. who was after the book, after the world's most precious secret.

Lottie reached out and touched my arm in a comforting manner as I must have looked like a frightened child. But it was the truth, I was frightened. If myths were real, then there were a lot of bad myths out there that could cause a lot of damage. 'The Sirens weren't just women who sang to passing sailors to lure them to their deaths,' Lottie told me. 'They had wings that looked like angels.'

I glanced at my pillow and saw the corner of my book. Was it time to tell them what I had discovered? Was it going to be the right choice? Making a snap decision, I reached out for the book and passed it to Hannah. 'I found this in a chair in the library back at the hotel. Saskia locked me in there, and I ended up discovering it.'

As Hannah opened the book, the note fell out. Picking it up and reading it, her mouth opened in shock. 'This is my relative!' she said brandishing the letter. 'Miss Ann Smith. My mother told me about a Mr Raleigh in my family.'

'Okay brilliant, but the letter itself, is it real?' I asked her forcibly.

She sighed. 'Here, what do you think?' The others crowded around her to read the letter.

'Oh crap,' Darren moaned the first one to read it. 'This is all we need and oh look, Tara has managed to bring them the information that they need,' he said angrily.

'At least I found it,' I snapped.

'But we're in a good position for them not to get it, right?' Macie asked, but no one looked at her. They were all thinking about the situation we were in and it was a complicated one at that. Here we were, knowing that our tattoos were not technology but instead were magical blood from myths. I also had a book in my possession which could give away the world's biggest secret and the people who were after this secret were right outside my room. It was indeed a conundrum, but what could we do about it? Was there even any way of getting out from under the British Museum without sparking any manhunt?

'So, what are we going to do about it? If myths and magic are real, if they gave us these powers from myths, then we have to stop the T.A.T from getting this secret, right? I got this book for a reason; Amjee said I was destined to find it. But what do I do with it?'

Hannah shrugged and looked at the others; they shrugged in unison.

'It's your call Tara, you are our leader,' Sam said with an air of disdain.

I frowned. 'Oh, come on, don't be like that. I know you don't know me and we've been forced to become a team, but we are in this together. Regardless that I'm classed as your leader we have to do this as a team, right? With everyone on board? Macie,' I began, making her jump as I addressed her. 'Are you with me?'

She bit her bottom lip. 'I still don't understand this myth stuff, but yes, I'm with you.'

Darren groaned, 'She's just saying that because you're her friend, and you're intimidating her.'

'How am I?' I asked, affronted.

'She's always intimidated by everyone,' he snapped, scowling at Macie. 'Well, I for one am not on board.' He folded his arms. 'I'm not going to say anything to the operators.' He said which surprised me, but the impression I got from Darren was that he was saving his skin, and not anyone else's. 'But if you go against them, then you'll be in trouble. Our operators are strong, and they are good at fighting and capturing. Look at how they caught us!'

'I agree,' Sam nodded. 'Tara, it's your call, but don't drag me into it.'

'Two peas in a pod you are,' Hannah said waspishly. 'Well, get out then.' She pointed to my door. 'If you aren't with Tara wanting to stop the T.A.T from finding this secret, then leave.'

Lionel, who was quiet throughout, hit Darren on the arm. 'We're a team dude. We don't have anyone else, but each other. There's strength in numbers. There are seven of us and four of them.'

I counted everyone in the room. Apart from Saskia, who I don't think anyone would like, Henry didn't seem to be part of Lionel's equation. 'Is Henry not part of the team?' I asked. Hannah scoffed.

'He's the T.A.T.'s golden boy. He was the first member to be inducted over a year ago. It's because of him that all of us were kidnapped, given our tattoos and sent here.'

That made me feel somewhat better, but Saskia's account of getting her tattoo worried me. She told me she hadn't been kidnapped. Was she lying? Or did Maynard and Lynn think that she'd come willingly?

Darren and Sam glanced at one another. 'As a team?' Sam asked him.

Without warning, Darren came up to me with an evil scowl on his face. 'For the record I don't like you and you are not my leader. But,' he put his hands up in submission, 'because I am a part of this team,' he said huffily looking at Lionel, 'I'll help the group.'

Sam nodded without comment. 'Good. Then let's have another look at this letter, shall we?'

Three hours later of endless arguments and pointless discussions on how to leave the base, how to find the secret, and what it could be, we couldn't agree on anything. The only thing that Lionel figured out was that this "pitted bay" may be in Asia, but whereabouts, he didn't know. 'I'll do some research,' he said and stifled a yawn. Everyone was tired, and the lights would be out by ten. They didn't have long until they had to go back to their respective rooms. Darren and Sam were also being most uncooperative with everything we were talking about, so at half past nine, I decided to call it a night. Darren and Sam left my room pretty quickly, pushing past me looking extremely sulky and didn't even bother to say goodnight. The girls and Lionel, however, bid me goodnight.

'We'll figure this out, Tara,' Macie smiled. 'Though it's going to take a while getting used to the fact that we've been injected with mythological blood! How cool is that!' She laughed, then closed the door behind her.

I fell against my bed and stared at the bland white-washed ceiling and thought about the day's events. I wasn't sure that having mythological blood in my body was a good thing. By all accounts, magic didn't exist. And no matter how I examined things, from any and all angles, there was no possible way of leaving this place unless we practically broke out. In reality, it was at least ten to one, and those were extremely unfortunate odds. Even if we did manage to leave this place, how were we going to get to Asia? It's not like we could get on a plane and fly there. These T.A.T people have amazingly good security. They would stop us before we even got to the glass lift.

About half an hour later as I was about to slip into sweet unconsciousness, there was a knock on my door. I pondered for a moment on who it could be until I heard her voice.

'Tara, it's Saskia, open up.'

I ignored her, pretending to be asleep. Knocking again a little louder, I gritted my teeth and went to open the door.

'Took ya long enough.' Barging into my room she glanced around, 'God it was so borin' in the 'otel.' She went to my desk and peering at her the mirror fluffing her hair. She glanced at me through the mirror then with a sneer turned and slowly approached me. 'And oh yeah, I forgot ter give ya this.'

Raising her hand she took a swing at me but I grabbed her arm in mid-air and shoved her away from me. 'Don't you dare hit me!' I shouted at her.

'You deserve it for rattin' me out ter tha' old bag on reception.'

Advancing towards her in a threatening manner, I said slowly 'Leave Amjee alone. You shouldn't have locked me in the library in the first place.'

'Whatever,' she said glancing around. 'Wha' a crappy room. Mine's obviously bigger, wi' better stuff in it.'

I scoffed, 'Hardly, the rooms are all the same size,' I said though I wasn't sure myself. After all, Darren had complained that my room was bigger than his, but I didn't know if that was true. 'Besides, I didn't know it was a childish competition to have better-.'

'Lynn said ya flew today,' she interrupted. 'I bet ya freaked out. Ya don't look much like a leader, that's why I'm apply'n for the position,' she said with a smarmy look.

'What?'

'Yeah. I asked Lynn about it; she said it was sound.' She picked up one of my hair clips that I had left on my desk and put it in her hair. 'Nah, this is tacky.' She checked my mirror again. Taking it out, she threw it on the desk so hard one of the wooden beads came out. Heading for the door and swinging her arse like a drunken donkey, she blew a kiss at me and with a small, 'Ciao,' left my room, slamming the door on the way out.

Fuming, I kicked the bed and grabbed my pillow, screamed into it. My wings then burst out of my back, ripping yet another t-shirt.

CHAPTER SEVEN

THE FOLLOWING MORNING THE PLACE WAS ABUZZ WITH people gossiping about one of two things. The first was poor Henry. He was still unwell and was being taken care of by the finest T.A.T. doctors. The second was Saskia, who was lapping up the attention like a deranged mongrel.

Dressing up like some tart out for the night in Bradford, with a low-cut bright pink top and matching hot pants, Saskia pompously burst into the refectory and shouted, 'Ariite people!'

Macie and I were sat at the table farthest away from her; I tried to duck behind Macie, but the Liverpudlian had already spotted me.

All eyes turned to Saskia as she strutted towards the breakfast queue, waving at people who looked at her as she walked, swinging her arse like a lame duck.

'Oh, good lord,' Macie said her mouth half open, 'why is she wearing that?'

Sighing, I shook my head and continued with my breakfast.

Moments later Darren, Sam and Lionel came over to us, stupid smiles slapped on their faces as they stared at Saskia. They seemed to be a bit friendlier towards me since we now had a common goal, but Darren was still off my Christmas list.

'Damn that Saskia is hot,' Darren said as he turned to watch her bend down to pick up some cutlery she dropped "accidentally".

'Nice arse, love,' Sam shouted out across the room.

Several of the older members turned to look at our table, giving Sam a cold stare, but he didn't seem to give a toss. He wolf-whistled as Saskia flicked her hair out of her eyes, giving him a sexy smile and a wink.

'That's sexual harassment!' Macie whispered.

Sam rolled his eyes, but Darren answered. 'She apparently wants to be wolf-whistled at and does she look offended? No,' he answered his question. 'Sam's given her a compliment. Now wolf-whistling to ugly girls? That I would find offensive to them because they don't deserve it.'

'Oh, forget this. I can't eat,' I said pushing my breakfast away as I suddenly felt ill. 'And you,' I pointed at Darren, 'are a horrible excuse for a human!'

'Tara darlin', where are ya flyin' off to?' Saskia called to me as she practically glided towards our table. I felt embarrassed by her and decided I needed to make a quick exit. This girl wound me up, probably more than Amanda, Beth and Heather did. And I didn't think it was conducive getting annoyed this early in the morning and sprouting feathers.

'Tara, don't go,' Macie pleaded. 'Stay a while longer.'

'Yeah, do stay, Tara,' Saskia said, placing her tray next to mine and grabbing a seat, pushed Macie out of the way. 'Sorry, 'bout that chick, wings only club 'ere. And 'ello, ariite lads,' she said glancing at Darren and Sam, who were practically drooling over her.

Macie smiled up at Saskia as she got pushed out of the way.

'Macie is sitting there,' I said to Saskia but she ignored me.

'So are you part of the T.A.T?' She asked, but the question seemed too complicated for them and they just stared at her. 'I'll make it a bit more straightforward. What's your name?'

'You can call me boyfriend.' Darren grinned at her.

Smiling at him she shook her head, 'Sorry but I don't date pug-fugly guys, but maybe Tara does?'

Gritting my teeth, I smiled politely. 'I'm going back to my room.' Standing up, Macie looked lost as I left her in the hands of Saskia. I didn't want to leave Macie alone, but I could feel the wings threatening to rip out of my back. I was irritated by Saskia in every way possible. She got to me easily, and she knew it.

I controlled my anger until I got back into my room. And as I screamed into my pillow the wings burst out of my back. I'd destroyed a third t-shirt. 'God damn it I'm like the frigging Hulk!' I shouted to no one.

Moments later there was a gentle knock on my door, but I wasn't in the mood to entertain.

'Sod off!'

'Excuse me?' Lynn said through the door. I moved and grabbing the handle, yanked the door open to see an irritated Lynn standing in the hallway. Her dark brown eyes flicked to my wings, and she huffed. 'Saskia annoyed you then?'

'How the hell did you know?' I frowned, yet slightly impressed.

'Just a good guess,' she said. 'Anyway, while you're um, winged, I suppose we should go, I have something to tell you.'

'If it's about Saskia wanting to take my position as the leader then fine, let her take it, she's welcomed to it.' I spat, as I took my uniform out of my wardrobe and threw it on the bed.

Lynn sighed in exasperation. 'Tara, what on earth are you talking about now? Saskia isn't going to be the unit's leader; you are.'

Frowning, I shook my head. 'Last night she told me that she got permission from you to apply for being the leader.'

Lynn laughed, 'No, she's not, you don't ask, you get chosen, and it was you. Henry, when he's better, is your second-in-command if you're unavailable, but we can talk about that later. I need to debrief you on what's going to happen during the next couple of weeks. You've got ten minutes. Meet me upstairs.' She closed the door, and I found myself smiling. I was the leader, not Saskia.

'Well, that's one up for me anyway.'

I met Lynn upstairs in one of the strange, floating glass rooms. Dave, Matt and Roxy were already there, sitting around a table, immersed in a deep discussion and all, for some reason, were wearing a navy blue uniform.

As I entered, Matt looked up. 'Oh well, she's already prepared,' he smiled.

Trying to hide my blushing cheeks, I nodded and went to sit by them.

'Right now Tara, we have to tell you the plans so you can tell your team and get some feedback from them,' Lynn explained producing papers from her desk.

'Why can't you tell them?' I asked her simply.

Moving to a desk in front of me, Lynn rifled through a drawer and pulled out some papers. She looked up at me with a furrowed expression. 'Because it's your responsibility, and you need to ensure that everyone listens to you. Sweetheart, you are the leader. As your operator, I can give you the instructions for you to tell the others. But it must come from you, no one else.'

'Ha yeah, tell that to Saskia,' I mumbled.

Ignoring me, Lynn placed the papers in front of me. 'Your training will begin today, in fact, this afternoon. You'll learn basic martial arts in Karate, Taekwondo, and Aikido. It'll make you stronger, should you need to use hand to hand combat in particular situations.' She pushed a beige coloured folder in front of me. I opened it up and spread its contents before me: a confusing amount of numbers, graphs, charts and bullet points as well as a map of two islands. 'This is where the team will be going for field training.'

I picked up a photocopied map of the islands and glanced at the name of it. 'The Falklands?' I looked back at the pictures. There were dots all over the islands, one pointing to Stanley, another to Bay of Harbours and also to the west, Weddell Island, as well as a few more.

'For two weeks,' Dave told me.

'You and your team will be let loose on a specific part of one of the is-lands,' Roxy began giving me a wry smile. 'You must survive the elements and complete your mission.'

'We've decided to give you one week of intensive martial arts training and then the team will be going a week tomorrow, but we can discuss that later. Here is the itinerary for the group. Both you and Saskia will be train-ing in combat flying from 7am to 9am and then again from 6pm till 7pm. The rest of the day, apart from one hour for lunch, will be your martial arts training. The others have their specialised training with these guys, but you won't have to worry about that,' she said looking at Matt, Dave and Roxy.

'Any questions Tara?' Matt asked me with a kind smile. He was a very good-looking man, but I'd still put Henry as my number one. I looked at him and glanced at his scar for some reason it was very prominent today. I had briefly wondered how he got it, but I had to focus on the situation at hand. Trivial things like that could wait.

'No, no questions.'

'Very well,' Lynn said, turning her back on me. 'You may go.'

I picked up the beige folder and left without another word. Clearly they had things to discuss, and now I had to go and find the others and tell them about the Falklands trip.

However, as I headed back down into the cafeteria, hoping that every-one was still there, I was told by an employee that I'd just missed them. I went to their rooms, knocking on each door, but no one answered. 'Where the hell were they?' Upon reaching the door to my room I discovered a small note and quickly reading it headed to the special training.

It took me mere seconds to get to the white cathedral-sized training room. I was on a rampage, pushing against doors so forcefully they almost cracked the walls. People jumped or yelped as they saw me heading towards them and muttered as I went by, but that only angered me more. Heading to the training room, I burst inside and immediately felt the air from the fan circulate around me. Glancing up, I saw Saskia in the air gliding gracefully, her white wings spread out like a graceful swan.

She beamed down at me, but there was a hidden evil grin mingled in there somewhere.

'Tara!' Macie yelled over the winds. 'She can fly, isn't that awesome?'

'No,' I spat with venom and walked towards the circus net.

The others were circled around the net staring up at Saskia in awe. Darren looked smitten with her. His eyes bulged from their sockets as she tilted this way and that, the wind brushing her hair behind her, whipping it up in a delicate way. I almost felt sick.

Walking over to the controls, I pushed the large red "OFF" button, and the fan died instantly.

Like me, Saskia wasn't expecting it and unlike me, instead of trying to flap to gain altitude, her wings suddenly disintegrated and screaming, she plummeted to the ground.

'YOU COW!' she screeched at me, as she crawled towards the edge of the net.

'What the hell did you do that for?' Darren yelled at me, defending her.

'You are not allowed to train here unless supervised by your operator,' I told Saskia as she gracefully jumped down to the ground. 'And you lot,' I turned on them, 'aren't allowed in here. This room isn't for you; it's for Saskia and me. Please leave.'

Storming towards me, Saskia stopped inches from my face. 'Yer so dead,' she hissed menacing tone.

'You listen to me,' I said closing the gap, so our noses nearly touched. 'I am the leader and you do NOT go off on your own just to prove to the others how special you are. We are all in the same boat. We have to train and we have field training a week tomorrow. If you step out of line, so help me I'm going to make your life a bloody nightmare, do I make myself clear?'

Seething with rage Saskia gritted her teeth and in moments, her brilliant white wings ruptured out of her back and she grimaced in pain. She hadn't been given that injection like the rest of us had, but she didn't cry out.

After asserting my authority over her, I expected Saskia to nod her head or to back away. She should have known by now that there were certain rules to follow, regardless whether she liked them or not. But instead of taking my command with good grace, she lunged at me. Saskia forced herself on me and pushed me back to hard, I lost my balance and fell to the ground. My head smacked the concrete floor and stars immediately burst into my field of vision, dazing me. Saskia began punching every place she could get to. I tried to hunch up into a ball, protecting my head and front, but there was nothing I could do to stop her. The others cried out in shock. Hannah and Sam came to my side and wrenched Saskia from me. And as pain erupted from my legs, arms and head where she'd kicked me, a tender hand was placed on my back between my wings and helped me to sit up. A frightened Macie looked up and down my body and lending me her hand, helped me up.

I spat blood from my mouth where Saskia had nicked my cheek and stared evilly at her as she was being held back by Hannah and Sam. My stomach, legs, arms and face continued to twinge with pain as I moved, but I was too annoyed to care.

Shrugging Macie's hands off me, I suddenly darted towards Saskia, my fist raised. Her eyes grew wide as she knew she had no chance to block me and with one punch to her cheek, I knocked her sideways. The mighty blow was too strong for even Sam and Hannah to keep their grip on her.

Saskia plummeted to the floor with a slap of her skin on the cold hard floor and bounced a few feet away, coming to a stop just beside the net.

There came a loud shout of 'TARA YOUNG!' and there in the doorway looking shocked and horrified, was Lynn. And she was very, very angry.

'She started it,' Saskia said pointing at me.

I tutted and rolled my eyes. 'Childish cow,' I muttered under my breath.

Unsure of what was going on, Lynn ordered everyone to get out of the room, apart from Saskia and me. 'Close the door and get back to your operators,' Lynn snapped at Darren who was trying to hear what Lynn would say to us. Regretfully closing it Lynn suddenly turned towards us. 'What on earth is going on, Tara?'

I saw Saskia smile and my anger grew even more.

'Saskia turned the fans on without you being here. I turned them off, she got annoyed with me, I told her to stay in line and she attacked me and yes, I know it was wrong, but I threw one punch at her.'

'Which I saw,' Lynn said. Sighing, she looked at Saskia. 'What was the first thing I told you to do when you got here?'

Saskia looked down at the ground, almost ashamed of herself, and mumbling quietly she said, 'Listen to Tara.'

'That's right. You don't EVER attack your leader, especially when she was obeying orders. I had also told you not to come in here without me, didn't I?'

'Yes.'

'Good, at least your ears work,' she snapped, putting her hands on her hips. 'Tara, go and get yourself cleaned up and meet me back here in an hour, Saskia, come with me. We're going to get you cleaned up; you've got your induction before Maynard leaves for a meeting. It was going to be tonight, but plans change. And a word of warning to both of you. If I hear that you two have been fighting again, by anyone, then so help me both of you will be in deep trouble! Understood?'

Nodding, I quickly headed out of the training room and went to clean the blood off my face and to get some tablets for the pain. Exactly an hour later, Saskia and I were back in the large white cathedral training room. Neither of us spoke and apart from the odd evil glance she gave me, I really couldn't care less. I was just happy I managed to sucker-punch her.

'Right, you two let's get going,' Lynn said happily as she fiddled with the level of the fan.

'Who's going first?' I asked.

'I didn't see Saskia so she can go first,' Lynn said looking up at her. Saskia nodded curtly and walked towards the ladders with a happy smile on her face. 'But bear in mind, I'll be turning the fans off after a while so try and stay airborne as long as you can.'

The wingless Saskia reached the ladder and gripped the sides. She then turned to look at me, and squinting evilly she issued a small grunt and her white wings erupted from her back. As I had, she evidently felt a difference after that last injection, which I gathered she had received during her quick induction.

'Cow,' I mumbled as I watched her go up so effortlessly. Consciously I hoped that she'd fall off the ladder, but by the looks of it, I wasn't so fortunate. Saskia was impatient to get to the top.

As Saskia walked to the fan's switch, Lynn turned them on. 'When you're ready,' Lynn called up, but within seconds of the winds gushing up to Saskia, she had dived off the platform, wings outstretched, gliding gracefully through the turbulent air.

'Wow, impressive,' Lynn told me as we watched.

I gritted my teeth as I saw Saskia tilt her wings left or right, changing directions with graceful ease.

Lynn moved and quickly turned the fans off.

Like before, Saskia gave an unsuspected scream. I laughed quietly to myself.

'Keep it up Saskia,' Lynn told her in an upbeat voice.

I noticed that after a while, Saskia couldn't keep airborne and then suddenly her wings disappeared and she fell to the net, screaming on the way down.

Frowning, Lynn went towards her.

'Why did me wings go?'

'I think fear overcame your anger,' Lynn said to her. 'Which was the opposite for Tara.'

'Black and white,' I said simply.

'Your turn,' Saskia growled and jumped down to the floor giving me a fleeting smarmy smile.

Striding confidently towards the ladder, even though I felt sick at the prospect of another panic attack from the falling phobia, I was determined to prove to Lynn I was worthy of being a leader. And I was going to prove to Saskia I was better than her at flying.

Climbing the ladder, I closed my eyes as before but tried to remain calm. After all, I had done this before and I attempted to remember the instantaneous and wonderful feeling of gliding on the air currents.

'Take your time Tara,' Lynn said to me in a gentle manner.

I heard Saskia mumble something, to which Lynn replied, 'Because she is afraid of heights.'

I could imagine Saskia laughing at this, giving me that extra boost I needed to reach the top without panicking. But when I arrived, I stopped just short of the top.

Opening my eyes, Lynn, who I saw through the ladder gaps, was standing by Saskia close to the fans, they were talking in low voices and I saw Saskia smile a little. I bet she was hoping I'd give up.

'Damn it, you can do this,' I told myself as I began to get sweaty palms and a racing heart.

Taking a deep breath, I climbed the last couple of steps and made a snap decision to do something utterly stupid. It was reckless by all accounts and I knew that Lynn may be angry with me, but at the end of the day, Saskia was my competition. I had to be better than Saskia. If I was going to be a leader, I had to stand up for myself. I had to take charge and show people I was capable of leading them, even though I still doubted I could do any of this myself. Shaking slightly, I forced myself to look ahead, to focus on my task. Leaving the last rung of the ladder, I stood up and took a few steps along the narrow platform. I glanced down and saw Lynn about to turn the fans on, but before she reached the button, I took a few steps and jumped off the end of the platform and into the air.

'NO TARA!' Lynn yelled as I plummeted towards the ground. The wind screamed through my hair and wings, my eyes began to tear from the sheer force of the wind. My heart rate beat frantically as I realised what I had done and as I continued to fall, I had to figure out the next step. I had to flap like mad. The net was getting exceedingly closer, far too quickly then I had planned out in my head. I spread my large, glossy black wings as wide as they would go and began to beat my wings, up and down, up and down, pushing the air below me to keep me airborne.

'I'm not going to hit it,' I called out as I began to stop in mid-air. My back instantly hurt as my new muscles were aching from their use, but I had now stopped myself from hitting the net and very slowly, I was beginning to rise.

'Come on Tara!' Lynn called enthusiastically.

It spurred me on, even though my back was killing me, my nerves begging to stop, I continued to flap up and down getting faster and faster. Then, as though I was programmed by instinct, my body straightened out and I actually began flying up towards the ceiling. It was such a euphoric feeling that I giggled like a child and began zooming around the room, tilting my wings to almost brush the walls.

'Stay up as long as you can,' Lynn told me from below.

Taking a chance to look down, I saw Saskia's shocked face. 'In your face, big disgrace,' I laughed.

I had no idea how long I was flying around for, but soon my back seriously became a problem. But instead of my wings disappearing all together like Saskia's, I made a hasty decision and decided to try and land.

Gliding down to the bottom, ensuring I dove down straight and trying to remember how birds slowed down to land, I leant forwards and with a little thump landed near to them, puffing from breathlessness. But I felt like a million pounds.

Lynn beamed. 'Very well done, I'm very proud of you Tara.'

Panting, I smiled back and quickly slumped to the floor, 'Damn,' I winced as my back ached terribly. 'That was fun, natural and painful all at the same time.' Reaching up, I wiped the sweat from my brow. 'Wow, what a workout.'

Saskia was gobsmacked. She stood like a melon, watching me catch my breath on the floor.

'I think you need a break,' Lynn told me. She looked at her watch. 'Go and get some rest and then have lunch. Martial arts training starts in the afternoon.'

'Okay,' I mumbled, straining to get off the floor.

Still with my heavy aching wings, I painfully folded them onto my back and left Lynn teaching Saskia how to fly. Dragged my sore, sorry self to my room I slumped down onto the bed and sometime later, felt the relief of my wings disappearing, giving my back a much-needed rest. Looking at my watch, it read eleven o'clock. I had an hour before lunch. 'Shower, I think,' I said to myself. A short time later, I shoved my hair up into a semi-dry bun and changing into some light clothes, I went along and knocked on everyone's doors to call for a meeting.

'What do you want?' Darren demanded looking irritated that I had bothered him.

'In my room now, I have something to discuss with you.'

'Do it later,' he said closing the door.

Putting my foot in the doorway and pushing it wide open with a bang, I said, 'Not later, now!'

I left Darren looking shocked at my authoritativeness as I went around to everyone else. Within ten minutes the team, minus Henry and Saskia, was in my room looking either puzzled or annoyed. I motioned for them to take out their earpieces and putting them away, I wasted no time in telling them that there was a way for us to get out of the T.A.T. facility.

'Training in the Falklands?' Lionel said looking puzzled. 'I wonder why all the way over there?'

'Does it even matter?' Hannah told him. 'We've got a perfect way of getting out. They'll take all of us, including Henry and Saskia-.'

'Interceding here,' Darren said as he was leaning against my wardrobe. 'What are you going to tell Saskia and Henry? If Henry, as Lynn explained to you, is your second in command,' he said sarcastically, 'then surely he has to be in the know too. So far we haven't got all the team here and we're already planning an escape? It's rude and also, rather stupid.'

'I'll talk to Saskia and Henry, separately if I have to,' I told him with a sour look. 'Everyone just stick to the plans that your operators have laid out for you. We don't want them thinking we're going AWOL until we actually do.'

'Good luck in talking to Saskia,' Hannah scoffed. 'She's a right cow.'

Lottie nodded in agreement. I couldn't help but smirk.

Darren shot Hannah an evil look. 'If you actually got to know her, she's hilarious.'

'Oh yeah, she's real funny alright,' Macie remarked. 'She practically shoved me off my chair at breakfast.'

'Because you are a pushover Macie,' Darren laughed then got a smack on the arm from Hannah.

'Enough. Everyone just please-' but I didn't manage to say anything further as there was a small knock on the door. Opening it, I saw the sweaty and bruised face of Saskia.

'Holy cow, what happened to you?' Darren yelped as he picked up my computer chair by my desk and gave it to her to sit on.

She slumped in it and wiped the sweat from her brow. Macie had to move as Saskia's wings got in the way. She shot me an angry look, but I just shrugged at her and mouthed, "Sorry." Saskia was part of the team and if she wanted to come into my room to talk, then she was welcome to.

'Wow Tara, you gave her a shiner,' Sam said impressed looking at her face. He gave me a small nod of approval. I guessed I was earning his respect at least, though Darren didn't seem too happy.

'Can we call it a truce?' I asked Saskia tenderly. 'You beat the crap out of me, I punched you. It's over, okay?' She nodded once then folded her arms, crossed her legs and huffed. 'Good.' Quickly, I moved on to explain the Falklands mission and the upcoming training that all of us would be given. Saskia remained quiet throughout my little pep talk and I just couldn't find a way to tell her about our tattoos and the book. So by half three in the afternoon, I called it quits. Everyone got their earpieces back, which Saskia didn't seem to notice nor cared that I'd hidden them, and I told the group to go and get something to eat as lunch was nearly over.

Macie, Hannah and Lottie were with me in the cafeteria, eating buttery mashed potatoes, spaghetti hoops and melted cheese. The boys had grabbed a snack-pack and went into the entertainment room to have their lunch.

Saskia, now wingless, was sat at a table by herself looking miserable. She was staring forlornly at her chicken salad, picking at it with her fork. I wondered why she looked so upset and guessed that maybe Lynn had shouted at her some more after I'd left the training room. We'd ignored her as she came into the cafeteria and had sat down on her own. No one mentioned her until Macie's worry and kindness shone through.

'Should we ask her over to our table?' Macie asked us. 'She looks really... upset.'

We all stared at Saskia. Knowing that we were looking, she stuck her middle finger up then turned around in her chair, so her back was facing us.

'Nope,' we all chimed in.

'Why is she like that?' Hannah asked as I made a small mound with my mashed potatoes and placed my fork in the middle of it to look like a weird flag. I'd had enough of this nasty food.

Hiding a smile, I replied, 'Probably because I kicked her arse at flying.' The girls looked up with inquisitive faces. 'I managed to fly without the fans on.'

'Oh, congratulations!' Hannah and Macie laughed together.

'It hurts a lot,' I told them, as I could still feel the new muscles in my back waiting to be used once more, 'but I did it.'

Lottie smiled. 'Wow, that's awesome!'

'Well, that cow isn't so cocky now is she,' Hannah said glancing at her. 'Telling me what to do...'

'Shh,' Lottie said lightly tapping her on her arm.

Looking around we saw Saskia get up and taking her tray, placed it on the rack by the doors then giving us the finger again, she walked off.

'Such a lovely girl,' I laughed.

As I finished my meal, the others went into their rooms but as I headed towards mine, I found the door wide open. My mind immediately went to the little red book. 'Oh crap.' Running inside, I saw Saskia sitting on my bed reading the little red book. My heart dropped. She held the clues to finding a very dangerous secret, and here she was brazenly toying with it, like a common library book.

Crossing her legs and waving the book in front of me, she chuckled and then picked up my key card and stared at it. 'You should make sure ya keep ya key card with ya at all times.' She held it up, playfully. I slammed the door behind me and reaching out, snatched the key card back. I tried to think of when I had it last, but my mind was more focussed on Saskia holding the book. 'Can't remember when you dropped it? Doesn't matter, but what does matter is your inability to look after this, especially something like this,' she said waving the book at me again. I instantly took my earpiece out and shoved it in my pocket and motioned for her to do the same. 'If you're not careful, it may fall into the wrong 'ands, like say, the T.A.T.' I went to grab the book but she held it away from me. 'Oh no, not for you. You can't take care o' it, obviously.'

Pointing to the book I spat, 'You don't even know what it is.' Trying to look nonchalant, I folded my arms as though seeing Saskia holding the book didn't bother me, but, in fact, it really was. 'And take that out!' I pointed to her head.

Saskia showed me her ears, which were empty, and smiled 'Uh 'uh, yes I do know about this book, and so does Henry,' she said with an evil grin. 'You're not the only one who knows about the book in the chair...'

Frowning at her, I leant casually against the door, all the time thinking of a way to get the book back. Or if that didn't work, hit her for pinching my key card and breaking in.

'You see, I 'ad a word with Amjee the night you left. We 'ad a little heart ter heart after I apologised for lockin' you in the library. Though wha' Amjee doesn't realise, and what both Henry and I know about, is that the T.A.T. is planning to use us to find this big secret.' She said quietly, waving the book. 'You know about us being Sirens right?'

Slowly I nodded. 'Hannah told me. I guess we all know now. But I don't get it,' I sighed frustratingly. 'When we grow wings, we are like Sirens, right? We fly. That's all there is, isn't it?'

'You idiot!' she said dropping her voice. 'Myths do NOT show themselves in this plane! It's a Golden Rule, the Golden Rule. Read that damn book!' she threw it at me and I caught it.

'I have,' I said irritably. 'I know about the magical plane and this one and that they've always been divided to conceal myths. And I know that in order to contain the balance only a certain amount of-.'

'-Myths should be in this plane,' she finished. Saskia stood up and moved towards me carefully. 'And do ya know wha' happens when the balance is shifted?' I shook my head. 'All hell breaks loose, literally. An' we are goin' to cause it.'

Her words sent a shiver down my spine. I didn't want to think about the type of evil myths that might come out of the magical plane should the world unbalance. However, as my eyes drifted to the little red book in my hands, my thoughts rested on the letter. 'Okay, I get that that's a big deal, but have you read that letter?' I asked her as I took it out and showed it to her. 'This huge secret is what the T.A.T. want. We have to get to it before they do. We have this Falklands field training thing in a week. We can leave when we get out.'

Saskia laughed then suddenly, there was a knock on the door making us jump and I heard Macie's voice, 'Um the martial arts training is starting, are you coming out?'

'Yeah, I'm just having a word with Saskia, be out in a sec,' I called.

'Don't say a word,' Saskia whispered as she looked in a motherly way at the book. 'And keep that hidden. Puttin' it under your pillow, it's bloody stupid.'

Grabbing the door handle, she yanked it open to see a startled Macie standing in the hallway.

'Worever you McDonald's worker',' she said making a W an M and another W with her hands and then walked off down the corridor.

'What was that all about?' Macie asked me as I clutched the book to my chest, looking dismayed.

CHAPTER EIGHT

THE FOLLOWING MORNING AT HALF PAST EIGHT, LYNN yelled in my ear to meet her in the training room.

Now that I could fly without the fans, the next task for me was to take off from the ground. Lynn had said, 'You will find yourself in places without high ground, so you need to learn how to take off within three steps.' Needless to say, this was an impossible task for me.

While Saskia was training to stay airborne for a long time without the fans, I was on a treadmill, running on the spot flapping like a demented bird.

'Why... am I... doing... this?' I panted heavily, completely out of breath as I fell to the floor when Lynn gave me a small break.

'You need to strengthen your new muscles for your wings and also you need to be able to run just as fast with them than without.'

'You expect me to do martial arts for six hours after this? You're having a bloody laugh.'

'Don't argue with me, just do it,' Lynn said waspishly and walked off towards Saskia, who had made a small scream indicating that she had fallen into the net again.

In pain and aching all over, I traipsed back to my room, having a quick shower and when my wings crumbled into a fine powder I met everyone in the gym room for martial arts. Dave and Matt were our instructors and drilled us in the basics for the entire morning and early afternoon.

I was about to drop after dinner, my bum was sore from being repeatedly kicked by Saskia, who was my sparring partner. My back was starting to cramp up every time I was flung on the floor or doing a small complicated roll and my arms and legs felt like lead and had dark purple bruises running up and down them. Suffice to say, I looked and felt like crap.

Macie ended up sitting out for a lot of it, she seemed so tired and put out. Somehow couldn't keep up with the rest of us and after a while, she didn't see the point in practicing. No matter how many times we all tried to cheer her up and tell her to keep going, Macie seemed low in spirit and energy.

After being kicked and punched for most of the afternoon, I was about to fall to the floor from pure and utter exhaustion when Matt and Dave called it off for a quick break. When I finally managed to drag my sorry carcass to my room, I realised I had about half an hour to chill out and eat something. Because afterwards I'd have a further two hours of running on that damned treadmill flapping like drowning duck.

I lay on my bed for about ten minutes before forcing myself up. Heading to the cafeteria, I asked for a jug of iced water and any food with chocolate in it.

'We've got a triple chocolate muffin,' the dinner lady said looking at me with pitiful eyes.

'That sound's amazing.' I stifled a yawn and winced slightly as my arm hurt.

'Been training hard?'

'You've got no idea. I'm going to seriously speak to whoever is in charge of making us do this, it's ridiculous.'

'I know but, no pain no gain right?'

Quickly downing my cold water and munching on my muffin, I headed back to the training room where Saskia and Lynn were already there.

'How long has she been up?'

'About half an hour, she's quite the athlete when she's focussed. And shouldn't you be on a treadmill with your wings out?'

'Yeah, yeah,' I muttered.

Collapsing onto my bed that night, I could barely move to get changed and within seconds I was out like a light.

'Ow... ow... ow,' was all I said the following morning, before, during and after breakfast.

'For God's sake, go and take some paracetamol and shut the hell up,' Saskia snapped at me as I slowly walked on the treadmill. I had barely enough energy to hold my wings up as they hung limp by my sides, dragging on the floor.

'Drop dead,' I bit back.

Lynn came into the room an hour and a half later, glanced at Saskia then turning to me said, 'Tara enough now, go and get some rest. Just do me a favour and keep your wings out for the remainder of the day.'

'What?' I yelled.

'Just please do it. I know it'll be difficult during the martial arts practices, but I want you to understand the differences with and without your wings, the balance and weight and to strengthen your back muscles.'

I headed back to my room, aching for my bed, but as I approached the red doors, I couldn't help but overhear part of a conversation between Roxy and Dave. Peering through them, which were thankfully ajar, I saw them talking in hushed tones at the top of the marble stairs.

'...Yeah, I know but this group is pathetic. Only Henry has the correct training and he's the one who could easily transform.' Roxy told him in whispers. 'The others are not there yet and they won't last a second.'

'Yes but Maynard had found something, something that will turn the tables in our favour. He's found a portal.' Dave spoke quietly making Roxy gasp in shock. 'Lynn told me the other night when Henry spoke of his mission to Norway.'

'We're half way there!' She squealed in delight. 'Is he going to go through it yet?' She asked him. I moved quietly and saw through the crack the delight on Roxy's face, but the conversation was confusing. What portal were they referring to?

'No, not until he knows the secret.' They stopped talking and after a while I realised that they had gone. Leaving me dumbfounded and feeling slightly sick, I headed back to my room and made a plan to call a meeting with everyone, including Saskia and Henry.

Over the following three days, everyone was feeling the drag of getting up early and training non-stop for the entirety of the morning and most of the afternoon. Every part of our bodies was aching to the point where cramps would ensue almost continuously. I didn't have the heart to give them such bad news about Maynard but instead I tried hard to encourage them to keep going.

Once or twice Darren ended up with his head in a bucket of cold water as he was always getting shouted at by Dave, who was telling him how inadequate his stances were in Karate.

'I don't give a flying kack,' he managed to mumble with the little oxygen he had as gills erupted from his neck.

On the third morning after Saskia's arrival, we had let her sit with us, on the one condition that she remained at least pleasant towards us. However, it was proving difficult; she was still as cocky as ever.

'Well, as far as I am aware, you haven't even been able to take off from the ground, unlike Tara,' Lottie beamed at me. I gave her a small wink but remained quiet.

It was a quick joyous occasion after I had managed the previous evening to take four running steps and flew off from the ground, but Lynn still wanted me to achieve it in three.

'Wha'…ever,' Saskia snapped making a W and an E with her fingers.

Biting back a retort, I looked over at Macie, who sat quietly eating her food. Like Darren, Macie was also getting shouted at for not getting the moves right, but unlike Darren, Macie didn't get angry, and instead she just withdrew in on herself and remained even quieter.

'You okay?' I asked her as Hannah, Lottie and Saskia got into a small argument on who would kick each other's arses in an actual Karate competition.

'Fine,' she mumbled.

'No, you're not,' I said quietly as I moved closer to her. 'What's wrong?'

'I don't think I can do this.' She began to cry. 'Everyone is working so hard and I feel like a complete and total idiot. I'm not very good at hand-eye co-ordination.'

That was the truth. On one move, we had to block with our right hand, grab your opponent's wrist with our left. And then we'd move to flip them backwards. But Macie messed up all the time and ended up on her back.

'Macie we can do this, don't give up yet, we still have until Wednesday, its four days away,' I said trying to be optimistic, but Macie only nodded in response. She didn't speak the rest of the day.

★ ★ ★

Wednesday was looming towards us and we were becoming progressively nervous, especially myself. Just the thought of this mission started butterflies flapping around my stomach, making me feel sick and unable to focus. And as we'd been so busy practicing, we hardly had the time to discuss how to break away from this mission. We hadn't seen Henry at all since my induction so I had no idea on which side he was on, our or the T.A.T's.

However, by Monday evening, just after dinner, I had a progress report from Lynn, Dave, Roxy and Matt and was glad to hear that everyone had managed to achieve their goals. Both Darren and Macie hadn't got shouted at during the entire day and Saskia had succeeded in taking off from the ground after four steps.

Due to our good behaviour and dedication, we had some free time and I finally called a meeting with everyone, including Saskia, in my room at midnight. The only problem was that Henry still hadn't been seen nor heard of his attack the previous week and I was getting exceedingly worried.

'Okay,' I called for attention as my room was very crowded. With our earpieces out and stored safely away, we were all free to talk but no one wanted to as they were unsure about where Saskia stood.

'Right, Saskia is on our side,' I told them first off. 'Also, there are three things we need to discuss: Saskia's discovery, what I overheard from Roxy and Dave and what to do when we leave on Wednesday.'

Macie put her hand up.

'Yes Macie?'

'What about Henry?'

Saskia sighed impatiently. 'We'll discuss it in a second,' I replied gently. 'Okay Saskia, tell them what you told me.'

Hannah and Lottie locked eyes on her instantly. Copying each other's offensive stance, folded arms and stern face, we all could see that even after training with her, they still didn't like Saskia for many different reasons.

As Saskia regaled them the tale of what she knew, the others listened to her in shock. It wasn't something you heard of every day, especially being told that who you were turning into, was breaking a Golden Rule and quite probably destroying the world along with it. Though, in truth, we didn't know why the rule existed, I was curious as to know who created it in the first place.

'Well, that's put a downer on my day,' Darren retorted. 'So fearless leader, what else have you got to tell us?' he asked, but there wasn't so much gusto in his words.

Taking a deep breath, I tried to recount the exact words that Dave and Roxy had said. 'I haven't told anyone, just so you know.' I began and quickly got through the conversation I'd overheard about Maynard and this portal and how they are half way there to their goal, most likely. Once I'd finished, they looked even more depressed and I was afraid that they may say something that they would regret. Especially Macie. Criticising her by

yelling, wasn't how to encourage her and for the past few days, the operators had been shouting at her until she finally got it right. But still, Macie's
happy spirit had been slightly broken. Hearing bad news like this wasn't
what she needed to hear. 'I know it sounds bad, but I think we can do this.
If we come up with a plan, I believe we can escape. All of us,' I emphasised,
glancing at her.

'No offence Tara,' Lottie mumbled, 'but it seems utterly hopeless.' Macie
sighed dejectedly. 'How are we going to escape them?'

Sam nodded. 'Lottie's right, our operators can take us down in seconds.'

There was a dark lull in our conversation until Lionel asked, 'What did
Roxy mean about Henry being close to transforming?' The others looked
up at me for an explanation, but I shrugged my shoulders. I wasn't quite
sure that I was becoming a Siren like Saskia had said. Regardless that we
were given mythological blood, I couldn't see it literally transforming us. It
was just giving us special abilities.

'Whatever it means, maybe Henry can tell us,' I said looking around at
everyone, but no one seemed to be as optimistic.

'Well, he'll be with us on Wednesday,' Macie perked up a little. 'If we
go on this mission to Falklands, he'll be with us right?'

I nodded. 'He should.'

Hannah shifted and coughing, drew attention to herself. 'Well anyway,
what is the plan for Wednesday, Tara? How are we going to get out?' I saw
everyone stare at me. I hated that. Since having these wings, all people seem
to do these days is stare.

'So far as I know, we'll be transported from me to an old World War
Two hanger in the late afternoon. The exact location isn't on the specs.
We'll just find out when we get there. Then from this hanger, a plane will
charter us to Lisbon and then changing from there we'll go straight to Stanley. If you want a plan, I'm sorry guys, but we'll just have to wing it. The
only thing I can suggest is that as soon as we get to the hanger, we try and
escape. We each have abilities and we know what we are capable of.'
Glancing at my watch, it read 01:15am. It was time for everyone to go to
bed. 'Just one more thing,' I began, putting my hand out to stop them leaving. 'We may not like each other, but we have to get along and depend on
each other, so for the meantime can we all please stop the arguing and bickering?' Shooting a glance towards Darren and Saskia they both nodded.
'Thank you. I'll see you tomorrow morning. Good night.'

Taking their earpieces they left silently and when Macie closed the door
behind her, I looked around my room and thought about the last few days

spent within the T.A.T. and the training they had given us. Who knew that they would even dream we'd come up with an escape plan. It was perfect, they'd be completely unawares and maybe if everyone pulled together, we'd get out of this, alive.

* * *

Tuesday afternoon felt hectic for all of us. The cathedral room was abuzz with workers flittering around from one room to another, carrying papers and talking excitedly. Of course, there was the odd yell of orders, and the snapping of fingers, but it was understandable. The whole of the T.A.T. were preparing for the mission and seemed to be on eggshells as they were on their best behaviour as the boss was watching them. Maynard strutted around the room in his pressed brown suit and cowboy hat, smiling in a triumphant manner. Occasionally he peeked over people's shoulders, nodded as his employees went by and yet I noticed he genuinely frightened all others with his presence alone. They eyed him cautiously and that spelt danger in my eyes. Maynard commanded attention, he just had this air about him. It was something I could never do, regardless that I was the leader of our little-mismatched group and because of his power over the entire base, I felt sick to my stomach. I knew why he was acting all high and mighty. He had already found this portal, whatever that meant. But it clearly was a big deal and that worried me.

I was sitting on a very uncomfortable stool by a set of double doors that lead into some ground floor offices. With my legs crossed, people watching for the hell of it, I was also feeling anxious. Lynn had expressly told me to not bother anyone before the mission. However, I couldn't help but watch the computer users from high above in the glass offices and laughing at them running around like ants. Though, I was thankful that no one noticed me sitting here and it was a nice reprieve after the constant staring from everyone over the past week. I had a lot of thinking to do and a lot of butterflies to digest. It was crazy that I had suggested to the others on wanting to escape, but I didn't see another way. The book and Amjee said that they were bad. So this would be our only chance.

We had been debriefed about the mission from Lynn and the other operators that morning. The meeting was, in a word, dull. We were told where to go while on the islands, where we'd be dropped off, where to find food and all that palaver. But as I sat there in that room half-listening to our operators, I could see the others weren't paying the slightest bit of attention to them either. They were completely ignoring them as though they had already started their own small rebellion in their heads. We had come to the realisation that we had been deceived by those we had come to depend and rely on. The T.A.T. and everyone who worked for them, including Lynn, Matt, Dave and Roxy, couldn't be trusted. And I couldn't help but feel uneasy when Lynn suggested that we take the rest of the afternoon to pack our things. I was done packing within an hour or so and I found myself here, waiting for my next command.

'Tara,' Lynn's voice sounded in my ear after half an hour of sitting there watching Maynard peer over at a computer screen that showed a list of places in the world. 'Please come to the cafeteria.'

'On my way,' I replied and standing took a brief glance at the people around and suddenly saw Maynard look at me. Seeing each other the way we did he didn't look happy that I was there and seemed to almost glare at me. His eyes were unwavering and cold. It was as though he knew I was against him in some way. I was tempted to pull a Saskia and give him the finger, but instead gave him a sanguine look and walked away feeling proud yet also feeling I had just signed my death warrant.

Lynn, Roxy, Matt and Dave had gathered the team in the cafeteria and surprised us all by throwing a small party for doing so well. Hannah wasn't impressed and neither was Saskia. Sharing the same folded arms and pout, I smiled as they started talking to each other in a polite manner. Perhaps people could get along with Saskia, but only in small ways.

'We're so pleased with you guys,' Roxy said raising her glass of orange juice; alcohol was prohibited in the base. 'To the new T.A.T unit, cheers!'

'Cheers,' we all said in unison.

'The new T.A.T. unit?' I heard Lionel whisper to Sam. 'Sounds like there's been one before us ey?'

'So then,' Lynn said as she came over to me, beckoning Saskia. 'We'll get you two kitted out tomorrow morning. Tara has already told you that you won't be leaving until late in the afternoon?' Saskia nodded. 'Good so you guys can have a longish lie-in.'

'Sounds heavenly,' I laughed in a nervous way.

Lynn picked up on this and gave me a brief hug, 'You'll be okay, I promise.' Saskia gave me a furtive look. 'And for once, you won't be shouting in my ear,' she added as though it was an added bonus for me. 'Well, you lot enjoy the food, sorry there's no music. Just make sure you get some sleep,' Lynn said hastily as she looked at her watch.

'Wait, what about Henry?' I asked, stopping her from walking away. The others stopped their conversations and looked towards Lynn and me, all waiting to hear what she had to say. 'He's alright now, isn't he?'

She turned to look at me and put on a fake smile. 'Yes, Henry is better now, but he doesn't really need to be with you on this field mission-.'

'Well then I insist that he comes with us,' I exclaimed and the others nodded. 'If he's part of our team, then it would be prudent to have him with us, to see how we are compatible with him, don't you agree?'

Lynn's eyes wandered from my own to look over my shoulder towards Roxy, Dave and Matt. Then a second or two later she nodded in a forced manner. 'Yes you are right, of course. I will see to it that Henry will be with you on the mission.' She glanced at the other operators and they nodded. 'Well, I'll let you enjoy the party.' Then without another word she, Roxy, Dave and Matt left us all in the cafeteria staring after them.

As soon as the doors closed, leaving just the eight of us, I pulled my ear-piece out, dropped it on the floor and stamped on it. The others copied me, stamping on their own as though breaking their own shackles of this place. 'Get ready guys,' I warned. 'Because as soon as we're able, we're leaving them and we're going to stop them from finding out this big world secret. We have to. We've got our own mission to complete.'

CHAPTER NINE

WEDNESDAY AFTERNOON CAME ALL TOO QUICKLY FOR everyone, especially for Macie. She looked as frightened as a kitten and practically jumped out of her skin when she was addressed by one of the operators, or when she saw Maynard. She even squeaked when I approached her to ask if she had everything packed.

'Hey, calm down,' I said soothingly as I met her in the cafeteria half an hour before we were meant to leave. 'It'll be alright.'

She nodded, twisting her hands over and over, looking pale as a sheet. 'I know but... I just... I'm really scared that something bad is going to happen.'

Putting my arm around her shoulders, I felt her relax a little. 'Nothing will happen and even if something did, I'd be there to help. I don't know how,' I admitted with a soft chuckle, 'but I'll do my best.'

Looking at me with tears in her eyes, she said, 'You are a good leader, Tara. I know that you'll help us.'

Hearing running footsteps, I turned in my seat and saw Darren and Sam looking worried. 'I have something to tell you,' Darren began breathlessly then began searching the cafeteria for anyone who would overhear. 'Maynard isn't planning to take us to the Falklands.'

'What?' Macie and I gasped.

Sam nodded. 'He's moving us to an underground bunker where we'll be "Staying for quite some time,"' he mimicked in a Texas accent.

Darren smoothed his hair back, looking nervous. 'We overheard him say it a few minutes ago, he didn't know we were there,' he added. 'He was having a quick chat with our operators.'

Thinking about what the boys had told me, there was no other explanation and no matter how many times I tried to tell myself. Otherwise, I knew the only outcome was that… 'He knows we plan to leave,' I whispered, feeling a wave of dread. 'He must know, or else why would he change plans so quickly?'

'I guess we'll know if Roxy and the others are on our side if they tell us the change in plans or not,' Darren mumbled.

Sam tutted, shaking his head in disbelief. 'But dude, how can he know?' Sam asked. 'We've all been careful, not to say anything. We took precautions,' he urged, pointing to his ear where the earpiece was no more.

Shrugging, I picked up my bag and digging around put on my black jacket. 'It doesn't matter. Go and tell everyone, but be discreet.' Sam and Darren headed off to talk to the others while Macie and I stayed put, waiting for our operators to arrive.

Within an hour, the others joined us but we remained astute in our conversation topics. We only talked about silly things. What good programs were on the T.V. if it was getting colder outside as we hadn't been above ground since we arrived; discussions that we didn't care being overheard. The girls even began discussing if shops had got all their Christmas decorations out. As crazy as that sounds, some shops are utterly stupid and would definitely have a singing Father Christmas in their windows by now. Then causing a bit of a commotion as all heads turned when they arrived, Lynn, Roxy, Dave and Matt entered the cafeteria in their uniforms under thick black matching coats. Like Maynard, they too commanded attention, which immediately put me in my place. The operators faces were rather stern and seeing us all surrounded by two tables in the corner, they made a beeline for us. I was apprehensive about the way they approached us, but I couldn't run, not just yet.

Lynn was the first to speak. 'Looks like everyone is packed up and ready to go.' She gave a hint of a smile, but I was unsure what it meant. I wondered if she knew we broke our earpieces on purpose. I told Hannah to let it slip to Roxy, that Saskia had the bright idea of packing our earpieces away. Although apparently Roxy didn't say anything to her and Lynn didn't say anything to either Saskia or me, which I thought was a bit odd. Lynn had berated me for not having my earpiece in and now, it was as though she didn't care. 'Let's move out,' Lynn called over our heads. 'To the Falklands we go.' Hannah caught my eye. It was confirmed. We couldn't trust our operators.

Leading us out of the cafeteria, people stopped and began to clap though I was unsure why. Were they being mislead too? Did they think we were going to the Falklands for our first mission? I didn't have a clue, but I instantly felt embarrassed. We all remained quiet as we got into the glass lift that would take us, "up top". It was strange to think that I didn't miss the outside world. Being stuck under the British Museum for all these weeks, you'd think I would have gone stir crazy, but I was so preoccupied, it didn't bother me.

As I looked through the glass lift to the people below, they gathered around, continuing to clap and wave us goodbye. I heard Macie faintly reply, "Goodbye," but I saw Lottie shake her head and warn her to keep her mouth shut, and so Macie remained quiet.

While the last sights of the secret T.A.T. base hidden under the incredible historical house of Great Britain, disappeared from view, I felt no sense of vertigo or fear of heights. Regardless of the situation I was in with the T.A.T, I'm glad I had conquered my fear and I'm very pleased that I'd learnt how to fly.

The lift stopped with a small click and as the doors slid open, we all filed out and walked into the cold back entranceway of the museum. Walking past the museum's security guards was a doddle. In fact, they almost seemed afraid of us; unable to look us in the eye. Instead, they shifted uncomfortably and stared at the marble floor. I thought it was strange behaviour from security guards but quickly gathered that the security guards must be employees of the T.A.T. I sighed and shook my head. I didn't like being feared. That's the feeling I got when they refused to look at me, fear.

Lynn told us to wait in the lobby while she was going to get the van. Glancing around, I noticed that nothing had changed since the last time I was here, apart from the fact that it was now freezing cold. Looking at my watch, it read 8:34pm 15th of November. It was a shame I missed Bonfire Night.

'Damn it's cold,' I shivered as a cold draught from the outside struck my warm body like a sledgehammer. Even with my jacket on it was freezing.

'D-don't c-complain,' Macie trembled through chattering teeth. 'We're outside the base.'

A large black van with tinted windows trundled down the road and stopped just outside. Roxy quickly ran out and headed towards Lynn, who was waiting patiently by the side of the road. The women had a quick private talk just by the van, and then Roxy turned and walked out of sight. Dave then opened the doors for us and I got another blast of cold air in my face. 'Okay guys, out you go.'

We hastened outside and both Macie and I almost yelled in shock as the bitter November wind took our breath away. It was relatively dark outside and I smelt the coming of winter; wet, damp moulding leaves and roasting chestnuts. I smiled. It was my favourite season as it also meant my 24th birthday was coming up at the beginning of December.

The van's driver got out and headed to the museum, passing us and waving at Lynn as he went by. He obviously wasn't needed anymore. Lynn then walked up to the van and got into the driver's seat. She beeped the horn a few seconds later.

'In you go guys,' Matt called from behind us as he huddled in his thick warm coat, ushering us. As the others went ahead of me, I stole a glance. He looked up and down the road in an anxious manner. It must seem a little strange; a group of people in black uniforms and bags coming out the back of the British Museum after it closed.

In our small group, we headed towards the van quickly and one by one we piled in. 'You're heading to an old World War Two air base,' Dave told us, trying to keep a light conversation. 'Henry will be meeting you there.' We took our seats, Saskia and I were at the front, behind us were Macie, Hannah and Lottie and the three boys were behind them at the very back. 'Roxy, Matt and I won't be going will you. We have other things to take care of,' Dave said. Macie gasped and he gave her a warm smile. 'Lynn is perfectly capable of taking you alone. Okay?' We each looked at one another, still refusing to say anything. It wasn't that we were afraid to, but Lottie had made a valid point earlier that morning. These people were our enemies now. They couldn't be trusted.

Dave and Matt hit the side of the van and Lynn started the motor. I heard footfalls and Darren came to the front and sat beside Saskia, who looked like she was about to throw up. Saskia always made it abundantly clear that she loathed Darren. 'How long until we get there?' Darren asked Lynn as Matt closed the door.

Lynn looked in the rear-view mirror and looked at me and replied, 'Two hours.'

★ ★ ★

Arriving at the frosty airstrip, nearly two hours later from a very uncomfortable, cold and silent ride, we parked by a huge corrugated iron-roofed building, which from what I gathered, was the hanger. So there was some truth to our little trip. We were to be taken to an old World War two airfield, but then we wouldn't be jetting off somewhere exotic.

Lynn turned the engine off and then pressed a finger to her ear. 'Something's gone wrong. You lot stay in the van.' She bailed out quickly; slamming the door behind her so hard it rocked the entire van. The others looked at each other apprehensively. The boys and Hannah peered out of the window to try and find out what was going on. Leaning over to see, we watched Lynn hurry off towards the shadow of the hanger, she then disappeared into the dark, and then there was utter silence. I felt a growing increase of anxiety swirl around in my stomach. The unease made my back twitch.

Then suddenly a piercing roar echoed around us, followed by two shouts of an angry female voice. I was frozen in my seat as did the others as we heard a strange animalistic screech that actually made the front windshield crack. Macie suddenly whimpered and put her hands over her ears.

'This is something bad,' she cried and instantly Lottie put her arm around her to comfort her, trying to calm her down.

The eight of us jumped as the van rocked from one single thud. Then seconds later, two bangs quickly followed suit.

'What the hell is tha'?' Saskia asked us, her voice sounded frightened which worried me. Peering into the darkness of the van was made worse by the damn tinted windows that let in little to no light from the hanger's flood lamp. But yet, I could make out the quivering forms of Lottie and Macie and bit my lip. 'I don't want to alarm you but those thuds sound like footsteps.'

'Footsteps to what?' Darren breathed heavily. He sounded just as frightened as Saskia.

Sam, who sat in the middle seat right at the very back, spun around to face the front. He frowned then moments later his eyes grew wide with terror. 'DRAGON!'

Turning around in my seat, I saw two things that I could not understand, yet all evidence to the contrary they were right there in front of me. The first was what I could only describe as a hairy beast with giant protruding claws that ran towards us and cleanly jumped over the van in one clear bound. But the second thing, which freaked me out the most, was an actual dragon.

We all yelled out in fear as this huge silver flecked mythological beast came barrelling towards us. Its large maw opened wide showing meter long sharp, jagged teeth. Shrieking again so loudly that it made the van windows shatter outwards in an explosion of glass. We screamed once more and ducked as flecks of glass showered us.

The van rocked wildly as the dragon thumped along the road towards us, none of my training kicked in and neither had it done for the others. We were all totally petrified, like stunned rabbits in headlights.

Hearing a deep, ragged inhaling of breath, blistering hot flames was suddenly spat as us, engulfing the van with such force that it turned over. The van was pushed along the road, causing sparks to erupt as the metal scraped on the concrete. I screamed in fright as my world was turned upside down; bags, hands and glass hitting me all over. We couldn't stay in the van any longer.

'GET OUT THE VAN! GET OUT NOW!' I yelled to the others, trying to unbuckle my seat belt.

Hearing the clicks and thuds of people falling out of their seat, Macie and Lottie were crying and looking at Hannah I nodded and she grabbed the girls and forced them out of the van. 'Come on we need to go,' she said, taking their bags and leaving the van.

'Got a plan oh fearless leader?' Darren snapped as we crept out of the wreckage of the vehicle. I turned a full circle but noticed that the dragon was gone. Everyone looked relieved, but not large mythical creature can just vanish into thin air.

'Get into the hanger!' I suggested. As long as we were safe inside something, then it would limit the dragon's freedom to more about.

'Hey, where the hell has it gone?' Asked Lionel throwing his bag over his shoulders and looking around nervously. I noticed he had a cut over his right eye, a trickle of blood seeped out and annoyed, he quickly wiped it away.

Shaking my head as I too looked around to see where it was, I brushed shards of glass out of my hair. I then took the little red book from within my jacket and shoving it in my bag, gave it to Lionel. 'Guard this with your life, got it?' He nodded. 'Now, get to the hanger. Saskia and I will look for the dragon.'

'And then what?' Darren asked.

'Try and find Henry,' I told him, shaking my jacket off, revealing my black uniform and motioning for Saskia to do the same. 'He's got to be here somewhere, try the hanger. If he's been tarred with the same brush as us, they will want to get rid of us all together. And also look after the girls.'

Nodding, he, Sam and Lionel ran off towards the hanger. I looked ahead of me down the black tarmac where sparkling frost reflected the light from the only orange floodlight from outside the hanger. Taking a deep breath, I started to run. 'COME ON SASKIA!' I yelled and heard her follow. Feeling both angry and upset, my wings erupted from my back and three steps later I was airborne.

Saskia caught up with me moments later and together we searched for the dragon below, but we couldn't see anything.

'Its bloody cold!' she complained, but I ignored her.

'We can't miss a bleedin' dragon, it's too big and silvery.' I paused to think as I remembered seeing that other 'thing' before the dragon. 'Maybe it was after that?'

'Wha'?'

Turning around, I hovered in mid-air to talk to her. 'The dragon was chasing something before it attacked the van, it was big and it had claws.'

She gave me a sceptic look. 'Where did it go?'

Searching on the ground, I spotted the van and pointed to the woods beside it. 'It went into there.'

'Well, a dragon isn't goin' ter jus' disappear,' she snapped angrily, her teeth chattering.

'So much for them taking us to this bunker of theirs,' I muttered then smiled at Saskia. 'I guess this is our opportunity to escape. Come on!' Diving down towards the tops of the dark, icy trees, I searched the ground for this thing with claws. It sent a chill down my spine at the thought of it. A black mass with claws that ran on two legs. If there was a dragon floating around somewhere, then maybe this creature was magical too.

'THERE'!' Saskia shouted from behind. Looking back she pointed to her left and searching the ground, I saw it. The black beast-like form slowly came out of the woods, looking around as though stalking its prey. 'LET'S GET IT!'

'No, let's not!' I shouted as Saskia dove past me, yelling all the while and attracting its attention. It wheeled around and stared at her, its cat-like eyes reflecting in a sliver of the moon above. It raised its hands waiting for Saskia's launch. As she plummeted towards it, her white wings flashed out beside her in a menacing way, but it grabbed her by the arms and threw her over its head. She landed on the ground, skidding slightly and came to a stop.

Worried that she may be hurt, I flew after her and landed beside her, stumbling a little. The thing turned to look at us but lowered its arms.

'What are you?' I yelled, throwing my wings out to my sides as a warning. Taking a quick glance as Saskia she looked a bit shaken up and had cut her cheek as she fell, but otherwise, she was unhurt.

'It's me,' it said in a soft male voice which sounded frighteningly familiar. He slowly took a few steps towards me and raised his hands showing that he wasn't going to attack. 'Tara, it's me. It's Henry.'

I gasped as I saw him. My wings fell to the floor with a soft thump, all aggressiveness had left me. 'Henry? Is this what you look like when your tattoo kicks in?'

'Wha'?' Saskia gasped in pain. 'It's 'enry?'

Approaching us, he came out of the shadows and into the light. I saw the familiarity of his stance and face, but his nose had become flat, he sprouted whiskers and had hair had all over his face and neck. It looked like some strange mane. But what really freaked me out were his hands. His fingers seemed slightly stumped with long scary claws protruding from them. It was as though he was turning into a weird lion.

'You need to get out of here,' he suddenly said and reached down to help me up.

'We know. The dragon.'

We helped Saskia up but shrugged us off and went towards Henry and slapped him across the face.

'Stop it,' I snapped, grabbing her hand as she was about to do it again.

'He hurt me!' Saskia screeched while pointing a threatening finger at him.

'You attacked me you freaking idiot. What was I supposed to do? Let you!'

'Enough!' I shouted, stamping my foot on the tarmac light a child. 'We need to get to the hanger and get the others.'

'Why the hell are they in there?' Henry asked as we hurried across the road. Saskia and I folded our wings back across our bodies to give us more speed. Looks like Lynn had trained us too well.

'I thought you were in there,' I panted. Making it to the large door of the old World War II hanger, Henry practically ripped it open for us. 'We need to get out of here. Maynard wants to send us to a bunker or something,' I told him.

'Yes, I know.' He replied. I stopped cold and Henry shook his head. 'Now's not the time to explain, come on!'

Inside the hanger, we saw three helicopters. Henry raced to the nearest one, climbed in and checked it out. 'It looks stable and the fuel gage is on max. I can fly it.'

Surprised, Henry didn't give me the chance to ask how he'd learnt, so instead I grabbed Saskia's hand and together we went in search for the others.

The hanger was large, about 300ft by 170ft. Besides the three helicopters, there were also long bars of rusty steel, old crates and a random old rusted car. At the very back of the hangar, on the far right was a door that was ajar. Wordlessly we sprinted to it and barged into an old disused office block. The smell of rot and mould was pungent and I also detected the hint of rust and petrol. The rooms were littered with debris like old faded crisp packets and empty squashed cans of beer. Looks like people used this once for a night out.

'Hannah? Macie? Sam?' I called and hearing muffled shuffling sounds, a few figures popped up from another office at the back.

'TARA!' Macie called as she pushed through an old door and raced towards me. Flinging herself around me, she began to bawl. 'I'm so scared. It's been horrible!'

'We've found Henry,' I told her, forcing her off me. I looked up at the others who looked worse for wear with cuts and forming bruises around their faces. 'Everyone, let's go.'

Gathering their things, Lionel threw my bag to me and nodding in appreciation, we went back into the hangar where Henry was powering up the helicopter. Running to it and ducking low as the blades began to whirl, the group jumped in and scramble for headphones, but Saskia grabbed me and spun me around.

'How are we going to get out? A helicopter goes up,' she pointed to the ceiling. 'It doesn't roll forwards like a plane.'

Pushing past her, I moved to the front. 'Which way are you flying out?'

'That way,' he pointed to a steel wall in front. 'Those are actually doors. This helicopter is on tracks. It'll move forward through those doors as soon as they are open. It's automatic. You have to push them back.'

Looking back at him, he gave me a broad grin and I wanted to hit him. 'Thanks for telling me,' I snapped and motioned for the boys to follow me.

'What are we doing?' Sam yelled as the blades quickly picked up, the whirling noise was becoming increasingly loud.

'Opening the doors to get out,' I pointed ahead.

Sam used his spit to melt the padlock that was strangely on the inside of the hanger. Once the chains were ripped away, myself plus Saskia, Darren, Lionel and Sam managed to push the squeaky doors as wide as they would go. It was an ordeal, as it sounded like nails on a chalkboard but as we finished huffing and puffing, everyone went suddenly quiet. My eyes found the horrified faces of Darren and Lionel, who were very slowly walking backwards with their hands out in front of them, as though guns were pointed at them. Then suddenly all three boys turned around and broke into a run, heading for the powered up helicopter that was now beginning to roll forwards on the tracks.

'GET OUT OF HERE!' Lionel shouted.

I spun around, looking at the direction they ran from and froze in horror as I saw the sliver dragon stare at us from across the tarmac. It stood proudly on top of the van, which was squished into a black metal pancake under its weight.

Saskia swore and tore off after the boys, but I stood my ground. Though I was scared, the dragon had to be distracted so the others could get out of here. A second or two later, I heard Saskia scream my name.

'TARA, WHAT ARE YOU DOIN'?'

'TAKE OFF, I'LL CATCH UP!' I shouted and making a snap decision, as I always do, I left the hangar and walked towards the dragon.

My body turned icy from sheer fear as a cold harrowing feeling crept over me, gripping my nerves and refusing to let go. I felt as though I was walking into a bitter iron sea that would soon drown me in moments. As I approached, the dragon stared me down. It sneered at me mockingly and launching into the air, landed with a thump quite close to me, unbalancing me slightly.

Hearing the whirling of the rotor blades of the helicopter, the dragon snapped its deathly jaws and looked past me, but I moved forwards, drawing its attention to me.

'You leave them alone!' I shouted, shaking from terror. It's striking yellow-flamed eyes found me and gave a strange cough as though it was laughing. Feeling the wind flow through my feathers the dragon opened its giant opaque wings and breathing deeply was about to belch fire as the helicopter was set to emerge from the hangar.

Taking a few running jumps, I swooped towards the dragon and halted in front of it, hovering like a kestrel, almost face to face.

'DON'T YOU DARE BREATHE FIRE!' I shouted angrily. Half turning my head, I saw Henry take the helicopter steadily out of the hangar. It began slowly rising into the air; the rotor blades caused a severe down draught, making it difficult for me to keep airborne. I had stared too long watching Henry manoeuvre out of the hanger and glancing back at the dragon, I knew was a goner. With no warning given, it opened its mouth and aimed at the helicopter, almost hell-bent on destroying it.

'NO STOP!' I screamed with all my might.

The dragon was about to admit a mighty blast of liquid flame, but then began to swing its long neck around madly, as though it was asphyxiating. Its tail lashed out and catching me in the stomach, threw me to the ground.

Dazed and in pain, I saw a figure with white wings descend towards me while light shone onto the dragon which continued to writhe on the ground, clawing at its throat.

'Tara,' Saskia said worryingly, turning me over. She grimaced then helped me up carefully. We hobbled past the dragon towards a rope that dangled down from the hovering helicopter.

Watching the dragon writhe in pain made me pity it but unsure of whether what I was seeing was true, the dragon's form unexpectedly began to ripple and shrink. Then moments later, there was a small form of a human where the dragon was, laid on the cold tarmac ground. It was a female with 1930's style brown hair wearing a one-piece black uniform.

It was Lynn. Lynn was the dragon.

'Saskia…' I croaked.

She shushed me then said, 'Yeah, I see her too.'

Nearing the top of the rope, the helicopter lurched upwards and I felt hands grab me and pull me up into it. Moments later the doors were closed I heard several people panting from exhaustion or terror. I felt something placed over my ears and I sighed with relief. The engine was extremely high-pitched and noisy. Enough to make your ears bleed.

'Shall we tell Tara?' I heard Macie asked. Her voice sounded odd. Reaching up, I felt headphones around my ears. That made sense. I remained on the ground for a while, being tended to by someone. Shaking from the cold and horror at what I had seen and done, I opened my eyes and found Macie in front of me and Hannah beside her, holding a First Aid kit.

'I saw Lynn… To be specific, I saw both forms of Lynn.' Groaning, I sat up stiffly, leaning against the door of the helicopter, my wings gave me some comfort against them, but not much. 'Henry, mind explaining?'

'I knew about Lynn,' he told us all, a collective gasp of shock came from the group.

'Dave, Matt and Roxy are they like Lynn, the dragon lady?' I asked as I looked at my left arm and grimaced at the sight of the blood that clustered around my elbow and dribbled down onto my uniform. Lynn had smacked me hard and I had hurt myself pretty badly. Though I was glad that I didn't break any bones.

Henry's head nodded. 'They are like Lynn, but they aren't a dragon. Each of them had different tattoos, so they'll be different myths. But Tara, I wouldn't put it past Maynard to hire powerful myths. So we should be careful. The book might tell us what we need to know,' he said.

That took me by surprise. 'Okay, how do you know about the book? I know for a fact that I haven't mentioned it to you.'

'No need,' he briefly turned in his seat to look at me with a smile, 'Amjee told me you retrieved it from the library.' He said in a matter-of-fact way. 'Amjee also said that you were going to be sent to a bunker somewhere in Britain. She found out this morning and relayed the message to me as soon as she was able. Whatever you heard from the operators, they had no intention of creating a team out of us. We've been an experiment and we've failed. And because we failed, we aren't needed in the base anymore, so they were going to send you to the bunker. Although they would most likely continue to send me on missions. But until two hours ago, I was their Golden Boy. Roxy found me snooping around Maynard's house near the museum. As soon as you reached the hanger, Lynn attacked me after she saw me. I'm now a threat to her,' he said more to himself.

'How can Amjee get messages to you?' Lottie enquired. It was a good question. I had been thinking it myself.

Henry chuckled. 'Everyone who is part of the T.A.T. whether part of a unit like us or our operators, are related by some type of myth. Amjee was part of the T.A.T about forty years ago. She has the uncanny ability of using telepathy to hear people's thoughts. A useful feature when relaying information to me.'

My mouth opened slightly in the shape of an 'O'. 'Well, that clears up a lot of how she knew the T.A. T. were the bad guys. And about Maynard and this secret. He has already found a portal, in Norway by the sounds of it.'

'I'm not sure about that,' Henry said with furrowed brows. 'He may have found one, but I'm not sure it was a portal. It vanished too quickly. But er, before we discuss this further, where do you want to go?'

Everyone looked at me and I felt a prickle of embarrassment creep up my neck. 'We need to get to Asia, but where in Asia, I have no idea.' I told them truthfully.

Henry turned around and looked at me, 'Well I have a suggestion. Let's go to Verona.'

I frowned and the others repeated the place.

'Oh I've always wanted to go to Italy!' Lottie squealed. 'Well, actually I've always wanted to go to Milan and check out Prada, Louis Vuitton and Dolce and Gabbana, oh and Dior,' she sighed contentedly. We all looked at her as if she was nuts. Realising this she shrugged. 'My family are wealthy,' and left it at that. I looked at Hannah for confirmation and she nodded once.

'Okay, fair enough. Um Henry, why Verona?'

Looking straight head, he shouted back to us. 'Amjee knows of a mission where Maynard wants to send Lynn and the others to Verona to capture Cupid. There's no way to warn him.'

'Cupid?' I scoffed. 'The little baby with the wings?'

Saskia burst out laughing, but no one else did.

'Cupid is a man who spreads love and joy and happiness,' Henry told me. 'I don't know what his connection is to Maynard and why Maynard wants him out of the way, but it's bad if he wants love out of the way.'

'Then how do we get to Verona?' Sam asked him.

Henry turned around and smiled. 'I have all your passports. Amjee warned me about Verona three days ago. Not that you all knew this, but as soon as you moved into the T.A.T. base, the operators took your I.Ds, driver's licences and you're passports. She managed to get them back and passed them onto me.'

The others laughed.

'Wow, you're full of surprises, aren't ya?' I said scathingly. 'So I guess we are going after a myth of love. Never thought I'd say that and not laugh.' Lionel smiled and turned his attention to Hannah, Sam and Darren, who chatted happily about going to Italy apart from Lottie and Macie, who rested against each other and closed their eyes. Saskia moved over to me looking troubled.

'Wha' about the secret we need to stop Maynard from getting'? Wha' about Asia?'

Nodding vigorously I agreed, 'I know, we can't ignore it. It is a top priority, but right now we need to stop Maynard and if we have an opportunity to do so, we have to take it. On the way, we can try and figure out this pitted bay and where the dragon descends into the sea.'

Expelling a lungful of air she nodded once then moved away, sitting away from the group to think. Glancing at the others, they looked shaken up and sordid. They were bruised and covered in blood from the glass. I suddenly felt a little queasy, and got up, gingerly moved to the front.

'Take us to Portsmouth,' I told Henry, 'or as close as you possibly can without being seen. We'll go by ferry to get to Verona, head to Spain and get another ferry close to Barcelona.'

He gave me a sideways look. 'Don't want to fly?'

I shook my head. 'Maynard could attack us on a plane, we'd put people in jeopardy. With the ferry, it's better, plus we'd be off the radar a little bit. Cameras at the airport and all that.'

He nodded. 'You're the boss.' Smacking him playfully, he smiled. 'I mean, yes Tara.'

CHAPTER TEN

HENRY HAD TIRELESSLY FLOWN TO THE SOUTHERN COAST of England towards Portsmouth. Although he happened to land in a park in the middle of the night, which I thought was stupid as we'd be surrounded by police and nosey civilians within seconds. But as it turned out, we were so far away from prying eyes; there was no one within sight.

As the rotor blades died down, everyone stayed inside and slept uncomfortably, either in the hard seats or on the floor. I noticed that it took longer for my wings to disappear and when they did, I huddled up in a corner and tried to get some sleep, but it was difficult. It had been a very trying time for all of us, and my mind was still buzzing from the fright of Lynn. I had never seen a dragon before, only sketches on paper and the CGI dragons on television. But seeing a real one frightened me more than I thought it would. Regardless that I had the mythical blood of the Sirens floating around my body, I was still mortal, and as Lynn showed me last night, I could still get seriously hurt.

As dawn's rays of orange and pink hue shone into the cabin of the helicopter, Henry, who was now back to normal, woke us up and told us to leave. Shivering from the cold, frosty morning, we took our bags and anything else that would leave evidence.

Digging in my black backpack that we'd all been equipped with, I pulled out a thick woolly jumper and smiled in relief as I was instantly warmer. I noticed the others did the same, and as we left the park, we came into a B-road where directly opposite us, looked like some weird 1970's buildings.

'Where to now?' Lionel asked out loud, and Henry pointed left.

'That way is towards Gosport, and then from there we get a ferry over to Portsmouth.' Hitching up his bag, he led the group on while I heard Macie mutter behind me. 'I thought Tara was the leader.'

Henry was kind enough to give everyone back their ID's, driver's licenses and passports, and soon we came to a bus stop and managed to find a bus to Gosport.

Waiting for the passenger ferry over to Portsmouth Harbour, the group split up. Some of us went to get money out of our bank while the others went to find a good place to eat at half seven in the morning.

By nine o'clock, we were in the warm munching on large platefuls of breakfast, feeling much happier and with it more hopeful of escaping the T.A.T.

Lottie asked to borrow the café owners phone to call up the ferry services to get us to Spain. 'Santander sound okay?' She asked us. We all nodded and fifteen minutes later, she'd booked us on the next ferry to Spain, one-way. Returning to her seat, she finished her tea. We all looked at her as though she was our saviour. She smiled. 'Don't mention it.'

The ferry from Portsmouth Harbour to Santander, Spain would leave at one in the afternoon and would arrive at eleven at night. We didn't need cabins to stay in as it was such a short crossing, but we all looked exhausted from sleeping rough in the helicopter.

'We can check into a hostel or hotel when we get there,' I told them as we made our way to the ticket office at noon. Lottie showed them our passports and her bank card and collecting our tickets, were told to follow the corridor towards the ferry that was waiting to depart.

'Damn its freezing,' Darren complained as we came out of the corridor and walked along the concrete path towards the awaiting ferry. I could understand him complaining; the harsh sea winds threw themselves towards us in an almost brutal fashion.

'Oh, shut up,' Hannah snapped at him as she grabbed his hand and dragged him to the port wall. 'The cold doesn't bother us you idiot. Not when we've… transformed anyway.' It's a word that Henry had mentioned before, and it shocked me at how truthful it was, for all of us.

'Not the point,' Darren said through chattering teeth. 'I'm cold now and I don't want to get into the water.'

'Ha! Some fish you are,' Hannah laughed at him, the others tittered.

'Okay, you two, calm down' I told them as though a mother would tell her children.

Approaching the boarding walkway, I saw someone out of the corner of my eye. Their appearance alone made me stop while the others carried on.

Looking up at the sky with a worried face was a man in his early twenties wearing an old army uniform.

'Tara wha' are ya...' Saskia began but she had stopped to see what I was staring at. 'Who da hell is tha'?'

Giving her a brief glance I saw her squinting at the man, but she seemed almost confused. Ignoring her, I continued after the others but the man, who was still in my peripheral vision, continued looking up at the sky.

I glanced up and saw nothing but the sun trying to creep through the dull grey clouds. Saskia came to my side and looked up at the sky too, but there was nothing up there.

'Who is tha' bloke?' she asked me as we turned back to look at him, still staring upwards. 'Wha' is he lookin' at?'

Shrugging my shoulders, I decided to find out myself but after I had taken a couple of steps Henry called to us. 'Hey, you coming or what?'

'Yeah, give me a minute,' I shouted back.

Both Saskia and I headed towards the man. I was curious to know what he was staring at and why he was wearing an old uniform. I wouldn't usually do this, but he gave off this strange feeling.

'Um good afternoon,' I said as I walked closer to him.

'Er Tara?' Saskia said cautiously, but I ignored her.

The man stopped staring at the sky and looked directly at me.

'This is going to sound weird but what are you looking at?' I asked stopping close to him.

He frowned at me and pointed at the sky, 'The bombs will be coming this way soon. The Blitz has started; it's only a matter of time.'

Suddenly from out of nowhere there was this God awful noise of an air-raid siren, wailing out its screeching sound from around me. Both Saskia and I clapped our hands to our ears and almost ducked from the impression of fear that we were feeling. Looking at the man, he nodded at me and walked off then suddenly disappeared and with it, the sound of the siren.

'What just happened?' I asked as the group sprinted towards us each looking horrified.

'What did you see?' Henry asked us as Saskia and I frowned at the place the man was just seconds before.

Explaining what the man looked like and what he said, Henry looked directly at me then glanced over to Saskia. 'Tara, your eyes are blue, same as Saskia's.'

'I 'ave green eyes,' Saskia snapped, but Henry shook his head.

'Why did you cover your ears?' he asked.

That shocked me also; they must have heard that, it was monstrously loud. 'Didn't- didn't you hear the air-raid warning?' I asked him, but Henry and the others shook their heads.

Gently lifting his hand to my face, he pushed my hair behind my ear. He frowned slightly then looked over to Saskia. Looking shocked, her hands snapped up to her ears and she yelped. 'I'm an elf! My ears are pointy!'

Copying her I felt my ears and they had become slightly pointed too. Grabbing the book from my bag I flicked through the pages and came across the page on the Siren Clan. Reading it, Saskia came behind me, looking over my shoulder and together we both read a small paragraph on the Sirens: "Not only can Sirens fly with their large and powerful wings. But, in addition, they can also see and hear ghosts among other mythological creatures and not only that they could command with their voice."

I found the last line somewhat stating the obvious. Anyone could command with their voice if they were loud enough. Saskia clarified what the book said and each of them looked a little worried but they didn't look as worried as I felt. The fear that I was becoming a Siren, becoming something monstrous, was palpable. My humanity was slowly being taken away and I knew there was no going back. Henry tried to give me a comforting smile, but it didn't work.

★ ★ ★

The ferry embarked Portsmouth on time. Watching England fade into the distance, I felt a certain bout of happiness as though I was leaving my troubles behind. Lynn, the T.A.T and Maynard were now all gone. Checking my watch it read half one in the afternoon and as England had nearly vanished past the horizon we went to the lower deck to relax or watch the boys play the arcade games.

Heading to one of the bathrooms, after drinking copious amounts of orange juice, I gasped looking at myself in the mirror to the ladies' room. Apart from the slow healing cuts and bruises on my face, my eyes were exactly as Henry had described. A startling azure. But what were also scaring me were my ears. Like an overnight phenomenon, they had become somewhat pointy as I'd felt them earlier. 'Don't panic,' I told myself firmly. 'Things will sort themselves out; you've just used your wings too much, that's all.'

Heading back to the others, I found the girls, minus Saskia, sitting around a table drinking milkshakes and the boys, minus Darren, drinking colas. Approaching the tables, out of the corner of my eye I saw Saskia come careening towards the girls and without saying a word, grabbed Hannah's arm. Yanking her up from her seat, she whispered in a panicked tone, 'Hurry up.'

Trying not to rouse suspicion, the rest of us followed a scared looking Saskia, who led us out of the warmth and up onto the windy and wet top deck of the ferry.

'What?' Hannah asked looking bewildered, wrapping her arms around her.

Saskia pointed out towards the sea. 'He annoyed me so I hit 'im. You'd better go after 'im.'

'What?' we all yelled.

Saskia peered over the side. 'Darren. I didn't want ta hit him so hard, in truth he was a bit of a wuss. But he lost his balance and well...' she left the sentence in the air, we were all stunned.

'What the-?' Hannah asked as without thinking she dove in.

Macie was about to shout out for Hannah, when I clamped her mouth shut. The last thing we needed was to draw attention. Looking around, we were lucky no one was on the same deck as us. Peering over, we saw Hannah meet contact with the iron cold sea and a minute later, she didn't surface.

So angry at Saskia for hitting Darren so hard that he fell overboard, Henry's tattoo burst out of his skin. Lion-like claws came out where his hands used to be and black fur spread all over his arms. Snarling in a big-cat like manner, Saskia cowered away from him.

'I'm so sorry,' she said almost crying. 'But he shouldn't 'ave sat on da side like he did,' she said trying to throw the blame on Darren.

'Lottie, Macie I want you to keep an eye out on the deck please. Go to the aft of the ferry,' I asked them. 'We have no idea if they are following... we can only hope.' I glanced at Henry. 'Calm down, please. It's not gonna help you being like this.'

Lionel and Sam were just as annoyed at Saskia as Henry was, but our collective fear overcame our anger.

Saskia was confined to the lounge area in a corner alone, watched over by Lionel, as the rest of us went onto another deck to discuss what we could do for them.

'So it's agreed then,' Henry finished after we all gave our input. 'If the girls can't find either sign of them by the evening, then you will fly down and re-track the ferry's course,' he said looking at me.

I nodded, but I didn't like the idea, even though I thought of it. Though Henry was supposedly my second in command, my current leadership skills lacked somewhat. I was still worried about my outward appearance and still freaked out that I could see ghosts. Clearly I was in no position to lead anyone.

★ ★ ★

By the time darkness fell, the ferry was thrown about through the raging seas like a toy boat in a bath. Lottie and Macie had kept a look out for Darren and Hannah for a few hours, but too cold and finding it pointless, they came inside shivering as they passed the buck to me.

'Tara, you have to find them,' Lottie snivelled unhappily, cuddled beside a heater in one of the lounges. 'We couldn't see them in the dark, not even with our magical eyes.' Tapping Lottie and Macie on the arm, silently thanking them, I looked over at Saskia, who was still in the corner of the lounge, sulking.

Henry kindly came with me to the cold windy aft of the ferry to ensure no one saw me. Shedding my woolly jumper, I jumped off the boat into the night. Before I hit the water, I thought of how annoying Saskia was and let my wings burst from my back and glided off into the night, calling out for Darren and Hannah until my voice went hoarse.

Flying as low as I could to the water against the frozen winds, I hoped for a flash of Darren's blond hair or a sight of Hannah's uniform amidst the spiralling foam. No sooner as I had thought that, on the brink of about to give up all hope, I got a face full of freezing cold water. Spluttering and flying higher, I stopped in midair. Hovering a couple of metres above the choppy waves I glanced below me. Both looking extremely odd against the dark iron sea were Darren and Hannah.

'Guys, you're alright?' I laughed with an edge of relief as I flew closer to them.

Darren nodded. 'Yes Tara, we're fine,' Hannah called up.

'Good, that's a relief,' I said waving my hand. 'Keep following the boat; we're going to get you back onboard soon. I just need a plan.' They turned to look in the direction of the ferry and nodded. 'Keep within sight of it guys, I know you can do it.'

Smiling in response, Hannah slunk back into the water while Darren half-dived, a light brown fish tail following his torso.

I met the others back on the top deck. Quickly and quietly slinking past the watchful eyes of the staff, Lottie handed me a large blanket to cover my wings and rushing back into the warmth, guided me into a small unused cabin. I soon discovered the guys had broken into this room so we could all talk in private.

Closing the door behind me, I noticed a miserable looking Saskia sitting on one of the camp beds staring at the bland, grey carpet. Sitting around her, the others watched me carefully, eager to hear what I had to say.

'I saw them,' I said through still chattering teeth as Macie gave me another blanket from the bed she was sitting on.

There was a great sigh of relief from all of them. Lottie even burst into tears, 'Thank God.'

Comforting her, Henry asked, 'What did you tell them?'

'I told them to keep the ferry in sight and we'll come up with a plan to get them back on board.'

Lionel nodded. 'Good.'

But the questions didn't stop there.

Henry furrowed his brows in deep thought then queried, 'Did they say anything to you?'

All eyes were on me. It seemed to be a collective eagerness to hear my answers. 'Hannah spoke but Darren kept silent. He was probably embarrassed about it though,' I said more to myself.

'Embarrassed about what?' Sam asked me looking intrigued.

'His merman tail,' I chuckled, but the other's weren't laughing with me and all turned to Henry, looking grave.

'We're going to have to think of another way to get them back, especially Darren.' I gave him an enquiring look. Henry sighed tiredly. 'I think Darren's fully transformed, but I can't be sure. At any rate, it'll take a long time for him to turn back to normal.'

'What?' Everyone shouted in alarm.

'Shush!' He growled, waving his arms at us to speak quieter. 'Once you have transformed into your tattoo it's difficult for you to become human again.' We each looked at one another, fearful of what we'd turn into. While Saskia and I were certain what we'd become, we had no idea what

Lionel, Macie, Lottie, Sam or even Hannah would turn into. Their tattoos were rather vague.

There was a short pause as everyone tried to think of another way of getting Darren back onto the ferry.

'Do you think they could swim all the way to Santander?' Lottie asked with bloodshot eyes from crying so much.

'I think they could,' I told her. 'Their tattoos were built for this type of environmental condition. It's like me with flying. I'm finding it much easier flying outside than I was in a high-ceilinged room.'

'Yeah, but man, you've got your problems too,' Lionel eyed me as I towered over him, which I hadn't really noticed until now. 'You are getting taller.'

'Plus,' Saskia spoke up for the first time, 'your hair 'as grown longer.' Everyone looked at me to confirm it as I ran my fingers through my black hair. What used to be shoulder length was at least three inches above my waist.

'Each time she becomes her tattoo, the more difficult it is for her to change back and that goes for the rest of you too,' Henry explained again. 'I mean, no offence Lottie, but you're getting smaller and you have slight feather patterns around your eyes.' She jumped in shock and touched her eyes then looked away, ashamed. 'And hell, I don't usually have black fur spread up my arms or growing a semi-mane.'

The group was silent for a while until, I shrugged the blankets off me and ruffled my wings. They all turned to me with expectant eyes, even Henry, who had so far been more of a leader than I had. 'We can deal with the collective depression of turning into mythical creatures later. Saskia and I are the only ones who can fly out there and grab them. We have less than three hours to get them out of the water and human before we arrive in Santander. They'll just have to stay in here until they become human again. Lionel, Sam, Henry, I need you guys to help them from the deck and back into this cabin. Does anyone have any objections?'

They all shook their heads. 'Good, Saskia, let's go.'

Together, Saskia and I took off into the bitterly cold night; Saskia spotted Hannah after twenty minutes of flying around. Hannah looked upset about something and kept glancing behind her nervously, but my vision was poor and couldn't see what she was looking at. Maybe she was waiting for Darren.

'Wha's goin' on?' Saskia asked her as I tried to search for Darren.

Hannah was about to say something, then put her hand up to shush her and moments later bursting out the water looking almost frightened, was Darren. Taking her hand, Hannah looked up and motioned for us to go; they then dived back into the water.

'Saskia, get high!' I yelled at her knowing something was wrong.

Just then, angry bubbles suddenly erupted from the dark depths immediately below us. I then saw something that made me feel like a small frightened child; large startling yellow eyes as big as dustbin lids rose out of the choppy sea. Flapping as hard and fast as I could, I flew towards the cloudy night sky trying to put as much distance as I could to this monster. My heart raced in panic as I heard the gurgling, rushing water as something came out of it, breaking the surface of the Atlantic Ocean with effortless ease. Then without warning, a huge angry scream pierced the night sending a shiver down my spine; its shrill voice made me clap my hands to my ears, trying to relieve the pain in my eardrums.

As I turned round to look at the source of the scream, I almost screamed myself at the sight. It was a gigantic slimy-grey sea monster, with spikes along high protruding ridges running along its long serpentine back. Snorting out water like a geyser, it continued to ascend out of the sea so that it was face to face with me as I hovered in the air, fear keeping me from flying off. Its huge hungry yellow eyes staring at me with spite and slowly opening its mouth it showed me Darren struggling to get out of in between its teeth.

Moments later I noticed Hannah surfacing a safe distance from the monster and issued a petrifying scream as she looked at Darren in the jaws of this enormous sea monster. Her scream broke through my fear, bringing me to my senses.

Turning, I caught sight of Saskia and flew towards her, I had a plan. 'I'll distract it, you get Darren, okay?'

'Wha?' she yelped. I could tell she looked scared, even in the darkness.

'Don't argue, just do it!' Flying away from her I dived down towards the mouth of the sea monster, it quickly saw me and moved its head smoothly, coaxing me with Darren. I was happy to see that he was still alive and conscious trying to beat every part of the monster he could get to, but without little success of causing even the slightest damage. Out of the corner of my eye, I saw a flash of white and heard a barrage of abuse coming from Saskia. The monster was angry, but now it had its attention on Saskia, giving me time to try and free Darren.

Camouflaged in the darkness, I flew towards the corner of the monsters mouth, dodging its spiky ridged head it lashed violently against Saskia's wasp-like attack. Its putrid rotting fishy breath was enough to make anyone pass out, and I tried my best to ignore it as I inched towards Darren.

'Don't,' he managed to gasp, lodged tightly within a gap of the monster's brown sharp teeth. 'Leave me.'

'Not the plan,' I shook my head, looking for a way to try and pry the jaw open, but Darren grabbed my hand to stop me. 'You can't stop her.'

'Her, who?'

'It's Roxy,' he gurgled in ragged breaths and that was all he managed to say. His eyes, which penetrated my frightened soul with fear, told me to fly away, but I couldn't do that. Saskia and I were the only ones who could help them. There was no way I was going to give up so easily, even if this monster was Roxy. Though I was stunned and horrified at this revealing secret, I had to understand that the world wasn't the one I was brought up in, it was magical and with it, it was also dangerous.

'TARA, WATCH OUT!' Saskia suddenly screamed from above, but it was too late. A huge black claw came out of the raging sea towards me, bringing with it a lot of frigid seawater, and tried to pick me out of its teeth as though I was a piece lodged food. Darren reached out and took hold of my hands firmly, unwilling to let me fall as the claw managed to briefly dislodge me.

'Cheers,' I smiled, but his wet slimy hands only gave me small purchase. I had to think of another plan. Glancing up, past the teeth that threatened to come down and chomp on us, I saw Saskia still taunting Roxy. But she was making her even angrier. Saskia wasn't giving me the chance to free Darren. 'THE EYES,' I yelled at Saskia, quickly thinking of a plan as I started to slip from Darren's hands.

Saskia smiled and bending her one wing back and tilting the other, she almost pirouetted in the air, hitting her right foot in Roxy's left squishy yellow eye.

In utter agony and close to being blinded, Roxy shook her massive maw with such force that Darren flew out of her mouth, heading towards the sea. From the saltwater that the claw showered me in, my wings was partially wet making them heavy and I knew it would be difficult to fly. I dived down towards the surface of the choppy, black, waters and plucked Darren out of mid-air. His fish tail wriggled underneath him as he reached up with his wet hands and grabbed hold of my arms for extra purchase.

'Get Hannah!' I yelled at Saskia, briefly turning back to see Roxy thrash around in pain, her eyes closed, screeching out a terrifying cry. Seeing the white flash of Saskia, she shot down like a bullet towards the sea and plucked Hannah out like an old waterlogged blanket. With difficulty, together we headed for the ferry and after a few seconds, we glanced back to see a blinded Roxy slinking back into the sea, the bubbles leaving the surface of the waters. 'She's gone,' Darren called up to me and I couldn't help but breathe a sigh of relief.

Half an hour later, we were all in the small cramped cabin. Saskia and I shivered together under four blankets while we had a conversation with Darren in the bathroom, his shiny, slippery tail flopped over the bath. We were waiting for him to become human again.

Henry felt mean depriving Darren of air, but he said it would be a quicker way for Darren to become human. He was right.

'He'll be okay,' Henry told us as Hannah, now normal, was silently crying on Lottie's shoulder. It was a very traumatic experience for her.

We had recounted what had happened with the sea monster and how I had managed to free Darren after Saskia's bold attack. Hannah had filled in the details when she had dived off the side of the ferry after Darren.

'I found him easy enough,' she began to explain, after drying her eyes. 'He's transformed, though it wasn't the first time,' there was a collective gasp; we all looked at her in shock. 'Darren first transformed in the swimming pool at the T.A.T.'

'Yes but Roxy had asked me all these weird questions,' Darren interjected from the bathroom. 'Then she said that I hadn't fully transformed yet and I think she's right. I think there's another step or something, I can't explain it.'

We each looked at one another, confused.

'Anyway,' Hannah said hurriedly, trying to push us through the shock, 'we can communicate through a particular type of telepathy, but it only happens under water. We decided to follow the ferry. Then sometime later, Tara met us and told us about getting back on the boat, but as soon as she left, both of us felt this oppressive presence in the waters. We couldn't judge the distance but after a while, we felt it getting closer to us. Within ten minutes, we heard her thoughts. It was Roxy and she was chasing us.'

All mouths were open, but they hadn't heard the whole story yet. Hannah, Saskia and I explained what Roxy looked like. They all shivered as one with each word that described her.

'What is Roxy anyway?' Macie asked. Lottie passed my bag and dipping my hand inside it brought out the little leather book. Flicking through some pages, I came across a picture of Roxy and felt a wave of sickness pass through me as I uttered the creature she was.

'The Leviathan.'

CHAPTER ELEVEN

ARRIVING SAFELY IN SANTANDER, WE PASSED THROUGH customs un-
scathed though still shaken up and decided to look for a place to stay for the
night. Heading into the town, there were people milling around leaving the
closing restaurants. Lionel pointed out a small hotel down a side street and
entering, found a middle-aged woman flicking through a Spanish magazine.

'Buenos noches,' she smiled, putting her magazine down.

'I'll handle this,' Lionel said, moving in between us to reach the front.
'Buenos noches,' he began then suddenly a string of Spanish flew out of his
mouth. The receptionist looked a little surprised but continued to smile.
Lionel then turned to me and said, 'She has four spare rooms for the night.
Will that be okay?'

I nodded and confirming the transaction, Lottie came forwards and held
out her card.

Guiding us along the corridors and up the stairs to the rooms, Saskia
poked Lionel on the shoulder.

'I didn't know ya could speak Spanish,' sounding mildly impressed.

Lionel frowned. 'You never asked me.'

'Oh yeah, so I'm going to randomly ask if you can speak Spanish. Anything else Tara needs to know?' She snapped. We came to the first floor, the
corridor softly smelt of rose.

'Hey, don't drag me into this.' I blurted out.

Lionel turned to face me, smiling slightly. 'I speak five different languages, Tara: Spanish, French, Italian, Vietnamese, Japanese and a little Chinese and Korean. Though I profess I'm not fluent in the last two.'

'Well, colour me impressed,' Macie smiled at him.

The woman showed us the rooms and between us, we divided ourselves up, the boys getting two rooms and the girls getting two rooms. Bidding each other good night, we closed the doors and tried to get a decent good night's sleep.

The following morning and feeling well-rested, we left the hotel by 10 o'clock and found a small café for a bite to eat. Sitting down at a table after eating our breakfast, Henry leaned towards us, a stern look on his face. 'We need to get across to Barcelona as soon as possible.'

'D'uh,' Saskia and I said together. I frowned; the girl was rubbing off on me. So sticking three fingers in the air, I counted them off. 'Plane, coach or car.'

'Expensive, expensive, expensive,' droned Saskia and I nodded.

'Not a problem,' Lottie smiled, but I shook my head.

'Your card can be tracked; we're trying to avoid that.' Pouting she nodded slowly looking down at her half-drunk glass of orange juice.

'Yeah Lottie,' Darren chipped in, 'stop waving your money around like some tart. You'll be asking for trouble.'

'If you can't say anything that's helpful, do not say anything at all,' I said loudly, sounding strangely like my mother.

Darren's mouth suddenly clamped shut and looking alarmed, nodded.

'Since when d'ya take orders from 'er?' Saskia asked him, but he shook his head, as though unable to talk. He suddenly looked absolutely scared and grabbed his throat beginning to panic. I frowned at him and then something suddenly clicked. This had happened before with Lynn. Just one word and Lynn had stopped in her tracks.

'Sirens can command with their voice,' I whispered, coming to the only conclusion. 'The book said that Sirens can command with their voice. I thought it was a bit obvious, but it's more than that. Saskia and I can control anyone and they'll do what we say. The Siren's voice lured sailors, but they won't do anything unless ordered to. Darren, you may speak,' I spoke clearly.

As though an invisible hand had been lifted from his voice box, he gasped grabbing his throat. 'That was horrible.' I gave him a sympathetic look, but he ignored me.

Saskia and I looked at one another, sharing the same interested look. It could be awful fun commanding people to do what we wanted. But as I thought on, I found that it was also a terrible thing to do; force someone to do something against their wishes wasn't right.

'So um,' I began changing the subject as Daren looked away from me, apprehensive, and that was something I didn't want people to see me as, an intimidator. 'What's the big deal about getting to Cupid before the others do?' I asked Henry, staring into his eyes, instantly feeling my cheeks blush. I took a brief moment to wonder what would happen if Henry hadn't been following me. Would I have felt the same way about him?

I knew on some level that Henry didn't like me that way, it was kind of obvious. And though this upset me, having a secret crush on someone, especially your "number two" wasn't a good idea. But I couldn't help it and as I glanced around the table, I saw that the others were feeling things for each other too. It was obvious that Darren was infatuated with Saskia. He couldn't take his eyes off her and defended her on every occasion, but we saw that his affection was not reciprocated with Saskia snapping at him and looking disgusted when he gave her a compliment. Lottie and Sam had exchanged goo-goo eyes from time to time, and in a cute childish way, tried to hide it. And poor old Macie was flicking her eyes towards Lionel, who was bashfully attempting to ignore it. If love was in the air within our group, it was permeated with it.

'Ever heard of a love-hate relationship?' Henry asked us, as I had practically paired up everyone in my head and thought how wonderful it would be if we all got along.

'Yes...' we said chimed together, curious to know where this was going to lead.

Henry leaned back in his chair, with a big know-it-all smirk on his face. 'Blame that on Cupid. If people get too infatuated with someone, they could hate them enough and have the potential to kill them. After all, love hurts,' he said giving me a small glance, 'and you hurt the one you love.' I instantly felt my face go even hotter and looked in a different direction.

Leaving the café, Lionel was kind enough to ask around for ways to travel to Barcelona to pick up another ferry to Genoa. Lottie insisted on flying to Verona, but I flatly refused. I didn't want to give the T.A.T. another way to find us.

Mooching around the town centre to see what the prices were for hiring a car, Sam and Lionel came back looking disappointed.

'Three hundred Euros for a week? Sod that,' Sam said, peeved.

Lottie sighed. 'Then go by coach. That's the only alternative if you don't want to spend so much money.' No one was paying attention to our dilemma as we sat by a fountain watching people going to work or simply having a wonder around. It felt surreal

'It'll take too long,' Henry and I said together.

'Any flyin' is not an option because…' Saskia began.

'Too expensive,' Henry and I said together.

'I didn't mean tha' type of flyin',' she snapped then folding her arms, looked away huffily. 'God, no one listens ta me!'

'I listen to you,' Darren said softly but Saskia was in "ignore" mode. 'Okay, how about the train!' Darren said clapping his hands. 'It can get us from A to B, with no money involved.' We all gave him a stupid look, so he filled us in. 'Courier!'

With Lionel asking for directions, as he was the only one who could speak Spanish, a nice old man told us of the European and International Courier Company situated near the outskirts of Monte. 'He said it delivers all over and not just flights but also train, or boat too.'

'Great,' Hannah, Lottie and Macie laughed at the ingenious of Lionel's foreign speaking.

'It's so incredible you can speak all those languages,' Macie practically drooled.

'Didn't you say you could speak Vietnamese?' Darren asked, overhearing the girls talking, as I looked through the little book for anything interesting. Actually I was secretly trying to find out what Dave and Matt could be. So far Roxy and Lynn had transformed into large mythical creatures and I was afraid that so would Dave and Matt.

Lionel turned around to answer as we headed through the busy city. 'I studied in Vietnam for six months as a transfer student back in college. My parents said it would be a good idea and it may help one day. When I came home, I continued to learn the language. It's quite fascinating.'

'Wow Lionel, your family are cool,' I laughed but he only responded with a small grimace.

'Oh, sod off!' Saskia shouted as two Spanish teenagers wolf whistled to her as they sped off on a muck-covered moped.

'They weren't whistling at you, they were whistling at Hannah,' Macie pointed out and instantly received a nettled look from Saskia.

'You won't be able to meet them,' Lionel continued ignoring the girl's bickering. 'They went abroad some months ago for business and I haven't heard from them since they left.'

'That's the same as my parents,' I said to him feeling a wave of uneasy panic.

'Same as mine,' Macie said sadly. And the topic was instantly dropped as the realisation that our parents may be in trouble, hit us like a tonne of bricks. The T.A.T. must have had something to do with it.

The couriers weren't difficult to find, but I got the suspicion that they weren't often used. The building was covered in pollution grime, giving it a grubby appearance and there was a broken window on the front of the building which someone had tried to patch up with some plaster board.

We went inside and waited until Lionel had asked a beefy gruff-looking man about any deliveries to Barcelona. Now and again the man would grunt and then looked past Lionel to us, especially us girls which unnerved me. Giving Lionel a ticket, he also gave him the instructions to get to the train station and then told us to get out.

'What a lovely man,' Lottie whispered scathingly as we left the building. 'He didn't like the look of us, did he?'

'Nope. Plus he smelt like a stale fart.' Saskia mocked.

Several of us rolled our eyes or groaned at Saskia's comment but thankfully, didn't argue with her.

Within walking distance, we picked up the ten relatively heavy parcels near one of Santander's train stations. The station smelt of diesel was quite pungent when you coupled it with the stink of fish from the market close by.

Lionel went off to talk to a station guard and came back looking angry. 'We're not going to be in any of the comfy carriages,' he spat, and then grabbed his ears as they began to grow; his tattoo was transforming him. 'We have to go in the very back of the train and be with the parcels.'

Squashed and cold, we tried our best to not complain during the four hours it took to get to Madrid, but it was difficult. Macie hated the cold and constantly shivered in the freezing carriage and Saskia hated being pressed up so close to Darren.

Alighting at Madrid's main train station mid-afternoon, we found a trolley to place the heavy parcels on and wheeled them over to platform five where the high speed, AVE train was going to Barcelona

'So, we've established that Roxy is a massive sea-monster,' Hannah started, trying to bring up an interesting topic, 'and Lynn is a dragon, but what about Dave?'

Henry and Sam looked at one another. 'We don't know what he becomes,' Henry told her.

'We've actually been discussing it, but all the things we've thought he could be just makes him seem superfluous, and he's anything but.'

'What about you three?' Hannah asked Lottie, Lionel and Macie. 'You were trained by Matt, what does he become?'

They each shrugged their shoulders.

'Whatever it is,' Macie said with a grave face, 'it's dangerous. Matt is a scary guy.'

The train to Barcelona was annoyingly boring. The carriage was bigger this time, but it was just as cold. Macie was sandwiched between Lottie and me, trying to keep her warm while Saskia took to walking on the spot. Darren was loving every minute of it. Saskia tended to wiggle her arse when she walked.

Henry, Sam and Lionel stared out of the window, glancing at the changing landscape from countryside to town and back to the countryside again. There was a strange oppressive feeling to the group and I couldn't help but feel it was my fault. I was the leader and I wasn't acting like one. As I sat there shivering next to the girls, my mind wondered on my meeting with Jeff and him telling me that I was the leader of this freakish group. Why me though? That is one thing that I didn't understand. Saskia was like me, but over the past few weeks I sussed out that she wasn't leadership material. Her focus was almost always on herself and never anyone else. Hannah seemed confident to be a leader, especially when I first met her but then when she found out who I was, she quickly accepted me. The others didn't seem to have the leader 'vibe,' so to speak, apart from Henry.

Bringing me out of my reverie, Lionel said calmly, 'We are almost at Barcelona. Just one more town to go through then we're there.'

'Finally,' Macie muttered. 'I'm so freaking cold.' Rubbing her back, I gave her a wan smile.

Saskia stopped walking and turned to face him. 'How d'ya know?' she snapped.

'He's psychotic,' Macie slipped up, making everyone burst out laughing.

'No, tha's wha' ya are,' Saskia spat nastily.

'Hey, there's no need for that,' I said angrily, glaring at her. Huffing, Saskia began walking on the spot again, turning her back on us. Lifting up my wrist, I checked the time. Lionel was right. We had twenty minutes to go until we reached Barcelona. But as I looked at my watch I noticed on the right-hand side was a small red light. 'Does everyone have a little red light on the side of their watch?' I asked out loud. The others checked their watches and nodded; however Henry became suddenly rigid, his face went deathly white.

'Henry, what's wrong?' my voice sounded fearful and the others immediately turned to look at him.

'We're being followed,' Henry said his eyes glazed over, talking more to himself.

'Well d'uh,' Saskia snorted at him but Henry looked like he was having a panic attack.

'Damn we're so stupid,' he growled, 'we've had them on our wrists for days and done nothing about it.'

The entire group suddenly grabbed at their watches and ripped them off. 'Oh my God,' Lottie said looking terrified. 'They'll find us again; they'll know where we're heading to.'

'No, no they won't,' Sam said trying to calm her. 'We've travelled too fast and on land, they can only track us if we have stopped for a long time. Why hadn't we thought about this and got rid of them ages ago?'

'We were too preoccupied with other things with Lynn and Roxy trying to kill us. It's an easy mistake though utterly stupid,' Macie replied as she put her watch on the floor and was about to stamp on it.

'Hang on, stop,' I said thinking of something. 'We need to ditch the watches but make it look like we're going off separately. When we stop at the next station, we get off and put them on different trains.'

'No, we'd place people in danger,' Henry told me sternly.

But I firmly shook my head, 'No we won't. They won't openly attack us in broad daylight. There's the Golden Rule remember. You can't expose yourself to people.'

Saskia snorted in laughter. 'Ya can't expose yourself ta people anyway Tara; ya get arrested for indecent exposure.'

Inhaling deeply and ignoring her, I turned my attention to Henry and the rest of the group.

'We could post them,' Macie said after a while.

'Ya know I'm goin' ta try an' ensure tha' ya don't utter a stupid word ever again,' Saskia said waspishly.

Macie's chin wobbled and looked like she was about to cry. But I cut across Saskia, glaring at her, 'Saskia don't make me order you to smell your own farts.'

Everyone burst out laughing, I even got a little titter out of Macie, but it still didn't help us in ditching the watches safely.

'What about an abandoned building?' Lottie enquired. 'We're being followed, we know that, but putting them into an abandoned building, we'd be okay.'

'I like it, we just have to find one,' Henry smiled.

An announcement in Spanish sounded through the speakers. We looked at Lionel.

'We're coming into Tarragona in a few minutes.'

I nodded. 'Good. We'll have to leave the stuff on the train while we make a run for a building of some sort, dump the watches and get on a train to Barcelona.'

A few minutes later, the train pulled smoothly into the station. Hopping off, we ran to the exit of the station and stopped outside, panting, looking where to go. Lionel went up to an old woman sat outside smoking a pipe and talked with her for a moment or two. She nodded then pointed to our right.

'Gracias,' he shouted then ran towards us, 'There's an old Roman amphitheatre up ahead on the right. We can leave the watches there.'

The amphitheatre was sadly crumbling away at the seams and no one seemed to care that it was there. It was accessible to everyone day or night, especially after I noticed old beer cans littering the dusty floor.

Finding a small alcove in the middle of the old ruined building, we turned around to head back when I suddenly felt a strange wave of fear and stopped midstride. The fear radiated from me, almost crippling me, making me unable to run away. Spinning around on the spot I looked around to see what made me so frightened, but I couldn't see anything on the ground, so then I looked up.

'Tara, what's wrong?' Macie whispered, as I noticed out of the corner of my eye, Saskia joined me and looked at what I was staring at.

'Can you feel that?' I whispered to her.

'Yeah.'

'It's a ghost isn't it?' Darren asked. 'Damn, this is creeping me out. I can't see them!'

I shook my head, 'No, it's not a ghost.' One by one, we looked up and saw them more clearly as they headed straight towards us. They looked exactly as the book described and I was not prepared to face these creatures. 'Time to go.' Hitching up my bag and running for the exit, the others were hot on my heels. As soon as we started to move, they screeched in anger; their prey clearly realising they were being hunted.

'What are they, what are they?' Macie screamed, terrified of being chased.

'Harpies. They're snatchers and are proficient at what they do,' I panted, still feeling the cold blanket of fear cover me.

'Oh crap,' Henry blurted out and I got the feeling that he understood what I meant. 'The T.A.T must have sent them. They'd use other myths to do their dirty work.'

'They've broken the Golden Rule. Why do they want to unbalance the world?' I asked myself, but there were more things to worry about presently.

'Tara, what else does the book say?' Sam demanded from behind us as we began to run up the stairs towards the exit, but we were slow and the Harpies were quickly descending on us.

Stopping for a brief second to wait for Lottie and Macie to catch up, I answered Sam's question. 'There are two of them, sisters, Aello and Celaeno. They're agents who punish and torture,' I whimpered.

'We need to get out of here and into the public, we'll be safe then,' Henry suggested but it was too late. One of them, unsure which sister, came upon us like a thundering boulder; blocking us from leaving, halting us in our tracks. There was a collective gasp from the group as it landed in front of us, its steel-like talons digging into the concrete like it was butter. The creature was hideous in appearance. With the body of a bird, the creatures' feathers were askew and splattered in dried blood. Its head, however, was that of an old gaunt woman with sunken red eyes, skeletal nose and tatty un-brushed black hair that fell around her feathery neck and bird body.

'Holy kack,' Darren whispered behind us. 'RUN!' he roared just as the harpy spread its vile smelling wings.

Turning around, we ran down the steps, only to scream in horror as the other sister swooped down towards us, making everyone run off in different directions. We were split up, which wasn't good, we were stronger as a team, it's how we trained.

Saskia, Henry and I went down on the right, Sam, Lionel and Lottie went left and Hannah, Macie and Darren went straight down.

'Duck!' Henry yelled tackling me to the floor as the harpy from behind dived towards us, trying to scratch our eyes out. Swooping off, I yelled out in frustration and my huge black wings once again erupted from my back, coupled with the feeling of my legs growing a little longer. Scrabbling to get up, I took a couple of running steps then jumped into the air and flew after the harpy who now seemed shocked that I was flying.

'Come here you feculent mutant bird,' I shouted as I twisted and turned in the air after it.

From behind me, I heard the familiar whomph of Saskia's wings. Seconds later, she was in the air behind me.

'Tara, what do you want us to do?' Henry called from below.

'Get the other one,' I called back. 'But don't get scratched, their talons act as a muscle relaxant!'

Looking down, I saw the others band together. Hannah and Darren stayed behind the others; they were pretty useless in this type of terrain. Henry and Sam, however, were ready. Their magical tattoo's activated.

Saskia caught up with me as I continued to tail the other harpy. Similar in appearance, this harpy had white cobweb-like hair. 'Wha' do ya want ta do?' she asked me as the harpy screeched in anger and fright at being followed by two huge half birds, like itself.

'I'm thinking!' I shouted back.

'Well, think faster!' she quipped.

The harpy quickly turned upwards and twisting in the air plunged towards me; an evil grin on its face matching the menacing sharp claws that were suddenly heading towards me.

'Crap,' I yelled tilting to the left quickly avoiding it. The harpy brushed past me and tilting quickly, doubled back. Without having any time to think about tactics, its sharp claws suddenly latched onto my right wing, piercing the skin and ripped out some of my feathers. The pain shot up my wing like daggers making me scream out in pain. 'Get off me!' I yelled at it, but my voice couldn't command, I was in too much pain and being unable to shake it off, I began to fall out of the sky.

'TARA!' I heard Henry yell out from below.

'I've got her,' Saskia called, as I saw her swoop down and manage to kick the harpy off my wing.

Incapable of gaining altitude as my wing felt like a floppy sock attached to my back, I bent my left wing around me to shield myself as the ground came quickly upon me. Bracing bone-shattering impact I was suddenly caught by someone, holding me in a protective embrace and sliding with me along the ground from their momentum. Panting in pain, I opened my eyes and saw Henry, holding me, his deep sea-blue eyes never leaving mine.

'I've got you,' he smiled. Everything seemed surreal at that point. In the back of my mind, I was vaguely aware of what was going on. I felt the vibrations of people running around. I heard the harpy's screams and saw the feathers fly, but the fact that Henry had gone out of his way to save me as he did, it was truly enchanting.

'GET OUT OF THE WAY!' Sam suddenly hissed, snapping me back to reality.

Rolling off me, Henry pulled me up and with a mighty roar, his claws and golden fur swept up his arms. Putting me behind him, I turned to see the grounded white-haired harpy half flapping half hopping, trying desperately to get to me, screaming out and dragging it's talons along the floor, digging deep groves. But it wasn't going anywhere. Saskia's right foot was pressed down on its back and with a waft of singed hair, I noticed that one of its wings seemed burnt off; Sam must have spat at it with his poison.

'Wha' do we do with it?' Saskia asked over its wailing screams for help from its sister.

Henry shook his head and looked back towards me. 'It seems to be after Tara. These things won't quit until they get what they are assigned to snatch. We need to kill them!'

With one powerful swipe of his claws, Henry caught the harpy in the stomach, ripping it open. It screamed out in agony for a few seconds then, fell to the floor and turned to dust. But the screaming still continued from its sister. Saskia took off into the air and tried to grab it, but it was too enraged with grief and hatred. The harpy blew past her and headed straight for Henry and me. Its face contorted with fury, its talons seemed even deadlier. It was within seconds of reaching us, but could Henry save us?

'Tara, tell it to go away!' Sam yelled at me.

Understanding what he was getting at I smiled and shook my head, 'I have something better.'

The harpy came within inches of us and willing for it to work, I shouted, 'Stop now!' As Darren had obeyed me before, so too did the harpy. It stopped attacking and landed on the floor close to me, panting heavily and frothing at the mouth. Though unable to go against my wishes, it was still angry and distraught.

'It's not going to go anywhere,' I called to the others. 'It's safe.'

'Ha!' Darren laughed. 'Not bloody likely.'

'Fine then fraidy cat. Go and get the watches,' I asked him as Macie, Lottie, Hannah and Lionel joined us near the bottom of the steps of the old Roman amphitheatre.

Darren had done as I had asked and bending down, I carefully attached the watches to its leg. It stared at me with hateful eyes and seemed as though it wanted nothing better than to kill me on the spot. Instead of delivering me back to the T.A.T. I stood up and gave it one final command; to fly back to wherever it came from and to not bother us again.

'Clever,' Henry laughed as it flew off into the greying sky, shrinking into the distance.

'Whoo hoo, Tara,' everyone jeered as we headed towards Barcelona on a nice comfortable train half an hour later. My wings had gone, but like some people experience phantom limbs, I was experiencing phantom pain. I kept moving my shoulder now and again and somehow it pinged with pain.

'Yeah and nice catch there Henry,' Hannah laughed nudging him in the side. 'You should have seen the look on your face when she was falling.'

'You two gonna go on a date?' Macie and Lottie giggled.

I could have hit them.

My face instantly turned a beetroot shade and I looked out of the window, trying to find something interesting to keep my eyes from the others.

Coughing and ruffling his hair, Henry said, 'I would have done the same thing for any of you. It's nothing special.'

Ouch, I thought, inwardly cringing.

There was an air of uncomfortable silence that now engulfed the carriage, no one knowing what to say to Henry's response. But ignoring this I said, 'Lionel, how long until we get to Barcelona?'

'Er...about thirty minutes,' he said, understanding why I changed the topic. 'We're on a slow train.'

I heard someone sigh next to me, it sounded like Saskia.

★ ★ ★

Jumping off the train as it rolled into Barcelona, we then headed on foot towards the port Muelle de San Beltrán. We felt a little safer than earlier. For one, we weren't going to be followed by our operators and secondly would have a clean sailing across the Mediterranean Sea.

When we arrived at the port, Henry took Lionel to find out when the next ferry to Genoa was while the rest of us waited by the main road. In silence, we watched the dozens of scooters, motorbikes and a few cars zoom past while they beeped at us. We couldn't believe how brazen these guys were.

'Pervs,' Lottie said smiling as one boy on a scooter did a double take as he drove past her and nearly crashed.

'Tomorrow morning at eleven,' Lionel told us as he and Henry jogged back with a handful of tickets and handed them out to each of us.

'On a Sunday?' Hannah asked him, but he shrugged.

'We should get into Genoa by Monday afternoon,' Henry added.

'I hope and pray that we don't run into Roxy,' Macie whimpered beside me.

'We won't,' I said looking down at her, hell, I really had grown taller. 'We had the watches on us last time and now thanks to the harpy, we don't. We just need to lay low and keep out of the water,' I warned looking at Darren and Hannah.

We found a nearby cheap hotel, Eurostars Grand Marina, which was really close to the port. Thankfully I got my own room, but I felt sorry for Hannah, who had to put up with Saskia in the room opposite me. I could hear Saskia's voice through the walls and cringed.

Heading out for some dinner later on that evening after a brief rest, we found a small little seafood restaurant La Barceloneta near the port and sat outside.

It wasn't particularly cold outside, not like frost bitten-England, but it was a clear night's sky; covering us in a sense of calm. The sights in Barcelona were just unbelievable. I had never been to Spain before; the closest place I got to it was Toulouse in France. It was refreshing to see a new country and actually stop and have the chance to admire it for its history and architecture.

As I looked across the small forecourt we were sitting in, I noticed boats for both fishermen and passengers from other European countries, tied up close to the café. Each vessel had their own country's flags flying gently in the night's breeze. Though after a while, I noticed that there weren't a lot of people about. And despite the fact that there were still cars parked in the car park opposite us, I didn't see anyone walking around.

When I confided this to the others, their reply was that it wasn't the tourist season, but people still went on holiday regardless of it being seasonal or not.

'Lionel, ask the hostess where everyone is when she comes round,' I hissed at him as Darren and Macie were having an argument about Roxy.

'She won't attack again and if she does, I'll be ready for her,' Darren snarled at her.

'But she almost killed you,' Macie said scowling back. 'You can't attack her with your tail, idiot.'

I slammed my hand down on the table making the cutlery clatter. 'Oy, both of you shut it!'

The conversation was immediately dropped. Though I was unsure whether it was my voice or the fact that we were drawing attention from the locals that silenced the all. The locals stared at us from their block of flats as we sat outside looking a little out of place. I noticed every now and again they'd mutter something, inhale on their pipes and continue to stare.

The hostess came around moments later to take our empty plates away and after a quick short chat with Lionel, the lady smiled and walked off.

'Well, she doesn't know,' Lionel told us. 'Business has been slow these days, but no one knows why. I mean she said in the city it's still buzzing, but on the coasts, it's pretty dead.'

As I wiped my mouth with a napkin, I suddenly stopped in fright as I saw Henry's face. His eyes were wide with shock, but there was a frown of confusion on his forehead. What was going on?

The others weren't angled to see what Henry was seeing. I sharply turned around in my seat, cricking my neck and there I saw him, skulking by the corner of the café, metres from us. Completely normal but looking murderous was Dave, Henry and Sam's operator.

CHAPTER TWELVE

HENRY AND I WERE JUST ABOUT TO GET OUT OF OUR CHAIRS when Dave put his hands up. 'Don't make any sudden movements.' Slowly walking towards us, everyone snapped their heads around and gasped as Dave walked into the dim orange light of the restaurant. He was wearing a denim jacket over a black high-neck jumper and black jeans; trying to blend in and look normal. But we all knew he was anything but normal. Henry and Sam never said much about Dave, apart from that he was extremely strong and was a black belt in Karate. But the man hardly spoke about himself and now that I thought on, Lynn never talked much about herself either. Of course, they knew everything about us but like a well-oiled cog, our operators didn't disclose anything that could be used against them. They had been trained in the art of silence.

'How the hell did you find us?' Henry demanded, and quickly moved around to protect us. But Dave shook his head and motioned him to sit back down. 'Don't cause a scene, Henry. Sit down and we can all have an adult conversation.' Dave chose his words carefully, but there were a lot of authority behind his voice and like a trained dog, Henry hesitated then sat back down. 'You lot are in deep trouble.' He said looking at me primarily. 'You have no idea what you have done.'

'We've run away from you trying to kill us,' I barked at him.

Dave gave me a fleeting look and smiled, 'Don't get angry Tara, this isn't the place. We wouldn't want to break the Golden Rule.'

'Hypocrite.' Saskia snarled. 'Ya harpies weren't a match for us and neither are you.'

Dave laughed. 'You may have escaped from both Lynn and Roxy, and our little feathery friends, but there is no point in trying to get past me, or even try to defeat me. So I'm giving you an option. Willingly come back with me now, and we won't harm you.'

Frowning Sam said, 'What's the other option?'

'There isn't one,' Dave spat at him. 'Not only have you cost the company millions of pounds and stolen a helicopter, but you've also gone off the rails completely; you need to be put into quarantine.'

'Ha,' I laughed, 'So that's what you call it? Being sent to a bunker is the same as being quarantined.'

His eyes narrowed.

'Oh yeah, I know about that,' I told him confidently.

'Your tattoos have become defective,' he said as though scripted. 'You need to come with me now to get you better.'

'Cut the crap.' I spat. 'Our tattoos aren't becoming defective. We are turning into myths from the blood you injected us with and we know you've been lying to us.'

Dave's lips curled showing his teeth, but he didn't falter, 'Come with me now, and we won't harm you,' he repeated.

Folding her arms indignantly, Saskia flicked her now long blond hair out of her eyes and stared right at him, 'Make me.'

'No,' I suddenly yelled as I realised what Saskia had done, but it was too late, Dave was already under her spell. Running towards us, we tried to scarper to get out of his way, plates, knives, forks and chairs all upended as we scrambled to move. Charging full pelt into the table, Dave turned around and snapped his eyes on Saskia; it seemed she was his prime target. She bolted, knowing her mistake and snorting like some crazed animal, he ran after her.

'CLOSE DOWN THE SHOP, GET INSIDE!' I yelled at the frightened looking hostess who had come out to see what was happening outside.

Briefly translating what I said, but Lionel having no need to, the woman screamed and headed inside, slamming the door behind her. We shooed the locals back into their houses as we watched Dave follow Saskia like an unrelenting greyhound follows a rabbit.

'What do we do?' Sam asked in a worried tone as everyone crowded around me, yet all staring at Saskia, who was unable to release her wings as there were still some people around.

'She needs to tell him to stop,' I shouted, hoping that she would hear me. 'I don't think I could tell Dave to stop, I don't think he'd listen to me.'

'But what do we do?' Sam urged.

'I don't know what we can do; we don't know what he can turn into.'

Saskia began screaming out, 'Get away from me,' and 'Stop Dave, leave me alone,' but there was no power to her breathlessness voice. Dave didn't want to hear her, he was incensed, enraged just like a...

'Oh no,' I whimpered suddenly, coming to an awful conclusion. I knew what Dave might be.

'What is it?' Lottie asked her eyes wide with horror, watching Saskia continue to run around, trying to get away from Dave.

'I think Dave's a Minotaur, look at how he's charging at her, like an enraged bull. The only mythical bull...'

'Is a Minotaur. Ah crap,' Henry muttered as though everything pieced together.

Lionel continued shouting in Spanish to the local people who gawped at Dave and Saskia, but their focus suddenly changed when whatever Lionel had said, got through to them. Within moments, they scarpered back into their homes giving us the chance to help Saskia in whatever magical way we could.

'Right, come on, we have to lead them away from here,' I told the others as I ran after Saskia, being careful, not to get in Dave's way.

'Tara, be careful!' Henry called. I couldn't help but smile at his concern.

Running full pelt towards her, I motioned for her to head towards a large steel warehouse that was situated right on the edge of the docks. Hidden in darkness, it would give us the chance to change without being seen. But Saskia suddenly tripped and fell; skidding along the ground carried by her momentum. She yelled out in pain but quickly managed to roll out of the way just as Dave charged right past her.

Coming to a skidding stop, Dave twisted to face her, and that's when it happened. Like Lynn had done before, Dave grabbed his shirt and began ripping it off, tossing it aside on the gravel-covered ground as though it was paper, but that's not all he did. Feeling almost physically sick, Dave dug his nails into his toned skin and began to tear it off. From where I was, I could almost hear the skin tear away from his muscles as though a nullified ripping of paper. I heard Macie and Lottie gag behind me, but still we all kept watching him change, rooted to the spot in terror, awe; an almost disgusting fascination.

His trainers split; rubber and plastic covered fabric ripped away from their soles and in their place, thick, shiny black hooves pushed out, looking like massive dinner plates against his shredded footwear. The sound of ripping continued as Dave still tore at his skin, but there was a reason for it. Underneath his torn skin wasn't blood, but instead dark brown hide of his tattoo.

Like Lynn, he was shedding his human part. Though, unlike Lynn, he wasn't growing as big as she got, but his muscles were immense. Bursting out of his chest and arms, I could now understand why he said we wouldn't be able to stop him. He was a bulldozer, pun intended.

Bellowing in pain and anger, two sharp horns came out of his skull, almost as though they were shattering it from the inside out. They grew and twisted around, just like a bulls horns and they pointed at Saskia.

'GET UP,' Darren yelled at her, but Saskia was still frozen on the floor, unable to move.

'What can we do? We have seconds before he charges again. None of us can stand up to him.' Macie cried as Dave was almost finishing his transformation.

'You guys get off the ground, get up somewhere high,' I told them as I ran after Saskia, with Sam and Henry hot on my heels.

A split-second later and grunting heavily where hot vapours came out of his now bull-like head, Dave was fully transformed, and we hadn't even reached Saskia. She was at least two hundred yards from us.

Henry quickly caught up with me and roaring like a crazed lion, black fur began to spread across his arms and his hands turned into beefy paws with sharp claws. Holding his right arm high in the air, he ran right towards Dave, poised to punch him.

'GET OFF THE GROUND, SASKIA,' I screamed at her as Sam went to Henry, giving him some backup.

Coming out of her shock, Saskia scrambled up and grabbing her hand; we headed towards the warehouse. But not taking four steps, we heard this almighty yell coming from behind us. Spinning around, I saw poor Henry flying through the air. Henry had received a hefty blow from Dave's powerful hoofed leg and suddenly crashed onto the ground.

'Saskia, get on the roof!' I yelled heading for Henry as Sam was now trying to taunt Dave into keeping his focus away from Henry.

'But, wha' about you?' she called back.

'Just get on the roof!' I screamed.

Running towards a bloodied and bruised Henry, I rolled him over to see what had happened to him and almost screamed. His nose was badly broken and hot blood seeped down into his open mouth. With his cheeks, hands and shoulders grazed badly from skidding to a stop, I put his arm around me and tried to lift him up.

'TARA, WATCH OUT,' Sam suddenly screamed.

I looked up and saw Dave begin to charge. He scraped his hooves on the ground and dipped his horns down to impale me.

'CRAP! Henry, come on help me out here, please,' I begged as Dave suddenly began to charge. He was within metres of killing us, stabbing us in the stomach so easily with those horns that even the thought of it made me feel sick.

Henry's groggy voice whispered in such a way it frightened me to the core. Staring up at me with his soft bottomless eyes in which only the brightest moment of the sun could penetrate, he wheezed, 'Leave me. He'll be after me; he was my operator.'

I shook my head. 'Don't be stupid.' I began to feel hot tears sting my eyes, but there was no point in wiping them away, I had other things to worry about, like surviving.

'TARA RUN!' Sam screamed at me again.

Dave was ten running strides away from me, I angled my body and hoped and prayed this would work. Unable to move Henry out of the way, this time I held onto him, willing him to remain conscious.

'Six...five...four,' I said, counting down the strides until the point where, I hoped, my plan would work, 'three...two...ONE.' I let my wings rip out of my back. Just as I had planned, the force of them caught Dave and managed to hit him square in the chest; causing him to fly backwards and fall to the floor not thirty feet away from us.

'Good enough for me,' I said, grabbing Henry and using my wings to bring him up to a standing position, but Henry wasn't having any of it and nearly collapsed to the floor.

Running towards us, Sam helped grab Henry and together, we hauled him off into the darkness, heading towards the warehouse.

'We can't bring him down,' Sam panted as we briefly glanced back to see Dave struggling to get up off the floor, 'but we can deter him until morning.'

'Don't... be... stupid,' Henry said quietly.

'We need to get him away from Dave, off the ground.' My eyes searched for something, and I saw the warehouse to my left. 'I can fly him up there, just give me a sec,' I told Sam as I ran off in a different direction and opening my wings, took off into the cold Spanish night air.

Circling around the top of the warehouse, I saw the others on the roof and breathed a sigh of relief. They waved me down. 'What's going on?' Hannah called to me.

'Hang on,' I called back as I dived towards Henry. Trying to get as much power as I could, I grabbed him around his chest and managed to sweep him off the ground. Now unburdened with Henry, Sam hastily began to climb the stairs.

I carefully placed the battered and bruised body of Henry on the roof and waited for Sam to reach us before I told everyone what was happening.

'A freaking Minotaur, Jesus,' Lottie said as she peered over the side.

Dave had seen us climb the stairs but was unable to do anything about it. He had tried to climb several times but shortly ended up breaking the first seven steps as they couldn't hold his weight. So, being bull-headed, he remained on the ground, too stubborn to give up and leave.

'We c-can't stay up here all night,' Macie said through chattering teeth.

Saskia looked like she was about to suggest something but then stopped herself.

'No, go on, what did you want to say?' I demanded from her.

'Wha' if ya got near enough ta 'im and blinded 'im?' she said looking at me and Sam.

'Hell no, I'm not gonna do that, he's my operator,' he frowned.

'Ex-operator,' Lottie corrected him. 'Do you think that Tara liked it when Lynn was chasing after her?'

Sighing, I rubbed my temple and tried to think, but I was coming up with nothing. Dave was being risky. Apart from fearing for our lives, the crazed Minotaur had been yelling and screaming; surely someone was bound to hear him and also wouldn't have someone seen me fly?

'Anyone got any ideas?' Hannah asked the group, but there was silence.

I flinched from the wind as Saskia's wings abruptly came out of her back. What annoyed her this time?

'Nothin' is going ta work now tha' he's fully changed,' she snapped angrily.

'I love it when her wings come out,' Darren sighed to Lionel, 'whompf,' he said trying to imitate the sound they made. Lionel clicked his cheek and ignored him.

'Can't we just wait until he changes back?' Macie asked everyone, but Saskia, for once, turned to look at her with sympathetic eyes. 'Lynn did, didn't she?'

'He's not goin' ter want ter change back, Macie,' she told her. 'Not when it's 'is job ter catch us. The T.A.T are desperate; they'll do anything to take us back to the UK. In fact, when we met our operators, they weren't human anymore, they were already myths, myths that the T.A.T. hired. If you ever saw them have a tattoo on their "body" it was pretence.'

'I never saw Lynn have a tattoo,' I said and Hannah and Darren nodded in agreement.

Clearing her throat, Saskia looked at us all. Her usual sassy demeanour had been deflated and now, looking bloodied and downcast, she had taken a more serious tone. 'Guys, I'm so, so sorry fer tellin' ya this an' I'm also deeply sorry fer the effect it 'as on all of ya. I didn't particularly want ta tell ya this because ya wouldn't 'ave believed me.' She took a slight pause and when she knew she wasn't going to be interrupted, continued. 'I knew full well tha' our operators weren't human because my Dad used ta work fer da T.A.T in da Experimental Department that now doesn't exist. ' She hurried as Macie and Lottie appeared lost. 'I saw them test on a unicorn in da basement of our house. But it's because I saw this tha' I broke the secrecy of da T.A.T. It was pure accident mind ya. Anyway, my parents were punished. I was placed in da care of da T.A.T an' all parents who were working with da T.A.T forfeited their children to be tested on. This is wha' I mean by saying I'm so sorry fer da effect on ya. All of our families were workin' fer da T.A.T in one way or another. It's why we were selected an' placed together in this group. An' since we left da T.A.T. their memories have probably been wiped. They don't remember us in any way, shape or form.'

I felt like I had been physically hit with a hammer and all the breath was knocked out of me. How could this be? It made no sense. My parents were in Europe on business; they frequented there a few times a year, only staying for three weeks or so before returning to their family home in Bristol. But now I came to think of it, I haven't heard of my parents in a long time. My stomach felt uneasy at Saskia's words and looking around; everyone looked just as shocked.

'Bull,' Macie snarled at her as tears began to fall thickly from her eyes. 'My parents are reporters. There's no way that has connections to.-'

'Back in da 1800's there were reporters who stopped mythical creature stories leakin' out in da world. Your parents did da same thin',' Saskia told her sadly.

'But my family are dentists and doctors,' Lottie said silently crying next to Hannah, who put an arm around her shoulders; comforting her.

''ow else can ya identify mermaid or centaur bones and teeth to humans,' Saskia said. 'No matter 'ow trivial ya thought our families jobs were, there is always a connection ta da T.A.T, ya just never knew it.'

'My parents were always out of the country on business,' I said to myself, but everyone was listening, even Henry. Hannah was bent over tending to his cuts on the flat roof of the warehouse. Everyone was silent as they let me try and figure out what Saskia had told us, to finally understand that our lives were never our own. They belonged to the T.A.T right from the very beginning. 'They went looking for them didn't they, for myths around the world?'

Looking at my face Saskia nodded, a single tear rolled down her scratched bloody face, 'Yes.' Each word of truth that uttered from her mouth felt as though I was both mentally and physically smacked. I had a problem with my parents being a part of the T.A.T., the organisation we were all against and that their minds now erased because of Saskia.

My head was aching with the painful information. I just wanted to go home, to cry into my own pillow. Just feel safe and try and believe this was one crazy dream. But it wasn't a dream. It was real, it was happening and it was hurting all of us.

'YOU UTTER COW,' Macie screamed; her voice being scoured hoarse by its shrill pitch. Macie suddenly dived towards Saskia, hands outstretched to grab her throat. Lionel and Lottie dove onto Macie trying to pull her off Saskia, who was going blue around the lips, but Macie shrugged them off as though insects.

'I'm... sorry,' Saskia tried to apologise, staring into Macie's eagle eyes, attempting to show her sincerity.

Then like a switch Macie stopped and withdrew her hands. Slowly she turned her head to me, her face was strangely lined with cracked and dry lips. I glanced down and saw her shaking hands begin to turn black. 'Tara, help me...' Macie whispered before a loud ear splitting screech made me flinch away from her, utterly scared. Though her scream may have been loud, it was the fact that it didn't sound human that scared me the most.

Macie suddenly stopped screeching, but her mouth was still wide open, as though issuing a loud inaudible scream that maybe only dogs or cats could hear.

Looking frightened, Saskia tried to comfort her. 'No, don't touch her,' I told her, motioning her and the others to back away.

'What's happening to her?' Sam asked his face shocked, staring at Macie in horror.

'She's changing into her tattoo,' Henry said sitting up to look, 'but into what I have no idea.'

Falling to the floor in silent agony, hazel coloured wings unexpectedly grew out from her shoulder blades. Feathers flowed over her face, neck arms and upper torso, all the while, a long snaky fur covered tail shot out of her behind.

'I can't... stand...' Macie tried to say as her mouth was contorted and shiny in the moonlight from above the Spanish skies. Within seconds her mouth clicked shut and joining her nose, a sharp yellow beak was in its place.

'What on earth is she turning into?' Hannah asked horror-struck.

All of us backed away from Macie, unsure of whether she would keep her head or not. But then I thought on. Though Macie was turning into a creature, she may not be able to retain her personality. Unlike her, Darren, Saskia and I were still human-ish to maintain our consciousness. Even Henry, who ended up sprouting golden fur on his face and arms and had large cat claws still kept his head. But whatever Macie was turning into, it was far from human.

As we crowded around her, unsure of what to do to, we looked on as Macie's skin delicately blended into fur and feathers like two colours of paint on canvas. Her jeans and jumper split from their seams, shards of clothes fluttering to the roof as through being mauled by a dog. After a few more seconds, all of us quickly realised why Macie had tattoos in the shape of eagle eyes and why we couldn't match it up to anything eagle related. It was because Macie was only part eagle. The other half of her, the back half to be exact, was a lion. Macie was a griffin.

On all fours and panting from the strain of changing shape, Macie's wings folded on her back and she slowly turned around and cawed at us in a penetrating eagle cry.

'Macie,' I said taking a tentative step towards her. Her golden eyes locked onto me and her head turned slightly, waiting for me to talk to her. Giving her a brief smile I said, 'Get the Minotaur.'

Clicking her beak, she slowly nodded and throwing her wings out to her sides, jumped off into the air. Turning sharply around she dove down towards the ground on the other side of the warehouse where unsuspecting Dave still waited for us below.

Running to the edge of the flat roof, we peered down to see Macie swooping onto Dave. Looking somewhat perplexed, Dave began to lash out at Macie as she flew back and forth; each time pecking and clawing at his arms which were protecting his face.

Yelling out in anger, Dave tried to swat Macie away like a fly, but she quickly manoeuvred out of the way. With each hit missing, Dave was getting more and more frustrated and suddenly, enraged, he jumped up into the air; his horns grazing Macie's right leg. Macie swooped away screeching out in pain and then turning around sharply, her eyes quickly fixed onto Dave, they were ablaze.

'She's going to give him hell,' Hannah laughed as we saw Macie perform a complicated little twist in the air and flew higher.

Bewildered, Dave had lost sight of Macie as he looked around, but then again, we all did. Apart from Lottie, whose eyes turned the blackest shade, to follow Macie's flight path.

'She's gaining height,' Lottie reported, her eyes locked onto her in the dark sky above us. Even though, it was a clear night, Macie was completely invisible against the twinkling atmosphere.

'Oh. Macie had banked right,' Lottie quickly told us,

commentating Macie's nightly flight.

'Okay, why am I hot?' Darren asked us.

'What?' I asked a little distracted, searching the skies for a glimpse of Macie.

'You're not,' Saskia snapped back spitefully not taking her eyes off Dave, who was still looking around for Macie, craning his neck and grunting in annoyance.

'Seriously, I'm really hot,' Darren said as I heard him stand up and walk away from us. 'What the hell, are you giving off that heat?' he asked, but none of us were paying attention to him.

Suddenly Lottie laughed, 'She's diving.'

All of our eyes then zoomed in and focussed on Dave. We wanted to see what Macie would do to him. An eagle's piercing cry sounded over us; my eyes darting to see where she was, but I couldn't track her. The buildings around us and the port close by, all but confused our hearing. It was as if Macie was coming in from all directions. As far as I could tell, Dave too was confused as he did a full three-hundred and sixty turn.

None of us were prepared for Macie's fast sneak-attack. Coming out of the shadows, by the port, Macie swooped over the dark churning waters with murderous looking eyes. Extending her claws that looked strong enough to rip steel like paper, she rushed straight towards Dave. With such force, she bashed right into him and sent him flying so hard and so fast, he had no time to react.

Dave smashed through the chained and padlocked iron doors of the warehouse below us, he seemed to have continued the momentum from Macie; bulldozing through boxes, crates and possible concrete. The sounds that rose up from beneath startled every one of us.

Spinning around, we heard another breaking metal sound BANG then closely followed by a gigantic SPLASH of the Mediterranean Sea.

'Holy kack, she smacked him through the entire building,' Darren yelled, as he ran to the edge looking over to the froth that rose to the surface.

Gathering around him we suddenly gasped as we saw a strange, brilliant blue light that shone from under the water. The light and a series of bubbles flowed out from just below the surface lasting for a few seconds and then the light vanished and then the bubbles. It was then we all realised that Dave had somehow, disappeared. But how and why was unclear. Even Saskia and Henry seemed confused.

There was a whomp of wings and a cold breeze from behind us.

Turning around, we saw Macie land gracefully on the roof. Giving us a pitiful cry, she collapsed onto the metallic ground and within seconds changed back into a human. I breathed a sigh of relief. She hadn't fully transformed into a myth. If so, she wouldn't have changed back into a human so quickly.

'Macie!' I yelled, running to my bag that one of the others had brought from the restaurant and dipping inside, pulled out a spare jumper as I ran to her. I threw it around her and gently picked her up. Either she hardly weighed anything or I was getting stronger. 'Macie are you okay? Can you hear me sweetheart?'

Everyone gathered around us, all looking scared for her apart from Henry, 'She's going to be fine. She just needs some sleep.'

Hannah and Lottie helped dress Macie while I shielded them from my wings. Macie was dressed thanks to the girls, but she was still unconscious. As I folded my wings back, I began to calm down and moments later felt the soothing feeling of the feathers falling off my back as they became dust. Rubbing my shoulders, I looked at Henry, who was leaning back against the side looking smug.

'Anyway,' Lottie began, 'now that Dave has gone, can we please go and find a hotel,? I'm freezing,' she said as her and Hannah walked off towards the stairs while Sam and Henry helped carry Macie. Saskia picked up Macie's bag and followed the others looking upset.

'I don't know why she's cold,' I heard Darren mumble to Lionel, 'she was emanating so much heat earlier on I thought she was going to self-combust.'

★ ★ ★

The following morning, after having only a small lie-in as Saskia bellowed through my door to get out of bed to eat breakfast, I grabbed all of my stuff and found everyone down in the breakfast room. My eyes found Macie, looking normal and happy.

'Good morning,' I said reaching to hug her. 'I'm glad you're okay. I mean you look okay,' I smiled back.

'I'm great,' she said as I sat down next to her while the boys went to get their food. 'Oh and just so you know, I understood what you were saying, I mean when I was a griffin,' she whispered looking around her.

I giggled. 'Griffin Macie and it was totally cool.'

'It was like I knew how to fly and dive and caw and everything,' her eyes lit up. 'It was as though I already had the instincts inside me. But I don't think I had fully become the griffin you know? I felt that I wasn't quite there yet.'

Understanding what she meant, I nodded.

'Well, you kicked arse that's for sure,' Hannah said giving her a high-five.

After a filling breakfast, the nine of us checked out of the hotel and headed to the port.

'Here's your key's to your cabins,' Lionel said passing them over to us. Smiling at me, he said, 'there's been a bit of a mix up with your room Tara; you're sharing with Henry.'

'What?' Both of us asked, not looking at each other, but Lionel ran off laughing.

'Here,' I said giving the key's to Henry, 'I'm going to find some new clothes. I won't head back to the room until two o'clock okay?'

'Sure fine,' he said looking a little lost.

I headed off with the girls to the onboard duty-free shops. Dior, Chanel, Gucci products stared up at me and I avidly stared back.

Saskia snapped her fingers in front of me, 'Oy! Snap out of it Carrie Bradshaw, I thought ya wanted some clothes.'

'Only if they're Prada,' Lottie and Hannah laughed.

The clothes section was at the back of the shop, but the clothes weren't particularly appealing.

'Does it matter?' Saskia said sniped. 'Macie is lucky tha' Hannah and Lottie's clothes fit 'er an' tha' I've got a spare uniform or else she would be walking around naked,' snorting she folded her arms. 'An' wouldn't tha' cause a stir fer Lionel, not tha' there'd be much ta see. She looks like a flat chested pigeon.'

SLAP!

The echo of Macie's whiplash hands scattered around the shop; people's heads turned in our direction and I felt a small pang of embarrassment for Saskia.

'I'm not taking your crap again. Speak to me like again and I'll slap your face so hard your brain will spin.'

I stifled a laugh as I looked at Saskia's hand-printed face. Macie had really cracked her one. Sulking like a child, Saskia's pouted face made it even worse for me as I tried desperately hard not to laugh.

After buying some clothes, the five of us headed out on deck and away from the majority of people on the ship, and then I burst out laughing. Bent over, tears poured down my face as the sound and image of Saskia being slapped by Macie, of all people, repeated over and over in my head. But I wasn't the only one laughing. Joining in, Hannah and Lottie were creased over. Looking over through my tearing eyes, Macie and Saskia's mouths began to twitch into a smile.

'I'm sorry,' I giggled wiping eyes, 'it's not really funny,' I said before bursting out laughing again.

'No, but it really is,' Hannah chortled.

'Oh, it's you who's laughing.' I heard Lionel's voice from behind. 'You've got a very loud, infectious laugh Tara. We can hear you from outside.'

'Cheers.'

'So you girlies got some clothes,' Sam said looking at our stuffed bags.

'What do you think?' Lottie laughed as she held up her three heavy looking carrier bags, 'plus we got a third off on a spa treatment,' waving her coupons like a fan.

'But its food first,' Hannah told her.

'Yeah, come and join us,' I asked the boys as we walked back inside.

Declining, they went off to an arcade next to a lounge area while us girls got some well-earned relaxation after a quick light lunch.

Feeling like I was being steamed like a vegetable, marinated in mud as well as thrown into a cucumber forest, we all came out squeaky clean for our next adventure in Italy and smelling-

'Vile,' Lionel said holding his nose.

Saskia looked affronted. 'Yeah? Well, so's ya face!' she barked.

Lionel frowned. 'Apart from having a monstrous headache I can hear freaking everything,' he said irritably, 'I can smell everything as well and you are making my eyes water.' Looking pale with a slight tinge of green he suddenly said 'I think I'm gonna be sick,' and quickly fled from the lounge area where we had met up.

'Don't worry girls,' Henry chortled, 'Lionel's feeling a bit irritated from earlier on.'

Macie perked up suddenly. Her eyes were wide in worry. 'Why, what happened?'

'He got angry that the three of us beat him at a shooting game in the arcade.' He shrugged. 'His tattoo acted up and he has been waspish since he came back, but perhaps there's more to it. Not to worry though,' he said to Macie, 'he'll be back soon.'

However, an hour later, Lionel didn't come back.

My eyes were locked on the main entrance to the lounge where Lionel had run out of and just as I was about to say, 'Where is he?' there came an announcement over the tannoy.

'This is a passenger announcement. Please can passenger Simmons, Henry Simmons, come to the reception desk. That's Mr Henry Simmons to the reception desk on the third deck. Thank you.'

Briefly looking at each other in confusion, we all quickly got up and followed Henry like the Pied Piper; all heading to the reception desk on the third deck.

'I'm Mr Henry Simmons,' he told the lady at the counter, flashing an identity card just in case she asked.

Looking concerned, she motioned him to the side to speak privately.

After a few seconds Henry jumped back in shock; turning to us he said, 'Its Lionel, something's wrong.'

Macie and Lottie clasped their hands to their mouths, looking troubled.

'Where is he?' Henry asked the lady.

'Public toilet on deck four,' she told him.

Sprinting off after Henry, we flew down the metal stairs; our feet thundered on the floor as we dodged past other passengers.

'Wha' happened?' Saskia asked Henry, as we barged past a small party of people who were nattering away in Spanish.

'He's locked himself in the bathroom; apparently he's been throwing up. The doctor was called for him, but he dismissed him and asked for me.'

'This way,' Sam pointed as we came to a fork in the corridor.

Hurrying down the bland but modern Titanic-looking corridors, we saw a small group of people banging on the door to the gents.

'Excuse me,' Henry said barging through.

'What's going on?' one grumpy man asked in a thick Spanish accent, his belly stuck outside of his neatly pressed trousers. 'I want to use the toilet.'

'Sir, go and poo in your room,' Darren snapped as he pushed past him to get to Henry.

'How dare you speak to me like that,' the man shouted, his face going red with anger and embarrassment.

'He didn't mean it sir.' Hannah apologised and steered the portly man away while Darren and Henry were trying to get Lionel to open the door for them.

As only the eight of us remained, Lionel opened the door and all of the boys went in.

Standing outside looking like hookers, we waited to hear what was going on and not fifteen minutes later, Henry and Sam helped an ill-looking Lionel out of the toilet.

'We need to get him to our room,' Henry said as he tried to reach for his keys, 'right pocket,' he told me.

Quickly shoving my hand in his right jeans pocket, I pulled out the keys and had everyone follow me to our room, which was tricky as I hadn't even been there yet.

'Is he alright?' Lottie asked as Lionel was in our bathroom throwing up and yelling in pain.

'Wha's wrong with 'im? Food poison?' Saskia drawled.

Sam and Darren remained silent, it seemed that they didn't know why Lionel was ill, but Henry seemed to.

'I can tell you what's happening,' he began, 'but I can't really explain it.' Taking a steadying breath, he continued, 'Lionel's tattoo has become thicker, the dog or jackal looks more pronounced. He's in so much pain he's throwing up.'

Rummaging through my bag, I brought out the little red book and began flicking through it so see what type of mythical dogs Lionel could be and soon came to the small Egyptian section of the book. On one page were the names of the gods and goddesses with their powers. Yet on the opposite page, were extra information such as M.I.A., F.I.T., L.I.T. and Cpd, in which on the bottom right of the second page was a key.

'Hathor, L.I.T lost in time, Osiris, L.I.T., Horus F.I.T. frozen in time, Isis Cpd, copied... here we go Anubis L.I.T.'

There was a brief pause between us, during which Lionel threw up again.

Cringing at the sound, I tried to drown out Lionel's retching by speaking loudly. 'Macie, do you know any other dog-like figures in Egyptian myth?'

Frowning in thought, there came a flush of the toilet and then looking pale and in pain, Lionel came out and slunk to the floor by the end bed.

Sitting opposite Lionel, Macie's eyes grew wide as she glanced at his neck. 'Hmm, it's not a dog. I really think it's a jackal. If I'm correct, it's attributed to Wepwawet,' she laughed. 'God of War. He wasn't a major god, in fact after all of these myths that were around Egypt ended up describing him as the son of Anubis. But apart from being good at leading and warring, he was the opener of ways.'

Glancing at the book I saw the name Wepwawet and on the opposite page it said Cpd.

'What does that mean, the opener or ways?' Lionel asked, shivering from pain.

'We'll just have to wait and see,' I said snapping the book closed.

CHAPTER THIRTEEN

WE MOVED LIONEL INTO HIS ROOM AND LEFT HIM THERE TO recuperate while the rest of us changed into our new clothes and headed for the restaurant to have some dinner.

'Ah ha, salmon and dill in a white wine sauce, roast potatoes and steamed vegetables, God come to mummy,' I said my mouth salivating as I dug into my food.

'I hate fish,' Darren grimaced as he tucked into his steak, egg and chips.

Giggling without spitting my food or choking, I swallowed and asked him why.

'Just all those little bones,' he shrugged.

'Liar, you just don't want to be slapped on a plate with a slice of lemon and served with chips,' I laughed.

The others burst out laughing as Darren scowled at me, but the corners of his mouth turned down into a disgusted grimace.

Taking a doggy-bag back for Lionel, which Saskia decided to play on the pun until Hannah clipped her round the head to shut her up, we all squeezed into Lionel, Sam and Darren's room.

'Here, we brought you a doggy-bag back fer da doggy,' Saskia laughed as she sat down by the door. 'Okay, last time I swear,' she said staring at Hannah's wavering hand.

'Thanks, I'm starving,' Lionel said wolfing down the food.

Having no room for the boy's hard beds, Saskia and Darren sat on the floor uncomfortably. Darren tried to sidle up to Saskia, but she moved further away from him towards the door. Then suddenly making us all jump, Saskia swore loudly and jumped a mile, colliding into Darren. Still in shock, she scarpered away from the door as though she'd on a red ant's nest.

'What is it?' we each asked her.

Looking scared, Saskia gazed at a small patch of the carpet by the door. 'Okay, that wasn't nice an' ya guys are sleeping in 'ere. Oh my God,' she shivered.

'Saskia, what the hell are you talking about?' Henry demanded, but ignoring him she reached for my hand and dragged me off the bed and pushed me towards the door.

'Put ya hand there,' she pointed to the floor.

Glancing at the others they each gave me a look that said 'humour her,' so I did.

Placing my right hand on the coarse beige carpet, I waited for something to happen but it didn't. 'What am I meant to see, hear, feel smell?'

Seeming impatient, she shook her head. 'Sit 'ow I sat, with ya back ta da door, ya legs out an' ya hands by ya sides,' she told me.

'Saskia, this is stupid,' I said doing what she asked, but as soon as I sat exactly how she sat I saw, heard, smelt and felt everything.

Instantly before me, the others had disappeared. The beds, carpet and small desk were in the same place but were somehow different; they looked newer. The room smelt like it was new too, with a fresh coat of paint on the walls. There were no cracks in the ceiling or patched discoloured blobs.

The sun was shining through the small porthole that cast a single beam of light into the room. Observantly, I saw that I had no shadow on the floor. Whatever I was experiencing seemed to be shown in my mind; I wasn't technically here.

I slowly got up and walked around the small cabin and noticed that one of the beds was untidy. There suddenly there came the sound of a lock clicking behind me and a young women, maybe a few years older than me, emerged out of the bathroom; a white towel around her. Within seconds, I realised she couldn't see me, or else she would have screamed.

Averting my eyes while she got dressed, I saw there was a small slightly-damp note by the bathroom mat that she must have missed. Going to retrieve it my hand passed through the note, 'freaky ghost powers.' I laughed to myself.

Leaning over I saw what the note said:

One's been spotted in Vietnam, just received a message from Maggie and Will. They are heading over there now. Ben and I will meet you there; we'll meet back up with you in Heraklion.

Kyle

The young woman had now dressed in a white shirt and dark grey trousers. By the way she was dressed; I had gathered I was in the past, about twenty years or so.

There was a sudden sharp knock on the door, 'Katie, are you ready?'

'Yes Rob,' she replied shoving a set of keys and some paper into a black handbag. She grabbed a small suitcase from under the bed and went to the door.

A tall olive-skinned man with a short moustache was waiting for her. Katie closed the door behind her, taking her suitcase with her. Making a snap decision, I tried to open it, only to find my hand going through it.

'You have ghost powers remember.'

'GARH!' I yelped. Jumping a mile, I turned around to see who spoke to me and saw a small girl with long jet-black hair and deep dark brown eyes staring at me. Her skin looked like paper, the purest of white, almost gaunt looking which matched her long white nightgown.

'You need to follow them, you have to learn the truth,' she said as she glided past me and went through the door.

Running after her, I passed through the door as though it was the air itself and looking to my left, saw Katie and Rob walk down the corridor. At a second glance, I noticed that suitcases lined alongside the walls outside the passenger's doors. I guess they were docking soon.

'Come on,' the girl said beckoning me.

Quickening my pace, I caught up with them. I was about to ask her what was going on, but she put her fingers to her mouth and pointed to Katie and Rob. She looked familiar in a way, but I couldn't put my finger on it.

Katie gave him a strange glance at a question I must have just missed. 'They are trying to find the disc aren't they, like that's going to help anything.'

'It should do, we have him Katie, we are holding him hostage. He is the only one who can translate it for us, after that, we can pass into the other world with ease,' Rob said enthusiastically. 'Just think of the powers we could have?'

She shook her head, her hair falling loosely around her face. 'I still think it's a bad idea.' Her voice sounded worried, but Rob didn't seem to pick up on this. 'Besides it might be years until he helps us translate the disc. It may end up being our children who pick up the slack.'

Throwing his head back, he laughed. 'Just think that one day they'll be helping us.'

'Please Rob, if any of us have any children, I wouldn't want them to go through what we are going through,' she sighed. 'If the Phaistos Disc is translated then we can kiss our world goodbye.'

Laughing, Rob stopped walking and grabbing Katie, pulled her close to him. 'Darling, nothing will go wrong. The translation will help us in more ways than one, but first, we have a dragon to get to.'

Continuing to follow them, the girl glided behind; keeping silent all the way through.

'Can I ask you some questions now?' I asked her quickly, hoping that Katie and Rob wouldn't say anything important.

'For the next fifteen seconds, yes,' she said smiling at me.

'Good so, just to clarify this is the past?'

'Yes, it is 1984. The boat is travelling from Cyprus to Egypt,' she told me.

'Right well, thank you for letting me know, I think.'

The girl laughed, 'You're more polite than the other girl.'

I was confused at first and asked, 'Saskia was here too?'

'Yes, I had to show both of you what was going on.' It now made sense. Saskia had experienced all of this before. It's why she wanted me sit where she sat.

'Alright,' I said, not sure what to do with that piece of information I asked. 'Just to clarify something else, these people, they are part of the T.A.T aren't they?'

She smiled simply, but I took that as a yes. So these were the people before us. My parent's names weren't mentioned, and if Saskia was telling the truth that our parents were part of the T.A.T then they may have known this Katie and Rob. But even if Katie and Rob were of the T.A.T. why was this girl involved? What connection did she have with them?

Now following Katie and Rob up a winding metal staircase, the girl suddenly disappeared but I wasn't worried about her, I was more interested in the topic that Katie and Rob were talking about. Maynard.

'Mr Maynard wants to move the facility to Carmarthenshire in Wales, out in the middle of nowhere,' Rob told her as they passed one deck and continued up the stairs.

'Understandable,' Katie nodded in approval. 'Though uprooting everything at this moment in time maybe isn't a good idea.'

'True, but those at the facility now seem to be in a stable condition. Let's hope the new additions will finally see our cause to help us. A dragon,' he chuckled, 'my, my how Maynard aims high.'

They became silent.

A couple of children suddenly rushed down the stairs bumping into Katie and making her drop her bag spilling some of its contents. In a hurry to gather everything, Katie looked at a photo of a group of people. Smiling sadly at it, she shoved it back inside her bag then continued to follow Rob.

They soon came out onto the second deck and walked towards a door which led outside. Everywhere I looked people was dressed in similarly styled clothes; it was definitely in the 1980's. Before heading out on the deck, Rob suddenly asked, 'I assume you read the note?'

'Yes, did Kyle send it to you via telegram or something?' Katie inquired.

'Did you put it in the bin?' he asked her a little firmly.

'Um, oh darn I don't think so,' Katie said looking shocked.

'Hang on,' Rob said, 'I'll do it.' Katie passed him the key and he took off.

'I'll be outside,' Katie called after him.

Heading out into the fresh morning salty air, it whipped at Katie's hair, but strangely enough mine didn't even flutter. Ahead of us was the mainland of Egypt. I had never been to Egypt before, but I had heard that Port Said was very busy with peddlers and tourist stalls. Looking up, I saw that Katie was serenely looking out towards the sea. She looked happy, content, although I saw there was something in her smile which she didn't want to acknowledge.

Standing there for at least half an hour Katie grew impatient but soon Rob came out on the deck, apologising for being late. He looked a little sweaty. Confused, I tried to ignore this as they began to strike up another conversation, lucky for them they weren't overheard through the howling ocean winds.

'I think we're getting close to finishing this operation,' Katie told him as they strolled to the front of the ship.

'You really think so, huh? And only after a few raids and five snatches of mythical cr-.'

'Codename please Rob,' Katie hissed at him.

'Sorry, M.C's and you think we're going to finish this? You're optimistic I'll give you that, but I don't believe we're through yet. Maynard has big plans for the other plane. He wants to get in there, but why, I don't know.'

'Well, we've done pretty well without this book that everyone keeps talking about' Katie smiled at him. I gasped. There was no doubt about it that she meant the red book from in the chair. 'Still, I say we should leave the other plane be. It worries me that Maynard is going to such extremes to get into the other plane, as well as trapping M.C's and trying to force them to open the portal. It'll be dangerous once it's opened. We don't know what's on the other side.'

'The new recruits will be M.C's soon enough,' Rob said offhandedly. 'They will be able to get us into the other plane if the disc fails.'

Katie looked slightly disgusted. 'They are just children,' she said sadly. 'It doesn't matter if they'll be full M.C.'s. I couldn't bear to see Lynn get hurt.'

My jaw fell open in shock. The new recruits were our operators!

'Well then help us to finish the job Katie, help us to get these beasts and win the war,' he said grabbing her arms and shaking her slightly. 'We need the world to understand our intentions and then the children can take the lead.'

'Oh bull,' she said shaking him off. 'You have crossed the line Rob. Don't you think it's wrong to use children? It'd be a suicide mission if we opened the portal. We shouldn't go there, just capture those who come into this world.'

'Which side are you on, Katie?' Rob said his voice changed to a menacing tone, taking a threatening step towards her, but before she uttered a word, there came an announcement over the tannoy.

'Can Mrs Katie Simmons report to the reception desk on deck three immediately. That's Mrs Katie Simmons; please report to the reception desk on deck three.'

My heart jumped into my throat. It was Henry's mother, it had to be,

Katie suddenly turned around and ran off, leaving Rob standing staring at her, an evil look on his face.

Not caring about Rob, I followed Katie through the doors, literally, and headed down to the reception desk like I had done only hours before.

'I'm Mrs Simmons,' she said looking confused as she approached the lady at the desk.

'There has been an incident in your room,' the lady said looking a little disturbed. 'Have you got your cabin keys on you?'

Frowning Katie nodded and flipped her bag around to look, 'Yes I keep them in... No wait; I gave them to a friend to collect something for me in my room.' The lady nodded and Katie gave her Rob's room number and where he was on the ship.

'The onboard police will need to have a word with you, please wait here,' she said then took the information away to a crew member to search for him.

Minutes later, two security crew members came towards her looking concerned. 'Mrs Simmons?'

'Yes,' Katie said frowning between them both. 'What's going on?'

'This way please,' one of them gestured to follow her.

Taking her to a small room in one of the corridors, she was asked to sit down.

'A child has been discovered in your room.' One of them said. 'Where have you been in the last half an hour?'

Puzzled, Katie told them where she had been, which from my point of view sounded pretty boring. 'And then I heard the announcement to come down to the reception desk...' she finished. 'What has happened, why was a child in my room?'

'Do you know a girl by the name of Annabel Cheswick?' one of the officers asked.

She shook her head. 'No, I don't.'

'Annabel was found by a maid in your room not ten minutes ago. The door was wide open when she went by. The child is dead.'

Katie gasped, clapping her hands to her mouth in shock, 'Oh my God!'

I felt a cold hand on my shoulder. Turning, I saw the black haired girl. She looked sad.

'You need to follow me now,' she said.

'You're Annabel aren't you?'

She nodded solemnly, a small tear rolled down her pallid cheeks. Offering me her hand, she led me out of the little room and together, we glided down to Katie's room where members of staff plus the captain and more onboard policemen surrounded the body.

Phasing through them, I screamed out in horror as I saw poor little Annabel on the floor, a pool of blood next to her head.

'Who did this to you?' I asked as warm tears splashed down my face.

Annabel looked pained at this question, 'Rob,' she said softly. 'He's not what he seems. He's not human.'

'Then what is he?'

'Cerberus, the Guardian of the Underworld,' she told me. 'If you noticed, Rob's attitude changed many times during his conversations with Katie. He can't help himself but lash out. After Katie had left him on deck, Rob was never seen again. He's working as a double agent, solely for Maynard. Maynard wants a war. He wanted the Phaistos Disc to be read out loud by the King of Minos himself and if that had happened, a portal to the magical plane will open. Maynard's goal is to get into that plane. But the real disc went missing in 1984; a fake one is in its place in Heraklion. Maynard still has his goal, but he's using all of you to become myths and to unbalance the world. When that happens, a war shall begin a war between myths and the T.A.T. It's inevitable now. The secret is in Asia and needs to be uncovered.'

'How do you know all of this?' I asked her, turning away from her body to look out of the small window where the blue waves danced out in the ocean ahead.

'Being dead has its perks. I've managed to find out a lot of information about the T.A.T. from following them and you. Watching you all grow up. I was killed by magic and I won't rest until this upcoming war is stopped. You and the others are the links to stopping it, even though you'll be causing it. But know this, this war will draw attention from beings who are not myths but who control them.'

'I don't understand.'

'You will when you have completed two tasks.' She said confusingly. 'I'll give you a clue. There is a reason why Lionel can speak Vietnamese.'

The scene around me began to change and I realised my time was up. 'Finish your task in Verona and you will gain an ally. Figure out the letter in Asia and understand your future then you must free the King of Minos. He's still being held captive in Wales. Tell the others about Rob and Henry's mum, and Macie and Lionel will want to know about their parents too. Good luck Tara,' Annabel said as she reached out to grasp my hand, but it passed through me.

I felt like I was being doused with freezing cold water. Gasping my eyes snapped open and I was in the room with the others. 'Holy kack!' I said jumping away from the door as Saskia had done.

'Weird wasn't it? Saskia nodded.

I stared at the patch of carpet where Annabel was found dead. Feeling bile rise up from my stomach, I grabbed the bathroom door and flung myself inside, throwing up and crying into the toilet bowl.

'What's wrong?' everyone asked me as someone grabbed my hair pulling it back as I threw up again, tears rolling down my face.

'She was just a child,' I cried, collapsing onto the floor of the bathroom, 'Rob, Cerberus, killed her for no reason, but why? She was barely eight years old.'

Collecting myself, Saskia and I had told the others what we saw. Apart from Macie, who burst into tears, Henry and Sam were silent throughout. Even after Saskia told us that our parents were involved with the T.A.T., they now had confirmation that Saskia was telling the truth.

Lionel's father, Ben, was barely mentioned, but it was nice to know that he and Macie's parents, Will and Maggie, got along so well.

Macie seemed to get instantly upset at the mention of her parents now. Ever since Saskia had told us that our parents' memories were wiped, the girls caught Macie crying when she thought they weren't looking. I felt her pain, we all did.

'There was a dragon in Vietnam though,' Sam said looking confused as he brought me back to a horrible reality, referring to the note that Katie was given. 'That's just odd.'

'Not really. You are thinking of the Western style dragon. There is an Eastern style too,' Lionel told him, 'dragons are quite common throughout Japan, China, Korea and Vietnam. The dragon is embedded very deeply into each country. In the Chinese or Mandarin language, you've got heavenly dragons called Tianlong, Shenlong for God dragon, Dilong for an earth dragon and many more.'

Putting two and two together I asked 'So "long" means-.'

'"Dragon" in both Korean and Chinese. And in Vietnam, though they speak Vietnamese, the country is heavily influenced by their northern neighbour, China. So they would use 'Long' for Dragon also.' Lionel asked looking confused. 'Why?'

'And also, does bamboo grow in Vietnam?' I asked him as I dived for the book which was on the bed next to Lottie. Annabel said there was a reason why Lionel could speak Vietnamese. Could he help find this pitted bay if it were in Asia?

'Um yeah,' he said still looking confused. 'Bamboo grows all over in Asia.'

'Are you having an epitome?' Macie asked me.

'It's called an epiphany and yes, well I hope so,' I said as I grabbed the letter and read it again. 'Lionel how would you say Dragon descends into the sea, in Vietnamese?'

The others looked astonished, each of them perked up as the conversation took an interesting turn.

'Wait, the riddle? Do you think it's in Vietnam?' He asked as he came over to me to look at the note. Nodding, I asked him again. 'Um… well if it's a pitted bay, as suggested, it wouldn't translate as Mr Raleigh has written. It would be more like the descending dragon bay and that translated to Vinh Ha Long or Ha Long Bay doesn't it, Lottie?'

She looked taken back. 'Just because I look Asian, doesn't mean I speak any of the languages. Honestly!'

'S-sorry,' he apologised, stepping on her toes, but I noticed her winking at Hannah. 'But anyway, it means Ha Long Bay and if memory serves, it's in the North part of the country. Clue, cracked,' he beamed.

Shocked for a moment, we each cheered and slapped Lionel on the back, or in Saskia's case patted him on the head like a dog, for solving the puzzle.

'Now all we have to do is get there; after Verona, of course,' I explained, which instantly wiped the smiles off their faces. I made a mental note to visit Wales and free King Minos after Ha Long Bay, but the more I thought about the tasks ahead, the more impossible it seemed we'd ever get there. The T.A.T could stop us no matter where we'd go. They had magic at their disposal. It was only a matter of time. This was proving more and more difficult with questions unanswered and secrets untold. What was Maynard really up to with this war? And what did Annabel mean about beings who control myths?

★ ★ ★

The ship docked at Genoa Port as planned on Monday afternoon. After scrambling off with the others, we were once again stumped for transportation to Verona.

'Okay, I think it's safe to say they probably have got to Cupid before us,' Lottie sighed as we wandered around looking lost.

Giving her a sour look Darren quipped, 'Thank you Miss Pessimistic,' but he didn't seem to have the will to snap at her.

'Um,' Macie said looking uneasy, 'let's just get off this road, I don't like it here.'

Somehow in our boredom, we had found ourselves in a back alley, behind some small extremely rundown houses.

'I agree with Macie,' Sam said in a nervous tone. 'We shouldn't wander off the beaten track.'

Upon turning around to head back the way we came, we saw at least seven people by the end of the road, huddled in a group.

They looked a little shifty as we approached them. Thinking that it would be best if the boys went first, we girls trailed behind them; not looking in their direction. Suddenly one of the men stepped out of the group and called out something. Not understanding an ounce of Italian apart from hello and goodbye, Lionel took over and politely spoke to him. But whatever Lionel said to him, made him angry and within seconds we were all surrounded by men; each looking threatening in their own way.

'He wants to know if we have any cigarettes,' Lionel told us in a calm way.

'We don't smoke,' Sam frowned at him.

Nodding slightly Lionel replied, 'Yes, but he doesn't believe us and wants us to give him money instead.'

Remaining silent, I tried to come up with some form of plan to get us out of this mess. I mean, they were only guys right? If I shouted for the police, they might end up running off, which I seriously doubted. Or they would beat the crap out of us, causing us to get mad and forcing us to reveal our tattoos, which was the most likely outcome.

I gathered from everyone's annoyed and nervous faces that they too came to the same conclusion.

'Just give him some money,' I hissed at Lionel.

'No,' Lionel hissed back, but that small, simple word upset the Italians and within seconds we were faced with three gleaming knives. Advancing towards us, they started speaking in hurried Italian.

As a group, we stepped away from them, ending next to a wall; we were cornered with the mean looking knives still pointed at us. How the hell did we get into this mess?

Suddenly one of the men grabbed Macie and held a knife to her throat. He spoke directly to Lionel.

'Macie,' Lottie and Hannah gasped unable to do anything.

This was the perfect opportunity for Macie to use her training in self-defence, but she was pretty useless at it from the start.

Macie tried to inch back from the knife as best she could, but the man gave her no leeway to move.

'Let her go,' Lionel snapped at him.

'Money,' the man said smiling evilly as he sniffed Macie's hair, making her whimper, a tear fell from her cheeks onto the man's rough looking hand which held her to him.

Without warning several things happened at once... Henry suddenly shouted out 'Lionel, no!' A hand then grabbed my arm, pulling be back but I lost my balance and fell over. Lottie screamed out, 'Macie,' but her scream was cut off by an agonising yell, as well as the quick succession of running feet.

Glancing up, as though everything was in slow motion, I saw Henry, Sam and Darren try to pin Lionel onto the floor. Attempting to move out of the way, Saskia held onto me. 'Stay here, you can't help her.'

Momentarily confused I thought... her who?

Craning my neck around the boys' blurry image, I saw Macie's flailing legs as she was being dragged away by the men as they fled around the corner.

'LET GO!' Lionel suddenly raged as he threw Henry, Sam and Darren off him. Hurtling to the ground, they hit it hard and rolled close to me. My mouth gaped open as I watched Lionel's quaking mass.

'He's turning,' Henry warned as he stood in front of me, protecting me.

'Henry, get out of the way,' I said trying to push him aside as I had to get to Macie.

But through the gaps of Henry's arms, I saw bits of shredded cloth from Lionel's shirt and jeans fly up into the air like confetti. And then in a blink of an eye, a large black pointy-eared jackal pelted down the street on all fours.

'Get after him!' Darren yelled scrambling to get up.

Running to the end of the road, we turned left, heading in the direction where Lionel had run off to. Not forty feet in front of us, Macie clung onto Lionel's neck sobbing into his side while he bared his teeth at the men who continued to brandish their knives at him.

The men saw us; their faces were pale and frightened. They began to shout at us in Italian, but having no interpreter as he was now some mythical dog, we could hazard a guess at what they were saying.

'I think,' Hannah told us as we slowly walked up to Macie and Lionel, 'that they are asking us to call off Fido.'

Smiling Sam nodded, 'Yes, I think you're right there.'

'Guys... help me,' Macie panted.

Unknown to us, as we approached her and Lionel, Macie looked like she was hugging him, but now that I looked more closely she was trying to stop him from attacking the men.

'Crap,' Henry said.

Everyone reacted instantly; all diving towards Macie and Lionel then suddenly and without warning there was a bright flash of light and then the men were gone.

'What... what just happened?' Darren gasped as we fell to the grassy ground together, as though we were in a large dog-pile.

With my entire body feeling as though it was made of jelly, I just about managed to stand up to get a good look at where I was. But glancing around all I saw were endless open fields and Cypress trees dotted around the edges marking the field boundaries.

'Um, where the heck are we?' I asked myself as I continued to stare at the strange surroundings.

One by one, the others stood and looked around them. As they parted, Lionel was lying face down on the grassy floor completely naked. I guess Lionel, like Macie, hadn't fully transformed either.

Henry shook off his jacket and placed it over him.

Going through Lionel's bag, the guys brought out some trousers and a top and helped him get dressed.

'He's a bit groggy and confused.' Sam told us as we sat in the field waiting for Lionel to feel better enough to walk.

'I heard him mumble something when we arrived,' Lottie said looking at Lionel through a gap between Darren and Henry.

Frowning Sam nodded, 'He said "Verona", but how the hell did we-.'

'The opener of ways,' Macie yelled suddenly her voice echoed over the fields, startling some birds close by. 'Lionel opened a way to Verona. He can transport us from one place to another. Oh well done Lionel.'

Lionel raised a hand and stuck his thumb up in the air.

'No way, are you serious?' Darren called to her, turning around and looking shocked.

'Well, it kind of looks like rural Italy,' I said looking at the Cypress trees that Nero imported from Syria all those years ago. 'But it just doesn't make any-.'

'Tara,' Henry said in an exasperated tone, 'need I remind you that you grow wings from your back? Not to mention you can see and speak to ghosts and by your voice alone, can command people to do your bidding.'

'I know but-.'

'Just, shut up,' Henry snapped.

'Meow,' Saskia laughed looking at him and me.

Feeling like a child, I remained quiet and tried to ignore him. Git, I thought menacingly as he soon led the group through the fields.

I smiled to myself as I knew he had no idea where to find a road to get us to a nearby town or village.

'Tara, why don't you fly up an' take a look,' Saskia said loudly but I ignored her as Henry said exactly what I was thinking.

'She can't, she'll be seen.'

Lionel forced us to stop moments later, 'Listen, I hear a car.'

Pushing through some tall grass, we emerged next to a small country road.

'Thumbs out everyone,' Hannah laughed as she Lottie and Macie were at the front, giving a sexy pose to whomever drove by. 'Oh, here comes a van,' Hannah said excitedly as she flicked her hair back like a shampoo advert.

'Where you go?' A man asked us as he wound his window down, stopping by our group.

'Verona' Hannah said smiling at him with perfect white teeth.

'Si,' he said motioning for us to get in.

Darren and Sam helped Lionel get into the back that was packed with boxes of roses, while Henry jumped into the passenger seat with: 'Gino, my name,' he said proudly. 'My Inglish, not so good, itsa small ah?'

Saskia and Macie stifled a laugh. Sighing, Lionel began speaking to him in Italian and after that, neither of them would shut up.

An hour's drive later, Gino told us through Lionel, that we were now in the middle of the City of Love.

'Ha whatever,' I snorted.

Staring at me through a small mirror, Gino asked Lionel a question.

'He wants to know why you don't believe it.'

'Believe what? That Verona is now called the City of Love? We all know why, it's why we're here. I just find it funny that the Italians have already got an excuse for everyone making out. Although, the French will be annoyed.'

Lionel translated and Gino looked sad and rambled off in Italian to Lionel again.

'He said he feels sorry for you that you don't believe in love. He prays you'll get...pain?' Lionel said frowning.

'Scusi,' Gino said shaking his head, 'I say ow, is good for you. Make heart sing.'

Demonstrating for us Gino began to sing; drowning out Saskia's complaining as she clapped her hands over her ears. Then dropping us off in the city, we said thank you loudly as Gino continued to sing as he drove off.

'So how do we find Cupid?' Macie asked as we looked around the dingy-looking city that was now inhabited by a God of Love which for some reason the T.A.T. wanted.

'Not a clue,' Darren told her, placing his hands on his hips and staring around.

Lottie laughed suddenly and pointed, 'Why don't we ask them?'

We turned and saw the most unlikely of couples. A balding, rotund man with a very wizened face holding hands with a young super-skinny blond with very long hair.

'It's rude to stare,' I said hitting Darren and Sam as they chuckled.

'Actually the Italian's don't find staring rude,' Lionel interjected.

I sighed, 'We're not Italians we're British and as such, have a sense of decorum to uphold when out of one's own country.'

'Shut up Tara,' Henry snapped as he led everyone towards the couple.

With a twinge of annoyance, I took a deep breath. Trying to ignore him again I followed the others but wondered when it would be my turn to lead the group. I caught Hannah and Lottie's faces, they looked confused and upset for me, but I shook my head. I couldn't get angry anymore, especially not in public.

★ ★ ★

Lionel didn't get much information out of the couple apart from when they first met. 'Just in the normal way, I guess,' he informed us as we walked off down the cobble streets. 'Met in a park, she was running, he accidentally tripped her up and it was love, at first sight.'

'People jus' don't do tha' anymore' Saskia said beating me to the punch. 'It jus' sounds so… lame.'

I smiled. 'I would have said mature cheddar cheese but either way,' we laughed.

'Oh, come on,' Henry said turning around to face me, 'we both know you fancied me Tara as soon as you saw me.'

Looking past him I saw Hannah and Lottie share a strange look. Henry was acting like an arsehole. What changed in the past twenty-four hours?

My eyes narrowed. I was getting fed up of him attacking me like this and here I was, taking it. 'Yes exactly, fancied, past tense,' I shot back, feeling my cheeks turn red and hot from embarrassment, I hated confrontations.

'Come on you don't need this,' Hannah said grabbing my hand and dragging me off away from him. 'Calm down,' she said soothingly, 'just ignore him.'

'I just don't get why he's acting like this to me. What have I done wrong?'

Hannah sighed. 'Lottie and I discussed it and we think it's because you knew something about his mother that he didn't and he's jealous. You have all these cool powers and you are the leader of the group and he isn't and he's acting up, trying to be all dominant.'

Scoffing, 'Really?' I turned around to see Henry looking at me, 'Arsehole,' I mouthed then turned to face the front again.

'That's not gonna help either of you, is it?' Hannah frowned.

'Does me,' I told her simply.

Finding a cheap hotel, which coincidentally was called Romeo e Giulietta, I decided to take Macie and Lionel out for a pizza. After all Macie had had a knife to her throat and Lionel went all dog on us; so I thought it would be nice to treat them.

'I'm going out,' I told Saskia, who unfortunately was my roommate again.

'Fine, I'm gonna stay an' read ya book.'

'Ah, ah,' I said snatching it up before she got her grubby paws on it. 'It's mine.'

'But ya don't read it,' she protested.

'I've read more than you think I have,' I told her truthfully.

I met up with Lionel and Macie outside the hotel and we ventured off to the city. We noticed without doubt that love was in the air. There were so many couples around us, either walking or on scooters, giggling, kissing, cuddling or laughing; everywhere you looked, in fact. Amongst them though were the usual walkers, gal pals and also a few teenage boys passed us, talking and laughing.

'What is it?' Macie asked Lionel as he started to chuckle.

'They think you two have nice legs.'

Both turning around, we saw them walking backwards looking at us. One of them, who weren't looking where he was going, hit a lamppost and yelled loudly rubbing his head.

Giggling we turned a corner and out of the blue, came face to face with...

'Gino?'

'Ah bella,' he said grabbing my hand and kissing it, then doing the same to Macie. 'Bella notte, beautiful night huh?' He smiled looking around at the couples holding hands and kissing.

'Er,' I replied feeling a little sick as some of the couples were close to being arrested for public indecency.

Gino said something in Italian in which Lionel translated.

'He's confused you don't have love for others.'

Feeling a little insulted, I told him what to translate. 'I do. I just have other things on my mind.'

Gino smiled, 'No one is too busy for love huh?'

'Well, I am,' I replied in a shirty manner.

Gino suddenly turned around and gave me a voluptuous red rose, 'Give it to someone you love huh?' He laughed, then smiling at us, walked off.

After having a delicious meal of Funghi Pizza that we all shared, we headed back to the hotel feeling happy and relaxed. Macie had worried me since the knife attack and Lionel on the sudden transformation. But both had told me that they were fine.

Bidding each other good night, I went into the room to find Saskia and Henry sitting on her bed. They quickly stopped talking, and as a child, Henry turned away, not looking at me.

'Did ya 'ave a nice time?' She asked as I took off my shoes and put my bag down on the chipped wooden desk in front of our beds.

'Yes we did. Bumped into Gino in town and he gave me that,' I pointed to the red rose in my bag. 'Then we had a lovely mushroom pizza at this authentic little Italian restaurant; apparently they've been making pizza there for generations. Then we mooched around and came back.'

Taking my top off, revealing my uniform underneath, I threw it on my bed, reached out to take the rose and laid down with my back to them. It irritated me that I had grown so much my feet were hanging off the bed.

'If ya 'ad such a good time, why are ya annoyed?' Saskia asked coyly.

Twirling the rose I still held in my hands, I cringed at her question.

Since I had walked into the room and saw Henry there, I instantly felt my back twinge; Saskia must be able to see my wings bulging from under the skin. Sighing, I flipped over and stared at them, 'Because he's here.'

Henry immediately frowned, 'I'm allowed to be here, I am the-.'

'Biggest git alive!' I shouted, still trying to contain my wings from bursting out of my back.

'I'm stepping up to claim leadership as you obviously aren't taking it seriously.'

'Ha, some leader you'd be.' I snapped. 'You can't fly, you can't see ghosts, you can barely fight a Minotaur; you haven't even changed yet!'

'Don't push me to get there,' Henry said angrily, fur suddenly glossing up his arms.

'Well, don't push me to make you get there,' I yelled back.

'Guys, please stop it,' Saskia pleaded but neither of us was listening to her.

'Well, don't make me want to change when I don't want to be pushed!' Henry yelled.

Suddenly many things happened at once.

The first was my wings splitting my shoulder blades apart for their huge and glorious entrance. The second was Saskia diving off the bed as my left wing caught an empty water bottle, made of glass that went careening in her direction. The third was that I felt a small prick on my thumb in the hand that was still holding the rose and the fourth was Henry lunging for me in which I smacked into the wall, cracking it. Winded I dropped the rose and I watch it slowly fall on top of Henry's head as he held me pinned against the wall.

CHAPTER FOURTEEN

BLISSFULNESS ENCOMPASSED MY ENTIRE BODY AS HENRY kissed me, holding me to him. I didn't care that Saskia was in the room with me. All I wanted was to be with Henry. Though he was only partially-transformed, I wrapped my wings around him, cocooning him in my soft feathers, giving us some privacy.

''enry, get off 'er!' Saskia shouted trying to use her commanding voice, but it didn't work. 'Oy get a room... jus' not this one.' I felt my wings being pried open, and sensed someone try to get in between us. But then Henry briefly jolted and hearing skin on skin, Saskia yelped and then all was silent until...

There was a loud knock on the door.

'What's all the noise... whoa!'

'Jeez.'

'Took them long enough.'

I heard the others enter the room. But really, I didn't care. It was not my problem. They were invading *my* privacy, not the other way around.

'How long have they been like that?' Sam asked.

'Oh about... get da hell out of my room,' Saskia snapped at them.

I had to give the girl credit. Even after Henry and I were making out, she still kept her famous sass-mouth.

'Don't you mean their room?' Hannah laughed.

'It's not funny, one minute 'enry 'ad Tara pinned against da wall, da next-.'

'Don't want to know that much detail,' Sam cut in.

'No, I mean he was attacking 'er-.'

'Again too much.'

That got my attention. Had Henry really been attacking me? My mind was full of nothing but the forcefulness of wanting to be close to Henry, to touch him and kiss him. Why had been attacking me if now he was acting like this?

'Dey angered each other,' Saskia explained.

'Okay, now I get it, cos of the wings,' Macie piped up.

''elp me, please,' Saskia begged them.

'What do you want us to do? Grab a crowbar?' Hannah asked.

'For God's sake this isn't a show!' Saskia yelled at them. 'Like I said before, no one jus' falls in love like tha'. An' those two, definitely not.'

My friend's wouldn't lie about something like this. This situation is wrong. It doesn't feel right. It's almost as if I was under a spell!

'Okay, I think Saskia's right... about the falling in love thing.' Sam spoke up. 'They must know we're here. We've been talking about them, but they aren't talking to us it's like we're invisible, as though we are not in their perfect world of two.'

I wanted this to stop now. Enough was enough. I was feeling exposed, as though my protective wall to block everyone's negativity against me that I'd created when I was in secondary school, was coming down. No. I didn't like this. I wasn't in control of my body and my feelings. This wasn't me.

'No, I mean they haven't told us to get lost. It's like they're in a trance.' Sam nailed it on the head and that was my cue.

I finally managed to pry my eyes open just long enough to see Henry's closed eyes. He was completely out of it. He needed to get a grip on himself. This had to end!

'Kack!' Macie gasped. 'Do you think Cupid has got to them?'

'Well, Tara must 'ave seen Cupid while she was out with you two,' Saskia pointed out. ''enry was talking ta me most of the night. But the kissing started in 'ere but I didn't see anyone else in the room.'

'So Tara and Henry were themselves leading up to-' Hannah began trying to suss it out.

'Uh oh, we have movement,' Darren warned everyone.

Somehow I had managed to get Henry towards the bed to hopefully unbalance us. I thought that if we fell, we would break apart from one another and I could end the spell.

And then suddenly, as I felt my back legs touch the bed Henry broke away. Both of us smiling stupidly and panting from lack of breath.

'Henry-' I began, and then he pushed me on the bed. And as his lips made contacted with me again, I felt the euphoric blissfulness once again and all rational thought went straight out of my head. All I wanted was Henry. I wanted to be there for him, to help him, protect him and support him... just like a boyfriend should be.

'Hey, Tara mentioned his name. I bet she's fighting the spell!' Darren shouted. 'Uh oh, the clothes are coming off.'

'You pervy git,' Sam spat at Darren, 'don't bloody help them!'

'Okay, we need ta separate them now,' Saskia said in a worrying voice.

'Why?' Darren laughed.

'Someone hit 'im,' Saskia snapped.

I heard the sound of a smack on skin which was then followed by an 'Ow,' from Darren.

My friends came around Henry and me as we took up both beds. I felt arms around my waist and ignored them as I tried desperately to end this spell. There was a strange feeling in the back of my mind that wanted to push the hands off me, to let the spell continue. But my rational mind was creeping back. 'On the count of three,' Saskia called, 'one... two... THREE!'

Pulling as hard as they could, they yanked us apart.

Henry flew back and collapsed on the floor with the boys and I collided with the girls, hurtling backwards onto my bed.

'What... the hell....' I gasped. In shock I slid off and backed away from them all, finally regaining the full reality of what had happened. Henry and I glanced at one another. He stared at me, just as frozen in shock as I felt.

'Tara, are you alright?' Macie asked her looking worried.

'What just happened?' Henry asked the others.

Out of the corner of my eye, Saskia pushed Macie and Lottie off her and shrugged. 'Oh, ya know, ya an' Tara decided ta make some sort of weird porno fer us. Quite disgustin' really.' Grabbing one of my t-shirt's off the floor, she threw it over to me. 'Put tha' on, other girl's boobs don't do it fer me, but there are three other guys present who 'aven't seen ya bare chest.'

Quickly putting the t-shirt on, I stood back from the others and pointed to the door. 'I need to be alone, please can everyone leave.' My voice sounded shaky. I was in utter shock of being pulled apart, from the spell ending so abruptly that I didn't know what to think or feel anymore. But when no one made a move to leave I said, 'Fine, then I'll go.'

I grabbed my shoes and striding to the door, pulled it open and slammed it on the way out.

I hastily put my shoes on and headed down the carpeted lemon scented hallway. I wanted to get away from them all, their stares, their judgement and their laughs at the horrible situation I was in. Not to mention I also wanted to get away from the person who I had tried so hard to bury my feelings from all this time. It was to ensure that Old Tara was never seen or felt again; she had a lot of unresolved issues.

Currently, however, I was confused about everything I was feeling. Love, passion, anger, irritation; I had been magically taken advantage of and that on top of everything else was too much to handle.

I was emotionally hurt and everyone just stood there watching me. Why didn't they stop us sooner? I remember him pinning me to the wall, the rage in his eyes scared me. He wanted to hurt me physically. I knew that much before that weird emotion took over my body, but I couldn't put my finger on what its name was. I would probably describe it as pleasure but not in a sexual way. It was as though my emotional barriers had fallen after placing them up a long time ago even before I met Henry. Yes, there was the occasional crush I had on someone. Sometimes complete and utter infatuation with a movie star, but there seemed to be no words to describe the hurt that gripped my chest. And it confused me even more.

Heading down a flight of stairs, I took a left and headed to the back of the hotel. Bursting out into the cold night air, I found a quiet place by an old water fountain where a small statue of Cupid was perched on top holding his bow and arrow.

I lay down beside it and cried. I vented all of my pain, all the emotional baggage I had with me from my old life, all those memories and feelings that had come back to haunt me. I knew they would someday but not now, not at this time.

'Mummy,' I cried out to her as she barged into our house in Bristol, taking her coat off the rack, throwing a hat and scarf on and grabbing her bag all in quick succession.

It was the 3rd of December, my eighth birthday. My brother had told me there was a surprise waiting for me back home, but I knew nothing had been arranged. My parents were always busy. But what hurt me the most and what my mother denies to this day is that my parents had forgotten it was my birthday.

'Mummy, please stay, it's my birthday.'

'No, it's not Tara. It's next month.'

'No Mummy, its' today. '

'I'm busy, Tara!' She shouted at me and began tapping her pocket looking for her keys. 'We have to go back to work. Your brother is at a friend's house tonight.' She found the keys hung up, where they usually were.

'But I'm going to be alone. I don't want to be alone,' I sobbed as I ran to hug her, to cling to her and not let her go.

'Why can't you just grow up Tara? You have to take care of yourself,' she snapped pushing me off and causing me to fall onto the floor. 'You will stay here until we get back from work. Do not leave this house and don't open it for anyone, do you understand? I've got the keys. We're going, now!' She called to my dad. Opening the door, Dad ran out before I got a chance to say anything and slamming the door closed, he locked it then left.

I suddenly understood the truth and meaning of being forgotten, ignored and not listened to. Of course, it happens to everyone throughout their life, but to an eight-year-old girl on her birthday, that day cut me deeply. After that, I never mentioned my birthday and over the years I always found that my parents had to quickly dash out of the house on the 3rd of December for work.

Another memory rose to the surface of my mind. I was thirteen and it was Christmas day. My brother and I were in the kitchen having some breakfast. The heating hadn't been turned on as Mum and Dad didn't want it on when they weren't there. A stupid rule I always hated.

'You haven't got any presents,' Nathaniel told me. 'I checked.'

Trying not to get upset I said, 'They have probably hidden them somewhere.'

'Oh, grow up Tara,' he chided me. 'When are you gonna get it through your skull that Mum and Dad just don't care about... us.'

'You were gonna say 'me' then weren't you?' I demanded as tears started pooling in my eyes.

He shrugged and returned to his breakfast.

'I hate you!' I yelled as I raised my hand and slapped him across the face.

Shocked, Nathaniel raised his hand and I cowered away from him. 'Ah, what's the point,' he said grabbing his cereal bowl and walking off. He called back, 'No one cares about you Tara, just let it go and get on with your life. You have to take care of yourself in this family. Don't depend on others if you want to survive.'

Nathaniel was seventeen then. Four months later when he turned eighteen, he left the house and never came back.

Another memory resurfaced; the results day for my G.C.S.E's. I was happy, for once. I passed all my grades, apart from French in which I got a D, but I didn't care. I had the grades to go to a College of my choice, or even continue in Sixth-Form.

All of my friends were going to join the teachers in the town for a drink and a party on the beach. However, halfway through, I got a call from Mum telling me that I had to be picked up early. I begged and pleaded with her, but she dismissed it and picked me up by the school gates.

'I passed my grades,' I told her, beaming with pride.

'And where are they going to get you?' she said in an icy way, not really paying attention as she drove me home.

'Well, anything I want.' I told her, feeling my happiness slowly slipping away from me.

'Don't get your hopes up. No one may want you in their college.'

I remember remaining quiet on the way home, staring out of the window, silent tears running down my face. And arriving back home, I headed upstairs and stayed in my room for the rest of the day. As hurt as I was, I created a technique which I used to stop anything bad actually upsetting me. I called it my steel barrier and I forced myself to ignore any negative remarks and comments about anything I was doing.

By the time I got into university two years later, my steel barriers had come down somewhat. I hardly spoke to my parents and found that I could live a new life, to make friends and be happy. And though I expected nothing and hoped for nothing, just ambling my way through, the fresh memories of Amanda, Heather and Beth flooded into me, making me cry harder.

For a brief moment, my barriers had come down for them; just enough to trust them so I wouldn't get hurt, but it didn't work. I had trusted them too much and it backfired on me again.

'Why...' I sobbed to no one, 'why do I get hurt, why do I even bother trying?'

There was a sound behind me and gulping some air, opened my eyes and saw a tall, fair-haired man wearing matching white trousers and top. He looked so sad when he saw me.

Taking a couple of steps towards me he bent down; bringing out a white linen handkerchief he wiped my tears away. 'Tara Young,' he said speaking so warmly and softly to me I couldn't help but give him a small smile as he said my name. 'I have seen you, I have watched you... so much pain.'

I turned away from him. Not wanting to meet his eyes. I knew who he was. In this world, how could Cupid not see how far I had fallen? But I didn't want him here. I had no need for him anymore.

'Please go away,' I told him gently as I closed my eyes and wished myself anywhere but Italy. I just wanted to be alone, to understand my own feelings and deal with this pain by myself. I heard him sit down. He wasn't going anywhere. It was so selfish of me to tell a God of love to go away, but glancing towards him, everything became apparent. 'Gino, did he do this?'

Smiling at me with such warmth that hit me like a blazing fire which instantly heated my cold body, he said softly 'I gave him the means.'

'The roses,' I said nodding as I pieced it all together quickly.

'I never left you Tara; love never leaves the ones who need it the most.'

'Please don't confuse me,' I frowned at him.

'You have been through so much these past few months and you've been all alone yet surrounded by friends,' he told me.

'That's so oxymoronic,' I laughed.

'But its true isn't it? You have walled yourself up. Not letting anyone in. That's why I sent Gino to you. Love touches everyone in one way or another and with it, I know everyone and what's in their heart.'

I snivelled. 'For a God you sure pick the wrong people.'

He shook his head, 'Gifted or not Tara, you needed me and my rose. You needed me to open your heart.'

'Was that the feeling I had?' I said more to myself.

'Euphoria, that's what my rose did to you and Henry. It helped open your heart to a new experience.'

'It hurts,' I said clutching at my chest.

'Love does hurt Tara, but it brings hopefulness. That's why the others are after me.' I wasn't sure that he was talking about Maynard. I felt a frown on my forehead, but he chuckled. 'I know what's in their hearts. I knew they have wanted me for their collection for some time. I can easily evade them.'

'If you can evade them, why am I here? Henry must have known that.'

He shrugged his shoulders. 'The Fates intervene in many ways, sometimes against things I have planned and sometimes with. I needed you here and it was done. I'm no prophet of your life, Tara, but I know what lies in store for your heart, in particular. You need love and the love of your friends to get through this.'

Biting my lip, I looked up at him. 'When Henry was injured and he lay in my arms, he felt so fragile to me that it scared me. Someone who has all this power yet was unable to defend himself. I felt something, but I was unsure of what it was.'

Sighing gently he replied, 'It was love Tara. Do not ever be afraid to feel it.'

'I don't want to feel it. I don't want to continue this anymore. What am I doing? What is my purpose?' I said angrily looking at Cupid. His warm smile never faltered. 'Why was I the one given wings? Why was I the one who was chosen to be the leader? I can't bloody lead! I can barely follow my own directions let alone tell others where to go. What do I do?'

He stood up slowly and turned to look at me. 'To hold out for more,' Cupid told me, his smile radiating warmth and love that I had never felt before.

'What,' I said shaking my head as tears poured down my face, 'what am I holding out for?'

'Everything that your life can give you,' he said quietly as he began to fade away. 'Hold out for everything and so much more.' His words faded with his warmth as he disappeared in a flash of blue light.

Staring at the spot where he had vanished, something happened that I had not expected. An arm came around my shoulders and hugged me and held me up. 'Hold out for us Tara,' Henry whispered in my ear, 'we need you...' Looking up through vision blurry, I saw Henry's startling blue eyes bearing down into my soul. 'I need you Tara.'

'You don't like me that way,' I shook my head, trying to back away from him. But Henry refused to let me go. 'You freaking attacked me!'

'I'm sorry but damn it, you do make me angry. You have the potential to be great and....'

'And then I was humiliated and you just stood there.' Henry couldn't rebut that. 'Look Henry, love has done nothing in my life apart from hurt me. You need to be with someone like Jennifer.'

'No,' he said forcefully shaking his head. 'I *want* to be with someone like you,' he professed.

But I still denied it. 'Henry, you were affected by magic. It's magic that pushed you and not your own feelings.'

'Its magic that made me see things clearly. Before I was unsure whether or not that we could work. Being in a team... it usually ends badly and I knew you were starting to have feelings for me.' I gave him a scathing look. 'Okay, but I knew you could have feelings for me the way we were saving each other's life. So I took the offensive and tried to stop you from liking me but Cupid and the Fates intervened.'

Cold November rain began to beat heavily down around us and the cold seeped to my bones, but my heartfelt warm with Henry being with me. I had liked Henry before all this magical stuff got in the way. I liked him for his courage, for his sincerity and for his instinct to protect his friends.

'Don't you feel something between us, Tara? Something that's not magic?' Before I could reply, I leaned forwards and his lips met mine. We kissed without magic and without Cupid. We kissed because our hearts told us to.

Henry apologised profusely about attacking me as he walked me back to my room. I was thankful it was only occupied by Saskia. She was propped up reading the little red book in bed and smiled as she saw us come in.

'Glad to know ya sorted everything out. You two okay now?'

I nodded.

'We don't need to worry about Cupid now,' I told her. 'He's gone back to the other side, I think. He knew he was going to be collected.'

'Collected?' Henry asked but we didn't know why he seemed confused. 'I thought he was going to be captured?'

'Same difference.' She sighed. 'I guess he came ta pay you guys a visit then?' I nodded again. 'So now I guess we 'ave to annoy Lionel enough to get us to Ha Long Bay, that's goin' to be interestin'.'

'Do you think he can?' Henry said, still holding onto me.

Saskia shrugged. 'Dunno, he "teleported us" I suppose would be da right term, only a few hundred miles, this next trip will be thousands, so ya guess is as good as mine.'

There was a short pause of silence then Henry whispered, 'I'm going to go to bed now.'

I turned to look at him, 'Okay,' I replied, my voice barely a whisper.

'I'll see you in the morning,' he said kissing my forehead. 'Get some sleep.'

Henry withdrew his arm from my shoulders and I felt a chill run down my spine. I grabbed onto his wet t-shirt and pulled him close to me, 'You can stay here tonight.'

'Hey, I'm not havin' you two doin' the rumpy-pumpy while I'm in 'ere,' Saskia suddenly shouted angrily.

Ignoring her, I stared at Henry, 'Can you stay with me until I go to sleep?'

Brushing my cheek with his warm hand he smiled, 'Of course I will.'

Henry closed the door and took off his wet t-shirt, showing his bare chest while I went into the bathroom to clean myself up and change into some drier and warmer clothes.

That night Henry stayed with me, cuddling me, holding onto me. His warmth filled my body, making my heart ache but in a good way. My heart was a muscle, after all, one that I hadn't used in a long time but now…now it was in use again and it hurt me. But as I was wisely told by Cupid, love hurts.

The following morning I woke up with an arm around my waist and I smiled. Henry didn't leave me. I was worth being with.

Turning around, I saw him staring at me. 'Good morning.'

'Morning.' I replied smiling at him.

'Yuk,' I heard Saskia yawn. 'Well, as least you kept quiet,' she said as I heard her pull the duvet off.

'We didn't do anything!' I snapped, feeling a little embarrassed.

'I was only pullin' ya leg, bloody bite my head off why don't ya.'

'Ha, don't tempt me,' I laughed.

'Nice to see we've got you back,' Henry smiled as he smoothed my hair from my face.

Saskia went into the bathroom and slammed the door, but then quickly opened it again and stared at us. 'When I get back out here I want you dressed,' she pointed to me, 'and you out,' she said to Henry then slammed the door again.

Henry turned around and threw a shoe at the bathroom door making her yelp from the shock. 'WAS THA' A SHOE? I SAID NO RUMPY-PUMPY IN MY ROOM!' Saskia bellowed from the bathroom.

Doing as she asked, Henry left the room and headed back to his own. After having a shower, Saskia came out and we sat on our beds just staring at the ceiling.

'What are you thinking about?' I asked her turning my head to look at her.

Scrunching her face, she said, 'I'm tryin' ta think of 'ow ta anger Lionel enough ta get us ta Ha Long Bay.'

I burst out laughing, 'You've got to be joking?'

'Nope, I'm completely serious.'

Sitting up, I looked at her. 'Maybe he can't, maybe it was a one-time thing.'

'Doubt it,' she said still looking at the ceiling. 'An' the annoyin' thin' is tha' he can't remember 'ow he did it.'

'What's confusing me is that Dave sort of did something similar. You know, disappearing with that bright light in the water. I don't think Minotaur's have that type of power, so there must have been another trick up his sleeve.'

Blowing out a large breath of air she nodded. 'Yup, came ta the same outcome. But I think I know why we won't be attacked, at least not while we are in a group.'

'They know we're getting powerful,' I smiled. 'Which is why from now on, they'll be cautious.'

'Exactly,' Saskia grinned. 'Soon we will all be able ta surpass the first stage of transforming and just fully transform anyway but I 'ad a look at the book last night an' there's something ya should know. If we save King Minos, after we 'ave discovered this secret in Ha Long Bay, an' he helps open a portal, we can't go. No human is allowed in the other plane. You have to be one of them, a mythical creature to gain entry. Do ya understand?'

'Yes but-.'

Saskia suddenly grabbed my wrists and shook them, 'Do you understand?' She said emphasising it. Frowning, I was about to open my mouth but then closed it. A small memory reached the front of my brain, replaying the whole thing.

Katie was talking about the Phaistos Disc and if it was being translated she, along with Rob and the others, would be able to pass into the other plane, the other world with ease.

'Oh my God, were our parents like us?' I asked, catching my breath as my head began to spin. 'Do you think they can transform too?'

Saskia shook her head. 'I dunno. Perhaps they 'ad tattoos also an' were given mythical blood. But it makes sense tha' we are in a group now, Tara. Our parents were part of the T.A.T, not jus' huntin' and trackin' other myths. The only thin' was tha' Rob was a mythical creature. He was Cerberus.'

Saskia let go of my wrists. 'Maynard is obviously plannin' somethin' big ta have Cerberus on his side.'

I nodded in agreement.

'In havin' a portal opened to the other plane, Lynn an' the others would 'ave access to a smorgasbord of mythical creatures. Maybe we should head ta Wales an' get ta King Minos first. It seems more important.'

I shook my head. 'No, Annabel told us Verona, then Ha Long, then King Minos. We need to listen to her. We need to get to Ha Long Bay soon, find out where that clue leads and see where it takes us next. The sooner the better or I have a bad feeling that all hell will break loose and I don't mean that in a figure of speech.'

★ ★ ★

We left the hotel late that morning and meandered around the city, but we had no idea what our next step was. Whether to eat, find a new hotel or shop, we had no idea. Although whatever idea we had we all knew that our money was dwindling. With Hannah and Lottie bickering about clothes, the guys were having a discussion with Lionel on how to transport us to Ha Long Bay, as neither of us had that kind of money to get us there.

Macie and I were on a round-a-bout in a children's play park near the hotel; our feet on the floor pushing us around in circles gently.

'I'm glad you and Henry have sorted things out,' she said softly.

'Me too.' Glancing at Macie I saw that she seemed rather subdued. I hadn't been paying at much attention to her since the knife attack and I felt sad that I hadn't had a one on one chat with her. Hannah and Lottie had told me that Macie had spoken to them, but by the sounds of it, Macie obviously hadn't been feeling as happy as she made out to be.

'Do you think that when this is over, we can lead a normal life?'

It was a question that quiet Macie would have asked and I tried to make light of it. 'That's a bit out of the blue isn't it? I thought you liked being able to fly.'

Sighing, Macie stopped us and turned to look at me. 'It's just that, I don't want this anymore. From finding out my parents, memories has been wiped and then being attacked by three of our operators. It's getting too much and I'm getting the impression that it's bearing down on the others too. Lionel doesn't seem to have the heart to help and I already know why.'

'Well then, don't you think you should say something Macie? We need to get to Ha Long Bay, like now.'

'No, we don't,' Macie said stubbornly. 'Can't we just go back home and forget all of this? I mean look what it's doing to us; look what Henry did to you? He attacked you and no one would do that if they didn't have a tattoo like his. He looks scary when he's angry and he could seriously hurt you.'

Macie shocked me to the point that I was genuinely upset at her openness. 'Macie, we're here for a reason, for that I'm certain.'

She frowned instantly. 'Are you? What's so important in Ha Long Bay?'

Flustered, I grabbed my long hair and put it in a ponytail, 'You know what's in Ha Long, the last piece of the puzzle. Something is in Ha Long Bay and we have to get there before the others do.'

'No, you and the others want to get there. I don't, Tara. I don't want to go there. I've had enough.' Macie suddenly got up and walked away from me.

'Macie, wait, what the hell,' I said grabbing her and spinning her around. 'Where has all this come from?'

Macie gulped and I could tell she was trying hard not to cry. 'Tara, someone put a knife to my throat the other day and I didn't do anything about it. I forced Lionel to transform and he went through a lot of pain.' Tears began to spill from her eyes and as I went to her to hug her, she moved away. 'I am a liability, even blondie would back you up,' she spat, nodding towards Saskia. 'I am the weakest in the group. It frightens me Tara, more than you know. I don't want to be part of the group anymore. I want out.'

'Macie, don't do this, please,' I said as she shrugged off my hand and walked away. 'Macie stop,' I said loudly in a commanding voice.

As though some invisible chains appeared from nowhere, Macie suddenly stopped.

'Please don't do this Tara, let me go' Macie told me, still standing, unable to move.

The others came round and asked what was going on.

'Macie wants to leave,' I told them.

Lottie hurried up to her, putting an arm around her stiff shoulders. 'Why Macie, we're in this together. We have to keep going. It's why we're here right?'

'Please Tara, let me go,' Macie said through tears.

'No,' I said plainly.

'Are you... have you stopped her?' Henry said looking at me in a strange way.

'She can't move. Not until she see's sense,' I told him stubbornly.

Saskia butted in between us all and stared at Macie, 'Wow, nice job. I really need to get the knack of commanding people.'

'Could I have a word with Macie,' Hannah asked, 'alone please?' Letting Macie go she fell to the floor and cried. Hannah shook her head at me as I went to try and comfort Macie. Giving up, I headed off with the others. Far away, I saw Hannah have an in-depth conversation with Macie so the rest of us decided to take a short walk to the park, to give the girls some space.

'That was really harsh Tara,' Darren told me looking annoyed. 'How would you like it being told not to do something in which you were scared of?'

I instantly thought of the first time Lynn told me to climb the ladder of doom and then jump off. 'I have been in that situation; I didn't like it, but I learnt a valuable lesson' I stated, shutting him up.

'I have an idea,' Sam said suddenly as he stopped walking. 'What if Tara could command us in more ways than one; not just Tara but Saskia too.'

'I'm not following,' said Lionel confused.

'What if Tara told you to change and take us to wherever we wanted to go?' He asked giving me a sideways glance.

'No, dangerous,' I said putting my hands up in protest. 'It completely wiped him out taking us a few hundred miles. A couple of thousand may kill him.'

'Hardly,' Saskia said shaking her head. 'We're a little more durable than tha' love. But I like da idea, it may work.'

'Um hello, don't I get a say in this?' Lionel said putting his hand up.

They all turned to me and I nodded. 'Go on then.'

Staring at me, he folded his arms and sighed. 'I think it's a bad idea.'

'Of course ya do, poor doggy,' Saskia mocked him.

Lionel frowned. 'So would you if you were being forced against your will to turn into a giant dog monster,' he snapped.

Saskia burst out laughing. 'Giant dog monster, yes I suppose ya were an' ya still don't remember wha' made ya change last time?'

Lionel clamped his mouth shut and faced away from her.

'Macie said that she forced you to change. Mind filling me in?' I asked him slyly. Not waiting for a reply I commanded, 'tell me.'

'Yes, it was Macie.' He began instantly.

'You are forcing someone again?' Henry said exasperatedly.

Lionel continued. 'When I saw her being taken away at knife point I lost it. I like her and I just wanted her back. When I got to the men, I snapped at them and they backed away leaving Macie on the floor. She went to hug me. I felt her kindness. I just wanted to get her away from them then you guys showed up and just when I willed myself to be taken away, Verona popped into my head and we were in the field.'

'I knew it!' Saskia laughed.

Lionel suddenly turned around and gave me an evil stare, 'How dare you!'

'Calm down Fido,' Saskia said flicking her hair out of the way. 'Thank god Tara made ya talk, or rumours would 'ave started ta fly.'

'Yeah and probably started by you!' Lottie whipped at her, but Saskia just shrugged.

Sam patted Lionel on the shoulder. 'It's sweet though, you liking Macie.'

'Get off,' he said shrugging him off. 'God damn it Tara, why did you make me say that?'

'Because now we know how you did it, how you managed to get us to Verona, now the next step is changing you.'

He shook his head, backing away from me. 'No, you didn't want to do it a minute ago. Why the hell do you want to do it now? And in the middle of a children's play-park in broad daylight?'

'He's got a point Tara,' Henry told me.

'A command is a command right an' it 'as to be obeyed,' Saskia said slyly. 'Just tell 'im to be quiet when he changes. There's a clump of bushes over there, we can hide there.'

Lionel looked worried. 'Please, I really don't like this plan.'

I shrugged. 'I'm sorry but you are our new travel agent and we need to travel,' I told him sadly. 'Saskia, get the girls, we all need to be with him when he changes.' Saskia ran off and I turned to the guys. 'No offence but if you want to keep your clothes Lionel, you're gonna have to strip.'

'WHAT?' he yelled, his voice echoing around the park, bouncing off nearby trees.

'Naked now or naked later, your choice,' Darren butted in looking smarmy.

Feeling embarrassed that Lionel had completely stripped, Lottie and Macie turned away to give him some privacy, being our lookouts. I tried to talk to Macie, to ask if she was alright, but she didn't look at me.

The others surrounded Lionel, blocking our view.

Saskia smiled as she gripped my right hand tightly. 'Okay, someone grab hold of naked guy.'

Henry held my left and squeezed. 'You had better get your words right,' he warned me.

I had been practicing what to say to Lionel in my head for the past fifteen minutes. But he was right, if I didn't get the words exactly, something could go horribly wrong.

'Is everyone holding hands?' I asked the group.

'Yup,' they all chimed.

'Good,' I said taking a deep breath. 'Okay Lionel,' I said to him peering over Sam's shoulder, 'you ready?' Lionel was squatting down on all fours, his head down breathing deeply.

'Just get it over and done with, it's gonna hurt like hell,' he grumbled.

'Okay Lionel,' I said breaking the conversation. Everyone held their breath… 'Transform into Wepwawet and keep quiet while transforming,' I spoke in a forceful, commanding voice.

For a few moments nothing happened then suddenly I heard a thump. I looked over and Lionel was bent over and he began to pant.

'Maybe you shouldn't have told him to keep quiet,' Lottie whispered in a frightened tone.

Trying to hide his pain he grabbed his sides, digging his nails into his skin. Short dark brown fur flowed all over his body. His legs elongated as well as his ears and mouth. Long sharp claws sprang out of his nails as they formed to become pads and within seconds he was the equivalent of Wepwawet.

Darren's hand was still firmly on his shoulder, but I could tell he was nervous.

'Take us to Ha Long Bay,' I ordered him.

Snarling he turned to face me, jet black eyes met my own, almost as if he was challenging my authority, but I didn't turn away. 'Lionel, take us to Ha Long Bay,' I commanded again staring him down.

'He's gonna do something,' Darren said as he gripped tightly onto him.

Placing his weight on his back legs Lionel began to lunge.

Holding each other's hands, I braced myself as suddenly I felt myself being yanked along with Henry. Saskia followed me but before we passed into the void where the blue light was, I heard 'I'm sorry!' and then suddenly cold-black salt water hit my face.

Floundering, Saskia and Henry had immediately let go of my hands and I was pushed under by someone who tried to reach the surface.

Feeling hands wrapped around my waist, I was pulled up towards the surface.

Gasping for air, I clung to whoever it was that was still holding onto me.

'Hannah?' I asked as I stared in the darkness where a soft bout of moonlight shed small light on the rippled waves.

'Guess again,' he laughed.

'Darren,' I said gasping for air as water threatened to pour into my mouth. It was one of my biggest fears; drowning.

'Let's get you onto dry land,' he said as he grasped my hand and began to pull me along.

Ten minutes later, I was clinging to a jagged rock and pulling myself out of the water, I flopped down to catch my breath.

'Sound... off,' I panted as I heard people gasping for air around me.

'Sam.'

'Henry.'

'Lottie.'

'The others are still in the water,' Sam informed me.

'What about Lionel?' I called out, but no one answered me. After a few moments, a bedraggled looked Saskia reached the small rocky shoreline, followed by Hannah. I waited for Macie but instead I heard someone crying.

Clearing the water from my eyes, I raised myself up to a sitting position and glanced at the wet bodies beside me. 'Hannah,' I said as I saw her curled into a ball by Sam. 'Why are you crying? Where's Macie?'

The moonlight reflected off her soaking face and shaking her head whimpered, 'She let go.'

Chapter Fifteen

'SHE WHAT?' In anger and my wings suddenly burst out of my back hitting Henry and Saskia who were on either side of me.

'Hey, watch it,' Saskia snapped as she forced my wing from her face.

I stared at everyone who shook water from their sodden clothes. 'I don't get it, why did Macie let go? We need to go back and get her.'

'She let go okay, so you let go,' Saskia said waspishly.

I frowned at her. 'No, it's not okay, it's not okay! We need to go back and get her.' Panic suddenly took hold of me as I was frantically thinking of what to do.

'Hey, speaking of our travel agent, where is Lionel?' Sam suddenly asked disrupting my thoughts.

A sound of water broke the surface and Hannah suddenly screamed. 'Something's got my leg,' she yelled. Scrambling to stand, she turned around and there behind her was a naked exhausted looking Lionel.

Henry and Sam rushed to his aid and pulled him ashore.

'I'm so sorry,' I said as I went to him, Henry and Sam covering him up.

Lionel's eyes flicked over to me then looked away. 'Don't make me go and get her,' he spat with venom in his voice. 'She let go so obviously she doesn't want to be here.'

Sighing, I sat down next to him looking out towards the little-darkened islets that dotted around in front of us. They were almost completely covered in shadow, apart from the tops which were struck by the brilliance of a beaming moon from above showing the dark green foliage on top.

It was a massive shock that Macie had let go and though I didn't understand why, I gathered that even after what Hannah and her had talked about, I really couldn't force Macie against her will. I knew she wanted to go home and to find a way to give her family back their memories, but I couldn't help her with that. We had a mission to do, with or without Macie.

'I'm going to take a look around,' I said standing up.

A hand suddenly grabbed mine; looking down I saw Lionel.

'No… stay here.'

With no forcefulness in his voice, I yanked my hand away from his. 'It's dark. It gives me an opportunity to find the shark's fin or whatever it is.' I looked up at Saskia, 'You coming or what?'

Darren had swum back to shore but was unaware that Macie had gone. I saw him do a headcount and he frowned. 'Hang on, where's Macie?' he asked me.

'She fell behind,' I said with contempt as I opened my wings and I jumped into the air.

Catching a cool current of some easterly winds, I climbed high above the bay; reaching towards the pinnacles of the scattered mossy covered islands. It looked as though dark green carpets had been placed on all of the islands, each smoothly caressing the odd shapes of the jagged rocks and though it was dark, it was a beautiful picturesque place. The moonlight shimmered on the still waters around Ha Long. Junks had grouped together and anchored in the small bays, fishing for squid most likely. It was so calm and tranquil that I wondered really what was out here that was so important to Maynard.

'What are we lookin' for?' Saskia called from behind me.

'An island that looks like a shark's fin,' I told her as I scanned the waters below. 'But I'm not sure if it looks like a shark from a bird's eye view-.'

''Ow about a Siren's eye view?' she interrupted with a stupid grin on her face.

'-Or from sea level,' I continued.

'I'll go up,' Saskia said, 'my wings may be visible to the floating villages.' She veered off to the left, her white wings tipped ever so slightly, where the winds carried her off in the direction she wanted.

I kept on a straight course but moved down several meters and stuck close to the islands, blending into the background. I only needed to flap my heavy black wings a few times as the winds pushed me along gracefully, silent as a barn owl.

Swooping here and there I searched the islands, trying to see if I could see one that looked like a shark. When suddenly I spotted something brown flying just above me. At first I thought it was a sea eagle as the birds were, according to Lionel, quite common around the islands, but it turned quickly in the air then began flying towards me. Hovering, I stopped to watch it and then suddenly realised I shouldn't have. Screaming at me like a banshee, it careened towards me.

'Ah KACK!' I shouted banking left, the winds favouring me, carrying me fast and up as I flew away from the thing that was following me.

Looking behind, I saw it, or rather her. A pair of golden brown wings that reflected the moonlight that streaked across her glossy feathers.

'Who are you?' I called to her, but she didn't reply. 'SASKIA,' I shouted, but having no idea where she was, I could only hope that my bellowing reached her ears.

Yelling like a mad woman, this girl flew fast, catching up to me within seconds. I dived suddenly taking a chance to glance behind me. She had followed, copying my moves, her hands outstretched to grab me.

I zipped around the side of an elongated rock that jutted out from the side of a rocky island and grabbed onto some protruding vines; quickly encasing my body with my wings so I couldn't be seen. I then heard the sweeping of wings and then a breeze of air. She had flown right past me. Counting a few seconds, my wings opened slowly and looking around I saw and heard nothing so I let go, then spreading my wings veered right and around the corner after her.

Smiling to myself, I saw that she had stopped too; hovering over the black waters she searched for me, but I wasn't there. Having the element of surprise, I flew straight towards her, my wings bent over my back like an attack from a bird of prey. Lunging at her, I elbowed her in the head. Her wings slumped and her body fell.

'Ah, kack on a stick!' I dived after her.

She was too high to survive the plunge into the water, I needed help. 'SASKIA!'

'I'm comin'!' I heard her panicked voice from above.

Diving right next to me, we each grabbed an arm of the brown-winged girl and hauled her away from the brink of the ominous iron sea.

'Who the 'ell is this?' She asked as we flew back towards the others, someone had cleverly lit up a torch so we could find them again.

'I have no idea, but she's one of us, a Siren,' I said looking at her. Saskia didn't look confused, instead her face showed worry.

'Who the hell is that?' I heard Darren's voice as we came in to land. The others cleared a path for us, but Saskia and I landed a little awkwardly and tripped up, sending the girl flying into some foliage close to us.

Panting from my exertion, I sat down and took deep gulps of air.

'No… idea,' I told him.

'But, she's one of you,' Lottie whispered looking scared.

Saskia frowned at the unconscious body of the brown winged girl, almost looking disgusted.

'So you two have no idea who she is?' Hannah asked, but then turned to Henry. 'Who is she?'

Henry had come towards me and sat down, looking to see if I was injured. 'Your guess it as good as mine. On this, I have no idea.' Turning to me he whispered, 'are you alright?'

I nodded. 'I'm fine, just a bit weirded out.'

'What are we gonna do about Macie?' he asked quietly as the others crowded around the girl.

I shrugged and stifled a tear that was threatening to pool out of my eye, 'dunno.' While I was flying around looking for this shark's fin, I was thinking about the "Macie Problem." She was part of the team. Saskia and I had discussed that if we are together we are stronger and without Macie, it would cause a problem if Lynn and the others attacked altogether. 'Lionel doesn't want to go back and look for her. So really, it's up to him.'

'He does want to,' Henry began, 'but he keeps talking himself out of it. If she didn't want to come then we couldn't force her.'

I opened my mouth to argue but then closed it. It was a difficult situation to be in. I was confused, angry and upset that Macie had suddenly backed out like this, no matter what Hannah had said to her. 'So I guess I can't force him either?'

Henry smiled sadly and shook his head. 'No Tara.' He put his arm around my wing and hugged me. 'There was nothing we could have done to make her stay with us without you verbally forcing her. It was a brash decision, I'll give her that, but what's done is done. We have more important things to worry about like this girl for one.' Henry turned to look at her and shook his head. 'Why is she like you? It doesn't make sense. I only knew there were two Sirens, not three.'

'Whoa guys she's coming to,' Sam said as the others backed away.

Henry let me up and Saskia and I carefully walked towards her, helping her into a sitting position. Opening her eyes, she scowled and suddenly lashed out at us, trying to scratch our eyes out like a cat.

'Oy, watch it,' Saskia said as grabbed the girl's wrists in mid-air. 'Don't mess with us ya little snot, you've got two Sirens, a vicious Egyptian dog, a merman, a man-cat thin' an' three other's with powers stopping ya, so don't push us.'

'Saskia,' I said frowning at her and pushing her away, I bent down, 'Do you speak English?'

Staring at me, the girl nodded.

'What's your name?' I asked her. I noticed that her eyes weren't blue like mine or Saskia's. Also, she wasn't as tall as us. I gathered that she hadn't been a Siren for long.

'Rhea, my name's Rhea,' she said still giving me a strange cold stare. 'What are you doing here?'

'Tha's none of ya business,' Saskia snapped, but I put my hand up to stop her.

'We've come to understand something,' I said vaguely.

Rhea scoffed, 'If you've come for the last piece of evidence, the riddle it's not gonna help you much, it's a dead end.'

'You know about the riddle?' I heard Lionel from behind me.

Saskia and I exchanged frightening looks. She mouthed Macie's name, but I shook my head. Though Macie left us, there was no way she would betray us like that, especially in such a short space of time. No, something was fishy and it wasn't Darren.

Pushing his way through Saskia and me, Lionel looked at Rhea and frowned. 'Only the people with the book know about the riddle and that's Tara and us.'

Her eyes grew wide as she looked at me, '*You're* Tara... Tara Young?'

I stiffened and stood up, my form towering over her. 'Yes, I am.'

'Then you're in some serious trouble,' she smiled as she stood up. 'Lynn is looking for you and she is fuming.'

I turned around to look at the others, but they seemed just as shocked and confused that this girl knew Lynn.

'How do you know Lynn?' Henry asked as he came to my side.

'D'uh she gave me the tattoo like ages ago, but she didn't tell me what it was for until a week ago.'

'It was a week ago we left London,' Lottie whispered to Hannah.

Rhea didn't understand this implication so she continued. 'Lynn then got three other girls and then after that Indian woman Amjee told us about the riddle, we got transported here. We got here like two days ago, found the island but we can't find the next part of the riddle, it's a dead end.'

All of us looked at each other in absolute utter confusion. Questions began to reel in my head. Lynn was using teenagers as part of the T.A.T, maybe some type of secret section. Also, it seemed that Lynn contacted this other group immediately after we took off in that helicopter to Portsmouth. But Amjee, telling them about the riddle, that made no sense to me, how did she even know? We only just found out that the riddle meant Ha Long Bay, so how the hell did she find out?

'We need to talk,' I said suddenly and grabbed Rhea's hand, dragged her off to a secluded place on the island, much to the objection of the others. 'Now, you're not to fly off, or backchat me or trying to claw my eyes out, okay?'

She nodded.

I sat down on a mossy, damp rock and tried to gather my thoughts. I needed the right information out of this girl or else we wouldn't get anywhere. If what she said was true, that the riddle was a dead end, then we were stuck with no idea about where the hell to go next.

'Um, you got a headache?' she suddenly asked me as she sat down on the floor frowning at me.

'No, I'm thinking,' I said as I pondered on the past ten minutes. She had attacked me but why? Did Lynn instruct her to? If not, then something was wrong and very confusing.

'Boy, that must hurt,' she quipped.

Annoyed my wings whooshed out to the side of me and I stood up, towering over her.

'You will tell me the truth,' I said in a forceful tone. 'Understand?'

Rhea gulped and nodded, 'Yes, I understand.'

'Good.'

Folding my wings back, I then sat back on the rock and looked at her sternly. 'How old are you?'

'Sixteen.'

'Are you in a group?'

'Yes.'

'How many including you?'

'Four.'

'Do they all have tattoos?'

'Yes.'

I paused for a bit while gathering the information she had already given me.

'Have they all changed yet?'

'Yes.'

'Into what?'

'Furies.'

'Erinyes or Furies there are slight differences.'

'Furies.'

Damn, I thought and tried to hide my shock. It wasn't good that they were Furies; vengeful personifications of the anger of the dead. That alone wasn't looking particularly good for us.

'Did Lynn ask you to attack me?'

'She told me not to let anyone near the island.'

I gave a small smile. I was close to the island.

'Amjee told you about the riddle?'

'No.'

'But you told us you did.'

'I lied.'

'Who told you about the Riddle?'

'A ghost.'

'Who's ghost?'

'Ann Smith's.' That struck a chord. Ann Smith… wasn't she the assistant to Mr Raleigh?

'Tell me about her?'

'We were in Wales in an old nuclear bunker and she was there. She came to me. She told me about the riddle and gave me the co-ordinates and we were transported here.'

'How did you transport here?'

'Cerberus, Cerberus transported us.'

A cold wind blew right through me, catching my breath, almost strangling me. The man, the creature who killed Annabel was still around. He must have holed up with the T.A.T after killing her.

'The others from your group, where are they now?' I asked her, feeling that my tone wasn't so forceful anymore, but her answer seemed to be truthful.

'In the cave on the island that looks like a shark's fin.'

Rhea suddenly scrunched up her face and yanked her whole body away from me. Scrabbling to get up, she spat ferociously. 'Why the hell did you do that?'

'I wanted answers and thank God I did force you or you would have continued to lie to me.'

Giving me the middle finger and about to storm off, I called her back and commanded her to sit down. Still thinking about the situation ahead, I stood up and rubbed my sore damp arse. Sighing heavily, I looked up at the beaming bright moon above me. Three fully changed furies against Saskia, I and the others were extremely worrying. There was only one option, but I didn't want to think of it, it was too horrible to imagine.

The lightly crashing waves and the eerie silence of the bay gave me no answer. Perturbed, I went back to the group with Rhea. As soon as they saw her they bombarded her with questions but she kept shaking her head.

'Nope, I'm not gonna say anything. Besides, I was already forced to say stuff because of her,' she said throwing a pointy finger in my direction.

'I know how that feels,' Lionel said darkly.

'Oh, shut up and grow up,' I snapped at him. 'You need us and we need you. You helped us get here, so thank you.'

'Well, sod your thank you,' he growled. 'It's because of you, Macie's gone,' he said shouting. Suddenly he bent over and fur began to creep over his back.

'You will not change,' I told him firmly. 'Calm down.'

Lionel fell onto the floor gasping, but he nodded, 'I am... I'm calm.'

'Wow, you can control them too?' Rhea smiled.

'Don't you even think about it, ya little git,' Saskia said almost growling at her. 'If I see ya screw up or do somethin' wrong, so help me I'll make ya wish ya were never born.'

Rhea scoffed and folded her arms, 'I like a challenge.'

'Be quiet both of you,' Hannah shouted. 'This isn't helping us. Tara, what's the plan?'

For once everyone was looking to me to give orders. I had to finally step up and take the reins of this adventure. If not, we would lose another member and we would be in big trouble if that happened. 'Rhea is going to take us to the shark fin-looking island and we're going to figure out this riddle,' I smiled at her.

'I told you. It is a dead end!' Rhea yelled in annoyance.

'Bull,' I barked. 'Ann Smith isn't going to send you off around the world just to come to a dead end, is she?'

'Wait, Ann Smith…' Hannah said staring Rhea.

'Yeah, it's a common name, but it is your dead relative,' Rhea said to her in a nonchalant way. 'She said 'hello' by the way.'

'Have I missed something?' Darren asked looking confused.

'Ann Smith helped Mr Raleigh with the downfall of the O.M.C. Well, they tried to and failed because it's still real, alive and it's the T.A.T.,' I told him.

Rhea's face went from confusion to shock and then she laughed. 'Okay, now that's utter bull. The T.A.T are the good guys.'

'Ignore her,' Saskia said nastily as she turned her back on her. 'So Ann is related ta Hannah an' I'm guessin' tha' Miss Ann Smith got her wires crossed an' talked ta Rhea instead of talkin' ta us.'

I shook my head, 'No, give the ghost some credit. They still follow us around you know, I think she got Rhea and the other's here for a reason, but we just haven't figured it out yet.'

'Well, the others are stupid nasty and boring,' Rhea said folding her arms. 'Old hags the lot of them.'

'Old, so you're the youngest then?' Lottie asked.

'Does it matter? I'm their leader and they have to do what I say. Lynn said so.'

'How long have you been together, I mean as a group,' Henry asked her.

Rhea stuck her tongue out in thought and looked up at the sky, 'About two weeks I think. They all came from the same backwater university while Lynn came to me especially because my parents were in the T.A.T.'

I looked at the others who seemed sad. We knew the truth about our parents now, but I didn't think that Rhea did. Though, strangely enough, Henry didn't seem sad, in fact, he seemed confused.

'These other girls, what are their names?'

'Heather, Beth and Amanda,' Rhea said.

Henry suddenly shot me a look of alarm.

I heard the words, "Uh-oh she's gonna faint," but I didn't get to find out who was about to faint as suddenly someone turned out the lights and my consciousness.

CHAPTER SIXTEEN

COLD WATER SPLASHED ON MY FACE AND DRIBBLED DOWN my chin. 'Hey Tara,' Henry's concerned voice sounded in my ears. 'Come on hunny, wake up.'

'Since when have you called me hunny?' I mumbled, shaking my woozy head. My eyes fluttered open to see a worried face hanging over me.

'You okay?' Henry asked stroking my head. It took me a second to register why I was on the floor and what had happened to me but as I recollected I frowned, feeling a strange emotion in the pit of my stomach. Was it jealously? Disbelief? Anger? A mix of the three? Or what it just intense shock? Amanda, Beth and Heather were part of my old life. In reality, they didn't exist in my new magical life. And yet, they somehow found a way, wriggled in like some maggot.

'Um, no, I'm not okay,' I said trying to sit up. 'Please tell me I didn't hear what I thought I heard?'

Helping me to sit up, Henry knelt behind me, keeping me upright.

'Some backbone you've got,' I heard Rhea's snide remark, but then shortly after, I heard a small thump then an 'Ow, you cow!'

'Stop fighting please,' Lottie said in a motherly tone.

I made a mental note to thank Saskia, only she would have the guff to smack someone.

'Tell me, how did you come across Amanda and the others?'

Saskia put her hand in front of my face, and shook her head. 'No, ya don't need ta know this crap. The fact that ya passed out, not only makes ya look like a pushover in front of 'er, it's gonna upset you further if ya hear something you don't want ta.'

'She's got a point.' Henry nodded.

'I need to understand.' Saskia lifted her hand and walked away, throwing her hands up in disbelief. 'Rhea, tell me about Amanda, how did you meet her? And don't lie to me.'

'We met in the bunker in Wales. I had already been inducted into the T.A.T. And I already knew who and what I was. Lynn told me I was going to be a leader over three furies. I bumped into one of them. She said her name was Amanda Winter. And I told her exactly what Lynn told me. That your old life doesn't matter anymore. What does matter is what you have been given and you plan to do with it.'

Lottie fidgeted uncomfortably and sitting down, hugged her knees. Since Macie had fallen behind, she had become subdued. She liked Macie a lot. Both had similar personality, kind and caring. To lose Macie was such an emotional blow to her.

'I explained that she was a Fury.' Rhea began, grabbing everyone's attention. 'She didn't know what she was,' Rhea continued. 'We walked to into the cafeteria together and I met the other furies, Heather and Beth. They were shocked about their new wings. Lynn hadn't told them. It was clearly down to me. I told them the brief history of Furies, that in Greek literature Furies were kind and caring, but when the Romans turned up, the name of Fury became a bad omen. Those who were claimed by the Furies had better pray to the Gods for forgiveness, cos they would drag their sorry arses back into the depths of Hades' hell.' She smiled slightly at that horrendous description. 'I told them that Maynard had been given the D.N.A. of the Fury and explained who he was.' Rhea's piercing eyes locked onto me. 'Of course your name came up. Amanda was desperate to know every scrap of information on you. It was like she was obsessed of finding out everything about you. It was pathetic.'

'Oy!' Saskia yelled. 'Watch your mouth.'

'Continue, Rhea.' I pressed and ignored Saskia's outburst.

'Lynn told me to give them a small induction into the T.A.T. I said that the T.A.T are the good guys who want to stop the myths from getting into our world. And to do that we have to stop them by going into their world but we can't do that until we know what's in their plane. Amanda wanted to know what myths the T.A.T. had to stop.' Rhea sat up and in a smarmy manner said, 'Lynn had told me, when I arrived, what myths the T.A.T had captured over the years. She trusts me you see.'

Saskia came back into view and with a threatening fist, held it up in front of Rhea. 'See this? It's gonna go in ya face if you don't get on with it! We don't have time for this!'

'The T.A.T have been housing dangerous myths for decades.' She continued and gave Saskia the finger who sauntered off in a huff. 'And they wanted to know about the facility.'

'What else did you discuss?' Henry questioned.

Rhea shrugged.

'Tell us ya little git!' Saskia bellowed.

'I told them I could see ghosts,' she said instantly. 'I told her about Ann Smith visiting me.' Hannah's head snapped up. 'Ann told me that Tara had found a book in the library of a hotel run by the T.A.T. She told me it was like some ultra-mega secret which she found out. The book has all the information the T.A.T need to stop myths getting into our world and screwing things up.' Rhea snorted. 'She told me not to tell Lynn.'

Hannah breathed a sigh of relief. 'Thank god Ann had some sense.'

'Whatever,' Rhea shrugged. 'Lynn suspected anyway. I think she just wanted confirmation.'

Steadying my breath as my heart was beating a mile a minute I went over the facts that Rhea had mentioned. 'Right, so my friends are Furies,' I said to myself, trying to will myself to believe and understand it, but I didn't. I was completely confused.

'Friends?' Henry questioned. 'After what they did to you? Ha!' He scoffed.

'Yeah Tara, they sound like utter tosspots, especially that Amanda,' Saskia told me, walking in front of me and staring at me with a hard look on her face. 'I wouldn't trust them as far as I could throw 'em.'

'Help me up please,' I asked Henry.

Taking hold of his hand, I stood up but clung onto him, my legs like jelly. I didn't understand that such information would make me pass out the way I did. Why did it affect me so much? 'Okay, we need to get over to the island,' I said to everyone. 'Rhea, lead the way.'

'Check this first.' Saskia passed me my sopping-wet bag. But looking inside everything was bone dry, even the book. Breathing a sigh of relief, I open the beginning of the book but didn't see anything that would help me discover the next part of the riddle. My eyes glanced to Rhea; her eyes were on the book, unwavering.

Making me a little uneasy, I slammed the book shut and smiled at her. 'Don't worry, we'll solve this riddle.'

Hannah and Darren were going to help Lionel, Lottie and Sam get across while Saskia and I helped Henry; all of us following Rhea. The only thing that worried me was that Rhea seemed almost happy that she was leading us to the island and I couldn't help but feel wary in the pit of my stomach.

Taking off into the breezy night air, Rhea dived down to an island close to where we were. From above I could make out that it would look like a shark's fin from the side.

Holding onto Henry's left arm, his hand squeezed my elbow. Looking down at him he gave me a cautious look; nodding slightly, I looked at Rhea's swooping shape ahead. She glided gracefully but at a few points, when there was a sharp blast of wind, she faltered and took a while to adjust her wings. I quickly got the impression she hadn't been flying long. I would guess about a few days if that.

The others were there before us, as Saskia and I had to circle a few times to land Henry safely on the ground. Landing beside him, I stared right ahead of me. Rhea had taken us to the rocky outcrop on the upper tip of the shark's fin. Covered in dew, the foliage shimmered with the balmy winds that swept softly across the bay. The pale orange moonlight glistened off the tops of the swaying trees and with the sounds of a babbling waterfall close by, I could imagine this place being extremely magical. But along with the calm serenity I felt from this island, there was a certain presence which got my back right up, something almost evil.

'This way,' Rhea said as everyone was ready to move on, apart from Darren and Hannah who stayed in the water.

As we trekked through the brush where birds twittered in annoyance as we disturbed their sleep, I thought about what I would say to my erstwhile friends if I saw them. I suppose I was still a little angry at Amanda and what she had said to me. But through all the things that had happened within this month Amanda had barely crossed my mind. I was too worried about being followed by our operators, then the ghost encounter; then Henry, Cupid and the Ha Long Bay secret. Now I was faced with the question of what I would say to them when I saw them? Hell, would I do anything if I saw Amanda? But on the other hand now that she was a Fury, I was in trouble. I knew what they were capable of.

Rhea's wings slowly disappeared as we headed deeper into the mini-jungle; the waterfall sounding louder as we walked. Henry, who was in front, turned around and gave me a wary look as if to say, "Be careful." Shaking my head he faced forward and clenched his hands into fists. He was ready for a fight, but the others weren't. If push came to shove, could I command them to transform to help me if Amanda and the others fought me?

'Through here,' Rhea said, as we came to the waterfall that was hidden behind a protruding foliage-covered rock. As she stepped through the drizzling waterfall she vanished instantly but I heard her footsteps continue.

Walking into a small cave behind the waterfall, that wasn't described in the riddle; we waited for the others who were bringing up the rear. The cave was very well hidden and was big enough to fit us all in, plus a few dozen people or more. The walls were partially damp from the waterfall, but the ceiling of the cave was dry with only a few completed columns of stalactites and stalagmites growing on the floor and cave roof. There were little nooks and crannies within the walls of the cave, but the chamber itself didn't continue very far, perhaps sixty foot or so, but no more than that.

Rhea continued on into the damp cave and stopped to face us and remained silent. After a minute or so the others caught us up and I motioned to Henry to stand beside Lottie, she didn't look very well. We all collectively shivered from a cold breeze that came from within the cave. My head turned to Rhea and I saw her smile evilly as she stared into the pitch blackness of the cave. Something was wrong, I could feel it. An almost dark depressive atmosphere suddenly enveloped us, nearly drowning us. It took a lot of concentration to keep my feet steady as my body screamed for me to run away.

'I don't feel so good,' Lottie whispered behind me.

'Er Tara,' Lionel's voice said urgently from behind me.

Turning, I saw Lottie crouched down holding her stomach, her strange owl-like eyes staring at me.

'Lottie, what's upset you?' I asked going over to her.

'Oppressive air,' she muttered. 'It's making me so angry, it's upsetting me.' Looking pale, I felt her forehead and yelped.

'Oh my God, you're burning up. Quite literally,' I gasped my hand feeling like it was just put into a roaring fire.

'Tara something's going to happen,' she said with wide frightened eyes. Lottie clung to my arms for support but hot pain seared through my skin and I quickly pulled my arms away before they got second-degree burns. What was happening to her? But all thoughts of Lottie were pushed out of my head as I heard three distinct thuds on the cave roof ahead. We weren't the only ones in the cave.

'Tara, Tara, Tara...' came a rasping voice. It was female, but it sounded gravelly and inhuman. 'All I've thought about is you. What you been up to Tara? Where have you been Tara? Made new friends... Tara?'

'Talk about stalker,' Saskia mumbled, but she sounded scared and that was worrying.

There was a whooshing sound and looking up, I saw three dark figures which clung upside-down on the cave ceiling, one of them had their wings open prepared to fly. 'Oh and look its Tara's group. I expected more of you, but no matter. I'll track the others down and kill them!' she spat with venom.

Gasping, I took a step back with the others as the figures crept closer towards me. I knew that voice though it was raspy and coarse. It was Amanda!

Three pairs of red eyes stared down at me, freaking me out to the point I wanted to scream, but I had to be brave, I had to see this through to the end, no matter what. They crept closer, scraping the rock with their long black claws. Nearly hovering over me, Amanda let go, twisting gracefully in the air, she landed on the damp ground, crouched with her leathery bat-like wings spread on either side of her. Her muscular tail, tipped with an arrowhead, swishing from side to side.

The only thing that still looked like Amanda was her face. The rest of her was some sort of weird mutant bat thing, or to those with mythical knowledge, a Fury. Hell's Daughters.

Inwardly cringing, I remained calm; I didn't want to show how afraid I was of her. Henry suddenly moved and came in front of me, protecting me.

A rippling sound came from her throat and she stood up from her crouch, her tail continuing to swish like an angry cat. 'My, my, Henry Simmons, the hottest guy in the university. Even in this dark light you look handsome.'

'Henry Simmons?' came another raspy voice from above.

Not bothering to look up, the other two figures came swooping down and landed behind Amanda, their red eyes fixed on Henry.

'Oh Henry, it's been a while and yet you haven't changed a bit,' Beth said, her weird serpent-like tongue sticking out to almost taste the air. 'Don't you taste yummy... you almost taste of fear.'

Henry remained silent, he kept his focus entirely on Amanda and she was loving it.

'It's nice to see you look at me Henry,' she smiled, showing pointy teeth, 'though why it's with caution instead of longing, hell knows,' she shrugged.

Rhea who was beside all three of them took a step forward, 'They want to finish the riddle.'

Amanda laughed and moved slightly to get a better look at me, 'You want to solve the riddle? Well, aren't you the smart one Tara? Always wanted to be best in everything? You were chosen by the T.A.T, you took Henry from me! I can smell you on him, it's disgusting!'

'I've never wanted to be in the T.A.T. if you knew what I've been through you wouldn't say that! And you leave Henry out of this! I didn't take Henry from you he was never yours in the first place!'

'YOU LIAR,' she screeched, her tail began to thrash wildly. Spittle flew out of her mouth. 'I KNOW YOU! You backstabbing slut!' she said viciously.

'Tara,' I heard Lottie whimper from behind me. 'I don't want to be here.'

'Aw. Let the little girl go, Tara,' Amanda said smiling at me. 'We can play cat and mouse. I've never hunted someone before. But it sounds fun!'

Daring to move, I turned around and saw Lionel and Sam near Lottie just looking at her, unable to touch her and I knew why. The heat she was emitting was overwhelming; the cave was gradually heating up because of Lottie. Coupled with the fear I was feeling, I was sweating profusely.

'Henry I think, I think she's changing,' I said in a frightened tone.

'Oh, this is priceless,' Amanda drivelled. 'And here I thought all you freaks had turned into your tattoos. Huh. I guess we're the dominant group then.'

That annoyed me. Spinning around I faced her, 'Ha, freaks? Have you looked at yourself in a mirror lately? You look like something hideous that got dragged out from the depths of hell.'

'Well, it was Cerberus who transported us here through the depths of the earth. So you would be correct,' she said, then unexpectedly within a fleeting moment, Henry was shoved out of the way, a whiplash hand flung him to the side. He hit the wall with such force I thought I heard something break.

Suddenly, a thick cord-like tail was wrapped around my throat, strangling me.

'TARA,' Lionel and Sam yelled from behind me.

'Let her go,' Saskia yelled in a commanding tone, but Amanda just laughed.

'That's not going to work little girl. You idiotic Sirens have no power over us Furies. We will command and take control of the T.A.T. Just like Lynn intends.' She sneered and pulled me close to whisper in my ear. 'Do you want to know how I became a Fury, hmm? I found your letter at Kevin's house. You only tore it up,' she giggled, squeezing tighter. 'I pieced it together and found your little secret. I managed to contact the hotel in London through my own means. The T.A.T became suspicious of us and we were captured and were made Furies. Doesn't revenge taste bitter sweet?' Her forked tongue lashed out and licked my cheek. 'Especially when our sole target has been you.'

'Don't... do this,' I gasped as Amanda's tail pulled even tighter against my throat.

'Oh, don't do what?' she sneered.

'Piss... me... off,' I said as I tried to pry her tail away from my throat. I was beginning to feel the same feelings when Darren had pinned my arms back the first time I met the group in the T.A.T. and Sam was about to spit his venom at me. I felt embarrassed, angry and upset. But I remembered what Saskia had once said, that there was another level that we could achieve and I could feel it bubble to the surface.

Lionel and Saskia ran over to see how Henry was. Rousing him, out of the corner of my eye I saw him move slightly. Thank God he was alright. Watching Amanda carefully, I tried to see the girl I used to like somewhere buried deep in the Fury that she had become, but I didn't see anything. Amanda Winters, the girl who used to dance to Chavy music, was long gone.

Flapping my wings to try and break free from her grip, I couldn't even get off the ground. Amanda had somehow become ten times stronger than usual.

I flicked my eyes to Rhea; she stood back as though she didn't want to get involved. Was this Lynn's plan with her from the beginning? For her to lead us to the Furies so they could kill us? My strained eyes searched the ceiling and I found Heather and Beth. They too remained silent but seemed almost eager to see what would happen to me. I let out a choking cough as Amanda's tail gave one more last powerful squeeze.

'Don't,' I managed to gasp but all Amanda did was laugh at me.

'See, who's better than you now? It's always been a competition, hasn't it Tara? Who's the strongest? Who can transform first? Who's the prettiest? Who's best for Henry?'

'You're insane,' I choked.

'Tara,' Saskia began in a calm voice, 'don't let her do this to you. We are more than this, achieve it and fight!'

I managed to smile and staring into Amanda's disgusting vampire-like face I uttered one word. 'Retribution.'

Using the last scrap of air I had in me, I yelled out in anger, frustration and pain. Every emotion that I knew I could use to tap into the unknown power to rid myself of my human form and transform me completely, I was willing to use. Amanda had to go and so too did Heather and Beth.

A strange power suddenly pulsed through my body that was quickly followed by a gust of wind, whipping my hair around me. I felt my wings grow and my body stretch. Rocks began to tumble down around me, falling on the others who didn't get out of the way in time. Amanda was one of them. She tried to dodge while her tail was still wrapped around my throat and there was an infinitesimal moment when she relaxed and I took my opportunity.

Yanking her tail from my throat, I gripped it tightly and sickeningly somehow managed to rip it away. I let it go in disgust as blood and sinew fell to the floor. She roared out in pain and anger.

Gulping deep breaths of air, my wings flung out to my sides I felt invincible, powerful and strong. My entire body was still buzzing with electricity, and the power still surged in me.

I was in control now; I was the most powerful one and, what's more, I understood everything. It felt as though I was given some ancient knowledge that I would never have gained if I hadn't had reached this level of power.

I knew what Hannah was. I knew her powers. I knew Lottie and Sam's too and I also knew what Henry was capable of. It was like I had been blessed with the gift of the Gods on a collective level. I understood the blood which flowed through me; it was warrior blood, otherworldly. Controlling my breathing, I gradually stood up and took in the scene in front of me. The first thing I noticed was that everyone seemed to have shrunk. I towered over them all, at least an additional head and shoulders above them, including Saskia who used to be the same height as me.

My eyesight was in one sense of the word, perfect. Everything was so crystal clear, so detailed. My hearing had even improved. I could even hear everyone's individual thumping heartbeats; at least four of them seemed scared. Maybe it was because of me?

My wings, which usually felt heavy, seemed almost light as though they weren't even on my back, but I could feel them, as well as the raw power that still continued to flow through my legs arms and back.

I peered down at Amanda. During my transformation, she had remained in front of me, unmoving, but I was unsure why. Looking over the top of her head, Heather and Beth were stock still, like statues.

'Are you ready to finish this Amanda?' I asked her, my voice didn't sound like my own anymore, it sounded softer, angelic even.

Amanda hissed and crouched down low, her teeth bared, her hands outstretched, ready to attack, 'Bring it on!'

In a flash, she slashed at me, cutting my right arm. I recoiled from the stinging pain and retaliated, not with my hand, but with my new powerful enlarged wings. Sweeping her away, I took the chance and turned sharply behind me. With one powerful flap, I was up off the floor and through the waterfall, flying up and out into the brightening sky. I had to get her away from the others, away from their sanctuary.

Heading high into the air, I stopped and turned around. Amanda was flying right behind me, screeching in a blood-curdling way. If I hadn't had already heard it, I would have been intimidated, but not in this body. I saw her career towards me, her black claws targeting my face, but I wasn't going to allow it. With a single flap of my wings, I forced a powerful gust of wind against her that caught her wings, spinning her in the air. Taking a while to correct herself, she circled beneath me then tore off around the island and out of sight.

Frowning, I tried to think of what she was doing. Diving, I followed her as she flew around the island and tried to picture where she would go, what she would do. But then suddenly, like a blinding light hitting my eyes, I saw in my mind's eye, a black-blurred figure striking me from above and as suddenly as it came, it passed, but I knew what it was and what going to happen. I waited for it, it wouldn't be long now. Hovering over the dark still waters, I took a deep breath and closed my eyes and paid attention to the sounds around me. Waters lapped gently at the rocky formations around me, fishermen putted around the islets, casting their nets into the bays; a cold breeze danced around my head, whipping over the tops of the limestone peaks bringing with them the scent of fresh foliage. It was tranquillity. The only thing I heard that wasn't part of this majestic scenery was the sound of the rhythmic flapping of what sounded like a monstrous bat coming from above, getting closer and closer.

At the very last second that I felt the air around me shimmer with her presence, I turned around and grabbed her throat with a quick thrust of my long right arm. My fingers wrapped around her neck easily and she shrieked like some dying bird; flapping her leathery wings against me, trying to pull away. But my grip was like a vice.

'I may not be the best at everything Amanda,' I told her calmly, as she clawed at my hands managing to draw blood. 'I may not be the most intelligent, the best-looking or the best person for Henry, but there is something I know that I am good at and that's understanding situations. And you fighting me right now is a stupid thing to do.'

Falling backwards, I dove towards the sea, taking her with me. Then with such power, I threw her into the cold black waters. Out of the corner of my eye, I saw Hannah swim towards the floundering Amanda. Breaking the surface of the water, she gasped as she saw me and I shook my head as she tried to help Amanda.

'Hannah,' I began, my voice changed instantly into a firm tone. She looked at me as though I had entranced her. 'Change into your true form and call Charybdis,' I commanded glancing down at her.

Looking shocked Hannah began to yell out in pain then suddenly sank into the waters below.

I glanced back at Amanda who was now trying to swim towards the nearest island. 'You think that you wanted to be like me?' I called to her. 'To be able to fly, to go off on missions and have adventures? You're wrong Amanda; there are so many things you do not understand.'

'I know… that this isn't the end,' she spat at me, her evil red eyes trying to bore into my head. 'I am in control, I always have been… you are just a pawn in his plans. Every step you are taking is helping him. And whatever you do to me, my father, Hades, will save me.'

'Daughter or not, you have no right to be on this plane. You bring corruption, pestilence and evil. There are no evil myths in this plane, Amanda. That is what I do know. And because of that, I shall send you to where all evil myths reside.'

Suddenly from the depths of the waterline, there was a great gurgling sound. Waves unexpectedly spat at us from beneath, casting up a wall of foam, soaking me in seconds. Shaking the water from me, I rose higher into the air and glancing down I saw the sea churning. It thrashed and twisted around in a clockwise direction; starting slowly at first, but quickly speeding up. The water pushed Amanda away from its centre, towards one of the islands. With her claws, she reached out and found purchase, then rising slowly, dried herself by flapping her wings and then suddenly took to the air, hurtling towards me once more.

'I welcome you to Charybdis, Amanda,' I called to her, forcing her to stop in mid-air as she looked down at the swirling vortex. 'Sister of Scylla, she is the embodiment of Poseidon's great power to rule the oceans and a gateway back to your father.'

Her eyes suddenly went wide and she took off in the opposite direction. I followed her with four powerful flaps of my wings and reaching out, caught her left foot and pulled her back. She flapped helplessly as she struggled to free herself from my grip. 'Don't you dare,' she begged. 'Tara, I'll come after you, I swear it. I'll drag myself out of hell itself to exact my revenge on you.'

Enraged, I dived down towards the centre of the swirling maelstrom and with all my might, threw her into its core. Amanda screamed as she splashed into the whirlpool. I saw her go round a full-circle before she disappeared.

Within seconds, I heard two ear-piercing shrieks from above. Getting out of their way, Beth and Heather plunged in after Amanda, not caring about what would happen to them. But before they got swallowed up by the raging waters, I caught Beth's eye. She looked almost pitiful, but I didn't understand why.

After Charybdis had her fill, the whirlpool stopped, throwing cold water and spray up into my face. It was refreshing, but there was something else I had to take care of.

'Hannah,' I yelled out into the rough waters below. 'Hannah, come here,' I ordered her.

Moving close to the water I hovered over it and waited patiently for her to arrive. I saw her; glistening with light as she surfaced from the dark waters beneath, riding a wave and coming up to greet me.

'How are you?' I asked her.

She nodded and smiled at me.

'Do you understand?

She nodded. 'Yes, I understand everything now. I've fully changed.'

Hannah looked normal though there were very subtle differences. Her hair was a shimmering golden colour, unlike her usual chocolate brown. Her eyes a deep-sea green and her face which seemed to have been chiselled by the finest of white marble.

'My blood,' she told me as we headed back to the island with poor Darren swimming behind in a state of shock, 'my blood is a water nymph. I can control the waters and I hear the entire ocean. I'm not as powerful as Poseidon, but near enough. But now I have reached this level, there is no need to become human again.'

My heart skipped a beat at her words. She was thinking on the same lines as me. Now that I had changed fully, I didn't want to go back to being a normal human. For all intents and purposes, I didn't belong in this plane of existence anymore, I belonged in the other world; it almost felt like it was my long-lost home.

By a command from me, Darren had become human again and with my new strength, I flew them both back towards the waterfall and placed them gently on the ground.

Lottie was still in pain while Lionel and Sam looked on hopelessly unable to help her.

'You should change her,' Hannah told me looking upset at Lottie's shaking body.

'I will give her the choice,' I told her softly.

'Damn girl you are huge,' Saskia said as she stood back from me. 'I saw you kicked Amanda's ass. Congratulations.'

'There is nothing to congratulate,' I told her simply. 'She went back home, I asked Hannah to provide a means to get her there and the others followed.' Bending down, I placed my hands on Lottie and felt her pain. 'Lottie, I am giving you a chance,' I told her quietly. 'You can change now or you can change later.'

'How later is later?' she asked me, her voice quivering. Though the Furies had gone, Lottie's mythological blood had kicked in and was forcing her to become her myth counterpart, but she was refusing to let it happen and it was causing her intense pain. The fear that Lottie had felt had pushed her tattoo to its limit. She had to change now to gain some relief.

Sighing I knelt next to her, 'Amanda, Heather and Beth have sparked off your change and you will not accept it at this moment in time but know this Lottie, the sooner the better. If you wait you will remain in agony but if I command to change you the pain will go away.'

'You know what I am, don't you?' she asked turning her head slightly to look into my eyes.

Sadly, I nodded. Her owl-like eyes and the heat she gave off, plus the fact that she was getting smaller, only led to one possible conclusion.

'Do it,' she sobbed, 'get it over and done with.'

'Lottie no,' Sam ran over to her. 'You don't have to do this. If you calm down, you'll feel better.' Holding her quivering body, being careful to not touch her scalding skin, she looked up at him and shook her head.

Stammering softly she replied, 'No, I won't.'

Sam desperately wanted to take the pain from her, but he knew there was nothing he could do for her. He shot me a look of contempt. As though this was all my fault. 'Can you make the change less painful?'

I shook my head. 'It's the same for all of us.' I knew that Lottie shouldn't be changed on this plane. Myths weren't allowed here. We belonged to the magical one and the more of us there were who change into mythical creatures, those on the other side would feel it and the balance would be tipped.

Raising my hand, I motioned Sam to move. Gently turning to Lottie, he kissed the top of her head, then standing up moved away from her, wiping his sweating brow. 'Lottie,' I said standing up and backing away from her while motioning the others to do the same, 'change.'

Lottie screamed in silent agony. Tears flowed out of her eyes and she grabbed her hair and began to yank it out; the strands fell to the floor then quickly disintegrated from the heat she was emitting.

'Lottie,' Hannah yelled as she tried to get near her to comfort her.

'Everyone back away,' I commanded them.

I glanced over towards Saskia and Henry who were cowering from Lottie. Rhea on the other hand seemed delighted, wearing an acidulated smile, but I didn't understand why.

Unlike my own, Lottie's transformation was long and by the looks of it ten times more painful. After all, she was turning into a creature.

'Do something,' Saskia yelled at me, the pain in her eyes made my heart hurt for her, but there was nothing I could do. We just had to wait.

Lottie suddenly stopped screaming and relief softened her face. Then as though greeting an old friend, she smiled and suddenly her clothes went up in flames; black smoke billowed around the cave making it impossible to see. Everyone began to choke. With one beat of my huge wings the smoke began to clear and I cringed away at the sight in front of me. Lottie was on fire. From an outsider's perspective, it looked like she was self-combusting. Flames erupted from her skin, burning and crisping it to a fine grey ash which fluttered to the floor.

'Oh my God!' Lionel and Darren yelled out in shock.

As though a vampire had been staked, Lottie began to turn into ash then, within seconds, her body was gone. Only a pile of cinders was left.

No one moved. Everyone was motionless yet verging on the pinnacle of shouting out in shock, or crying from the horror of what they had just witnessed. The only thing I heard was slow breathing with quickened, scared heartbeats.

Glancing down at the floor and searched for a few stones. I picked up each one and held them in my hands tightly. After a half a minute or so they had become rather warm from the pressure. I placed the stones around the pile of ash and gently blew and there in the middle was the cutest little yellow bird, all fluffy and vulnerable.

'What is she?' I heard Henry whisper in a frightened tone from behind me.

Not wanting to disturb the stones around her that were still keeping Lottie warm, I leaned away from her and turned to stare at him. The others grouped together, glancing in a frightened way at Lottie's small form. Hannah was silently crying as Darren comforted her. Sam and Lionel had turned pale as wax. 'Lottie is a phoenix. In truth Lottie, the human, is gone. But the blood that's in her has taken over and she has been born again.'

'From out of the ashes the phoenix rises,' Darren uttered gently.

Smiling I nodded. 'In time Lottie will grow, rather more substantially than normal birds. But there is a price which she has paid,' I said sadly.

'She won't be able to turn into a human will she?' Henry asked me, his voice cracking with anguish.

I stood up and looked at him. His face was contorted in pain, but he already knew the answer. 'Not like we used to. Lottie has fully changed, like Hannah and I. If there is a way to turn her human, I don't know it. But I won't be able to change her back, even if I commanded it.'

Sam looked away, but I saw a small tear rolled down his face. Before it reached his chin he quickly wiped it away. 'Will she keep her memories of being human?' He asked.

I shrugged my shoulders. 'It's all up to Lottie. Though her body has gone, her spirit, her mind is still in there somewhere.' Glancing at her I suppressed a sob. I hated what I had done to her, but there was no other choice.

Sam knelt beside her. 'She looks cold. We need to build a fire.' Henry suddenly scarpered off while I picked up each stone and pressed them into my hands. Moments later he came inside and began to rub some sticks together. And with Darren and Lionel helping, they made a fire.

Placing the stones around the fire, I picked Lottie up and placed her in the fire.

'WHA' DA HELL ARE YOUS DOING?' Saskia screamed as she tried to get to the fire.

Restraining her with ease, Hannah forced her back. 'Phoenix's need a lot of warmth when they are born. Even mythical birds such as these are vulnerable to the cold climates on this plane or the next. Please Saskia, let Tara help her.'

'But you're burnin' her all over again,' Saskia yelled, tears flowing down her cheeks. I didn't realise that Saskia was so upset for Lottie. To me, Saskia didn't seem capable of liking anyone to the point of crying for them, but I guess Lottie had touched all our hearts in some way or another, Sam especially.

Gently walked to Saskia, I put my hand on her shoulder. 'Come and look.'

Everyone carefully gathered around the little campfire. Several gasps of shock came from their mouths as they began to see Lottie's fluffy, yellow, down feathers being replaced by young adult ones.

'Talk to her, Hannah,' I said to her softly. 'She is your best friend. Maybe you'll be able to give her some memories back when she is an adult.'

'And when will that be?' Sam asked darkly.

Pondering on the sight of Lottie and her already rapid development I said, 'Maybe a few days or so. Though, it'll be interesting in how she will be able to communicate with us.'

Darren frowned. I was about to explain to him when Henry got there first.

'She's a bird and birds don't speak,' he told him looking sad.

'Um parrots speak,' Darren retorted.

'She's not a parrot,' Saskia shouted at him.

'No, but she's special,' Sam said sadly, stopping everyone from shouting. 'She's always been special.'

'She has.' Hannah cried softly.

Not wanting to crowd them while they were crying over Lottie, I stood up and backed away from the group. Lionel gave me an evil stare as I left. His hated hurt me. He was blaming me for the ordeal I had put Lottie through.

Leaving the cave, I decided to walk down to the tip of the island instead of fly. When I came to the top, I noticed that the new, fresh morning was fast approaching. It had become significantly lighter since my fight with Amanda but, after everything that had happened this past night, I still had a job to do; I had to solve the riddle. A few moments later, Saskia and Henry caught up with me. I smiled. I had heard them talk about whether to follow me or not. The only down-side to having super-hearing was that you would inevitably hear something you didn't want to.

'Hey Tara, wait up,' Henry called.

I stopped by a large clump of tall grass and turned to face them.

'Tell me,' Saskia said softly as she came closer to me, her eyes showing so much apprehension. 'Tell me what it's like.'

I knew what she was talking about, but I was unsure if she was ready to know what she would be leaving behind. Expelling air, I turned to look at her, or rather look down at her. 'Saskia, the power is unreal. My eyesight has improved, as well as my strength and my hearing. I even have the ability to see the future at points when my own life is in danger or when there are things I need to see in order to understand.' Saskia frowned in confusion and shaking my head I got straight down to it, 'Saskia, I don't think I can become human again. Just like Lottie, this is the end for me.'

'But what about Hannah?' Henry demanded looking angry. 'She's still human.'

I shook my head again, 'No she's not. She is a water nymph. One of the daughters of Poseidon. Hannah belongs to the sea now. It's almost cruel to ask her to come with us.'

'For God's sake!' Saskia yelled in frustration. 'The group number is dropping like flies. I blame this on Macie. This is all 'er fault.'

Henry sighed and closed his eyes shut. 'I just want to know where this is all leading. We've had bits of information left, right, and centre and we're still no closer to why the hell we're here. I thought you said that Annabel talked of a war. Shouldn't we do something about that and try and stop it?'

I smiled. 'We're here because we have no choice. By pure accident, the T.A.T. have created their own enemies, us. Annabel told us that we will both cause and prevent the war. I shouldn't be here in the human world, but things must continue the way they are going, regardless.'

'Our world is the human world,' Saskia quipped, but I merely shrugged my shoulders. I had no reply for her, so I continued.

'Back in the 1980's, our parents tried to get hold of this Phaistos Disc but it was lost. The disc was one of the ways to get into the other plane. Maynard is now using us to open up a portal to it and spark a war. The myths will come here to fight us. We're not meant to be here. I can feel it. In any case, we need to find out the second part of the riddle.'

'The bamboo trail,' Saskia gasped.

Nodding, I pointed towards the point of the tail. 'I need to head down there and start searching in the right way. Though, if it's anything as crazy as the chairs then well, you best leave it to me.'

'Oh hell no,' Henry shook his head. 'I am not going to miss this. Besides you may need my claws,' he held up his fists, waving them in front of me.

Saskia folded her arms and gave him a pathetic look. 'Henry, by the looks of Tara, she can rip ya in two. Forget ya little kitty claws, Tara's got uber muscles. Did ya see wha' she did to Amanda's freaky devil tail?'

I cringed away at the thought and turned away from them and began to walk off. I didn't want to remember what I had done. It was in the past and I had to look towards the future.

'Hey, Tara wait up,' Saskia called as they trotted after me.

CHAPTER SEVENTEEN

THE THREE OF US REACHED THE VERY TIP OF THE SHARK'S fin, but searching the area, I did not see any bamboo which puzzled the hell out of me. Henry and Saskia also looked frustrated and started looking around on the floor for evidence of bamboo, but I looked to the south to the other point of the fin. I stared at it for a long time but still came up with nothing.

Annoyed with the silence Saskia bellowed, 'Wha' the 'ell are we lookin' for?'

Giving an exasperated sigh, I turned around and calmly said, 'Find the shark that's out of water; keep a weather eye open and be prepared for some swimming. We will have reached its fin by a bamboo trail. X will not be the start, but it will be the end of your beginning.' I suddenly groaned and shook my head. I had been thinking like a human. 'We're going about this the wrong way, literally. We need to go underwater to get to the shark's fin.'

'Huh? But we're on it,' Saskia asked in a puzzled tone.

'I mean underneath it,' I said looking down. 'The sea level has changed, plus a shark has many fins, dorsal, pectoral. There must be sea caves or tunnels underneath this island. I need Hannah.'

After calling for her outside the cave, Hannah appeared a few minutes later, her face like stone. I felt horrid taking her away from Lottie, but I needed her. 'When you were in the water did you notice anything strange about this island?'

Hannah's eyebrows rose in awe and she nodded. 'Yes but how did you know?'

'The riddle,' Saskia interjected. 'Big gob over 'ere,' nodding towards me, 'said tha' there might be tunnels under the island.'

Hannah nodded. 'No, not human-made tunnels. However, there is a cave system underneath. I could feel the currents passing through it.'

'Okay, will ya two stop with the human-thing? I'm startin' to feel insulted,' Saskia snapped.

Hannah looked surprised. 'You think that way too? That we aren't human anymore?'

I nodded sadly. 'Yes. I wonder if Lottie feels the same way,' I asked myself.

There was a moment or two where I thought about the others and whether they'd have the same feeling and wisdom as Hannah and I. But Hannah tapped me on the arm, reminding me of my plan. 'You called for me Tara. What do you want?'

Minutes later, Hannah dove down into the dark, cool waters. I had asked her to go under the island and see if she could see anything out of the ordinary, specifically a tunnel.

'She's been down there a long time,' Saskia groaned as we sat on some rocks near the water's edge close to where Hannah dived off.

'Water Nymph,' I told her sternly. 'She'll be alright.'

Henry and I weren't sitting together. In fact, since I had changed, there were two things I noticed instantly. For one, he barely looked at me and the second he wanted to keep some distance between us. My brain felt completely confused. There was one side of me where I wanted to spend some time alone with him, but the other side of me wanted nothing to do with him. It was as though I was repulsed by him because he was still human. Mentally shaking my head of these thoughts, I tried to focus on what was going on around me.

There were five fishing boats that were within sight of the island, but with their human eyes, they wouldn't be able to see us sitting on the rock waiting for a Water Nymph to spring out of the water. But what did concern me, was that pretty soon, more boats will be making their way to and fro to the little harbour as the night wore on. We needed to get this over and done with quickly.

'Um Tara,' Henry said snapping me out of my focus. 'I want to ask you something.'

Glancing towards him, I caught his eyes shining in the moonlight. He was staring straight ahead, determined not to look at me. 'What is it?' Mentally pleading for him to look at me, but he didn't.

'Would you change us if we asked you?' Henry asked me softly.

It wasn't something I expected him to ask. I stood up, towering over him, 'Only if you asked me.'

Henry finally made eye contact with me. 'Do you know what I will look like?'

I nodded once. 'Yes, but you and Sam-.'

'Sam?' he interjected, 'you know what he is?' Henry asked his mouth hanging open slightly.

'Yes, he's a-' I didn't manage to finish that sentence as I felt what I could only think of was thunder rumble up from beneath me. I stood stock-still, listening, but I heard nothing but the soft lapping of the waves against the island and the putting noise that came from the fisherman close by. 'Hannah,' I whispered. 'Something's wrong.'

Saskia and Henry suddenly jumped up and ran to the edge to peer over the side of the small rocky cliff, but my eyes snapped to a figure, dressed in Victorian clothing with odd looking spectacles, a walking stick and very heavy moustache. He stood ten feet away from me with a look of concern on his face. There would be only one name for this ghost; it was no surprise that he was here.

'Hello, Mr Raleigh,' I said inclining my head.

'Forget hellos, your friend is in danger. The cave has collapsed she didn't figure it out. She's in trouble.'

Out of the corner of my eye, I saw Saskia stare in shock at Mr Raleigh. Henry stood up and looked at where I was looking at, but his eyes passed through him, unable to see.

'Mr Raleigh?' Henry asked in a quizzical way, 'but isn't he that man who made that ridiculous riddle?'

'Ridiculous? Ha,' Mr Raleigh snorted in a pompous manner. 'I'll have you know Sir that it is not ridiculous. Only the person who could figure out the chairs is meant to follow the rest of the riddle into the waters.'

'But she's a Water Nymph,' Saskia said as though it was the answer to Hannah's problems but Mr Raleigh shook his head. 'Hannah can breathe underwater, she's magical. 'ow come she is in danger?'

Mr Raleigh frowned a little. 'Water Nymph or not, there are spells and enchantments down there that renders her powerless with those types of abilities. Only a true Siren can go down there. Only true Sirens can breathe underwater.'

'She can't breathe underwater,' Saskia snapped at Mr Raleigh; thinking he was completely deluded.

'You're a Siren, a Siren of the sea. Not to mention Tara's immortal.' He sounded impatient. 'You wouldn't drown; only by magic can an immortal be killed.'

Saskia and I were both stunned into silence; Henry on the other hand looked confused with the looks on our faces.

'Uh oh, what have you been told?' he asked behind me.

'Forget that, just get down there!' Mr Raleigh shouted. 'Go Tara, before it's too late.'

About to fly off, Saskia shouted, 'Take ya bag, ya might need it,' she said throwing it at me.

I looked at Henry and sighed. 'Damn it, I have to go.' Spreading my wings I jumped off the cliff.

'Tara, come back, you'll drown,' Henry called after me.

But before I hit the water, I heard Saskia say, 'No she won't, she'll be fine.' I took a deep breath and plunged headfirst into the calm sea, my body was instantly saturated with salt water. I swam down using my wings for extra momentum; pushing me through the water. Reaching the bottom in seconds, I searched for an entrance to the cave, but I didn't see anything. Passing colourful flitting squid, ancient coral and old sunken boats, I began to swim around anti-clockwise around the island then suddenly, a great torrent of water began to push against me, forcing me close to the jagged rocks of the island. Using my wings, hands and feet, I back peddled away from the current and decided to look around. As I went around the current, I noticed something odd about the rock-face. Near a large clump of coral that was bedecked with multi-coloured stones that I managed to see in the hue of the morning sun, there was a strange door-like opening. 'Bingo, I've found the opening,' I thought as I swum towards it, seeing a large enough gap for me to squeeze through. Spooking some tiny shimmering fish that flittered around, I pushed my large body into the perilously dark cave. I quickly realised that my new perfect vision didn't include night time vision and, what's more, I was wasting time.

Feeling around the rocks I used my wings to test how big the opening was but I still couldn't see. 'Damn, I need some help.' I thought, panicking that I was running out of time. Then, not two minutes later and completely without warning, something fell into the water above me, sending disorientating bubbles flourishing around. Something cold and slippery grabbed my hand and pulled me deeper into the cavern. My face was grabbed and lips pressed against mine blowing fresh air into my lungs.

Pulling away in shock, whoever it was gently lifted my hand to their face. I yelped, leaking bubbles out of my mouth. It was Darren!

'Can you hear me?' More bubbles escaped from my mouth from the surprise and he laughed, 'The telepathy only works if our bodies are connected. Use your thoughts to talk to me. And as far as I know, Sirens can breathe underwater, but that's why I'm here anyway. Saskia heard every thought when you got into the water. She said that you needed help, and here I am.'

There was no way I was going to inhale water though strangely enough I felt as though the air was sort of unnecessary. But Darren struck a chord. 'Saskia can hear my thoughts?' I thought and Darren laughed again. 'Well, that can't be good.'

'See, it does work.' Darren took his hand away from me, but I wasn't done with him yet. I grabbed his hand and held it tightly.

'Hannah is trapped down here, but I can't see in the dark and I have no idea how to solve this riddle yet. You need to help me.'

'Yeah, sure fine, don't get your wings in a knot,' he said, then taking my hand like a gentleman, he tugged me forwards into the murky black of the cave. Veering left and right, I gathered that he was taking me around rocks and through other parts of the cave, but it was horrible, claustrophobic and dark.

I felt that we had stopped moving in the water, but I saw nothing apart from the black. 'I see her; she's right in front of us under a rock.'

'Guide me to her, maybe I can lift her free.'

Darren carefully guided me through the blackness, telling me now and again what to be aware of and then placed my hands on a large rough rock. With some difficulty, I placed my feet on the sandy ground and finding some purchase on the cave floor began to push it up.

Darren informed me what to do during the entire process, but I couldn't see what I was dealing with.

'I need light,' I said and then added quickly, 'can you see anything odd around here?' I asked him ensuring his hand was firmly on my head.

'No, well... apart from some odd-looking gaps in the rock which may lead outside of the cave, but they are blocked, why?'

'Go and see if you can unblock them,' it was a request, not an order.

'Yes, master,' he slurred then taking his hand away from me, I felt a rush of stirred water and the slickness from the end of his tail as he swam off.

A few moments later, a striking beam of light came right into the cave which hit a mirror and then reflected off that and struck another. I smiled as soon the cave was lit up with pure morning sunlight. Darren went around and brushed off the algae and seaweed that clung to the other mirrors and I quickly saw the extent that Hannah was stuck. A huge rock had pinned her down in betwixt some rather pointy looking rocks and she looked in terrible pain.

'Don't worry, I'll get you out,' I mouthed to her.

Finding the right way to lift the rock, without crushing her, Darren came over and together we lifted it just long enough so that Hannah could get out. Letting go of the rock, it smashed down onto the floor; sand erupted around me, blurring my vision. Waiting for it to settle, I felt something odd like something hot and prickly attacking my body, but as soon as this sensation began it quickly faded.

Hannah's eyes quickly darted to Darren and without warning he doubled over in pain; his eyes squinting shut and suddenly in a blast of bright red light, Darren was human again and completely naked.

Trying to avert my eyes, Hannah quickly dashed over to him and giving me a strange look for the briefest moment, grabbed Darren and took him back out of the cave.

Turning round, I began to follow her, but unexpectedly the cave began to rumble. The sounds like muffled thunder pinched at my eardrums with silt and sand exploding around all around me.

Hannah stopped and turned around just as she was about to get out, she was waiting for me.

'Keep going,' I mouthed to her, urging her on.

Nodding, she swiftly made it out of the cave, before the entrance was blocked by several large rocks that had come loose from above. Heading right to the blocked entrance, I tried to bulldoze my way through but after a while it proved impossible. Even my new strength was no match for the tonnes of rock. Trying not to panic, I searched for another way out and was thankful that the crumbling cave system hadn't displaced the mirrors.

With the sand beginning to settle, I swam back to the large rock that Hannah had been stuck under and tried to find some sort of way out, but there was nothing that I could see. From what I gathered, the cave was just one large chamber.

I moved around the large rock to see if there was any possibility of getting out, like maybe a smaller gap that I could punch through, but after looking I saw that there wasn't a gap. There was, however, a strange looking symbol, like an arrow which had been weathered away by the water that passed through the cave… and this arrow, pointed up.

'Oh my God… what, an idiot,' I thought smiling. The rock which had fallen on Hannah must have been a booby-trap which she'd blundered right into; but whether by mistake, fluke or accident, the rock revealed a perfect hole, that led to another chamber which I stupidly hadn't noticed until now.

Kicking off from the sea-bed, I rushed at the hole and burst out of the water, inhaling good clean air that hadn't been forced into me by a merman. 'Gross,' I said to myself, thinking of his slippery fish lips. 'Henry needs to kick his arse.'

Turning a full circle in the water, I looked around and I saw that the light from beneath shone feebly into the new chamber, casting shimmering water ripples on the chamber walls. Swimming to the edge of the hole, I hefted myself out and plonked my bag on the ground and collapsed next to it, trying to calm my nerves.

'I'm stuck under an island with the only entrance and exit blocked,' I told myself. 'Oh joy.'

Pulling the bag from under me, I opened it up and to my surprise found one of the torches from the helicopter that Henry had flown. I flicked it on, amazed that it was still working but what astounded me further still, was the chamber itself.

'Holy kack,' I gasped.

The walls of the chamber were covered in symbols and strange swirling patterns that looked familiar but had no meaning to me. As though I was developing a habit, or maybe a nervous twitch, I brought out Mr Raleigh's book and flicked through the pages, hoping to find something interesting, but the only thing that fell out was the letter and a random piece of folded up scrap paper. Curious, I opened it up and mentally hit myself, 'Oh you idiot,' I said again. Everything came flooding back to me. The weird markings on the chairs. I had made a written copy of them. Glancing at the symbols on the walls, they all matched with each other but as quickly as I figured this all out the adrenalin rush ebbed away. I didn't know what they meant!

'Well, there wasn't a Rosetta Stone on the chairs,' I said out loud, 'and aren't any decipherment's in the book so… they are… where?'

Getting up, I stared hard at the symbols but none of them looked like anything Egyptian or Greek that I might be able to take a stab at. They were completely alien to me. Even to my new mythical brain they made no sense.

Sweeping the torch around the chamber, a blink of white light struck the corner of my eyes for a brief moment, and then it was gone. Repeating the same moment, slowly I caught the reflection of another small mirror that was imbedded into the ceiling. Turning the beam to the mirror, it flashed down into the chamber beneath; illuminating the large rock that Hannah was trapped under.

I stuck my head under the water and with the torch poised over the surface. I saw to my bewilderment it was the Rosetta Stone I was looking for. There embossed on the top were symbols from the chairs and the ceiling and so too were the Roman alphabet.

Taking a few loose rocks from the side of the chamber, I propped up the torch and pointed it right at the mirror. Diving down, I peered at the symbols which corresponded with the others.

As first glimpse, I thought it would be a piece of cake, but I was wrong and I knew it was going to be a tedious task. I shouldn't have thought that this would be easy; the chairs, after all, knackered me out. Planning the task ahead, I sighed in annoyance. I would need something to write with so I could decipher the symbols. As I didn't have a pen on me, which apparently every woman carries in her bag, I had to dive down to the stone, find the symbols, memorise how they look, get out of the water and scrawl each one on the side of the wall where I could find space, matching it with the letter.

Needless to say it took me quite some time and after half an hour, I was extremely tired but as soon as I finished, I sat there and stared at the letters on the wall and began to slowly translate them. However, after a while I got confused as they didn't make sense.

The symbols didn't seem to follow the lines of a sentence, not in its structure at least. With Japanese writing it goes either top to bottom or right to left, and with English, as well as the majority of other languages on the planet, it was written left to right but this was, odd. They seemed to be, boxed like some stupid puzzle you'd find in a newspaper and each set of symbols looking like some weird So-Do-Ku puzzle.

The letters didn't seem to make any sense at all. They were all jumbled up as though they were... 'Frigging anagrams. God I HATE anagrams!' I shouted to myself.

Trying to go about it methodically, I grouped each set of symbols into numbers and began with the ones on the left at the top.

'Right so I have…E…F…O…B…R…E. Efobre,' I said to myself. 'What the hell is that? I stared at it for ages until suddenly my ancient brain kicked in. 'Ah 'Before', okay nice thing to start out with,' I smiled sheepishly.

Grabbing my rock-pen, I went to the other side of the chamber, where I found out quickly that there were no other exits, and began to translate all of the sets of symbols.

After what felt like two hours, I came up with "Before humans, the Ancient's ruled the land and divided the world into three."

I quickly guessed that 'three' meant three different planes. The other plane which we were going to end up in, the human plane that we were in now and the Underworld or the plane I sent Amanda's sorry arse.

Crossing out each deciphered set of symbols, I continued on with the next. "With the birth of myths in which the Ancients created for the humans, the humans then gave worship. But soon renounced their belief –thus war was brought forth. The Ancients decreed that myths must be kept in the magical plane and sent forth a key to open a door to the mythical world."

'Ohh,' I said as I deciphered the last sentence, then squealed in joy as I translated the next few sets of text. "The Phaistos Disc was bequeathed to the humans so they may travel to the Ancients and plead forgiveness. Thus, when they did, they became Gods and Goddesses of the Ancient Worlds."

'Holy crap,' I gasped.

When I first read the word "Ancients" I thought it meant the true Gods and Goddesses of the world, and not just Roman or Greek deities, but also Egyptian, Norse, Japanese, African and Celtic. But it seemed there was a whole other group of people, who were the rightful Ancients of the world. 'Man, this is getting deep,' I thought to myself, perplexed. 'My group are just ancient fodder compared to the true Gods and Goddesses.'

Still confused, I translated the last few sets, which looked different from the other sets, but they weren't particularly helpful… "The end of the X has just begun, say the magic words and be prepared to run."

'What magic words?' I asked out loud to no one, but there was no answer. Frustrated, I sat on the floor and stared at the last translated lines. Gazing around the entire chamber I saw no way out and also no more symbols to help me. There was nothing else. 'Come on Tara, think,' I told myself in a strong manner. 'What else is there?'

I groaned, feeling miserable that I couldn't figure out this wretched puzzle. 'Avarda Kadavra,' I laughed but nothing happened. 'Ahh think! What else has symbols?'

This time, I did actually smack myself at my stupidity. There in front of me, a little soggy from being splashed as I dived into the water several times, was the piece of scrap paper.

After translating it, I laughed out loud. 'This is so lame,' I said picking up my bag and torch and took a deep breath. 'Open Sesame.'

Internal thunder trembled around me instantly. Cracks that split the ceiling like fork-lightning were shaken loose and began to collapse. Large chunks of symbol-covered rock fell around me. Yelping, I side-stepped out of the way and picked up my bag as I judged the moments each rock was about to fall and then I saw something green which poked out from the ceiling.

'Wow, its bamboo,' I exclaimed, recognising the foliage.

More rock tumbled and fell into the water below, splashing me. Opening my wings and trying not to let any rocks fall on me, I jumped into the air and grabbed hold of the bamboo and dragged myself up through a small narrow gap between the thick knotting canes. Folding my wings back tight against me, I used the torch and crawled up through what looked like a knotted tube of bamboo which seemed to lead in a slanted way, heading north towards the main part of the island. For about twenty minutes, I crawled on my belly and squeezed through the vibrant green canes, when suddenly I smelt the whiff of salt air.

Snapping back some spindly looking stems, bright warm sunlight welcomed me. Hauling myself out of the tunnel of bamboo and onto clean dry land I fell to the floor and laid there catching my breath. 'I don't... ever... want... to do that... again,' I panted and closed my eyes as I rested on the ground.

As I got into the small cave past the waterfall, I was welcomed with an exuberant 'Tara!' from the group and was immediately bombarded with twenty questions.

'What happened?' Was the first one I wanted to answer, but as soon as I opened my mouth another followed.

'Did you solve the riddle, is there another part?'

'Can you breathe under water? It didn't seem like it from Darren's perspective,' Rhea quipped.

I glanced at Henry who had remained quiet and he quickly looked away from me. I made a mental note to have a quiet word with him.

'Alright guys enough with the questions,' I said to them firmly, raising my palms to stem their words. 'I'll answer them in a minute.' My attention turned to the little fire that was made earlier. Walking towards her the others parted showing little Lottie asleep in the embers and hot stones.

'She's been asleep since you left,' Sam told me. 'We've been talking to her but she... she doesn't seem to be acknowledging us,' he said sadly but I wasn't buying it.

I knelt down and got as close to the fire as possible. 'Lottie, I know you're depressed and you can fully blame it on me-' one eye slowly opened and it stared right at me, 'but you're not in pain anymore.'

'No, I'm just gonna be stuck as a bird for the rest of my life,' Sam said suddenly.

I frowned and saw everybody looking at him. Sam clapped his hands to his mouth, apparently shocked.

'Wha' did you jus' say?' Saskia asked, but he shook his head and I quickly knew why.

'That is amazing! Oh well done Lottie,' I beamed at her.

Wearing a mixture of Sam and Henry's clothes, Darren stepped into view looking thoroughly confused. 'What's going on, I don't get it?'

About to reply to him, Henry beat me to it. 'She's throwing her voice, like a ventriloquist. I've seen it before with Odin's ravens. They could only speak if someone who was capable of speech was near them, but out of all of us, Lottie picked Sam.'

'Well she wouldn't have picked me.' I laughed.

'You got that right,' Sam snapped at me.

The others giggled finding it funny, but staring at Lottie, I picked up on her unhappiness. Once again I was to blame for something I had to act on with little or no alternative.

'Lottie, I have to ask you this and I would like a straight answer. Do you feel wiser, do you know more?'

'Yes,' Sam spoke for her, 'Yes I do know more.'

Hannah and I shared a look and I slightly nodded. 'Any way,' I wanted to change the conversation. The group needed something else to focus on. 'The riddle... was weird, similar to the chairs and also exhausting, hence why I'm a little late. But there is one thing that's new and it kind of freaked me out.'

'Oh, this can't be good,' Hannah said, who seemed perfectly fine apart from the fact she was clutching her waist, like she was getting some sort of stomach cramp.

I nodded. 'The God and Goddesses of mythology; their image, their blood that we've been given, well it's like a strange cycle,' I said to their confused faces. 'Beings called Ancients created the Gods and Goddesses of mythology. It is most likely what Annabel had talked about. Knowing about the Ancients is the secret that Maynard is after. The knowledge of the Ancients existence and how to get to them. The Ancients gave a Phaistos Disc to humans, to act as a key to visit the Ancients. But when they did, they became Gods or Goddesses.'

Saskia's face lit up in understanding, 'Ahh, so tha's wha' ya mean by ancient fodder. I can hear ya think, so please don't think soppy sex things when you're talkin' to 'enry,' she added, then seeing the way I reacted she ploughed on. 'But tha' is deep. I guess I would be freaked out.'

'Okay, confused dot com over here,' Rhea shouted out. 'The gods and that lot, they are infallible right?'

'Oh, the little girl can make big words,' Sam said staring at her. Quickly looking at Lottie she clicked her beak. 'I didn't say it, Sam did.'

I moaned at their childishness and continued. 'Maybe now, but the gods used to be humans- humans who returned to the ancients and who worshipped them.'

Darren glanced at everyone before he asked, 'Okay I'm thick, what does infallible mean?'

Henry took a step towards him, folding his arms. 'Infallible means completely perfect, can do nothing wrong.'

'King Arthur's sword Excalibur was infallible,' Hannah added.

Rhea frowned and shook her head, 'King Arthur didn't exist.'

'Yes he did.' Henry interjected, 'Excalibur is a real sword. Right Tara, continue.'

'I think Maynard wants to become a God. It's the only explanation for it. He wants power.'

Lionel asked to see the little red book and passing it to him; he whizzed through it and then promptly closed it. 'Nope nothing about the Phaistos Disc or the Ancients.'

'Well, there isn't going to be anything in there if the Ancients were before humans and then the humans became Gods and Goddesses,' Sam told him.

'So what else did this riddle indicate?' Lionel asked me.

'Apart from an Ancient creating the Phaistos Disc for King Minos, the riddle also pointed out that it was then that human belief and religion began.'

Saskia looked right at me and gave me a small smile back. She had also talked to Annabel that night on the ship. We both knew what that meant, and so did the others. Rhea on the other hand looked shocked and shied away.

'What do you know?' I demanded from her.

Cringing at my tone she said, 'King Minos is being held in Wales. He was in the facility we were staying in while waiting to leave and come here... DAMN IT!' she yelled. 'Why do you have to keep doing that?'

'Because you wouldn't have told her the truth if she had asked politely,' Lionel grumbled. 'We don't trust you Rhea, isn't it obvious?'

'I never asked you to trust me,' she shouted back. 'I never wanted to be this,' she said gesturing at her body. 'I used to be normal once. Whatever that is. '

'None of us wanted any of this,' Hannah said softly. 'But we can't change that...'

I folded my arms, my eyes shifting between Rhea and the floor. 'We already knew that King Minos was in Wales, but not where,' I smirked, forming a plan. 'That's our next port of call.'

As the others began to prepare to leave, I moved over had to Henry. 'We need to talk,' I said to him quietly as the others gathered around Lottie. Nodding, he followed me out of the cave and we headed away down the trail. I stopped by some sweet-smelling flowers and faced him. 'What is bothering you?'

'You, doing that,' he said looking up at me. 'Looking down at me as though I'm a lowly human. Your eyes have changed against me.' He slumped against a leaning tree. 'I feel like I can't protect you anymore and I should be protecting you... If I'm being honest, it hurts me.'

My heart was heavy. I knew he was feeling that way because deep down, Henry wanted to be the protector. Throughout our travels, he was the one to catch me when I fell; to help me when I was down. He was that sort of guy. He was chivalrous and men like that don't come along very often. But though I understood him, I was feeling the same thing as Henry. As the leader and a Siren, I felt that I had to protect everyone. 'Henry, I get it, but you have to understand that this is how it is. I'm sorry it upsets you. There's nothing I can do.'

Henry's face fell and there was an uncomfortable silence between us. Folding his arms, he paced back and forth in front of me kicking dirt and thinking all the while. To be honest I knew what he was thinking, I had been thinking the same thing too, but I didn't want to voice it, I didn't want it to end up like that. Quietly he said, 'I'd feel differently if I changed.'

I shook my head, 'No Henry, don't think like that. Why shorten your time being human just to try and prove a point?'

'If there was a chance of you becoming human again, then it wouldn't matter would it?' he asked, tilting his head like a curious puppy.

Looking away from him I tried to think about this rationally. If there was a chance we could all be human again, the question I had to answer myself was... did I want to? My life had been epically destroyed, university was out of the question, I had no job, I hardly talked to my brother or my parents and now that I knew about the magical world, could I leave it all behind? I had no real reason to give it up.

'We'd all be happy again,' Henry finished but he didn't sound happy. 'What are you thinking about?' he asked as he looked at my confused face.

'You are presuming everything; us becoming human and with it our lives going back to the way they were. It won't Henry. Everything has taken a turn for the worse. Macie's gone, Lottie, Sam and Lionel hate me and this group has one extra addition we could do without.'

'Not to mention we are going to be in for some rough weather,' he said in a matter-of-fact way.

Completely off topic, I turned to face him to ask him what he was talking about but his face said it all. I saw what he was looking at and gasped out loud. There, in the distance, rolling towards us like some monstrous black beast, was a huge thunderous looking cloud.

'Something's coming for us.' I began to back away. As soon as I said that a great gust of wind blew at us, nearly forcing my wings to open it was that strong. 'Get back to the cave!' Together we began to scarper up the hill and back towards the waterfall.

Chapter Eighteen

Running pell-mell into the hidden cave on the top of the hill, Henry and I turned around to see the dark cloud cover the island. It was no ordinary cloud that was for sure and I was beginning to panic that that cloud was because of me for disturbing the cave or… 'Hannah,' I said quickly, piecing the puzzle together. 'It's for you,' I said as though handing a telephone over to her.

She stood up and came over to me, all the time staring out towards the darkness that had suddenly descended into the bay, the morning rays vanishing like a puff of smoke. In the distance, I heard the waves bash against the rocks; a far cry from the gentle lapping they did not ten minutes ago.

'I can feel it,' she said in a whimper. 'But why, I don't understand.'

'The letter,' Lionel said raising his hand to get our attention, 'the letter said, "keep a weather eye open". I think we were meant to leave as soon as we found out the riddle.'

Saskia nodded, 'Mr Raleigh told us that there are spells and enchantments in the cave. Both Hannah and Darren got hit with them. Maybe it's a form of cheating.'

'He said that only I could get into the cave,' I added. 'I bet the book is magical, placed with the same magic as the cave. It makes sense.'

Then at that precise moment, a horrendous deep clashing pang of thunder rumbled over our heads, as though threatening to tear the sky in two. I felt the vibrations course through me like an electric volt and quickly glancing at the others, they felt it also. The loudness of it almost gave way to the sense of a great and powerful presence, like it was commanding everyone's attention that it had arrived.

'I, I have to go,' Hannah said in a strange voice.

Darren stood up and offered his hand to Hannah, 'I'm going with you.'

Smiling, Hannah took his hand and he helped her up. 'I don't think I go alone, thank you.'

The others were confused and looked between them and me, but I kept silent. This wasn't my command to give. This was what they were created for. Whether it was the sea itself that was beckoning Hannah to it or a God or Goddess in which their DNA flowed in them, I could only guess. But whatever it was, I wasn't a part of it.

Even though the Siren in me cowered away from this almost regal presence, it wasn't calling for me; I was only half of water, the other half, I was of the sky.

Joining hands, Darren and Hannah walked out of the cave in silence and past the waterfall. A single tear rolled down my cheek and quietly I said, 'I will see you two again soon.'

'Wait, what's going on?' Lionel shouted as he moved to follow them, but I spread my right wing out, stopping him in his tracks. Lottie squawked in protest, but the sound was lost to the waterfall and howling wind that pushed itself into the cave.

The waterfall enveloped their bodies and in that brief moment, when they were still in this world, I heard Hannah whisper, 'I'm home.' In a blinding flash of light, they were gone as so too was the stormy weather, vanishing quickly and leaving nothing but the gentle sounds of the water lapping against the rocks, coupled with the calm stillness of the morning air.

'Wha' the 'ell was tha'?' Saskia demanded. 'Where 'ave they gone?' She stormed towards me and stood by my side; the pair of us looking towards the waterfall.

'I believe they've gone home. Probably to the mythical plane. Darren would now be fully changed.'

'You could have stopped them,' Henry yelled at me. 'Why didn't you?'

Snapping my head to look at him I said calmly, 'It wasn't my place to order them to stay. Hannah got called by something or someone that was extremely powerful and Darren followed. It was simple as that.'

'No, it wasn't,' Lionel interjected. 'That's the third member of our group that's gone. How the hell are we going to win this war with only the six of us?'

'There are seven of us,' Rhea said quietly from beside the fire.

'You're not part of our group,' Lionel snapped at her. 'In fact why the hell are you still here? You've done the damage you wanted to inflict on us, so why don't you sod off and leave us alone?'

'Where should I go?' she shouted back. 'I can't go home cos my family don't know I exist. I can't go to school I can't do sweet F-A!' she yelled and with a cry of pain as her wings erupted out of her back.

'Are ya okay with this, with Hannah and Darren goin'?' Saskia asked me quietly so that the others didn't hear.

I shook my head. 'No, I'm not. But there is no time to think on the past Saskia, we have to keep moving, regardless if our number is dwindling or not.'

'Do yous know somethin' about everyone's departure?' she asked as we moved away from the others.

I glanced at her and shrugged. 'I can only speculate. Hannah was called by something which we have no knowledge of. My assumption is maybe the original myths called her.'

'So myths, such as Water Nymphs, took her?'

'Maybe, I dunno. Darren went along with her because I think he felt some pull towards it too. I believe we'll see them again, but I don't know when.'

Saskia sighed and moved to stand in front of me. 'You feel a pull to the magical plane?'

I nodded. 'So did Hannah. You will feel the same if you changed and so would the others.' Turning around I looked at Lionel who was sitting by the fire with Sam and Henry. Rhea was on the opposite side of the cave looking glum, but her mind had wandered. 'I think we should keep an eye on Rhea,' I told Saskia quietly. 'I don't trust her. She may be like us, but she's tainted. She lies and we need to ensure she doesn't do a runner.'

'Ya think she'll go back ta Lynn an' da others?'

'It's a possibility and the percentage of it is extremely high. She spent some time with Lynn and I've gathered that she wants to keep close to her, kind of like a mother figure.'

Saskia frowned and looked almost, ashamed. 'I felt the same thing with Lynn; or maybe like a big sister. But I felt I could trust her, but after all the things we 'ave found out an' been through, I wouldn't ever trust 'er again.'

'Okay guys, saddle up,' I said loud enough for them to hear me. 'We're moving out now. There is no point in us staying here we still have some things to do. Lionel,' I said looking at him, 'I need you again.'

He sighed heavily as though he knew this was coming. 'There is one thing I want you to do,' he said looking worried, 'don't change me back.'

'What?' Sam and Henry gasped.

But Lionel shook his head. 'I know but what if we need to make a quick getaway? You need me in that dog body, not like this. I'm useless like this. Besides, the last time you changed me I felt as though...' he stopped and stared at me with pained eyes, 'as though I could fully become a myth. Like I could reach the next level.'

I nodded in understanding.

'But you won't be able to talk to us,' Sam said to him, 'you can't communicate like Lottie can.'

Lionel shrugged his shoulders, 'Better that than being gouged by the King of the Minoans.'

'He's not evil,' Rhea said quietly. 'I... I've met him, only briefly, but I know he's not evil, he's just upset.'

'Well d'uh! Tha' dude got kidnapped about two decades ago, of course he's upset,' Saskia said waspishly.

'Two decades ago?' Rhea asked her looking confused. 'But Lynn told me that...'

'Tha' wha'? He came by for a quick visit?' Saskia rounded on her. 'Look, I hate to burst ya bubble but Lynn is a lying cow. All of the operators aren't human. Lynn is a dragon, Roxy is da frigging Leviathan, Dave is a Minotaur an' hell knows wha' Matt is.'

'Lynn's a dragon?' Rhea asked, almost shouting.

'Way to go with the crash test on the secret lives of the operators,' Henry smiled.

'Meh, the kid's gotta learn,' Saskia shrugged.

'I ain't no kid,' Rhea snapped at her.

'You're younger than us, ergo a kid,' Saskia said. 'Anyway, I believe Tara ordered up a side of dog, let's get this over with.'

Grabbing our bags we huddled around Lottie.

Through Sam, I'd ask her to tell me if she would get too cold once we reached Wales. I knew Wales and at this time of the year, it was going to be freezing for everyone, but strangely not for me. Being mythical, I was neither cold nor hot.

'Hang on, before we do this,' Lionel said putting his hand up, 'do you know where this place is? I mean the last time I just thought Ha Long Bay and we got here but ended up in the sea, I don't want to make that mistake again.'

Everyone looked at Rhea, she shrugged her shoulders. 'All I know is that it was an old nuclear bunker somewhere in Wales. That's all I got from being there. I didn't see any road signs or anything, I was drugged.'

Henry and I scoffed; we both knew I had experienced something similar not too long ago.

'I know someone who can help with that,' I said to him, 'but Henry's going to have to do the talking.'

'Me why?' he asked looking confused.

'We're going back to my university. We need to talk to Kevin. He knows a lot of Welsh histories. I'm sure he'd know something about a nuclear bunker,' I told him giving him a sly glance.

Lionel nodded, 'Just tell me where to go…BEFORE you change me,' he added.

Nodding Henry told him exactly where to go, so bracing ourselves, I nodded at Lionel. 'Are you sure about this?'

Lionel's eyes looked sad but he shook his head, 'I can be of ore use to you as this Egyptian dog than a human. Besides, I feel more comfortable as a dog,' I felt Saskia's eyes on me, '- just do it.'

'Okay, ready guys,' I said to them, 'Lionel, change into Wepwawet.'

Lionel's back twisted into an arch. He yelled out in pain; his eyes cringing, his teeth bared. Rhea had never seen Lionel change before and was both shocked and awed by the changes to his body. Like some odd werewolf movie, Lionel's skin dissolved and was quickly replaced with dark coarse fur. His legs crunched as the sinew and the bones were elongated; his skull crackling with the extra bone and brain mass that was added. With my new hearing, I heard everything that was happening to his body and it made me feel slightly sick. Coupled with loud screams, ripping from Lionel's throat, within a few minutes he had become the giant dog.

'EVERYONE HOLD ONTO HIM,' I shouted grabbing onto Henry as he linked with the others. I plunged my hand into the fire and grabbed Lottie quickly, just as Lionel lurched forwards; the brilliant blue lights erupted before my eyes, almost blinding me.

'TARA, HELP ME!' I heard a familiar voice but it came and went so quickly that I was momentarily stunned at how familiar the voice was.

We collapsed in a heap in what looked like a frozen wasteland but as I quickly got up, my legs feeling like bendy willow branches, I realised we were in Wales, in a field just behind my old university. Gathering from the cloud cover, with a pale silvery moon lurking behind them, it was the middle of the night.

I shoved Lottie in my jacket and asked her to speak up if she was getting cold, but quickly looking at Sam he shook his head.

'Okay, did anyone hear tha' voice?' Saskia said standing up, wobbling slightly.

'Yeah, I did,' Henry said putting his hand up as he rolled off Lionel who was splayed out on the frozen ground.

'It was calling out for Tara, whoever it was,' Sam told me, giving me a strange look. 'It wasn't any of you guys was it?'

Rhea shook her head, 'Nope and I'd never ask for her help anyway,' she spat.

There was the sound of a whip-like smack, hand on cheek and Rhea yelled out in pain, 'Bloody stop hitting me!'

'Don't say such nasty things then!' Saskia shouted.

'GUYS!' I yelled, trying to stop the argument, as I just figured out who the voice belonged to. 'The voice... the voice who called out to me. It was Macie.'

'Holy kack you're right! It was Macie's voice,' Henry said looking shocked. 'But,' he quickly looked around him, confused, 'she's not here, so what does that mean?'

'She's trapped,' Sam said and pointed to my jacket, indicating Lottie was talking. 'I felt her with us for a brief moment as we crossed over. That bright light, it's the passage, like a tunnel between this plane and the next. Its how myths like Dave and Lionel can travel from one place to another. They pass into a rift in space and Macie is stuck in it.'

'But how do we get to her?' Henry asked us. I shrugged. To me it seemed like a one-way entry... you can get in, but you can't get out. If there was a way out, Macie wouldn't have called out to me for help.

'Not sure, I'll have to have a think. Let's just get some place warm at least,' I said seeing Rhea shiver, as a bitter wind whipped up my hair like a blackberry sorbet.

'Where the hell are we going to find someplace warm in the middle of no-where?' Saskia asked, her teeth beginning to chatter.

Henry scowled at her. 'We aren't in the middle of no-where. Our university is just down that hill,' he pointed. 'Besides, I took a walk once around this area. There's an abandoned coal mine not too far from here. See up there,' he pointed behind us high on a hill. In the moonlight there was a heap of discarded coal, where old rusty carts were thrown askew; tendrils of ivy partly encased them. 'Beyond there is an old abandoned farmhouse near a small copse. It'll keep the elements out.'

As we walked through the dark in the middle of the Welsh countryside, my mind was focussed entirely on Macie. She was alive, we knew where she was, but she was trapped.

'I have to get her out of there Lottie,' I said to her as I tightened my jacket to keep the cold out, 'I just have to.'

Down in the valley were flickering lights from my small university town and now and again, I would see the headlights from cars passing along the main road which was a good few hundred yards away from us. Other than that, it was completely secluded.

From the outside, the farm screamed out 'neglect' but I gathered that there was a reason why it was abandoned. I had a funny feeling it had something to do with the Cold War, which was why there were nuclear bunkers scattered around the country. Farmers were cast out of their homes back in the 1950's to secure the bunkers; many families were destroyed because of it.

Barging through the front decrepit door and almost breaking it, we headed through the slate covered hallway towards the back of the house; where thankfully, though also extremely run down, was where we found the kitchen. It was appallingly mouldy and looked like it hadn't been lived in for decades. The door opposite led into an old living room. It was dark, musty and full of mildew, but the ceiling above hadn't collapsed, so this is where we decided to camp until we got information from Kevin.

'I'm so cold,' Sam said as he pointed at my jacket. I hugged Lottie closer to my chest, hoping that I wouldn't squash her, but Sam remained silent.

Between them, Saskia and Henry made a fire in the hearth. It had taken a while getting rid of the old damp rotted logs, but being helpful, Henry had taken an old chair and smashed it on the floor, the pieces of wood splintering so easily that really there was no need to break it with such force. Men!

Lionel lay down on the floor beside my feet and yawned. I didn't blame him for being tired; he had done so much for us already. Sam bent down and patted him on the head, then went off in search of more wood and returned with old pieces of rotted furniture which he placed in a tripod-looking pile on the floor away from where Saskia and I sat.

'Rhea, can you close all the doors and curtains if there are any left,' I asked her.

'What if there aren't?' She asked not looking like she cared.

'Use ya initiative idiot,' Saskia snapped at her, 'we need ta make sure no one can see any light, ya got tha'?'

'You're the idiot,' she snapped back. 'You want us to choke to death from the smoke?'

Saskia gave me a quick glance, but I turned away from her. I didn't want an argument. I just wanted to find out how to get to Macie... maybe King Minos could help? It was definitely something to think about.

Stomping out of the kitchen, Rhea went off to sulk.

The boys made a circle of bricks around the hearth for Lottie, getting the material from the kitchen. Henry kept the fire going with broken wood and other random material Sam had found.

'Lottie's getting really cold,' he said looking worried. Plucking her out of my jacket pocket, I placed Lottie into the heart of the fire. She cooed gratefully then snuggled down.

'Thank you,' Sam said staring at her, smiling.

Coming back into the slightly smoky room, Rhea flopped down next to me. 'All of the doors and windows are closed, so if I don't wake up tomorrow, its cos I've asphyxiated' she said irritably.

'Oh an' wouldn't tha' be upsettin',' Saskia retorted nastily.

The small fire began to grow and I noticed that so was Lottie. She was close to the size of a little owl and I hoped that by tomorrow, she'd be big enough to fly.

Within the flickering flames, I saw something in Sam's eyes, something that the others didn't pick up on. He cared for Lottie more than he let on. The others, I think, saw Sam being concerned for Lottie, but I could almost go that further mile and say he might even love her. Though, through the situation we had found ourselves in, outcasts and runaways from the T.A.T, our group quickly shrinking as though the world was picking us off one by one, it was nice to see that two people could be happy with each other. The only depressing point was that Lottie would forever remain in that bird body, unable to hug or kiss anyone. Damn, I felt so horrible. This was my fault. Everything that happened in our group, my group, was my entire fault.

Rhea hated me because I got rid of Amanda, Heather and Beth and was left friendless because our group hated her and wouldn't accept her. Lottie hated me because of the way she was and her best friend had gone. Lionel hated me because I'd transformed him into a huge dog and caused him pain and embarrassment. Sam was beginning to hate me because he would never be able to love Lottie as a human and Henry… Well, Henry and I were complicated. Not your usual run of the mill boy meets girl, girl falls head over heels for boy and boy and girl get together. It was more, boy meets girl, girl meets boy and girl transforms into a mythological being; boy and girl… don't fall head over heels in love. I mean, for the love of Mike, couldn't we get a break, just to have at least one happy something in our lives that would make all of this pain worth it?

I glanced at Henry and suppressed a sigh. I closed my eyes and tried to visualise him not there. That I was by myself. Perhaps it was best for everyone that I was away from them then maybe things would sort themselves out, without me there to mess everything up.

'So, what do we do about Macie?' Saskia questioned breaking the silence.

I still had my eyes closed, pretending I was listening to the telly while sitting in my kitchen back home with a roaring fire in front of me.

'Tara, what do you think we should do?' she pressed.

Regrettably, I opened my eyes and saw that everyone was looking at me. It surprised me that no matter what I had done to my friends, they still wanted to include me. I shook my head. 'King Minos is the only thing I can think of.'

'Ha!' Rhea barked out a laugh, folding her arms as though she knew better. 'That old freak won't help you.'

Sam gave her a hard stare. 'Don't you mean he won't help *you*?'

'Why Rhea?' Henry asked gently, ignoring Sam.

'Because,' she said like it was the answer, but with all of us staring at her she huffed in annoyance and explained. 'That old dude hates the T.A.T. If what you say is true, that he's been in there for what, twenty-odd years then he aint gonna help ya.'

'Well, all we can do is ask nicely,' I told her.

'Yeah, like that's gonna work,' she scoffed.

'At least try and be more positive,' Sam told her in an irritated way. 'You've been nothing but arrogant, selfish and a downright pain in the ass.'

'Yeah, you've told me,' she said offhandedly.

Sam flicked his eyes to the fire where Lottie was sitting, calmly looking at him. He chuckled softly and smiled. It didn't surprise me that Sam could hear Lottie's thoughts; after all, Lottie was very magical. Although, I did wonder why Sam didn't tell the others. And was keeping it a secret.

'Okay, so we need to find this nuclear bunker then.' I began, but suddenly everyone looked away, even Lionel wined and placed his paws on his head. 'So, Henry and Sam and Saskia, it's down to you three.'

'Why us? An' wha' the 'ell do ya want us ta do?' Saskia demanded looking annoyed.

Rubbing my hands over my eyes I said, 'I can't waltz up to Kevin and ask him where this nuclear bunker is. I can't hide these fecking wings anymore.'

'Saskia and I can go. Sam can stay with you guys,' Henry told me, giving me a fleeting glance.

Not wanting to argue with him I nodded. 'Wait until morning. We need to get some sleep.'

'Yeah and food, I'm starving,' Rhea said stifling a yawn as she laid down and curled up.

One by one the others went to sleep around the crackling fire; only I stayed awake. Even though I was tired, or maybe the better phrase for it would be frigging knackered, I wanted to watch over them, just in case.

Standing up, I moved carefully out of the living room and headed outside. From the smell of oncoming snow, I could guess that the Welsh air was freezing as I stared at the cloudless sky above. My eyes fell to the ground; it was already covered with a white sheet of crunchy frost. My breath streamed out of my mouth as I exhaled the crispy air and for some strange reason, I felt content. Though we were in a disastrous situation, a third of our group gone, I liked being outside alone, surrounded by this quiet darkness.

'Where's Tara?' Saskia whispered as I heard movement from within the house.

'She's probably gone for a walk. Go back to sleep,' Henry yawned as I heard him roll over.

'I'm worried about 'er,' she said in a strange tone, it almost sounded as if she was genuinely concerned. 'There's somethin' off about 'er. I can't put my finger on it.'

'She's keeping her distance from us,' Sam mumbled. 'She doesn't want to get hurt.'

'Hurt? She seems fine,' Saskia scoffed.

'No, she's hurting, she's hurting really bad,' Sam told her. 'Lottie, Macie, Hannah and Darren, we were all like family in a way. They're all gone and she's taking everything to heart. She's blaming herself for this.'

'Fer wha,' fer them leavin'?' Saskia asked.

'I had a word with her,' Henry spoke softly. 'To put it bluntly, she's changed, not just in looks but also mentally. She's grown up, not in a sense of being more of an adult, but she's become wiser. She knows what I'll turn into, what Sam will turn into. She's carrying the weight of the world on her shoulders and that little git over there isn't helping.'

Rhea was snoozing and from her breathing I could tell that she was still completely unconscious. I was glad that she didn't hear their conversation. I wanted to be like that, completely unaware of the things people were saying. I didn't want to hear them talking about me, them knowing how I had changed and how they were seeing the real me. The one who had to lead them into battle, a battle that was fast approaching and one in which I had no idea what we were facing.

As soft droplets of sadness rolled down my cheeks, I slid down the wall and I hugged my wings to my body.

★ ★ ★

The following morning a warm hand pressed down on my shoulder. Opening my eyes, I saw Henry and Saskia staring down at me with pained worried eyes.

'Are ya okay?' she asked me, offering a hand to help me up. I didn't take it but nodded at her.

'Were you out all night?' Henry asked as he gently touched my right wing, and then began to brush away some frost that coated them.

Trying to change the subject of my segregation from the group, I asked 'Are you two heading to Kevin's?'

Saskia nodded. 'Yeah then we're gonna bring back some food. Any suggestions?'

'Anything that we can cook over the fire.'

'Got ya,' she said smiling at me. 'Oh and ya should see Lottie, she's grown overnight.' With that, Saskia and Henry walked off into the freezing morning, heading down into the valley where my small university was hidden.

Standing up and feeling somewhat achy, I headed back into the house and came across an interesting scene. Sam was holding Lottie in his hand as she bobbed up and down as though trying to fly. I smiled at her development and went to join them.

'Nice growth spurt there Lottie, but your wings aren't fully mature yet.'

Sam smiled and replied, 'She knows but she just wanted to stretch her wings.'

'When do you think she'll be able to breathe fire?' Rhea said as she flicked through my little book.

'Put that down,' I shouted at her. As though she got an electric shock, Rhea dropped the book. 'Didn't your mother teach you to keep your nose out of other people's business?' I asked, snatching the book off the floor.

'I'm sorry, I just wanted to know what Lottie does,' she said as though I had hit her.

'Well, she doesn't breathe fire, she emits it through her wings,' I said glancing at Lottie.

'Cool,' Sam said looking at her. 'Then you can build us fires instead.'

'Sam,' I sighed, sitting on the floor next to Lionel who was looking sad and depressed on the floor. 'I know you can hear Lottie's thoughts.' His eyes went wide and opening his mouth to try and explain, I put my hand up to stop him. 'I figured it out. I'm not stupid. I kind of gathered that Lottie would attach herself to someone with bird-like qualities, not to mention that you are smitten with her.' Sam looked a little bashful and stroked Lottie's head. She eyed me curiously but didn't speak to me through Sam.

Sam, however, suddenly frowned. 'Bird-like qualities? But my tattoo is a snake,' he said looking shocked.

'Yeah, I know,' I said as I laid on the ground on my side and stared at the soft ashes that Lottie had made a small nest out of.

'Tara, do you know what I am?' I nodded. 'Then please, tell me what I am,' he begged.

'If I did you wouldn't understand what it does and to be quite frank, for the moment in time you're better off not knowing and the same goes for Henry.'

'I don't care about what Henry will turn into. Just please, tell me what I will become,' he asked sounding angry, but I didn't have the chance to explain.

In a flash, Lionel leapt up from his melancholy manner and growled. His hackles were up and his teeth were bared, his head pointing at something behind me. I shuddered as though someone had walked over my grave and inwardly cringed. 'This isn't going to be good. Don't we ever get a frigging BREAK!'

Without warning the front door burst open in an explosion of splinters. Moving to the door of the living room which led out into the slate corridor, I spread my wings covering the others preparing to fight. When I heard nothing, I walked slowly into the corridor and faced Matt.

Lionel quickly moved in front of me, snarling with drool dripping from his jowls. I heard Sam stand up and his zipper go. He must have placed Lottie in his jacket. Rhea moved past me and tried to sneak away, but it was too late, Matt had already seen her.

'Well, well, what do we have here?' he said as he strode down the slate-lined hallway towards the kitchen. 'A Siren and a half, a Wapwawet and a confused looking human, oh this should be fun.'

'Say my name, arsehole,' Sam growled, his tattoo erupting immediately; his eyes turning red and his tongue splitting into a fork.

Matt chuckled, 'I'm sorry, Sam.'

'So, what do I owe the misfortune of your carbuncle?' I hissed like an angry bird.

Matt laughed again and shook his head, 'Now I would say keep your temper Tara, but it's gone beyond that,' he said, his face contorted in an angry stare, his teeth gritted, 'it's gone way beyond that.' His hands balled in anger and said with a deep breath, 'Listen carefully, I'm only going to ask this once...' Matt laughed in mirth as he reached with his right fist up to the top of his head and opening his hand grasped the crown of his head, as though he was digging into his skull, 'can you guess what I am before I transform into my true self? Because if you can't... you all DIE!' With that, he backed out of the house and suddenly with a sickening crunching sound he jammed his left hand into his skull and slowly, with blood dripping down his arms and pooling onto the floor, brought out what looked like a weird black twisting horn.

Rhea screamed and tried to make a hasty exit, but Sam grabbed her arm and made her stay put. Lionel continued to growl at Matt's transformation, but I got the impression that Lionel was also feeling the same thing I was. Apart from being utterly freaked out I was also queasy.

Yanking the strange horn that continued to grow out of his head and with a couple of quick tugs, Matt pulled it out completely and to my consternation it wasn't a horn at all. It was an antler, like from a deer.

'No,' I gasped, 'it-it can't be!'

'Tara, what do we do?' Sam asked hastily as he looked like he was about to spit venom.

But what could I do? Matt was a Celtic God! There was no way we could defeat a God, even collectively.

I glanced at Sam. Was he ready to become his tattoo? Would he be able to handle it and if so, would he want to become human again? My thoughts quickly turned back to what I was thinking the previous night. I was changing everyone before they were ready. If Sam got stuck in his form, he would hate me forever. He wouldn't be able to hug Lottie or even touch her; he may even kill her.

'Sam, do you want to change?' I asked him, keeping my tone normal, emotionless.

Matt suddenly lifted his other arm and dug his hands into his skull and with a second lot of blood that dribbled sickly down his face, began to pull out his other antler.

'Will it help us? Will it help her?' he asked quickly, looking at his jacket.

I stopped myself from crying angry tears. It was happening all over again. First it was Lottie, then Lionel and now Sam. Why was I destroying everyone's humanity?

'With the three of us, yes it will,' I told him, feeling my heart breaking just that extra bit as I knew he would do anything for Lottie even to giving up being human.

'Do it,' he said staring down at his jacket then quickly unzipping it. He passed Lottie over to Rhea but not before kissing her ever so softly on her head. 'I'm doing this for you, I want to keep you safe,' he said.

Struggling to free herself from Rhea's grip, he shook his head, 'No Lottie you can't help. You're too little; you haven't grown into your adult feathers yet. Please, just stay with Rhea. Do this for me. I don't want to see you get hurt.'

Rhea held the struggling, flapping Lottie to her chest, looking unsure.

'DO IT,' Sam yelled as he ripped off his top.

Lionel turned around to stare at Sam and winced as though he was in agony.

'Sam, I'm so sorry,' I said, chiding myself. 'Sam,' I said looking into his red eyes, 'transform.'

Sam yelled out in agony and fell to the floor, writhing in pain. His muscles tensed and bulged under his skin.

'No,' said a shocked voice. My head snapped in the direction of the voice. It was Matt and he looked scared, scared of Sam's transformation.

'Lionel, give Sam some time to transform, sick him!' I pointed to Matt.

Barking with delight, Lionel took two long lunging strides and collided into Matt, toppling him head over heels.

'Rhea, take Lottie and get out of here,' I shouted at her, but she shook her head.

'I, I want to help, I want to fight.'

'You're not strong enough-.'

'Then change me,' she cried, her eyes wide and determined.

'No,' I yelled stubbornly, 'get out and protect Lottie.'

Folding my wings back so I could fit in the hallway, I ran towards Matt and Lionel who were having a wrestling match on the cold and frosty floor. Nearly reaching them, I suddenly slipped; my right foot flaying out under me as I stepped in Matt's blood. Unbalanced, my momentum carried me forwards towards Matt and Lionel. Like a bowling ball to pins, I knocked into them, making them fly part. Lionel was on his feet in seconds and lunged towards Matt who was struggling to get up, but for some reason, he kept falling over as though something or someone was preventing him from standing.

'Sam,' I laughed as I glanced behind me and staring through the hallway and into the kitchen, I saw torn clothes; Sam's clothes.

'Damn it,' Matt gasped as Sam, completely invisible due to his speed, kept swiping at Matt. Deep lacerations appeared on his face and arms; small rivulets of blood seeped out of his wounds and gently spotted the white frosty floor. Sam was helping, he had got his wish and I was grateful for it.

'Lionel, back off a bit,' I told him as Lionel's head whipped from one direction to another trying to keep up with Sam.

'Times running out you fools,' Matt laughed as antlers were now fully emerged.

Then without warning, Lionel and I were flung backwards; hitting the ground with such force, it felt like the aftermath of a huge explosion, like a shockwave. Matt laughed manically, then stretching his left hand out, snatched a strange half-bird half-reptilian creature out of the air which struggled and squirmed in his grip.

'Sam,' I yelled out as I scrambled up and headed towards him, but Matt quickly got up and put his hand out to stop me getting any closer.

'One more move and I'll snap his neck,' he said, the smile wiped off his face. Glancing at Sam he turned him over, examining his bird-like face and snake-like tail, 'How quaint, a pathetic little Cockatrice. No wonder this group was a failure.'

'What are you talking about you moron, you created us!' I snapped at him.

'Did I?' He asked as he threw Sam away like a piece of old cloth. 'You created them Tara. You are doing this to everyone, don't you understand? All this,' he said raising his hands out towards the sky, 'it's all because of you.'

Biting back a retort I accepted what he was saying. After all, it was true. 'I know this is all me. I know that everyone would still be human if it wasn't for me. But this, all this,' I said mocking him as I raised my arms, copying him, 'is to prevent you from destroying us.'

Tilting his head to the side, Matt gave me a strange look, 'Well, if you think so.'

Rhea's hurried footsteps grew louder as she approached the doorway. In one hand she was holding the frail-looking little body of Lottie; her hand was covered in scratches. In the other was my little red book, half open. 'Tara, he's Cerenum, the Celtic horned-God. Break his antler's off,' she suddenly shouted.

I wanted to hit her. 'I know!' I yelled, but Matt started laughing.

'Too late.' Grunting like some strange animal, Matt began to grow. His arms, legs and torso appeared to double in height and his muscles seemed to double in strength. Long, muddy-brown hair, grew around his antlers and fell to his shoulders. His eyes became an oval shape, turning a deep mossy green.

'Lionel, get Sam and Rhea out of here, I have to deal with this antler freak.'

Matt laughed, his voice booming over the deserted fields around us. He tilted his head back and breathed in deeply. Then as quick as lightning, his hand flew out towards me trying to grab my neck. Ducking just in time, the swoop of his hand ruffling my hair, I turned away from him and taking two steps, took off into the air; adrenalin pushing me on. It annoyed me that I didn't have a vision and see it coming, but I could figure out how that worked later. Within seconds, I heard a groan behind, which sounded like a tennis player exerting his energy. Then he grabbed me. With a momentary look behind me, I saw Matt gripping my ankles, trying to pull me down and it was working. 'Get off me,' I said, trying to shake him loose, but my words were ineffective.

Like a waterlogged bird, my continuous flapping wasn't getting me any-where and with one violent yank Matt pulled me down to the cold, hard ground winding me in the process.

Gasping for breath, Matt groped my legs, trying to pull me closer to him. 'You are so beautiful Tara,' he laughed, 'even when you were human.' Dis-gustingly I felt what could have been drool fall onto my legs, but then I felt the same sensation on my back too. Opening my eyes, I saw that it had started to sleet.

Heavy padded paws came thundering towards us and then swiftly, the heavy body of Matt flew off me. Craning my neck, I saw Lionel rolling around, biting and clawing at Matt's face.

'Leave me be, you disgusting mutt,' Matt yelled, quickly grabbing Lionel by the throat then throwing him into the farmhouse wall. Through his sheer size and power, Lionel broke the wall. Bits of limestone, dust and concrete fell to the floor. He gave a small yelp as he collided with the wall but shak-ing it off, charged again.

For the briefest moment, Matt was distracted. Scrambling up, I folded my wings back and took a few steps towards him, aiming my wings slightly, to catch him in his side, but within a split second, as I aimed, he somehow managed to catch my wing and began to bend it back. I screamed in pain as he tutted at me.

'Same old Tara, you tried that trick with Dave. And let me tell you, he wasn't a happy bunny.' Grabbing my left arm, he twirled around and threw me against the farmhouse wall like he had done to Lionel. But instead of the wall partially cushioning me, it was too damaged to stop the momentum in which I was thrown and it broke; brick and mortar falling all around me as I hurtled through the wall, landing in the damp and forgotten front living room.

'Tara!' came Rhea's voice as she barrelled her way through the debris.

'Get out of here Rhea or you're going to get killed,' I mumbled as I slowly tried to get up.

Throwing the book aside, Rhea began to help lift the bricks off me and then grabbing my jacket, helped pull me up to a standing position. 'I've told you before,' she said looking angry, 'break his antlers.'

'What the hell will that do?' I asked, shaking dust out of my hair.

'It'll,' she began, then bit her lip as though she was revealing a deep se-cret, 'it'll kill him,' she said simply. 'I read it in the book.'

Laughing her off I pushed her aside, 'The book would never say that, you can't kill an immortal. He's a God-.'

'He has a weakness in this world,' she shouted at me.

Without warning, there was a sudden bright ball of orange light and like a rocket exploding,

Rhea was flung back against the opposite wall along with Lionel sprawled across her body, his side bleeding out. Coughing through the brick dust, I peered outside and saw the twenty-foot horned body of Matt. His feet were now hooves, his legs which looked like they belonged to a deer were covered in short, brown fur. There was hardly any part of him that resembled a human. Matt had fully transformed. This wasn't good.

Not having time to stop and check on Rhea or Lionel, I stumbled out of the debris-filled living room and walked back outside to face Matt. My eyes started from the bottom and slowly looked up towards the sky, his figure casting an eerie shadow over me.

'Ready to die, Siren?' he snarled, as he took a fighting position.

'Bring it on,' I sneered.

His deformed vine-like hands reached down to grab me, but I ducked right under him. Turning around, I Karate-kicked him on his leg. Giving a painful howl, his leg nearly buckled under him, but he turned around and tried to swipe at me, catching me on my left wing and forcing me back. Doing a strange little cartwheel, I righted myself and taking two strides, went off into the air and flew left, just before he made a grab for me again. I flew high over the farmhouse and looking down, saw his angry face.

'Come down and play Tara,' he roared up at me, 'or watch your friends die!' His words wrapped cold dread around my heart. I can't lose anyone else. I thought as he faced the farmhouse and began walking slowly towards it.

'NO!' I screeched as I dived towards him, the wintery flakes blurring my vision as I flew quickly towards him. 'YOU WON'T HURT THEM!'

For the slightest second, Matt glanced up at me and smiled. Before I even managed to change direction he jumped into the air and grabbed me and in an instant a brilliant blue light shone around me and the farmhouse suddenly vanished before my eyes.

Matt was still holding onto me but then threw me to the ground. I bounced a few feet and skidded to a stop.

'TARA!' Macie yelled from in front of me.

My eyes fluttered open and I saw her standing there, staring at me with fearful eyes. But though I was concerned for Macie, I had to process what was going on. There was nothing around me, no trees, no sky, just whiteness. It seemed I'd been forced into some sort of unnatural white void.

'WATCH OUT!'

Hearing his breath behind me, I rolled over to the right, just in time, before a big stomping hoof came down, millimetres from my head. Scrambling to a standing position, I looked at Matt; he gave me an evil smile. 'Just where I want you,' he raised his arms.

'TARA, GET OUT OF THE WAY,' Macie yelled again. Suddenly there was an almighty screech, mingled with an eagle's cry. A fleeting glance to my right and I saw Macie quickly transform into a griffin. With one leap, she was in the air and hurtling right towards Matt. Taking the opportunity, I spread my wings and jumped high into the air and charged towards Matt intending to rip his antlers right off his head. I didn't trust Rhea, but as she had been with Lynn and the others I gathered that she must have known something about the group.

Macie dug her beak into Matt's neck; thick blood gushed out and flowed down his body in a torrent. He writhed in agony, lashing out at Macie, trying to rip her wings off, but she dodged out of the way each time. Macie, it seemed, had been practicing flying.

I was inches away from Matt's right antler when a flailing arm caught me in the face and smacked me away like a fly. Spiralling out of control my hand reached out to grab onto something and caught his antler.

Pulling myself up, I smiled at my sheer luck and placed my feet firmly on his head. Grabbing it with both hands, as though pulling out a stubborn weed, I yanked with all my might, pulling it clean out of his skull.

Matt screamed in pain and threw Macie and me off in an instant. We both crashed to the floor and rolled out of the way as Matt began to sway. He suddenly toppled towards the ground, a pool of blood splashing out from his skull.

Not taking any chances, I yelled in frustration as I got up and ran towards his remaining antler. My heart was pounding in my chest from fear and my adrenalin pumping through me giving me strength. Macie whipped around and screeched out in an almost deafening sound. Together we lunged towards his remaining antler. Macie clamped her beak hard on the top while I grabbed the bottom. With all our might, the pair of us pulled the remaining antler out of Matt's skull. Matt's hands flailed around. He yelled out a piercing scream, as though he was dying and suddenly and without warning the brilliant blue light burst into my vision and together, Macie and I hit the cold sleety ground of Wales, right next to the farmhouse.

CHAPTER NINETEEN

ACHING ALL OVER I ROLLED TO A SITTING POSITION, TRYING to catch my breath and also to think about what I had just gone through. But sitting there with sleet falling softly on me I couldn't think. What the hell had just happened? One minute we were here, then in some white-void room thing, then back here.

Macie was still in griffin form, shivering slightly.

'Are you okay?' I asked dropping the blood covered antler that was still in my hand. I wiped way the gunk on the snowy ground. I really was in need of a shower.

Macie nodded slightly and moved her left paw. It was bleeding.

'Ah, well change back and you should be fine,' I said, gingerly standing up. 'Just need some warm tea and- oh crap, LOTTIE!'

Springing into action, all pain ignored, I ran to the door and burst into the half-demolished living room. Lionel was still laid across Rhea, unconscious. Glancing at Rhea's hand I saw Lottie and gasped. Lottie's tiny fluffy head lolled to the side; her small pink tongue poking out of her beak. 'Oh no,' I cried, pushing away the broken furniture to get to her.

Reaching out I grabbed her and turned around. Staring around I was still surprised to see that the fire in the hearth hadn't gone out. Moving to it, I placed Lottie inside the embers and began blowing gently on them to get the fire going. A few feeble flames flickered around her, but she hadn't stirred. 'Please, please live,' I cried, tears rolling down my face. Walking with a limp, Macie hobbled into the living room her golden eyes locked on the fire and its occupant. She emitted a piercing eagle cry and came closer.

'It's Lottie,' I said, placing some kindling into the fire. 'She's a Phoenix and needs warmth in the first stages of her development. Rhea was holding her and I told her to leave but she didn't. I guess when Matt attacked Lionel, Rhea got in the way.' Macie cried out as she looked over to see Lionel's limp body draped over Rhea. Moving through the debris, she nudged Lionel's side. Lionel whimpered a little and I distinctly saw and heard Macie sigh in relief. She tilted her head as she saw Rhea and didn't seem to care and nudging Lionel again, returned to me.

Macie cooed softly and laid beside the fire, all the while looking at Lottie in a curious way. A few seconds later, Lionel began to stir and with it, so did Rhea.

'You guys alright?' I asked. Lionel's tail gave one weak wag and slowly, he got up whimpering. Rhea, on the other hand, groaned in pain and sat up, holding the back of her head. Macie turned her head so one golden eye locked onto my face. She pointed her beak at Rhea and then looked back at me. 'That's Rhea,' I told her but she must have been confused as to why we were here, but a lot had happened in the past twenty-four hours. I had so many questions and puzzles going through my head and this new wisdom that I had wasn't helping me very much. As I kept thinking about the white-void I recalled what Sam has said last night. Macie was stuck in a tunnel where myths like Dave and Lionel could travel through to get from one place to another. It made sense as it wasn't like travelling to the magical plane. Myths didn't have that kind of power. Only Ancients did and with it the gift of the Phaistos Disc that was bequeathed to the myths a long time ago to travel back to the magical plane. The disc was before the known myths of today, that much I knew, but if humans went into the other plane they would become a God... My heart suddenly quickened as I realised Maynard's plan. He wanted to become God!

Lionel managed to get up and I told him if he could, to go and sniff out Sam. Macie snapped her head around to look at me, but I shook my head. 'There's no point in explaining things to you now. Wait until the others have come back. We are all wondering why you ended up in the white-void.'

I don't know how long I was on the floor, staring at the fire, figuring things out, and upsetting myself more and more as I came to devastating conclusions but I noticed that as the fire steadily grew, so did Lottie. Breathing a sigh of relief, I laughed. 'Ah, you're alright,' happy tears flowing from my eyes. 'Oh, thank God.'

Hearing a small feeble cheep, it was Lottie confirming it.

'Macie, stay with Lottie, I need more firewood,' I told her as I wiped my tears away and went outside. There was snow on the ground now and it was coming down heavy, but I saw Lionel's paw prints going around in circles, as though following Sam's scent. But I couldn't see Lionel. 'Lionel!' I called, looking around me. 'Lionel, where are you!' I heard a bark that came inside the house. Frowning I went to investigate and saw to my horror that Lionel found the crumpled body of Sam amongst some debris in the kitchen. Picking him up carefully, I brushed the dust and grit off him and tucking him under my arms, took him to the fire. I felt his little heartbeat thump softly against my hand as I smoothed his crumpled feathers. 'You were very brave today Sam,' I told him softly, trying to make him comfortable on the floor. Rhea was sat away from Macie looking wary. She made no sound as I came in with Lionel and Sam and instead sat on the mouldy floor, hugging herself to keep warm.

'Rhea, its cold, come and sit by the fire.'

She shook her head, remaining silent.

Macie, who hadn't turned back into a human yet, and I was beginning to wonder why, was sat next to the fire looking at Lottie in a puzzled way.

'You know, if you turned back, you could help me.'

Crooning slightly she nipped at my torn and bloodied jacket, which I didn't see the point in wearing anymore as it was practically ripped to shreds. 'Ah right well, we don't have any clothes to offer you. We lost your bag in Vietnam.'

Macie screeched out in annoyance, but I put my hands up, 'Sorry but you shouldn't have let go.' Macie suddenly stood up and began flapping her wings and stamping her paws on the ground, she was irritated but I didn't know why.

'Could you not do that, you're going to injure yourself further,' I snapped at her.

A despondent Macie sat back down again looking disgruntled. Lionel sat beside her and placed his head on her back, both of them watched protectively over Sam and Lottie.

Standing up, I decided that I had to somehow block the gaping hole in the living room. Heading into the kitchen I took off the old rotting door and placed it horizontally across the hole, then went in search of other flat things to insulate our "den". I headed upstairs, with some difficulty as the ceiling was so damn low, and took some boards that were blocking up the windows. Once these were in place over the hold and I was satisfied it would keep out most of the cold I stoked the fire and added more wood. With the living room door closed, I say with the others, watching the fire like a natural television.

I tended to everyone's injuries. Lionel was the worst out of them all. It looked like his ribs on his right side were broken. I guessed the damage happened when Matt rammed him into the wall.

Rhea had just been knocked unconscious and it was nice to have some peace and quiet from her. She looked like she was in pain, probably from a headache, but she refused to talk to me.

Lionel, Sam, Macie and Lottie soon fell asleep and having nothing else to do, I managed to retrieve my book from under the debris and began to read it. I had read the book before but skimmed it rather than properly reading it. Each page I read each mythical creature I thought I knew was detailed in Mr Raleigh's meticulous way. For instance, I didn't know that faeries looked like butterflies or moths, to the non-believer, or that Silkies gathered together in Scotland on the North coast every few decades for a massive celebration and to do the Highland Fling. Some information like that was a little trivial, but others were useful: like how to distract an ogre, throw a stick and it'll leave, or to get Pixies to stop asking ridiculous pestering questions, just ask them a riddle!

The book was jam-packed with such information but in the Celtic section I found I was right in knowing that the book did not, in fact, have anything on how to beat the horned God. Rhea had got the information while spending time with our operators.

Halfway through the book, I came to the Egyptian section which I had flicked through before, however there was information I had missed out about the Gods and Goddesses. I read that although they were in charge of things like birth, fertility or death and destruction, there was a small sentence below each one, which showed their personality trait.

The God of the Underworld, Anubis was "an utter lapdog." The Goddess Sekhmet was a complete flirt. Osiris was a party animal, Hathor was a loudmouth who cursed at everyone and Set was the irritable bleeder, how ironic, with a constantly broken nose which when he sneezed, sprayed blood on whoever was in range.

I was creased up with laughter as I read all of this and as I continued to read more, I felt that I'd like to meet these guys. After all, they were human once too- maybe they would be able to help us.

Six hours later, I heard approaching footsteps and Saskia's loud voice, 'What the hell happened here?' Half snoozing, I smiled and pushed myself up to a sitting position.

'Tara!' Henry yelled, his voice sounding panicky as he ran into the room, practically crashing through the rotting living room door. Looking frozen and carrying bags of food were the forms of Saskia and Henry.

'Oh, thank God,' he said as he looked at me then both him and Saskia's mouth fell open as they stared at Macie.

'Holy hell,' Saskia said gaping at her.

'Macie?' Henry said looking between me and the quizzical griffin by the fire. His brow furrowed in confusion, his mind probably spinning with questions.

Nodding slightly and clicking her beak in response, he ran to her and hugged her feathery neck. 'Oh dear God, we thought you'd jumped ship, what the hell?' he asked withdrawing, staring at her with a mixture of confusion and awe.

'While you two were having a boring little trip to Kevin's,' I began, placing the book down beside me and turning to face them, 'Matt turned up.'

'WHAT?' Saskia and Henry both yelled.

Nodding I continued, 'Yep and we had a little brawl and Sam ended up changing,' I said nodding to his sleeping form next to the fire.

'Wha'... wha' is he?' Saskia asked looking somewhat repulsed.

'A Cockatrice,' Henry told her quickly. 'Cool but weird. Anyway, Matt turned up?'

'Yeah, in all his form and glory and I mean form. He was the Celtic Horned God, Cernenus,' I said with a cringe.

'Jeez, a god? 'Ow the hell did ya survive?' Saskia asked me as she and Henry came and sat down on the uncomfortable flagged floor next to me.

Sighing, I shook my head, 'It wasn't easy. Sam asked to be transformed and he played his part very well and was exceptionally brave, but after Lionel got shoved through a wall. Rhea had previously told me to break his antlers off and as I was about to, I was suddenly magically in this white-void. Honestly, it was bizarre. The sky, if there was one, was white, the ground white also, there was nothing with colour, but that's when I found Macie. And together we kicked his arse, broke his antlers off and for some weird reason ended up back here.'

Henry and Saskia both looked confused. I had expected at least one of them to give me some explanation but inwardly sighing I shrugged my shoulders. 'I'm completely confused. Anyway, Lottie was on the brink of death. Lionel looks like he's broken his ribs on his right side. Sam is now just resting and Macie is well... still a griffin,' I said tilting my head at her. 'She hasn't got any clothes and I think she doesn't want to walk around naked.'

'Bull,' Saskia said turning around to look at her, 'ya can't transform back can ya? Either tha' or ya don't wanna. Feel comfortable as a griffin do ya? Givin' up on humanity are ya?'

Macie clicked her beak in defiance then looked at me reproachfully.

'No, I don't think she's fully changed, but anyway, I don't want to get into this,' I said rubbing my temple from a slight headache that was beginning to form. 'So can you two enlighten me on your excursion to Kevin's?'

Saskia and Henry came in and sat by the fire, placing the bags of food on the floor and taking out their contents. 'We have fruit, milk, orange juice, chocolate, granola bars, bread and four tins of spam.' He listed.

'I don't like spam,' Saskia complained.

'Don't eat it then,' I snapped at her.

Henry made a little cough stemming the tension. When we were silent he told me his story.

'Kevin was in a lecture, or so we were told.'

'Tara, your university is really... small an' weird.'

Henry and I chuckled. 'Yes it is.'

'So we hung around until after it had finished but found out it was the wrong lecture room. We lost track of him but found him a few hours later after trying his house, friend's house, the student union.'

Laughing I said, 'Let me guess, he was in the library.'

Giving me a small smile, he nodded. 'Yup, so he took us back to his, gave us some drinks and some biscuits and we asked him where the nuclear bunker was and you're right, he knew exactly where it was, or close to. It's on a hill, not far from here, about a few miles due north.'

'So you guys had a nice little trip, got fed and watered had a nice chat while the rest of us were battling for our lives, well that seems fair,' I snapped, my temper changing in an instant, but as soon as my temper flared, I shook it off. 'I'm sorry; I'm just so tired and hungry.'

Saskia nodded. 'Yeah, we understand. Tha's why we tried our best ta get back 'ere as quickly as we could but in da town it was snowing quite bad an' it took us a while.'

'Here, have some spam and bread,' he offered it, but I shook my head.

'No, not until the others are awake. We need to share it out equally, it's only fair.'

Saskia folded her arms and stared at me as though I was insane. 'Hunny, today hasn't been fair on ya. So take wha' ya need. Wales isn't devoid of food,' she laughed as she grabbed a green juicy-looking apple from the pile in front of Henry.

I fell asleep minutes later but was shaken awake after what felt like only a few seconds.

'Tara, everyone is up alive an' kicking. You gonna wake up now?'

Sitting bolt up, my eyes focussed on the small half-frozen group. 'Hey everyone, what time is it?'

'About half past six. You've been asleep fer four hours. It's also dark enough fer us ta fly,' Saskia said.

'Right, now that our freak leader is awake, can you explain to me why there is a griffin sitting next to me?' Rhea asked irritably.

Frowning at Macie I said, 'I won't tell you Rhea. I want Macie to explain to you; in fact she can explain to all of us why she is here. When I met her in the white-void she was human, then changed into a griffon to help me. Now she won't change back, but I don't think she's given up on being human. She's just being obstinate.'

Saskia tapped me lightly on the shoulder, 'So can I do it?'

Macie screeched at her, but I ignored it. 'Go ahead, I want answers. We deserve to know what the hell happened, Macie. Oh and Sam,' I asked casting my eyes over to him, 'I know you said you didn't want to be human, but I'm giving you a chance. Do you want to turn back?' His weird scary red eyes blinked at me than with some difficulty, he nodded his head. 'Okay then.'

Henry grabbed his bag and his torn clothes, which were acceptable for him to wear indoors for now and chucked them over to him. Saskia and I looked at each other and I took off my blood covered jacket and threw it towards Macie.

'Oh, I saw some old sheets while I mooched around the house while you were asleep,' Rhea said getting up. 'I'll go and get them.'

'Thanks.' I felt somewhat shocked that she'd offered to help but didn't stop her.

Rhea left quickly closing the door to keep the heat in. I turned to Sam and locked eyes on him. 'Sam, change into a human,' I said in my commanding tone.

Screaming and yelling like a strangled chicken, Sam shed his feathers and like my own, they disintegrated into a fine ash on the floor. Within moments, there shaking heavily, was a naked Sam.

I averted my eyes and waited for him to cover up and after a small, 'Okay,' from him, I looked round.

'Are you alright?' I asked him.

He hugged his knees to his chin, nodding slowly. 'That was fun,' he said giving me a strange smile. 'I mean not the agonising bit, but the power and knowledge I had while I was a Cockatrice. Seriously cool. Oh and for the record, it's a very odd feeling, shrinking.'

'Noted.' I took a loaf of bread and a tin of spam and threw it over to him. 'Feed Lottie as well.' Picking up another tin, I hastily opened it and prising out the contents, threw it to Lionel. He gobbled it down in one bite and whined. 'I'm sorry but that's all we have for now. You can have some bread though, but I don't think your stomach would like fruit.'

A few minutes later, Rhea came back with a light blue sheet that looked strangely new and threw it to Macie who snapped her beak at her in annoyance.

'Alright Saskia, off you go,' I said to her lazily.

Smiling evilly at Macie, Saskia licked her lips. 'Macie, change back into a human, now!'

Macie screamed in her ear-piercing way. All of us with hands suddenly clamped them to our ears. I felt so sorry for Lionel who howled with pain as Macie ripped and tore the wooden floor beneath her.

Her eagle scream soon became human-like and so did the rest of her body. 'You... bitch!' Macie panted in pain as tears poured from her eyes. 'Don't you know how painful it is?' as she wrapped the jacket around her first, then put the sheet on her.

'Nope, but don't worry,' she said in a sad way, 'I'll find out soon enough.'

When Macie had calmed down, I knelt beside her. I had to get to the bottom on why she left us. 'Okay Macie, the first question we want to know is, why did you let go?'

Macie opened her mouth then closed it quickly and looked around the room. 'Where are Darren and Hannah?'

'They aren't here, they have their reasons. But I'm asking you a question,' I said a little too loudly.

'Well then maybe we should wait until Hannah get's here,' Macie said folding her arms in defiance.

Henry glanced at everyone, confused. 'And why would we do that?'

'Because Hannah let go of me,' she barked. Macie seemed to have come out of her shell pretty quickly, 'It's not the other way around,' she told the stunned room.

Rhea put her hand up and pointing to Macie asked, 'Who the hell is this girl?'

Feeling my blood boil with anger I replied, 'She's a liar.'

Macie's eyes snapped wide open in shock. 'I am not a liar. Hannah let go of me!'

'Hannah wouldn't do that,' Sam said pointing at Lottie. 'She was consoling you before we left Verona. Why are you being such a cow?' he asked.

Her mouth fell open but Sam pointed at Lottie. 'I am not a LIAR,' she roared and cringed as she was about to change. But Saskia was quick and commanded her not to. 'Hannah shook me off. She wanted to leave me behind.'

'First, it's let go and now it's shook off,' Sam said as Lionel began to growl. 'Which lie are you using Macie?'

Saskia interjected. 'Ya let go, tha's wha' Hannah told us. Not only tha', I heard ya say, "I'm sorry," like ya were sorry fer lettin' go.'

'I heard that too,' I agreed, studying Macie's voice and body language. The others nodded.

'Yeah? Well, Hannah said that, not me. She said "I'm sorry," then shook me off,' Macie told us, holding fast to her story.

Lottie who had been sitting patiently in the fire suddenly got up and lunged at Macie, trying to scratch her eyes.

'GET OFF ME!' Macie screamed as she tried to beat her away.

Reacting quickly, Sam leaned over and grabbing Lottie, held her to him, whispering to her to calm down.

'Lottie?' Macie asked me and I nodded. 'You'd attack me?' she shouted her, but Sam held Lottie still. 'I thought we were friends! Of course you'd choose Hannah over me, she's your best friend.' Macie then rounded on me. 'I thought we were best friends.'

Saskia put her hand up. 'Tha' would be me.'

I groaned. 'You're making it worse, Saskia.'

'You have missed a lot since you abandoned us,' Henry said bitterly.

'I didn't abandon you. Hannah… shook… me… off,' she said monosyllabically. 'And oh look, she isn't here to tell you otherwise.'

'We wer' 'appy tha' ya came back. But now, we want ya ta sod off,' Saskia said folding her arms.

I clipped her around the head. 'No, we just want the truth. Stop being so nasty!' I nagged. All this shouting wasn't helping my headache. I had no choice. I had to force her. 'Macie, tell me the truth,' I commanded her.

Macie stared right at me. 'Hannah shook me off.' There was a collective audible gasp, she had been telling us the truth.

'Wow, she isn't lying,' Saskia said looking shocked, rubbing her head where I'd hit her. 'So where does tha' leave us?'

I shrugged my shoulders. I didn't have the foggiest.

'Now we've got that all wrapped up, are you going to fill me in or do I have to watch from the sidelines?' Macie asked me as I tried to think about why Hannah would have shaken her off and left her in the white-void.

'One question I want you to answer,' I said to her calmly, 'the white place, what is it?'

Macie glanced at the floor in thought. 'I'm not sure, but I've come up with some theories,' she began. 'The flash just before Lionel transported us, it's a portal-.'

'Yeah, we kinda figured tha' out,' Saskia said but I hit her again.

'Don't interrupt,' I quipped.

'Anyway,' Macie said loudly, getting the attention of the room again. 'I think you have to pass through the portal, to a type of plane to get to where you're going. Think of it as a stepping stone from one place to another.'

'So there are other planes then,' I said to myself. 'That confirms the three planes. In the cave wall in Vietnam, when I translated the pictograms, it said that there are three planes. Originally I thought there was the magical plane, this one and the bad plane where Amanda went.'

'Amanda?' Macie asked surprised, but I ignored her.

'But perhaps the white-void is like customs at an airport.'

'Nice analogy,' Henry nodded.

'Lionel,' I said glancing at him, 'did you know about this or even think it was possible. I mean,' I said trying to phrase it so he could give me a straight answer, 'did you see a white plane the times we passed from one place to another?'

Everyone stared at the large black dog on the floor. It was difficult for him to communicate with us. So I had to think of questions in which he would somehow manage to reply with a yes or a no, in whatever way he could.

Lionel nodded his head once in reply, but it annoyed me. Why hadn't he told us before? I wanted to ask him, but he would never be able to reply to me, not in detail anyway.

'Right, so are you going to fill me in?' Macie asked looking between the three of us.

'I'll do it,' Henry said putting his hand on my leg, making me shiver, then instantly taking it off. 'Let's see… after you left we bumped into Rhea here,' he said indicating her.

'Oh, thanks for including me,' she snapped.

'She is a Siren too, recruited by Lynn and had three others in her group which are now no longer here.'

'They are in the deepest parts of Hell right now, where they belong,' I said bitterly. Shocked that I had said something so horrid, Macie gave me a reproachful look. I explained, 'They were Furies, Hell's lackeys if you will. They were also my friends or ex-friends from university.'

'That Amanda girl?' she asked me.

'Yes, she, Heather and Beth had turned into their tattoos which they were given only a week or so after me,' I said not delving into it too deeply. 'What's done is done and they're gone.'

'So,' Henry said continuing, 'during the fight Tara had with Amanda, she transformed, and what you are seeing is the end result,' he motioned to me. 'If and when they transform, Saskia and Rhea will look like Tara.'

'Yeah, nice upgrade,' Macie said smiling at me. 'Anything new?'

'Sometimes I can see things before they happen, like visions. I'm stronger. Can see and hear better and also Saskia can read my thoughts. I think it's a Siren thing as the others can't, apart from Darren, strangely enough.'

Macie stared at me in a pitiful way. 'She hears your thoughts?'

Saskia rolled her eyes. 'Yeah, it's not pretty.'

'And you've grown taller and your wings are huge.' She stared at them.

Nodding, I looked at Henry to finish filling her in.

'Hannah transformed into her tattoo. She is a Water Nymph and conjured up Charybdis which swallowed up Beth, Heather and Amanda. Lottie was in agony because of the powerful atmosphere the Furies were surrounded with and asked to be changed. But she grows a lot every day,' he said staring at her. 'And now she can communicate through Sam.' Macie nodded in understanding but remained quiet. 'Then we tried to figure out the riddle, which led to an underwater cave system. Hannah dove in and became trapped beneath the island. Tara went in to save Hannah and then she figured out the riddle. But then Hannah was called by a powerful myth, we think, and with Darren they both vanished in a flash of light. Tara says they have gone to the other plane.'

There was quiet between us for a moment then Rhea said, 'You forgot to mention the riddle, you know, what it said.' She moved forwards and taking a banana and two slices of bread, made a banana sandwich and looking famished, wolfed it down.

Meanwhile, Henry explained about the Ancients, the Phaistos Disc, the portal and the origins of the Gods and Goddesses of mythology.

Macie's eyes went wide with horror then gasped, 'But that's... that screws us up completely we're like...'

'Ancient fodder,' I told her.

'But what about the myths that are animals like me and Lionel?'

Henry shrugged his shoulder, 'If you have the power to create Gods from humans why not create myths from animals? I mean if you think about it the Cockatrice is the answer to the question, which came first the chicken or the egg,' Henry laughed.

'Not funny,' Sam snapped, shivering slightly.

'I don't get it,' Rhea said looking confused.

'Both come from eggs idiot,' Saskia said irritably. 'Chickens and reptiles, it's a freak of nature. Chickens are warm blooded and reptile's cold. It's weird.'

'So Hannah and Darren are-.'

The others looked at me. 'They may be in the magical plane. They went in a flash of light but before Hannah left, I heard her say, "I'm home" so I'm confident in saying they've left Kansas, Toto.'

'So you guys ended up here?' Macie asked looking at us, getting back on topic.

'Yup and Saskia and I have found a nuclear bunker,' Henry told her.

'Um, why?'

I nodded at Rhea, but she was looking at Macie, frowning.

'To have a word with King Minos,' I explained to her. 'Rhea told us about it. Probably one of few things she's told us which is the truth.'

'Hey!'

'Anyway, he's the only one who can translate the Phaistos Disc and shed some light on our situation with this war between the T.A.T and everyone else. Plus, we need to free him.'

Frustrated that I only got little information from Macie about the void, we ate and drank the food, equally sharing it with the others and began to prepare for the flight to the nuclear bunker.

'Do you want me as a griffin or human?' Macie asked as we packed up our stuff, about to leave.

'Um, it's up to you,' I said not really knowing how to answer her.

Saskia poked her head around the mouldy doorframe, an evil glint in her eye. 'Macie, transform in a griffin,' Saskia commanded quickly.

'AHH, YOU BITCH,' Macie screamed out as she collapsed to the floor in agony, the jacket and blanket fell to the floor. Rhea dove for it and kicked it away with her foot.

'SASKIA,' I shouted at her over Macie's screams, 'THAT WAS COMPLETELY UNCALLED FOR!'

'Whatever,' she said storming off with a smirk on her face.

Glancing at poor Macie, she erupted in feathers; her face changing crudely into an eagle's head, her body elongating into a lion's. I crouched down beside her, whispering to her. 'Macie, if you can feel the next level to become a true myth, you need to tell me. Do you understand?'

It took Macie longer than normal to change into a griffon, but once she finished, panting from the pain she laid on the floor crooning sadly. Refraining from patting her on the head like an animal, my wings shuddered with anger as I barged out of the living room and caught up with Saskia. 'What the hell?' I yelled grabbing her shoulders and spinning her around, looking down at her threateningly. 'You really have no idea when you change into your tattoo Saskia, it canes; it hurts like hell and you commanding her like that without her being prepared? Dear God why don't you think?'

Saskia flicked her hair out of her face and stared at me, 'No you're right, I don't know 'ow painful it is, but I'm not apologisin'. I don't trust 'er an' unless I speak to Hannah I WON'T trust 'er.'

'But she told the truth, I made her,' I reasoned with her. Sighing, I put my hands up to stop her retort which I could see coming from a mile away. 'I know what you are getting at. But just please, shut up.'

Turning away from her, I began to walk off when she grabbed my left wing and tugged.

'What now?' I yelled at her.

'How much does it 'urt?' Saskia asked, her tone of voice scaring me as it sounded so defenceless and alone.

'You'll find out soon enough,' I told her and walked off.

'Everyone ready to go?' Henry asked as he gathered everyone outside in the freezing cold night.

'Yup,' we each said, Sam giving a thumbs up on Lottie's behalf.

'Hang on!' Rhea called as she was the last to come out of the dilapidated house. She brought my bag with her and threw it around her back. 'I'll carry it for you,' she offered.

Shrugging, I didn't particularly care.

Henry counted heads and nodding when everyone got into a line said, 'Okay well, we can either fly or walk.'

'Fly,' Rhea, Saskia and I said all together.

'Plus, I'm not asking Lionel to take us there. He's still injured.'

Macie pawed the ground, but I had no idea what that meant. Maybe she wanted to walk?

Henry stared up at the clear night sky; his breath misted in the air. 'Well then Lionel, Sam and I will have to go with you lot then,' he said looking at us. 'Not that you'll like it Sam, but you and Lottie will be safe on Macie. Lionel, I think, can go with Tara as she's strong enough to carry you, and you two,' he said looking at Rhea and Saskia, 'will have to carry me.'

Macie tilted her head and snapped her beak at me. I hadn't forgotten that while Henry was filling in the gaps for Macie, he didn't mention him and me.

Moments later we were all in the night sky with Henry pointing out directions on where to go. Passing over lit houses that were warm and comfortable, I envied the residents; living normal lives, watching television, only having to worry about work and bills. If someone had told me only a year ago that I would end up being a Siren and preparing for a war of myths, I would have thought they were crazy.

As the houses began to thin, it became difficult to find where the bunker was, so Henry decided it would be a good idea to land in the "general" area which Kevin has described.

Half an hour later and with Saskia, Henry and Rhea shivering from the cold, Lionel sniffed out the entrance, which really wasn't an entrance so to speak. As it was a secret bunker, there was a hidden hatch door under a load of shrubbery, which looked like it had been recently disturbed. Being the only one with the strength to break the heavy metal door, I went to the front of the group and balling my hands into fists, punched the door handle twice. The door caved in with a loud bang that echoed over the majestic Welsh countryside. I moved it aside and stood out of the way.

'Ladies first,' Sam said offering.

Saskia scoffed and pushed past him. 'Look like a chicken, act like a chicken,' she said and headed down into the dark staircase below the hatch. Clunking down the metal stairs, we followed Saskia. I felt a little angry that she was leading everyone, but there was no point in arguing with her now.

Henry closed the hatch doors behind us and we were thrown into total darkness.

'Okay, I can't see a thing,' Saskia said stopping. There was a collected 'oof' or growl, or a snapping of beaks as we collided with each other.

'Hang on,' I said, bringing out my bag and feeling for the torch.

'If you're looking for the torch it's in the front pocket,' Rhea suddenly called. Finding it, I flicked it on and illuminated the concrete bare walls. I pointed the torch down the stairs, catching Saskia's creepy reflective eyes. Before her, the stairs ended abruptly and at the bottom was another door.

Hurrying down the steps Saskia reached the door and tried the handle. 'It's locked,' she said, turning towards us.

Huffing in annoyance, I eased my way past everyone, careful not to step on anyone's paws or feet and reaching the door. Grabbing the handle and pushed hard. The whole thing flew off and bounced across to the illuminated corridor in front, cracking the walls from my strength. I inwardly smiled at Saskia's shocked face. Hearing Rhea clumping down the stairs, followed by angry growls and shrieks, she came out into the lit corridor and after turning around in a three-hundred and sixty degree circle took a left and walked off.

'Oh hey, wait up,' I called as everyone piled into the corridor and followed Rhea, leaving me behind with Henry.

'She had better be taking us to the right place,' I heard Sam mumble.

As Rhea and the others' rounded a corner and vanished out of sight, my heart jumped into my throat. Just like before when I saw Amanda attacking me in the air, I had a strange vision. In it I saw Lynn standing in a puddle of blood. While I stood there trying to think about what I was seeing, Henry passed me with a cheeky grin, following the others.

'Hey, come on, let's free King Minos.' Henry walked around the corner and vanished from view, but his face was added to my vision of Lynn and the blood. I had made a horrible connection and I knew that the blood belonged to Henry.

Racing around the corner to face a long concrete tunnel-like corridor, I saw Henry about to turn left and screamed out his name to call him back, but it was too late. A loud intense sound of a fired gun rang in my ears. Henry staggered back towards me holding his chest and then crumpled to the floor, blood spilling out of his torso, pooling on the ground.

'Henry,' I whispered in terror. Willing my legs to move, I ran forwards but came to a skidding halt as Lynn emerged from a corridor on the left, holding a gun and pointing it right at my head.

'Lynn,' I whispered my voice barely audible and took a step back. Fully transformed or not, Lynn was dangerous either way.

Lynn smiled and cocked the gun, raising it higher. She seemed unsure of where to shoot, my heart or my head.

Henry writhed in pain on the floor. I took my eyes of Lynn and the gun and glanced down at him. With his legs thrashing out, trying to find some ground, he slipped in his own blood and winced. 'Tara, do it now,' he said through gritted teeth; sweat poured down his face. 'I'll live, do it NOW.'

Lynn, still holding the gun, turned at an angle to look at his agonised expression and gave him a bittersweet smile. 'Aw, poor baby. And here I was thinking that everyone, including you, had changed.'

'Lynn, don't do this,' I said trying to back away, but she flicked the gun in my direction, making me stop, frozen to the spot.

'Ah ah,' she said shaking her head slowly, 'don't make me shoot you too early. You may be classed as an immortal, but hunny, even magic can solve that little conundrum.'

Trying not to frown as guns weren't magical; I tried to think of why she would wait to shoot me. Did she want information out of me? Did she want the book that was concealed in my uniform pocket?

'What are you waiting for?' I heard Rhea yell. Hurrying out from the corridor where Lynn came from, she came to a stop beside her, a smile creeping on her face. Ever so gently, she reached up and tapped her ear; it was then that I knew. All the times Rhea had kept silent, Lynn was listening to our conversations. Lynn was telling her what to say to lull us into a false comfort with her. Though we didn't trust her, we had, in a way, let our guard down. Everything clicked into place; the attempting to be helpful; getting sheets for Macie —she must have gone outside to briefly talk to Lynn, to update her or have a conversation on how to trap us. I felt so dispirited and shook my head at her. I was angry at her betrayal, but angrier at myself for being so stupid.

'Tell me Tara,' Lynn spoke softly, her eyes never wavering off mine, 'how did it feel when you threw your best friend into the mouth of hell?'

She waited briefly for me to reply, but when I didn't, she continued, 'Pain, sorrow, happiness?'

'Shut up,' I seethed, balling my hands into fists.

She laughed mockingly. 'Is the big bad Siren going to command me?' She tapped her ears, indicating something inside. 'Unlikely. I know all your little tricks.'

Quickly glancing at Henry I realised his beating heart was slowing down and his breathing becoming slow and fitful. He was dying and I had no plan.

'Where are the others, my friends?' I asked, my eyes locking back onto Lynn.

'Dave has them,' she said clicking her fingers.

Dave, in his Minotaur form, came skulking into view carrying a large light-blue sheet that had been turned into a makeshift sack.

'Saskia, Macie?' I cried out, but there was no answer.

Dave and Lynn laughed. 'Oh, they can't hear you,' Lynn smiled at me, 'they've permanently drifted off into the land of nod.'

Dave was holding the blanket with some extra different coloured cloth between his brown furry hands and then it hit me. 'The Blanket of Morpheus.'

'Oh well done,' Lynn mocked. 'You've read the book then.'

My eyes stabbed into Rhea's. She must have been leaking information from the book to Lynn when I was fighting Matt.

'So, you've changed,' Lynn said to me, her tone of voice almost sad. But her eyes gave away her true emotion. She was scared.

'Yes,' I told her calmly, trying to think of a plan. I looked at Henry again. His head had flopped to the side, his eyes staring at me, almost pleading me to do something. But I couldn't, not yet. I needed a distraction, just something small to put Lynn off for a second. I tried desperately for indicate with my eyes to Henry to grab the blanket, but he didn't seem to get it. I returned my attention to Lynn.

'Bigger wings,' she said inspecting them like a judge in an animal fair, 'giving you an advantage for longer flights but a disadvantage for speed. Also, you've grown taller. Another disadvantage. Your voice has changed. It's softer, more enticing for males.' Lynn looked out of the corner of her eyes at Henry. 'Anything else?' she asked casually, as though talking to two friends in a café.

'Hearing, eyesight and the ability to see the future,' I told her, shifting the weight on my left hip as I began to formulate a plan.

Lynn scoffed, 'You don't have that power.'

'Actually,' Rhea piped up, 'she does. Didn't you hear her call out for Henry, moments before you shot him?'

So Lynn didn't know about my little psychic gift, advantage, me.

'How often does it happen?' Lynn snapped, giving me a curious look.

But Rhea spoke for me, 'Only when she's in danger.'

Lynn quickly put her hand up and silenced her. 'No, not always. She wasn't in immediate danger.' Lynn's lips turned into a small smile and she looked at Henry's dying body on the floor and then turned back to me. 'Have you got a connection with him? Oh,' she said laughing derisively, 'that's sweet; the dying boy and the heroine −about to die herself. Oh, this reminds me a little bit of Romeo and Juliette, or Anthony and Cleopatra − and I'm the asp,' she said raising her gun slightly higher.

'Actually,' I began, 'I think Rhea would be the asp, after all, she's the vicious snake.'

Rhea's eyes narrowed and taking one step, smacked me in the face. It wasn't hard and it didn't hurt but it gave me the opportunity I needed for a distraction. I span around and tripping up crumbled to the floor beside Henry. As I fell I ensured my left hand was palm down by my head, my right hand underneath me and with my left wing covering me, I looked right at Henry.

'Tara?' Lynn asked quickly, as I heard slow hesitant steps towards me. 'Tara?'

'Wow, looks like I'm getting as powerful as she is,' Rhea said in a smarmy voice.

My heart skipped with joy as I next heard two sets of footsteps and one set of hooves heading towards me. 'Grab the blanket,' I mouthed to Henry, 'when I say.' He nodded ever so slightly in understanding even though he was in a lot of pain and when I suddenly felt hands on my shoulder about to turn me around I blinked at Henry. A small smile spread on his face –it was time.

Pushing on my hands, I brought my body off the floor with ease and swung my legs under me like a street-dancer, kicking Lynn square in the chest pushing her up and away. Such was my power that the kick caught all three of them knocking them off their feet. Dave, as I had planned dropped the bag on the ground close to Henry.

'HENRY, GRAB IT!' I yelled, hoping and praying that he had enough strength left to get up. Rolling over as quickly as he could, he reached out and grabbed the cloth that Dave had dropped and yanked it back, yelling in pain as he did then fell to the bloody floor. He had no energy left; his life was slipping from him.

Glancing quickly at the others I could see they were rousing from the spell of Morpheus's blanket. I saw Sam, we'd need him too. I had no choice; Henry would die if I didn't change him.

'SAM, HENRY TRANSFORM NOW,' I commanded loudly.

Saskia, Macie and Lionel scrambled out of the way and charged towards Lynn and Dave who were struck with shock at what was happening. Macie pounced on Dave, trying to rip his throat, fluttering her wings madly to disorientate him. Saskia went up and punched Rhea right in the face, but Rhea was just as strong as Saskia and quickly recovered. Both of them fell to the floor and were rolling around punching, hitting, slapping and pulling each other's hair and wings, while Lionel ran right at Lynn bowling her over and sending her flying against a wall.

'Saskia,' I said to her while Sam was screaming in agony, ripping his shirt off to change. But as he did so, I saw his neck. His tattoo had vanished completely! What was going on? Glancing at Henry, who was in double the amount of pain, I also saw that his tattoo's had gone. Was that because we were changing into our true forms? Did that go for Hannah, Darren and Macie too?

'Saskia, immobilise her,' I called as I went to Sam, who had inadvertently dropped Lottie as he changed.

Grabbing Lottie, I shoved her on my shoulder, 'Grip it as tight as you can, don't fall off,' I told her as I turned my attention to Henry but Saskia had come into my peripheral view. As I had my back turned to grab Lottie,

Saskia had immobilised Rhea in the best way she knew how; head butting her.

'Damn, tha' felt good,' she smiled as she kicked the blanket of Morpheus over Rhea's body.

Holding back a laugh, I turned my attention to Henry. I could feel the power erupting out of him. It wasn't an evil power that I felt; it was more of a thundering presence like Hannah had felt in Ha Long Bay.

Though he had been shot in the stomach, the DNA from Maahes, the son of Sekhmet, wasn't letting him follow Anubis into the Underworld. As I was aware from the Ancient side of my brain, Henry was in for some big changes and it started out with his size.

Once again, golden fur rippled across his entire body. His arms and legs grew rapidly along with his torso and a small bullet popped out of his stomach and fell to the floor with a clink; the hole healed within seconds. Claws ripped out of the ends of his fingers and he roared deafeningly, like some angry beast.

With his legs resembling a lion's hind legs, Henry stood up and shook his half-mane, half-beard that flowed down from his face. His eyes were like a cat's, oval green and striking; staring right into your soul. Henry had grown to my height, which I found slightly disconcerting.

Smiling at me, showing new white pointy feline fangs, he said 'Thanks,' his voice sounding so melodious to my ears, I wanted to listen to him speak for hours. Then pushing me gently aside, he lunged towards the fray between Lionel, Macie, Lynn and Dave. Staring around quickly, I noticed too, that Sam was missing.

'LIONEL, MACIE, SAM GET OUT OF THERE,' I bellowed to them. 'HENRY CAN HANDLE THEM, LET'S GO!'

From my shouts, the fight stopped briefly. Henry ploughed into Lynn and Dave, sending them flying in the opposite direction. Hesitating for the briefest moment, Macie and Lionel turned tail and headed towards me and feeling a weight on my other shoulder, I quickly turned to see Sam's weird form perched on top of it, his red eyes staring at me.

'Henry is the embodiment of warfare and destruction,' I told him. 'I don't want anyone to be around him when he gets angry.'

Macie, Lionel and Saskia ran ahead of me and down a corridor that looked like it was a tunnel.

'Where are we goin'?' Saskia asked the only one out of us who could talk.

'If anyone has any ideas, squawk or bark or whatever,' I said as the tunnel was about to split off into two. But before we got there, there was an almighty BOOM from behind us; the aftershock throwing us off our feet. Suddenly the tunnel ceiling cracked. Bits of brick and dust rained down on us as parts of the old Cold War bunker started to fall apart.

'Damn,' Saskia yelped as she scurried to get up, 'was tha' 'enry?'

'Yup. KEEP MOVING,' I urged them onwards as I led, not daring to waste any time within a small radius of Henry. Lionel barked and turned quickly right, almost skidding into the wall in front.

'LESS CLAW MORE PAD!' I shouted at him, grabbing the fur between his shoulders and yanking him up.

Lionel snapped at me from pain, but this was no time to get involved with the RSPCA. 'MOVE IT,' I bellowed as another thunderous boom came from behind us, followed by another loud roar; one that sounded so ferocious, so familiar I hesitated for a moment and Saskia smacked right into me. Lottie and Sam dug their claws into my shoulder to keep from falling off as I pitched forwards.

'Wha' the 'ell?' she said, scraping herself off the floor and pushing me forwards with the others who had stopped to wait.

'It's Lynn,' I told her, my heart racing from fear for Henry. 'She's turned into a dragon.'

'Well then, 'enry's got his work cut-out fer him. I thought we were in a hurry?' she asked me, coming into view; her face looking scared.

'She can't fly,' I said thinking about Lynn's little talk with me earlier, 'she's at a disadvantage.'

'So?' Saskia asked, looking like I had lost the plot.

'I need to stop her,' I said making a snap decision. I looked at the others and sighed, shaking my head. 'Find King Minos, I'll catch up with you later.'

'TARA, NO! COME BACK!' Saskia yelled after me as Lottie and Sam each let go of my shoulder.

I pelted back towards the sounds of the fight, the sounds of mythological creatures biting, snarling, roaring and demolishing the tunnels of the abandoned nuclear bunker of the 1950's.

Rounding the corner, I was met by a horrendous scene. Rubble from the ceiling and walls were everywhere. Scorch marks flared up in both directions of the tunnels. Dave was down, thick blood spilling out of his mouth and ears. His jaw looked like it had been broken and his horns had been ripped out of his skull. On the floor, Rhea was still under the blanket out for the count. But my attention quickly turned to Henry and Lynn who were locked in such an epic battle that it was difficult to see who had the upper hand.

Lynn had pretty much demolished two floors of the bunker. The upper floor tunnel was caved in from her sheer size, but no matter how much of the bunker she destroyed, Henry still had the opportunity to fight back.

She had deep bloody scratches all over her face with viscous looking liquid dripping to the floor, forming a small pool on the debris littered ground. Lynn's long tail thrashed out, as she quickly locked her jaw around Henry but putting his hands up, he stopped her in her tracks. Henry held her mouth open; holding her vicious set of teeth apart, her tongue close to licking his face.

Lynn then began to inhale deeply, 'HENRY, LOOK OUT,' I screamed, knowing she was about to breathe fire.

Caught off-guard from my voice, Henry backed off, with moments to spare as she threw a stream of scalding fire towards him. Grabbing him, I pulled him towards me, using my wings as a shield from the heat of the fire.

'Tara, you'll burn,' he said looking shocked, as the fire raged on behind me.

But shaking my head I told him, 'I'm immortal remember. I can't die from a little heat.' The fire suddenly stopped and I folded my wings back, turning swiftly around to face Lynn, but she was human again. She raked the floor beneath her for some ripped clothing and tied it around her chest and hips. Scratched, bloodied and bruised, she looked close to death.

'Henry,' she hissed as she fell to the floor looking exhausted and in pain, 'don't think your bird-bitch can save you. You are no match for me,' she laughed pathetically.

Henry put me behind him, as though he was protecting me and took a confident step forward. 'You have a choice,' he said, his voice filled with power and authority. 'You can continue fighting and die here in this abandoned bunker, or you can listen to reason and live.'

Lynn scoffed and spat on the floor, 'Listen to reason. What is so important you have to tell me? You know nothing. You childish assholes know NOTHING!' she shouted.

Suddenly, I got annoyed. All the things that she had kept from me that myself and the group had found out by clues and little pieces of information we stumbled upon over the past few days, came tumbling towards me; almost crushing me. I hated being lied to and kept in the dark. I wanted answers from her and damn it, I was going to get them.

'TELL ME WHAT YOU KNOW!' I commanded her, stepping out from Henry's shadow and facing her head on.

Lynn bit her lip and shook her head as she began to mumble, the words trying to escape from her mouth, the words of truth.

'LOUDER,' I shouted.

'It's a cycle!' she burst out. 'I used to be human. Jeff, Amjee, some of the group's parents; they were the cycle before me. We all used to be human, me, Dave, Matt, Roxy. But the Goddamn T.A.T did this to us. We've been on a leash for years, always doing what he wants!'

'We knew that already.' I said, coming out from behind Henry to face her. 'I guess that the dragon that was found in Vietnam in 1984 was the DNA that was put into you?'

She nodded pathetically.

'Lynn, we knew the T.A.T are bad and I know about Maynard and his plans to get into the other plane.'

She began chuckling madly then spat blood on the floor. 'The T.A.T. are bad, yes,' she laughed, 'well done on figuring that out,' she snapped at us. 'But...' she sighed, her head dropped, downhearted. She was giving up. 'They have a hold on us. We have to work for them. If we don't, they'll kill our parents.'

'WHAT?' Henry and I asked in shock.

'My parents are still alive,' Lynn's voice cracked. 'They don't know who I am, but does that matter?' she lifted her head; tears fell from her eyes and into the smashed concrete floor below. 'I would do anything for them even if, even if I'm not human anymore.'

'But you're human now,' Henry said to her. Lynn shook her head, not bothering to argue with him.

'This cycle about our parents,' I said hurrying her along, 'what do you mean?'

Lynn tried to move, but yelled out in pain and instead kept still; taking a moment to calm her shaking body. 'The T.A.T., they have screwed up, trial and error.' She said bitterly. 'Jeff and Amjee, they are the failed attempts on previous experiments to turn them into myths. The majority of the parents from your group were the employers of the T.A.T. who went out to collect myths, collect them alive or dead. Their job was to bring them back to the T.A.T to collect their D.N.A and help turn people.' Lynn slumped to the floor, her breathing was laboured but neither Henry nor I made a move towards her. Lynn laughed lightly and shook her head. 'And you can thank your mother for who you are. All of the T.A.T's parents used to be myths and your parents, Tara, found a cure to turn them back into humans.' she sniggered. 'Maynard has been using you to get to your parents to kill them. But he failed.'

Henry's furry hand squeezed my own, trying to convey to me that everything was going to be alright, but this was heartbreaking. My parents were myths and they left me to save themselves, without telling me what was going on? I closed my eyes and took a deep breath.

'Why, why go all through this?' I asked her, my eyes still closed.

Lynn paused and finally I saw her lift her head and smile evilly at me. 'A plan from the very beginning. Maynard needs to get into the other plane. The Phaistos Disc is being required as I speak and though the King has been silent for years, he *will* talk. But as a failsafe we've discovered Maynard needs a portal opened by the right people. You provided Rhea with the answer that Maynard has been searching for. The Ancients. We used you Tara. Letting you escape, and by attacking and provoking you to turn everyone into myths. *You* are unbalancing the world, you will be punished. And when there is enough myths in this plane the Ancients will open a portal and the real myths will come through and will kill you and Maynard will become a god.'

CHAPTER TWENTY

HENRY TOLD ME TO CALM DOWN OVER AND OVER AGAIN, but I didn't understand. All I was doing was breathing, wasn't I? I saw Lynn in front of me in her ragged make-shift clothes, giving me a harsh look. She was in no position to attack us now; her energy was zapped.

'Tara, Tara, look at me,' he said, his words flowing over me. I didn't understand what he wanted. 'Tara!' His pitch reached my ears, but my brain refused to acknowledge what he was saying. I knew that I was sat amongst the debris-filled tunnel, just staring straight ahead but then Lynn staggered up and hobbled out of view. A loud growl sounded beside me, but nothing connected. Henry, the weird black lion thing was shaking me. The old 1950's lights above me began to flicker. There was some part of me that knew I had to get up, but I didn't really want to. I just needed time.

A smart stinging sensation erupted on my right cheek. I blinked coming to my senses.

'Tara, get up, we need to get to the others,' Henry yelled, pulling my arm. I let him haul me up and drag me away. As my shoes slapped along the concrete, I tried to piece everything together. My parents were myths. There's a cure to be human again and Maynard wants to become a god.'

Henry seemed to know where we were going. It sounded as though we were following barks, chirps and yells and approaching a long dark, almost oppressing corridor, we came to a thick metal door. The bolt had been scratched open. The door was ajar, a single, feeble beam shining out from the crack.

'They're inside,' he told me.

I stopped outside briefly and shook my head of the fuzziness. There was too much information to deal with. I had to accept what I had heard and get on with it. There were more important matters to deal with. 'I know. I can hear them.' I whispered. Taking tentative steps, we walked into the dimly lit room; our footsteps echoing off the walls.

'Ah and the Siren approaches,' came a deep voice. It wasn't a scary voice or a threatening voice. It was an almost docile one, but it was full of sadness.

Moving inside, the light from within flooded my vision and shielding my eyes, I saw that Saskia and the others were crowded around a large bearded man with a kind and noble face. He was the King of Minos. But what was surprising to see, was that he appeared human, although somewhat larger than most people.

'Welcome Siren,' he said inclining his head.

Smiling at him, I walked further into the room, which was completely bare and dismal looking. 'It is nice to finally meet you King Minos,' I replied.

His smile met his eyes and he gestured me to come forwards. 'I had the pleasure of meeting your parents a long time ago,' he said glancing at the others, 'and of course your mother,' he told me in a warm voice.

'I am so sorry you have been down here for all these years,' I said sadly, knowing of his long and lonely imprisonment. On the floor, I saw broken chains that had fallen from his red raw wrists and ankles. 'But now you're free, you can return home.'

His face fell a little and I was unsure of what he was thinking but then: 'Your friends call you Tara,' he glanced at me carefully. 'It has a powerful meaning, did you know?'

I shook my head gently.

'You have a destiny Tara, to be a guardian of the world. After all, you have her blood in you,' he said, his brows creased slightly. 'I know why you are here, why you are all... here...' he said turning to glance at everyone, changing the subject quickly again.

'Do you know of this war?' I asked him hesitantly.

The King nodded sadly. 'I have known of the war for some time. It was brought to my attention many, many years ago when humans found a way to enter our plane and become, more...'

'But,' I stopped him, 'I know your secret. You were all once human too. That the Ancients turned you into myths. Why are you so against us becoming myths?'

The King chuckled, 'My dear, I am not against killing the purity of you changed humans. After all, this isn't your fault. But the truth is we cannot allow the rest of you to become full myths. Think of the imbalance the world would be thrown into.'

'Please,' I begged, making him return his attention on me. 'What do we do to stop this?'

'Turn yourselves into humans again,' he said simply. 'Your mother was working on a cure was she not?'

I nodded and the others gasped in shock. Lottie chirruped quietly and flapped her wings. She was so desperate to become human again.

'Then go to her. Find out the secret of your cure before the war starts.' I didn't know where my parents were. Last time I heard they were in Europe but that would be anywhere. If Maynard wanted them, they probably went into hiding. The only way I could think of to reach them was my brother, but how could I explain the situation without giving anything away?

'Sir,' Saskia asked timidly stepping towards him, 'the war, when will it start?'

Sighing, he looked at her, helplessly. 'When you have all transformed. I know your plight,' he said gently to her, taking her hand. 'Just don't get angry.'

A shiver ran down my spine. I looked at the others and even caught Henry's eye. 'Have you all... are you all fully...?' I couldn't finish the sentences but in their own way, they each nodded. 'Oh my gosh, I'm so sorry, I'm so, so sorry.'

'Do not feel bad, Tara,' the King said. 'It was inevitable, just as stones are washed by the sea. There is a reason for these things.'

Not wanting to look at the others, I looked at Saskia. 'If the others have all changed into full myths, then it's just you Saskia,' but I saw her shake her head. Then I remembered. There was one other who hadn't changed yet... 'Rhea.' She was a Siren and she was capable of fully changing. 'Henry,' I whispered.

'I'm on it,' he said and without another word, quickly left.

'It's Rhea,' I told the puzzled group. 'She's not part of our group, but she's still like Saskia and me.'

There was a collective sound of acknowledgement, but everyone kept quiet apart from the King, who was mumbling to himself. Then quickly standing he looked at the door. 'The dragon' he said with an angry voice. 'She knows.'

As old as he seemed, the King sprightly hurried after Henry, the rest of us, a little stunned, quickly followed.

'What is it?' Saskia asked me as we sped out of the blackness of the corridor and back into the flickering tunnel.

'It's Rhea,' I told her. 'If she leaves we're screwed.'

'NO!' came a loud tremendous roar from up ahead. Suddenly there was a brilliant flash of blue light and then it was gone.

Rounding the corner we saw Henry and King Minos alone in the debris-filled tunnel, both gaping at a spot on the floor metres in front of them. Morpheus' Blanket was ripped. Rhea, Dave and Lynn had vanished.

'Damn,' Henry said in frustration turning around to face us.

'Does anyone know where they could 'ave gone?' Saskia asked, cutting in front of him.

Henry gave me a brief smile. 'London. I know Lynn. She'd take Rhea back to the museum.'

★ ★ ★

Now able to leave his prison, the King of Minos followed us back out of the nuclear base. The fresh winter night air of Wales cleared my thoughts completely. I had to make a plan to get us into the museum; we needed to stop Rhea from changing.

'Ah, smell that fresh air,' the King said inhaling deeply. 'How I have longed for such an emotion as freedom. It is good to be out.'

'Are ya goin' home now?' Saskia asked him as she glanced up at him.

'Yes. I am going home, although where home is, I am unsure,' he said looking down at her. 'My home was the Palace of Knossos, the greatest palace in all of Crete. I was worshipped and praised by my people daily. The festivities we had,' he smiled, 'bull-leaping was my gift to them. It was a great and joyous sport, but also a dangerous one. Only those with great courage could do it.'

As the King reminisced, I took Henry to the side to talk to him.

'We need to get into the museum, undetected… the only one of us capable of doing that and at great speed is Sam.'

The King of Minos smiled and raised his arms. 'I am being summoned back to the magical plane.' Lowering his arms, he glanced at all of us, smiling in a fatherly way. 'I want you all to solemnly promise that you will all work together and to try and stop this impending war. I know that the magical community do not want to fight with you, but they will do as commanded by the Ancients, just as any troop is instructed by their leader.

Tara, you have a destiny. Just know that everything happens for a reason. You will know what to do when the time comes to make the ultimate decision for all of you. Goodbye!' In the middle of our circle, he left our world in a brilliant blue light. I felt emptiness when he left. It was like a helpful guide had finished a tour and now we were left on our own to contemplate the information we had been told.

With Saskia shivering, we went back into the bunker and searched around for anything useful we could use to get Sam and the others into the T.A.T. headquarters under the British Museum.

The annoying lights still flickered as I headed off with Saskia, which adding to my headache. I was tired, hungry and bruised and no matter how many times I told myself "I'll find the time to eat and sleep," there was no goddamn time. There was always something.

'So, wha's ya plan?' Saskia asked. I knocked down a solid steel door with one quick kick; the room behind it revealing an old kitchen.

'Sam is the only option we have,' I told her, as we moved on to another door.

Saskia chuckled ruefully, 'There's a problem with tha.'

'He can't communicate,' I said peering into the unused room, but everything looked like it hadn't been touched in years.

'Yeah, but also, he'll be seen,' she said in a matter-of-fact way.

Calming myself before I slapped her for being stupid, I humoured her. 'How?'

'Well okay, not seen visually, because he's invisible when he wants ta but, the lift in the base has pressure sensors. If ya even breathe the sensors kick in.'

'Is there a way in?' I asked her as we approached another solid-looking steel door on the left of the corridor.

'Maybe,' she shrugged, 'but I need ta see wha' their computer equipment is like. I might be able ta tap into their security system an' mess up their computers which communicate with the lift. Givin' us some time ta get Sam in there without them noticin' an' then cause a disruption fer us ta go in with Lionel, grab Rhea an' leave.'

I laughed, 'You sound like a computer hacker.'

I lifted my leg and kicked the door hard. The metal buckled; the hinges snapped and the door caved in, falling to the floor with a loud echoing BANG!

'Tara, I *am* a computer hacker an'-' she began, but suddenly shut up. As I had felt for a light switch by the side of the wall and flicked it on, Saskia smiled, 'Welcome ta my domain.'

The room which we had forcibly entered was full of computers, but the strange thing of it was that they didn't look old; they looked new, like the ones from the Cathedral room.

'These aren't old like everythin' else in this God forsaken bunker,' Saskia jumped around looking giddy as she touched the slightly dusty monitors. 'Ah, technology,' she said almost lovingly.

'You're such a closeted geek,' I told her as I casually leaned against the broken door. 'I had no idea you were into this stuff.'

She beamed at me and walked around the room checking the wires. Bending down, she picked up a thick black wire and followed it with her eyes. 'I 'ave internet but there is a problem.' She stood up and placed her hands on her hips. 'You know at university ya have ya intranet? Where all the computer rooms are on da same system?'

'Yeah…'

'Well, so is this,' she told me, moving the black wire with her foot. 'It's the main lead which connects to the T.A.T. server, I'm sure of it. There is a down side an' an upside to it though.'

'We have to access all of their files but they will know we are here and see what we're doing?' I asked randomly thinking ahead and she nodded.

'Yes to the first an' sort of to the second. It will take them sometime ta figure out tha' their system is being hacked or used. But the problem is… tha',' she said pointing above me. Spinning around, I turned to look at what she was pointing to and my heart sank. It was a camera. 'It's not on,' she said quickly, 'but I wonder 'ow long it will take fer them ta turn them on.'

'I didn't notice,' I said sheepishly.

'I've counted ten so far. They aren't in all the rooms, just the ones tha' matter.'

'Oh,' I suddenly shouted, clapping my hands and making her jump. 'Question, how long do you think it would take you to get into their system before they figure it's us?'

Expelling air she shrugged. 'I can scramble the signal by usin' the homin' beacon on the little hand-held computer tha' they've left behind,' she nodded at the device beside her. 'It only works when the thing is turned on, but I once asked Lynn, they put homin' beacons in everythin'.'

'Gits. But, I have an idea; we need to move one of these computers into a room with no camera. I want them to see that we aren't here when they turn these cameras on.'

After finding the others quickly, Saskia and I told them about the plan, the only problem was that all of them seemed to have something to say, but none of them could communicate with us.

Macie and Lionel roared and screeched at me in protest to the plan. 'It's not my fault you can't frigging talk! Henry,' I said as I turned to face him. Though he kept quiet during the planning brief, he hadn't said whether he was for or against it. 'What do you think?'

'The King said that we all had to stick together,' he said avoiding my question, 'this plan is the only one we've got-.'

Lionel barked, but Henry shook his head. 'I know that you have a plan mate, but you can't talk. If there were a way for you to communicate to us then, that would be great but there isn't.'

'Oh my God,' I said as it suddenly occurred to me, 'Why didn't this knowledge kick in sooner. I am such an idiot.'

'I could 'ave told ya tha',' Saskia said giving me a sideways glance.

Closing my eyes and ignoring her I opened them and looked at the others, 'The book mentioned something about telepathy. Darren uses it and Lottie does too,' I said looking at her.

'Wha' of it,' Saskia shrugged.

Grabbing her hand with my left, I placed our hands on Lionel's shoulder...

'...you stupid cow, I could have told you that telepathy works, that's how we've all been talking to each other but you three are too damn idle to even think about it.'

'Well, holy mother of Mary,' Saskia laughed as she looked at Henry, 'I can hear 'im.'

Frowning Henry put a hand on Macie and instantly smiled.

'Are you still with Tara? I'm really confused with you guys at the moment,' Macie said, her voice so crystal clear it was as though she was standing right next to me... well in human form anyway.

'It's nice to hear your voice.' I smiled at her. 'So how do we do this?' I asked Lionel as everyone gathered in closer so we could all get in a word or two.

'I don't think you should do this computer hacking crap,' Sam voiced in our minds, 'just let me get in and get out.'

'You can't,' Saskia snipped at him, 'The lift is pressure sensitive. As soon as ya get in they'll know somethin' is in there. Regardless of ya being invisible or not.'

'How does she know that?' Lionel asked giving me a puppy look with his head titled.

'She's a closeted computer geek and also a tech-nut, just let it be,' I told him.

'So, actually Tara's plan would be the way to go,' Lottie said to us. 'But I don't like the idea of Sam going in alone.'

'He won't,' Henry smiled at her, 'I'm going there too and so is Lionel. The three of us can get Rhea and bring her back.'

As the others went to get the equipment for Saskia, I sat down heavily on a chair and closed my eyes. There were so many things to prepare for. We had to get these gismos up and running and ensure that the T.A.T. didn't home in on us. Saskia need only hack into their system and bring their computers down for a few minutes, during which time Lionel had to transport Sam and Henry to London. Sam then had to break into the museum and create a diversion. Henry and Lionel will wait five minutes before they break in themselves and kidnap Rhea. This plan was all down to the assumption that Lynn believed we had left this facility.

'Are you alright?' Macie's thoughts passed into my own.

I opened my eyes to see Macie's head on my leg; her eagle eyes looking lost and confused. Giving her a watery smile, I patted her gently. 'I have too many thoughts that's all.'

'Is it about Henry?'

Scrunching up my face, I shook my head. I wasn't sure if I should tell Macie what was going on between Henry and me. In reality, it had nothing to do with her and I didn't want to burden her with my love life, no matter how unclear it seemed to the others. 'No,' I replied, 'it's about the plan, that's all.'

Moments later, Henry and Saskia came in with everyone's bags and promptly tipped them upside-down, spilling the random contents of gadgets and tools on the floor.

'Right, let's get to it,' Saskia smiled as she sat on the floor and began working.

Sam and the others quickly followed behind and sat with Macie; all of them seemed to be in a deep discussion about something, but I didn't particularly want to know what. I was still lost in my own thoughts about my parents, Rhea, the war… and Henry. Glancing at him now and again, I saw that he was looking at me in a cautious manner, but I didn't understand why.

I groaned loudly and lay back on the floor, folding my wings around me like a cocoon. I wanted darkness and quiet. In truth, I wanted to be alone but I couldn't leave the others, not now. How I longed to just leave and fly off somewhere. To sit, perhaps, on top of one of Wales' highest peaks and think. Just until I had cleared my thoughts. But I couldn't and it was frustrating. I was still angry at Lynn and Rhea; annoyed that I hadn't seen through Rhea. I was too trusting, it was my only flaw.

''enry could ya pass me tha' Phillips screwdriver please,' I heard Saskia ask as the sounds of clanking metal echoed around the room. 'Thanks. Oy you,' Saskia said, raising her voice, 'bird lady. Are ya just gonna fold up like that or are ya gonna help?'

'What do you want me to do?' I asked, not unfolding my wings.

Saskia muttered a few choice curse words then after a short pause said, 'never mind, um Tara, we have a visitor.'

Unfolding my wings completely, I sat up and spotting Annabel by the doorway. Lionel and Macie looked at up at where I was looking at and seemed to have finally reached the point where they could see ghosts too.

'Annabel?'

'Tara, I'm sorry to bring you such bad news. It's about your parents,' she said softly. 'Maynard found your father this evening. He believes your parents had the Phaistos Disc.'

I felt my eyes grow wide in shock. That was a lot of information to absorb. 'My father? Aren't my parents together?'

'Your parents had split up. They knew Maynard wanted the disc and were giving him the run-around. Your father was in Europe. Though he didn't have the Phaistos Disc. I watched as he contacted your mother when he knew that Maynard was after him. Maynard now thinks that your mother has it instead.'

I stood up and she took a step away from me. 'And does she Annabel?' I said gently, 'Where is my mother?'

Annabel looked away, unable to meet my eyes. Although a pained expression etched on her face. 'She left for the other plane, with the disc. But that isn't the reason why I came here.' Annabel paused slightly then looked so sad. 'Tara, I'm so sorry but, Rhea killed your father.'

Saskia, Lionel and Macie each cried out in shock in their own way. Henry was the only one who couldn't see ghosts, but gathered from the sound of our cries, it wasn't good.

'H-how? He's meant to be part of the T.A.T. right? A myth?'

She replied sadly, 'A myth can be killed in this world with the right type of magic. I'm so sorry, Tara.' She voiced what Lynn had said earlier.

Collapsing to the floor, Henry came and hugged me as I cried into his soft furry chest. Smoothing my hair, he rocked me gently and repeatedly told me that it would be alright but I didn't see how. No one moved or said anything for a long time as they heard me sob uncontrollably. It was the first time I had ever lost a loved one. I wouldn't wish it on anyone. It was as though someone had literally grabbed hold of my heart and was trying to physically pull it out of my chest. The loss of my father was so unbearable; I found it difficult to breathe.

Sometime later, my sobs turned into silent crying and I started to calm down. No one had seen me break down like that before, apart from Henry, and I had no doubt that they were shaken to see me in such a state.

Saskia managed to find me a glass of water and I gratefully took it. 'Thank you,' I mumbled, smiling she nodded and sat back down on a computer chair. 'I'm sorry guys.'

Henry shook my gently. 'No, Tara, don't apologise for that, anyone would have done the same thing.'

I shook my head. 'No, I can't get like this.' I took a few deep breaths to try and calm down. What happened, happened and I couldn't change it. 'We have a job to do.' My voice wavered and Henry hugged me and kissed me tenderly on my forehead.

'Go and lie down for a bit,' he said softly. 'We'll wake you if there's anything important.' I tried to stay awake. I had to focus on the task at hand, but tiredness, exhaustion and the death of my father caught up with me all too quickly.

Chapter Twenty-One

'Are we going ta be wakin' her up soon?' I heard Saskia's annoying voice ring through my ears like a high-pitched bell, which ironically woke me up.

'Let her sleep,' Henry soothed. 'She needs her rest.'

'But as much as I hate ta say it, Macie's right. We need ta make a plan after we get the little git from London,' Saskia stated.

I didn't mean to fall asleep in the computer room, but my brain needed time to think. As I slept I had discovered something terrible, something which threw a spanner into the works. Including Saskia's own plans.

'I've told you already,' Henry said, sounding angry.

'No, you've explained to me ya suspicions of 'er plan about me. I want ta hear 'er say it. See it come right outta 'er mouth an' why she won't take me with 'er. We know she wants ta go to the other plane ta get the disc an' I know she'll leave me behind!'

I had made my choice then and there and saw no other way. Opening my wings wide and standing up to my full height, the group jumped at the sudden movement.

'Everyone, I've been thinking about this. About the plan. Getting to London and grabbing Rhea. There's a flaw, a big one, that I hadn't seen until now.'

'What do you mean?' Henry asked.

'Maynard cannot get into the other plane without the disc, so far as we know. If he cannot find my mother, he will assume she's gone into the other plane. The only way he can get the disc is to blackmail my mother to bring it back. Ergo Maynard will be coming after me and with it, all of you will be put in danger.'

'Then wha' do you intend to do?' Saskia demanded as she folded her arms, frowning at me. 'Go an' confront him at the T.A.T. an' have a show-down with 'im?'

I remained quiet; it was exactly what I was planning to do. Within seconds, everyone started to shout, or bark or chirrup, or screech at me, but I shook my head definitely.

'This doesn't concern any of you,' I shouted them down. 'Rhea was the one who killed my father and no doubt on Maynard's orders. I know that you want us to be a team and I respect that, but this is *my* fight, not yours.'

Henry reached out and took hold of my shoulders. 'Think about what you are saying, think about what you are doing? We have no idea what he is capable of.'

I shrugged him off. 'I know what I'm doing. Maynard's had this beef with me from the beginning. This is my fight guys. If it was any of you, wouldn't you want to do the same?' They each looked at one another. As soon as I finished talking there was a distant BOOM up above us. Fine dust rained down from the ceiling.

'Wha' in the 'ell was tha'?' Saskia jumped.

After a few seconds interval, there was another tremendous BOOM, knocking all the lights out in the corridor.

'I can't see!' Saskia shouted.

'I've got a torch,' Henry's calm voice came from beside me then a beam of light shone towards us showing dust shimmering everywhere. Henry threw another torch to me and grabbing our bags, we left the room in a hurry.

'What's going on?' Macie's thoughts entered my own, as I felt her head touch my hand.

'I dunno, but it sounds as though we're being bombed.'

'We can't be,' Henry said irritably.

'The T.A.T, must know we're here still. They are destroying the bunker. They're forcing us out.' As soon as I said that, another loud BANG came from above us. The floor shook violently, almost unbalancing me. 'We need to get out of here,' I said, my torch flicking around the tunnel, checking out rooms that we had been in, but showing nothing helpful to our situation. 'Damn,' I panicked, feeling my stomach churn. 'Lionel you are going to have to take us somewhere. And no, I don't know where,' I added. 'They are after me; they're flushing us out to get to me. Damn it, you're all in danger. I have no choice,' I said more to myself.

A furry hand suddenly grabbed my own and together, we all stopped.

'Don't you even dare,' Henry said looking deep into my eyes, my soul finally understanding. Whatever strange feeling I had towards Henry when he was human had completely gone. My heart lifted, as though it had its very own set of wings, but what I had in mind for the group could destroy us. Shaking his head in defiance, 'Please, don't,' he begged.

'Wha'? Wha's goin' on?' Saskia asked her voice filled with panic.

I stood back away from the group the base continued to be bombarded with more debris raining down around us. I left go of Henry's soft hand. I hated making snap decisions, but they had never let me down before. Henry shook his head, pained eyes meeting my own. He knew what I was going to do, but he didn't stop me. He knew it was the only way.

Initially I wasn't sure if this would work, but Lionel's ability far exceeded what Lynn and Maynard would ever hope to understand. Lionel was the opener of ways. Not just in this plane, but the magical one as well. I took a deep breath. 'Lionel,' I said in a commanding voice, 'take everyone and go to the other plane and don't come back here looking for me.'

'NOOO!' Henry yelled as Lionel, snarling from being given a command he didn't want to do, pounced on the others.

Everyone screamed, yelled, screeched or roared out in pain and sadness before the brilliant blue light swept them away and then they were gone.

★ ★ ★

The booms continued up above me and I sank to the floor crying. I had sent everyone away; I had forced my new family to leave me. I was taking a big risk, especially with Saskia and Rhea. It wouldn't have mattered if everyone had transformed in this plane or the next; it's the fact that we existed as myths that would create a war. But I knew if I got to Rhea before she transformed, I could stop this whole thing from starting.

Slowly getting up off the floor, and with the explosions still sounding above me I knew I had to face them head on. With no time to lose, I hurried down the labyrinthine corridors. I needed to get to the staircase and up to the surface. But as I approached them a few minutes later, to my dismay the stairs had been demolished. The heavy metal door leading to the stairs was crumpled, like paper on the ground with rubble from the stairs littering the floor. But not only that, what twisted my stomach with cold icicles was the sight of strange claw marks that were cut deeply into the walls.

Before I could react to what I'd seen, I had another premonition. A ropy-tail was wrapping around my throat, choking me but not strong enough to kill me. I could smell putrid breath and feel it hot and sticky on the back of my neck coupled with that voice which made my blood turn cold. I couldn't understand why or how this event should take place. But the fact that it was going to and that I would be completely on my own, worried me more than anything.

Blinking, I turned around in a circle and saw nothing at either end of the corridor, but my heart palpitated as I felt the atmosphere enclose me. It was as though there was no escape from this oppressive feeling. It sucked everything that was good from the world. There was no light, no warmth, and no kindness. And what was left was cold, dark and malevolent. This sensation was the grand entrance of a daughter of Hades. She had arrived and had found me here. Sniffing me out like a hound to a rat. I tensed, waiting for something to happen, for it was inevitable.

Then I heard her voice, rasping and close by, but with the torch I could only see certain things. 'Hello Tara, aren't you going to welcome me back home? After all, this was where I was made.'

Trying not to jump in fright, I turned around slowly and saw Amanda, in her complete Fury form, behind me. Holding back a gasp, I stared at her and saw a significant amount of damage had been caused to her face, arms and torso. It looked like she had literally been through hell and back.

'How... how did you get up here?' I asked her, unsure of what to make of all of this. I tried to listen for the others, Heather and Beth, but it seemed that only Amanda had made it out.

'I have friends in low places,' she smiled evilly. 'You know it's funny,' she began as she started pacing on dinosaur-like hind legs, a new ropy tail swishing back and forth. 'Every day on earth seems like a year in hell. And do you know what I did in hell, Tara?'

I saw it happen before I physically felt it, but what was worse, I couldn't stop it.

'I FOUGHT DEMONS!' she shouted and like a viper, slapped me across the face so hard I flew into the air. Crashing into a brick wall; concrete and dust fell around me, the torch clattering to the floor just out of reach. 'They are wimps,' she laughed as she came towards me, her talons scratching the floor. 'Though you can't kill demons, they were fun to beat up. I just imagined they were you and I became oh so powerful.'

The ropy tail, which had evidently grown back while in hell, gripped around my throat and with it, she pulled me to my feet, then lifted me clean off the floor.

'You… won't… kill me,' I choked, unable to catch my breath. 'Maynard needs me,' I said but she just laughed manically.

'Stupid bitch, who needs you?'

'I do,' said a strong male familiar voice. 'Let her go, or I'll kill you.' The sound of a rifle cocking echoed off the broken walls around me.

'Who the hell are you?' She demanded, her eyes twitching in the direction of the stranger.

But he remained silent as he took a few steps towards us. Amanda was distracted. With one sweep of my left wing, she relinquished her grip on me and I fell to the floor. Taking deep breaths, I turned my head around and in the dim light recognised the last person in the world I expected to see. 'Run,' I tried to shout to him, but Amanda suddenly stomped on my back and left wing, pressing me down into the concrete floor. I tried to flap to get away from her, but she was too strong.

Craning my neck to look up at him, I saw that he was entirely focused on Amanda. He didn't run away in fright, he didn't even seem surprised. Did he know about our parents? He had to know something at least. 'They've killed Dad. Nathaniel… please, run,' I gasped, looking into the eyes of my brother.

'I won't tell you again, let her go,' Nathaniel said forcefully, raising his voice. He held the rifle steady at shoulder-level, taking aim.

Amanda laughed maniacally, as though it was a joke; shaking her head she told him, 'You can't kill an immortal. Especially a daughter of death.'

'Wanna bet bitch?' he said and fired.

I saw the bullet rip through her left shoulder; impacting into the wall behind, the brick smashing on collision. Amanda began to laugh, but then her smile faded quickly; her face contorting into an anguished look and suddenly she started to scream. Her tail thrashed around in agony. Stumbling back, she lifted her talons off me. Taking the chance, I scrambled away from her towards my brother and turned back to.

Amanda's shoulder bubbled like heated plastic and then her steely grey-tinged skin began to melt, falling to the floor and smouldering like hot acid on impact. Too shocked to move, Nathaniel came over to me; grabbing me by the upper arm and dragged me away from her as she screamed in extremis. Placing me behind him, he raised the rifle to Amanda as she collapsed writing on the floor. Her arm suddenly completely came off, thick black blood gushed out and began to fizz as though it was dissolving.

Looking at her stumpy arm through the torch light, I could just about see the rest of her body slowly begin to melt too. The stench was overpowering. It smelt like burning flesh mixed in with rust. Amanda's incomprehensible screams echoed along the tunnel. 'What have you done? What have you done?' She bellowed. I couldn't look anymore, hated or not, Amanda shouldn't die like this. It was why I wanted Charybdis to swallow her and the others whole. It was quick and without pain.

'Vile scum like you have no idea about the Tears of Pandora. And you call yourself a myth?' Nathaniel hissed.

'Put her out of her misery,' I shouted at him feeling sick as tears flowed down my eyes. 'Please, Nathaniel!'

Nathaniel obliged, 'Burn in hell,' he spat and shot several rounds towards her. I heard the fizzing of her blood splatter on the floor, choking her to silence and then a heavy thump. I knew that she was gone, the sizzling noise of her dissolving body the last residual sound.

Looking away, I retched, bringing up the remains of my last meal.

'Breathe through your mouth,' Nathaniel told me gently.

Wiping my mouth clean, I sat there on the floor and cried. It was such a horrible way to die... 'It was acid,' I said slowly as Amanda's body continued to bubble and dissolve.

'Pandora's Tears,' Nathaniel told me, 'one of the only known substances to kill a myth.'

The book had stated that when Pandora looked into the box that God had given her, she cried black tears. Those tears were acid and could eat through anything but...

'But what about the bullet? It was made from metal? Surely the acid would have dissolved that too?'

'Not metal that was made from Hephaestus,' he told me as he knelt down to see if I was alright. He checked my face, arms and legs and then looked at my wings; touching them gently along the top, then the rest of my feathers. 'You seem to be in good condition.' He stood up and offered his hand to me.

Taking it, I stood up. 'Well, that's nice to know, just don't use that weapon on me,' I snapped.

He frowned. 'I ain't no mercenary and I wouldn't kill my own sister.'

'Ha,' I barked, gingerly standing up. 'You've never given a damn about me before now. Had a change of heart?' He didn't reply. 'Well, whatever the reason, you being here has shed a whole new light on your character. I don't even know who you are anymore. Last time I heard, you were in the States as a banker or whatever. And yet here you are, in the middle of Wales in an old nuclear bunker with a gun that can kill myths and you are staring at a fully grown Siren and you're not freaked out.'

He gave me a reproachful look. 'The banker thing was my cover,' he said then looking away from me, he slung the rifle over his back. 'Still have a grudge against me haven't you? Are you ever going to grow up?'

'Coming from a guy who won't mature until he's forty! Speak for yourself. Are you going to explain to me why you are here? Or is a secret like everything else in my family?' I retorted irritably.

Spinning around to face me, his look made me shut up. 'I didn't come here to argue with you. I came here to save you.'

'Well, you did that after a fashion. So I guess I will say goodbye and leave you with your myth-dissolving rifle,' I growled, grabbing the torch and heading towards the demolished staircase.

'I wouldn't go that way if I were you,' he said in a smarmy way.

Sighing I stopped and turned around. 'Why wouldn't I want to leave the way I came in?'

'Because there is an ambush waiting for you,' he told me. 'That banging was them – trying to scare you to come out.'

'Yeah, I figured that. They want me to get to mum.'

'I know,' he scratched his head, avoiding eye contact.

I bent down and picking up a large piece of debris from the stairs I hit it with my other hand. It exploded in a shower of dust. Nathaniel just stood there looking bored, he didn't seem to care. 'How long have you known about me?'

'Years,' he said his face impassive.

I can't deny it took me by surprise. Here I was thinking that my family was normal but really they were all attributed to the T.A.T. in one form or another. But I wondered if Nathaniel knew everyone. I had bit my tongue enough. He had to know. 'Dad's dead.' I whispered, my voice barely audible.

'I know.' His face didn't eve reveal an inch of remorse.

'Don't you care that's he's dead?' Nathaniel didn't say anything. 'How did you find out he'd died?' I demanded.

Scrunching up his face, the only family trait we had. 'I have my means.'

'And Dad didn't tell you to save me,' I asked knowing that there was no way he could have been contacted by anyone who would have known.

'No. Amjee did.' That shocked me. 'Mum and Dad told me who they were and who they worked for about month before I left home. Amjee contacted me after discovering about Maynard's plans for Dad. She knew where you were. She's been spying on the T.A.T. for years. Dad always told me that if anything was to happen to him, to find you. So I teleported and ended up here.'

'Okay, how the hell did you teleport?' I asked, folding my arms. 'You sure as hell don't look like a myth.'

Giving me a sad smile he shook his head. 'I'm not, I never will be.'

'This is just too much information to handle in under twenty-four hours,' I shouted, clutching my head and closing my eyes trying to remember everything. 'I find out Rhea was against me the entire time. Lynn told me about Maynard wanting to be a god. And if Rhea turns into a Siren, the war will start.' I stopped suddenly and looked at Nathaniel. I had to think of a way to ask him... but from the little sleep I had got over the past day; my brain couldn't come up with a suitable question. Even my ancient brain was at a loss- so I just came out with it. 'So, you knew about me, Amjee and everything else? Did you know I'd become this?'

'Yes. I knew mum was a Siren. She and Dad were friends with Amjee. Since Mum and Dad had been in hiding since the summer, Amjee contacted me the day you arrived at the hotel in London and has so far, kept me in the loop. She lost you a few times, especially when you went off the radar, but figured that you had completed the task set out for you.'

I couldn't believe what I was hearing. My parents and my brother knew I would end up like this and no one told me! Not to mention putting me through hell and for what? To keep the truth from me! My parents and my brother were spiteful when I was growing up, but why?

'Mum and Dad made a contingency plan, should something happen to them and they were unable to help you,' he told me. 'That contingency plan is me.'

Sighing, I walked towards him, 'I'm so confused right now. Why does everyone seem to know everything and I don't? It is some cruel cosmic joke that I get left in the dark?'

'Come with me,' he said offering his hand.

An old memory flashed into my head. Nathaniel had offered his hand to me once when I was a child, when he was a nice brother. It was a bitter November morning and Mum and Dad couldn't take me to school. They slammed the door in my face when they went to work and I was left alone in the house with him, but he was in bed. Hitching up my backpack and grabbing some change off the kitchen counter for lunch, I headed outside and walked the three miles to school. I was only seven. Nathaniel must have woken up and seen that I was gone and came after me. Before getting to school, there was a horrible junction with no traffic lights or footbridge to cross the road. When I stopped to cross the street, looking left and right, I stepped out into the road. A car almost hit me, but I was unaware of it. Nathaniel, out of nowhere, grabbed my hand and pulled me back onto the pavement. He shouted at me for being so stupid as to walk to school and why I hadn't waited for him. I couldn't give him an honest answer and began to cry. Nathaniel hugged me until I calmed down, then offering his hand, helped me cross the road and took me to school. It was that moment when I began to appreciate having Nathaniel around. But that feeling was quashed months later when he decided to catch the bus to school with his friends, leaving me to walk to school alone.

I looked at Nathaniel's outstretched hand and quietly told him, 'Don't offer it, unless you promise you won't leave me.'

His eyes showed so much regret and sadness, but giving me a small smile he said, 'I've been cruel to you Tatty,' using my nickname that he hadn't used in years. 'You're my sister and I love you. We have to stick together on this and see it through. Come with me, I want to show you something.'

I took his hand and he guided me down the tunnel. I had no idea where we were going, but he seemed like he did and I remained silent throughout. There were still a load of questions I wanted to ask, but at the moment, I was comfortable being shown the answers instead of finding them out for myself. Also remaining silent, it gave me time to think about the others. A deep pang of pain hit my stomach, making me feel sick. I felt so guilty doing what I did, but I didn't see any other way. Although what I didn't understand was why didn't Nathaniel ask me about the others? Surely if he knew that I was in a group, then he would ask where they were.

Shaking that question aside, I continued to let my brother lead me.

'There is someone you didn't notice when you were down here,' Nathaniel told me, as we came to the broken tunnel which led to the place where the King of Minos was kept. 'She's been waiting for you to see her, because when you do, everything will make sense.'

Still holding my torch, Nathaniel led me into the corridor and took me into a small room. I gasped as I saw dozens of moths fluttering around me. 'Whoa.' I yelped trying to duck as some headed right for me to get to the torch's beam. 'Where have they come from?' I asked as I was beginning to get freaked out that they'd fly in my hair.

'Don't you get it?' Nathaniel asked his voice tinted with concern at my lack of knowledge.

'Um, no,' I snapped, irritated.

'Do you believe in fairies?' he asked.

'Of course I do!' But no sooner had I said that, then the hoard of moths suddenly attacked me. Fluttering around me at a much quicker pace, as though annoyed, they dive-bombed towards my head; their soft wings silently brushing my face. 'Oy, get off,' I shouted, but it didn't stop them. 'What is going on?'

'If you don't believe, you won't understand,' he told me, his voice serious.

Still trying to bat the moths away, it quickly dawned on me what I was seeing, or more to the point, wasn't seeing. I had read it in the book. 'Oh my gosh, they're fairies!'

Quickly, Nathaniel grabbed my torch and flicked it off. I expected to be thrown into pitch darkness again but instead, the whole room was full of what looked like glittering fireflies. They gently flew around my head in a circle, tinkling softly like wind chimes as they went.

'Thank you for believing in us,' they all began to sing. Their voices were so small but together, they made my ears ring with their beautiful enchanting and melodious tones. It sounded like pure magic and with it the entire room was filled with their blue-ish white glow.

'So how come they are down here?' I asked laughing as they began to braid my long hair, weaving in and out and giggling all the while.

'Because of me,' a strong booming voice said. A fairy with long grey hair, who was about the length of my hand and taller than the others, flew towards me. Holding my hand out, she fluttered gently onto it and stared up at me, smiling. 'I am the Mage of this small clan of fairies,' she told me.

'Small?' I asked looking around at the dozens of lights. 'But there's so many of you.'

The Mage smiled sadly and shook her head, 'We have been dwindling ever since two little girls captured us on a photograph many years ago.'

'I remember that,' I said wide-eyed as she looked so sad, her delicate spider web wings drooped.

'It was terrible for us. The O.M.C got involved and tried their best to confiscate the photograph, but the media had already been involved. Since then, we've been hiding in plain sight. Only humans who believe and who can keep our secret can see us. And because the human world is based on science and not magic, you do not see what it right in front of you,' she said a little sternly. 'Being a Siren, I thought you would have instantly believed in us.'

'I'm sorry,' I said earnestly. 'Sometimes I forget what I am.'

Giving me a small smile she nodded.

'So, the reason why my brother can teleport and knows everything about me,' I said raising my wings slightly, 'is because of you?'

The Mage nodded. 'My brothers and sisters and I are in debt to your mother and father.' The word father was a quick stab to the heart. I could feel the tears well up again, but I pushed them down. If my father was a myth and he died on this plane then where did he end up? Did he end up in the magical plane? Or was it someplace else? The Mage reached out and placed her tiny hand on my thumb, trying to console me as I started to panic thinking about where my father was. 'Yes, I know it is sad. Your father was a good man and terribly brave. He saved us many years ago and returning a favour, he and your mother asked us to protect your brother in case the T.A.T. came after him if his secret was learnt.' That stunned me a little, what secret was Nathaniel hiding? 'It was a great torment to us when they took you last month. We could not prevent it.'

'So when did Nathaniel know of your existence?' I asked her, Nathaniel looked away from me, a pained expression on his face.

'When he was four. Your parents kept you out of the ways of magic to keep you safe, but there were times when Nathaniel had to be with you to protect you.'

I shot Nathaniel a look and he nodded slowly. 'So all those times you left me, no scratch that, mum, dad and you left me, was to cavort with magical beings?'

'It was to keep you safe,' he repeated the Mage's words. I wanted to hit him but restrained myself.

'When Nathaniel was eighteen he wanted to do what he could to stop the T.A.T.' She continued. I noticed that the fairies around me slowed down as though listening to her every word. 'He went undercover in Europe trying to track down Maynard, leaking any information to Amjee and Jeff when he could.' I understood that part. It was the year that Nathaniel left the house. As far as my parents said, they only heard from him now and again. The Mage looked angry and clasped her hands behind her and tutted. 'We tried everything to thwart their plans but Maynard was always one step ahead of us, like tonight, for example. We didn't find out about Rhea until it was too late.' I nodded trying to understand everything but this conversation was unnecessary. I had to get to the T.A.T. base and confront Maynard myself, as I had planned. 'Have the others transformed?' She asked, snapping me from my thoughts.

I nodded sadly. 'Yes, all of them have. They are in the magical plane now, with my mother.'

'Why are the others in the other plane?' Nathaniel said quickly, making me jump.

Shaking my confused foggy head, I filled in the details from the riddle in Ha Long to when Nathaniel turned up. 'I sent them away so they could be safe. Maynard is after me. The others would be in danger if they stayed with me.'

'The Ancients' the Mage said with a quivering voice. 'They have not been heard of for a very long time. And for Mr Raleigh to give you a riddle to show you the origins of mythology and the Phaistos Disc,' she smiled, 'it's exactly the type of thing he'd so. As far as I am aware there are only a few cultures around the world which discuss the Ancients and how they came to be. Searching for a legend in Vietnam of a dragon, Mr Raleigh found the cave but knew he was unable to finish his quest. I helped him place enchantments around the cave and his precious red book where he kept everything magical he had learnt. However, there was a catch. Only the first person who touched the book could gain entrance into the cave.'

I smiled slowly. 'Yes I figured that one out, with a little help.'

She nodded. 'But my dear, you have to stop Rhea from transforming and stop the Ancients from opening a portal for Maynard to go through. He cannot be turned into a god. He will wreak havoc on the world for sure.'

'There's something I don't understand,' I began, thinking quickly. 'If the disc is the only known object that can open a portal, how did I manage to send the others into the magical plane? I didn't use the disc and I'm not an Ancient. I just commanded Lionel to take the others in the magical plane and he did it.'

Nathaniel and the Mage shared a strange look. After a moment, she finally said, 'You have a powerful name Tara. I'm not sure if you know this, but you have a great future ahead of you. You can be a guardian of the world and with it, you have special abilities.' Frowning I explained that King Minos had said something similar and she nodded with a polite smile. 'But does Rhea have that power?'

She shrugged her tiny shoulders. 'That I am not sure, but Tara that is something that you need to find out on your own.' Taking a deep breath to steady my nerves, I nodded. 'Very good. So, what is your plan?'

'To go to the T.A.T. base and confront Maynard and Rhea,' I said, but in all honesty, it wasn't going to be so simple. Nothing is ever as straight-forward in my life anymore.

Nathaniel put a sturdy hand on my shoulder. 'I'm coming with you. I may not be magical, but the fairies can teleport us to wherever we want. They can give us magical coverage until we get inside.'

'I'm going to have to fight Rhea,' I told him confidently though my heart quickened at the prospect and I started to feel sick.

'In the act of doing what is right, one has to realise the cost of not acting at all.' The Mage said wisely.

My nerves were wracked though I didn't show it. I understood what the Mage was saying, but it wasn't helping me.

Between the three of us we came up with an idea. It was loosely based on the plan I had earlier with Saskia and the others. And though the Mage didn't know much about computers, she did know how to use magic against them to act like a virus and destroy their security systems.

Nathaniel reloaded on Hephaestus bullets with the Tears of Pandora. The Mage had magicked up some garments for me, as the ones I had were pretty tatty and had also healed my cuts and bruises. The only thing I was annoyed about was that she couldn't give me any time to sleep. That was something I desperately needed.

'Do you have any weapons?' Nathaniel asked me, as all the fairies gathered around us, preparing to teleport us to the T.A.T.

'I can slap good,' I said raising my hand, but his grave face quickly brought me down to earth. 'No, I don't. I fly, I command, I flick my hair. That's about it.'

He didn't seem to be happy. 'Have you had any training?'

'Combat training,' I told him. 'But there must be some weapons around here somewhere. It's a secret bunker.'

The Mage sent a few fairies off to find a weapon for me while Nathaniel checked, my now very tattered bag, to see if there was anything useful. He looked at the little red book. 'So this is the book that Maynard was after.' He flicked through it and laughed at a few pages.

'He must have known that Mr Raleigh had found a place that mentioned the Ancients and wrote it in the book, but he didn't know where neither the book nor the cave was. It's been helpful.'

Moments later the fairies came back with a crossbow and a quiver of arrows and some canisters of knock-out tear gas and one canister that was unlabelled. 'That'll do. I'm no good at aiming, but I can try.'

'Good, use them,' he said quickly, 'we'll need them.'

Picking up the crossbow I fitted a quarrel and aimed carefully at a spot on the far side of the room. The arrow zoomed through the air and smacked into a nearby concrete wall sinking at least a foot deep. Reloading, I put the safety catch on and slung the quiver of arrows over my back. 'There, you happy?'

'Never,' he replied.

Ignoring him, I began to mentally prepare myself. This had to go flawlessly, there couldn't be any mistakes. I repeated small phrases in my head. Snappy ones that got to the point and had to be followed, like, 'knock yourself out,' or 'run to France' or 'go to the toilet.' I wanted to avoid hurting people if possible. Not everything had to end in violence.

'Are you ready?' The Mage asked me as she came in between Nathaniel and me. I placed the book back into the bag.

'She's having kittens,' Nathaniel giggled.

'Shut it,' I snapped and his mouth clamped up. 'You have no idea what I am capable of. Just don't get in my way.'

His eyes widened in surprise at my tone of voice, but he remained quiet. Well, he had to. I had shut him up.

The Mage tutted. 'Sibling rivalry won't get you anywhere,' she said wisely. 'You must work together.'

'Okay, I'm ready,' I exhaled a deep breath and nodded. 'Send the virus, please.'

The Mage nodded and lifted her hands up, the fairies copied her.

'Nathaniel,' I looked at him, 'you may speak, but watch what you say to me.'

His mouth opened and he smiled, 'You're scary.'

Smiling back I replied, 'You have no idea.'

A short while later, the Mage brought her arms down and nodded, 'It is done.'

'Give it a few minutes for pandemonium to kick in,' Nathaniel said and I nodded, not wanting to lose my concentration. Closing my eyes, I tried to get a feel for what was going on, hoping that these Siren powers could extend as far as London, but I wasn't picking up anything. I had to be there.

'Right, let's do it,' I said grasping Nathaniel's hands.

'As you wish,' the Mage said and quickly, the fairies began to dance around us, turning invisible and then a bright blue light came up from the floor, swallowing us up and WHOOSH. Wind hit my face with the force of a tornado; the blinding blue light pounded against my eyeballs. But as quickly as this sensation started, it stopped. Both the light and the wind had gone.

Still holding onto Nathaniel, I tried to get a sense of where I was. I smelt varnished wood and also something else familiar, something like rubber like I was in some type of gym perhaps. I took a small step, the din of my shoe echoed. It sounded like I was in a big room.

'I think,' I began to whisper, my voice shivering through the void of black that surrounded us; 'we're in the training room.'

'Training room of what?' Nathaniel asked, his voice gently bouncing off the walls.

'Of the T.A.T.,' I told him.

'How the hell can you know that, its pitch black,' he chuckled.

'It smells familiar, plus we're at an advantage point,' I said to him, as I let go of his hands. 'We're above the main computer room. The Mage explained that she can give us about ten minute's tops. We need to find Rhea in that time and...'

I suddenly stopped talking as I heard footfall coming towards us.

'What is it?' he asked a chill in his voice.

Grabbing around in the dark, I found his hands and pushed him behind me, 'Footsteps.'

The footsteps got louder and soon they were right outside of the door. I couldn't tell who it was, but I knew it would be trouble.

'The ambush,' I asked him hastily, 'do you know who was waiting for me?' Thinking about the people who had a gift of magic, I counted them off. If Lynn and Dave had left with Rhea and Matt was gone... That just left Roxy. Could she transform without being in the water?

'No,' he whispered quickly, 'the fairies didn't tell me.'

With a deafening crash, the double doors suddenly flew open, banging on the walls; the loud clamour echoing off them. 'And why not?' Came Roxy's sultry, disturbing voice. Light suddenly flooded into the large training room. My eyes adjusted quickly, but I was still unable to move as Roxy's sneering smile glued my feet to the floor. 'Oh, please continue,' she said, her hand on her hips, moving in a swanky-way towards us. 'I'd love to know all your little secrets,' she said seductively.

Glaring at her, I spread my wings aggressively and look a step towards her, stopping her in her tracks. 'Not another move,' I growled. The smile faded from her lips. 'Well, look at you... in your human body. Such a change from that disgusting slimy sea-bitch you were the last time I saw you.'

Throwing her head back, she laughed manically. 'Oh Tara. You've come along in leaps and bounds. It's just a shame that you're going to die.' Her body began to quiver and she slowly started to grow in size. 'I guess she *can* transform without water,' I answer myself.

'I don't think so,' Nathaniel said from behind me.

'Meet my brother,' I smiled as he brought up the gun and shot her right in her half-transformed head. Like with Amanda the bullet didn't stop, until it whizzed out behind her head, smacking into the wall behind.

'Oh my God,' I gasped as her eyes rolled back into her skull. Momentarily standing there, her body twitched. The bullet hole in her forehead began to fizz and bubble and subsided lower and lower before our eyes.

'We don't have time for this,' Nathaniel said, gruffly grabbing my hand and pulling me forwards and out of the training room.

'I cannot believe you did that,' I said, feeling sick as the memory of how Amanda was killed replayed in my head.

'Grow the hell up Tara, this is war. There is no time for happy endings or sad eulogies to a freaky cow who wanted to kill you. It's kill or be killed and frankly, I can't lose another family member.'

My heart ached at his words, but there was no time in dwelling on it. He was right. This was the pre-emptive attack that the T.A.T. were not expecting. For all they knew, we were still in the bunker... but why then, had Roxy turned up?

'Nathaniel I need you to get behind me,' I told him, 'you don't know where you're going and I can stop the bullets.'

'Don't be stupid,' he said, still pulling me along.

Heading down the darkened corridor, with only the red safety lights to guide our way, I abruptly stopped and yanked my hand away from his. The force of it nearly toppled him.

'Look, I am the leader, not you. So do what I say!'

Giving me a strange vacant expression, I turned around and beckoned him to follow me. As we approached the glass corridor, I crouched down and peered through the floor. Like frantic ants whose nest had been discovered by an anteater, the T.A.T. were running around trying to get their systems back up. They didn't even notice that Roxy had been shot or that we were still alive and in the building. Inwardly smiling I came up with a plan that would throw them into utter chaos.

'Grab hold of my waist, I'm going to give you a flying lesson.' Nathaniel did as I asked, but he didn't look happy about it. Inching forwards, I brought up my right fist and smashed it down heavily onto the glass beneath me. It shattered into a million pieces. The sound was almost deafening. Nathaniel and I fell through the corridor's floor, raining thick shards of glass upon them. The people below screamed in panic and ran out of the way, cowering to protect themselves. Opening my wings, I flew upwards and out of harm's way, but someone had seen me.

'SHE'S UP THERE!' I heard a man yell.

Twisting into the air and hovering with Nathaniel still gripping tightly around my waist, I glanced down. I saw the usual office workers run out of the way, ducking and dodging as they tried desperately to avoid the sparking computers. The glass had demolished the screens and delicate instruments, rendering them useless. That was one less job done. But I also saw a small army of people in black, coming out of the archway, carrying rifles and kneeling, aiming at us.

Zooming around the room, I brought up my crossbow and fired below. I felt Nathaniel grope around my hip and soon saw a gas canister being thrown into the fray. On contact with the ground, yellow gas erupted from it, flowing around people as they frantically tried to escape. Within seconds, the floor was completely covered in yellow-looking smog and dozens of people had collapsed like bees in a smoke-filled hive.

'I'm going to drop you into that,' I said to Nathaniel, as I began to circle around, 'hold your breath.'

'Bring it on!' he shouted, as I dived down into the gas, twisting around so that he landed safely and swooping back up again.

Guns suddenly began to spit bullets around the room; the metal bouncing off bullet-proof screens or embedding into walls or nearby bodies. People screamed in panic or pain as the fight began. Searching the ground, I couldn't find my brother, but hoped that he would be okay.

As I turned around to repeat another circle above, the chaos continued below me, although unexpectedly, I heard an ear-splitting roar that shouted my name. The sound of it sent shivers down my spine. I knew who it was and I knew that I had to win this fight. Flying up, I perched on top of an elongated light that was attached to the ceiling with thick metal cables. I looked down at Lynn and bared my teeth.

Lynn was in dragon form. In all her splendour and glory, she was still scary to see.

Regardless that she was my ex-operator, or that she used to be in my position, Lynn was an enemy. She had to be dealt with and quickly. I didn't have time to mess around. I had to get to Rhea and stop this war from raging.

Suddenly catching me off guard, Lynn shot a savage stream of multi-coloured fire at me. Quickly jumping off the light, I headed straight towards it. With a single twist, I whipped my wings around and blew the flame back towards the ground. Lynn roared out in shock and tried to escape, but it was too late, for all of us.

The fire touched the gas covered ground. Hell knows what was in the compound of the vapour, but the entire room erupted in a massive explosion. Gigantic columns of flames quickly raced towards me, emanating colossal heat. Cringing, I shielded myself with my wings, waiting for the shock wave to come. When it did, it was with such devastating force as though napalm had been detonated. I crashed through the ceiling of the T.A.T. and into the rear lobby of the British Museum. Screaming in terror from the hot blast that propelled me with such force, I landed in a crumpled heap with ignited debris from the floor and ceiling falling around me. Wailing sirens blared above my head, attached to twirling blue lights; showing that there was an intruder in the building.

My right arm felt like it was being stabbed with an especially large blade of glass. Coughing from the dust that settled around me, the hole that I had made, was still crumbling into the base below. Slithering away from the edge, I gingerly sat up, slowly pulling my right arm from beneath me. I resisted the urge to throw up as I saw the damage to my right elbow. Sticking out and covered with blood, which dripped from the puncture, was a bone.

'Ah damn,' I groaned, struggling to get up, but my body refused to move the way I wanted. Ripping the bottom off my shirt, I made a small bandage around my elbow and putting one end into my teeth, grabbed hold of the other and pulled quickly. Clenching my teeth, I screamed as the pain shot up and down my arm. Tears fell from my eyes and ran down my gritty cheeks as I pushed the bone back in under the skin. Then with a click and another spurt of pain, my elbow joint felt better, with the agony beginning to abate. Shaking off the chill that crept around me, I looked at my elbow and moaned in pain. A massive bruise had formed on the skin, but magically the bone had set back. Tenderly, I moved my arm. It hurt, but it was bearable.

Coughing, as I was inhaling dust and smoke, I saw a continuous plume of fiery smoke that billowed out through the Tara-shaped hole in the ground. Black soot reached up to the cathedral room's white walls. It looked like I had missed most of the fiery blast by inches. It had engulfed everything.

Peering down, I saw the devastation. The room was unrecognisable. Practically everything was destroyed: desks, tables, chairs, computers, the glass offices, the lift, even the archway. Debris covered bodies were strewn all over the room. No one was moving; I started to panic…

'NATHANIEL!' I screamed, unable to distinguish him amongst the bodies and my tear clouded vision. 'NATHANIEL!'

I continued to scream until my voice was hoarse, but there was no reply. 'You'd better not be dead, or I'll kill you myself,' I shouted, testing my wings so I could fly down to the wrecked room of the T.A.T. below to search for him. My wing-joints panged with some discomfort, but they were able to keep me airborne for a while. Landing gently, I tried not to step on the bodies as I hobbled around looking for my crossbow which had flown out of my hand. Suddenly, over the wailing of the intruder alert above me, my ears picked out another familiar sound. The sirens of the police.

'Oh crap,' I gasped, my heart skipping a beat; panic and bile rising up my throat. What would they make of all this? Of me? My mind began to wonder and I could picture a hospital and crazy doctors and experiments on my wings. Shuddering, I pushed it aside. It would never get that far, I'd never allow it.

After a brief few seconds of searching the debris ridden floor, I found my crossbow. I was thankful that my quiver of arrows was still on my back, but as I continued searching for my brother, I heard the museum doors burst open with such force that the hinges were broken off. The sound was quickly followed by the scurrying of heavy footfalls on the tiled floor above; it echoed in the destroyed cathedral room. I closed my eyes and cringed as I heard the sounds of guns clicking and then:

'DON'T MOVE!' shouted a man with a deep scary Cockney accent. 'DROP YOUR WEAPON!'

The only word that was going through my head was, 'crap,' repeatedly. The T.A.T. was meant to be a secret and myths, like myself, were meant to remain just so. How would they react to me? Well, there was only one way to find out... I dropped the crossbow to the shattered floor.

'Sir, it's... it's just a big bird.'

'Oy,' I shouted, beginning to turn round.

'I SAID DON'T MOVE,' the man shouted again.

'Fine, but I'm not a big bird. I'm not yellow with an American accent and I'm not friends with a fluffy elephant or a grouch that lives in a garbage can,' I called up to them.

'Shut your gob,' the policeman shouted. 'Someone get me some rope and pull her out.'

'That's northern,' I laughed, but I heard someone's hand move smoothly on the barrel of a gun. That shut me up.

'What are you? This some sort of prank?'

'Forget that,' the Cockney man snapped. 'Hands in the air, you're under arrest for breaking and entering, and for destroying public property,' I then heard the clinking of metal and chains; they were bringing out the cuffs. Not that they would work on me, I could break them instantly, but I didn't want to give them any cause for a scandal on London's finest. 'You do not have to say anything. But it may harm your defence if you do not mention when questioned something which you later rely on in court. Anything you do say may be given in evidence-.'

'Um, I have something to say,' I said loudly. Flexing my wings slightly, I heard the sound of guns clicking again. 'I don't need a rope.' Throwing my wings out, I took two steps jumped into the air and shot through the hole, landing on the other side. Five policemen, jumped back, yelling in terror and fright.

'WHOA, WHOA, WHOA!'

'THIS IS NOT A HUMAN SIR! THIS IS NOT A HUMAN!'

They blanched at my appearance. Tall, azure-coloured eyes, pointy ears and large black flyable wings.

'STAND YOUR GROUND!' The Cockney man shouted. Putting a face to the voice, I looked him up and down. He was tanned with short brown hair. His black body armour, helmet and gun gave him a striking appearance, but I wasn't frightened of him, not in this body. 'Okay everyone, calm down!' he ordered the others. 'Now you,' he pointed his gun at me, 'put your hands up.'

'It's a mutant freak Sir,' a small policeman said, his voice quivering with fear.

Looking down on him I gave him half a smile, 'That's not very nice. I'm not a mutant freak,' I spat, but it was the wrong thing to say.

The scared-looking policeman levelled his Heckler and Koch 93 sniper rifle and fired, the small bullet piercing the shoulder of my damaged left arm.

'DON'T SHOOT!' someone screamed, making them all nervous.

'Son of a bitch,' I cried, twisting away from the sting.

The pain wasn't what I expected. On T.V., when you saw people getting shot, they were in absolute agony, and most, in complete and utter shock. But for the past half an hour, it wasn't shock I was experiencing anymore, it was annoyance. These humans should not be here, they needed to leave.

Inhaling a deep breath, I glanced at my shoulder and picked out the bullet like a fat thorn —yelling out in pain all the while. Flicking the bloody covered bullet to their feet, I looked down on them and placed my good hand on my hip. 'That wasn't very nice and completely uncalled for,' I spat. 'Are you going to apologise?'

The policeman gave me a frightened stare and gulped.

'APOLOGISE,' I ordered.

'S-sorry,' he stuttered. Looking gobsmacked that he'd spoken, he clapped his hands over his mouth. I smiled.

'Stand down Miss,' one of the policemen said, pointing his rifle at me in a threatening manner. 'We don't want to shoot, but will do unless-.'

'I'm not your enemy,' I interrupted him. 'You will all listen to me and do what I say,' my voice boomed. 'There was an exploded boiler in the basement. There was no intruder. This is all you will remember from tonight. You will not remember my face or even the concept of speaking to anyone when you got here. Do you understand?'

'Yes,' they all said in unison.

'Good, now get out,' I shouted, pointing to the broken doors.

The small group of policemen filed out of the building in silence. When the last one had left, I turned around and dived back into the hole.

CHAPTER TWENTY-TWO

LANDING AMONGST THE WRECKAGE AGAIN, I PICKED UP my fallen crossbow and wafted my wings at the smoke that was blurring my vision. The more I stared at the charred remains, the more anxious I felt that he wasn't alive. 'Nathaniel,' I cried out. 'Come on, say something!'

Making me jump, I heard a strange noise over to my right and glancing, I saw a burning table that was moving slightly. Someone was alive.

'Nathaniel?' I shouted, manoeuvring around the bodies. Grabbing the table with my good arm, I threw it away easily, revealing a shaking burning Lynn; though in agony and in human form, she was still alive, but only barely.

'You... clever bi-' she gasped, unable to finish insulting me.

I inwardly winced at her wounds. Her face looked like it had melted on her right side. Her 1930's curly hair was reduced to cinders showing singed skin and patches of skull. In fact, the whole right side of her was extremely burnt. If I didn't recognise her voice, it would be difficult to tell it was Lynn.

'Where's my brother?' I commanded.

With a substantial amount of pain, she replied with a small shake of her head, 'I don't know,' she whispered. Closing her eyes, she tried to steady her breathing. 'Do you know... what the gas was?'

Ignoring her, I searched around, trying to locate Nathaniel's clothes or shoes, anything that I could tell me he was here at least, but I saw nothing that belonged to him.

'I asked you... a question,' she breathed heavily.

'What?' I spun around, staring at her. 'No, I don't know what the gas was,' I snapped.

'Magic gas,' she laughed laboriously. 'Highly flammable. You found it at the bunker... didn't you?'

I frowned, nodding. 'Well, aren't you stupid? You shouldn't have belched fired at me.'

There was an ominous creak from above and then suddenly a tremendous crash. Part of the ceiling caved in further. Plaster dust spewed out at every angle, my heart jumped a mile from the sound. Using my wings to cover me, I flapped them and blew the dust away from me, but it didn't help much.

Trying to breathe through the dust Lynn said softly, 'I didn't know you could throw my fire back at me. That... was impressive.'

'Uh huh yeah. I'm... going to find my brother and you... you can stay here, I don't care-.'

'I'm going to die,' Lynn said, making me stop. 'I inhaled the gas, it exploded a lung. I shifted back into a human. When my time is up here, I'll turn to ash. I won't go to the other plane.'

The breath was knocked out of me. It didn't occur to me that Lynn would die. She was severely burnt, that's true, but she was a dragon, she was magical. I thought she'd be able to change into a dragon and heal. I was stunned to realise that this was Lynn's end. It was a horrific way to die and I felt sorry for her. Lynn had tried to kill me at least three times, but I believed that people, humans or other, deserved a peaceful passing. But Lynn's was so terrible it shook me to my core. Looking at her two tears slipped softly down my face. 'I'm so sorry,' I whispered.

Giving me half a smile, she mouthed the words, 'Thank you,' then remained silent.

I stayed with Lynn right up until the last few seconds of her human life. Lynn's eyes wearily opened and she looked at me, her eyes pained with regret. Lynn was carrying out orders from Maynard. I was no fool. She did what she could to help her parents and that was what I was doing as well. She was just like me. Trapped in an iron-clad contract by a maniac bent on becoming all powerful. We were both used like puppets, but I had more friends who worked as a team. Lynn and the others worked alone.

As Lynn's breathing became laboured, I reached out and held her hand and nodding, gave her a smile. 'I forgive you.' A moment later, her eyes closed. Her last breath escaped her lips and slowly she turned into ash that fell gently to the floor. Lynn, my operator, the might silver dragon, had died. 'Even an immortal can die,' a female voice said from behind me.

Spinning around, I saw Rhea standing on a smouldering body; her face, impassive. With brown wings outstretched in a menacing way, she glared at me; glancing at my shoulder and arm.

'I see you killed Roxy in the training room. Tears of Pandora, the same method used on Amanda. Now that was genius,' she laughed, an evil smile appeared on her face. Rhea hadn't changed yet, and I knew there was a chance I could stop her.

'How did you know about her?' I blurted out.

Rhea laughed again and began walking towards me, disrespectfully standing on the dead bodies as though they were stepping stones. 'Oh, I have my ways. Amjee!' Rhea was looking over my shoulder. Turning around I saw a small figure shuffling down the dust-filled corridor that led to the cafeteria. Rhea giggled behind me. 'Amjee has been particularly useful to us. As soon as I was able to command people to do what I want, Lynn told me to force Amjee to do what Maynard asked. We had to find out where the Phaistos Disc was and had an idea that it was in your parent's possession. We couldn't find your mother, so we went looking for your Dad. Your Dad didn't have it and then, would you believe it, your mother then went into the other plane with the disc. GUILTY! Well,' she said folding her arms and shaking her head for emphasis, 'you can imagine the bitter disappointment. So the only way to split the group up was to force you to see that Maynard would come after you. And predictable Tara sent her friends to the other plane and forced Saskia to change.' She smiled sweetly. 'We used magic to imitate a bomb over the bunker if you didn't know.' She laughed at me then stared at Amjee. 'Everything has gone according to Maynard's plan. I will change, the Ancients will get annoyed and open a portal and Maynard jumps into the portal and thus he becomes a god.'

Rage, pain, hatred and remorse were but a few emotions that were currently running through my heart. This was not something I was emotionally prepared for. However, the only thing I knew I had to do was to stop Rhea, at all costs.

'He'll never get that far,' I seethed and leapt towards her.

Rhea took off into the air, twirling around and bringing out a gun, she fired. Dodging the bullet by millimetres; feeling the hot stream of air as it passed by, Rhea yelled out in frustration and flew up through the hole in the ceiling. Before I followed her, I turned to look at Amjee and shouted, 'SNAP OUT OF IT AMJEE AND FIND MY BROTHER!'

Folding my wings against my body, I flew out of the hole. Doing a small loop-de-loop in the air, I caught a glimpse of Rhea's feet as she flew out of the broken double doors of the demolished back entrance of the museum.

'Ah kack.' Twisting in the air I flew after her.

Rhea flew out into the cold November night, heading up and over the bright and electrified busy city of London. Unable to feel it, the freezing, snowy wind blasted in my face instantly as I flew higher over the tall buildings, forever keeping Rhea in sight. She was straight ahead of me, climbing higher towards the clouds, but why? Why didn't she turn around and shoot me again, or for that matter, why hadn't she turned into a Siren? What was going on? Was I missing something?

My poor left arm pained me as the snow fell onto the bloody bandage, seeping onto my skin. Ignoring the pain, I flew faster, my wings more powerful than Rhea's. I quickly caught up to her.

Withdrawing my crossbow, I aimed and fired. The sound of the shot whooshed over the busy streets below, silent against the night time traffic, but it missed her by half a foot and Rhea retaliated.

Turning around, flying backwards in a cocky manner, she began firing at me.

I banked to the left and flew behind a large red bricked building; bullets smashed into the windows, people screamed from the roads below as they were showed with glass. For that instant, I lost sight of Rhea, but that wasn't worrying me. At that split second I got a vision, of my own impending doom. My eyes saw a tall tower though the snow was making it difficult to know exactly what tower it was. But it was surrounded by old buildings and the Thames River was running in front of it next to a bridge. Rhea came swooping down and fired her gun, it missed but it confused me and I flew into the tower and fell. She then pounced on me and we fell to the ground. As she reached for her gun, she kneed me in the stomach, I stumbled back and she brought the gun to my head.

I shook myself from the very frightening and vivid vision; clearly I had to get to her before that even happened, which would be soon.

Skimming the tops of the modern buildings, I heard people yelling from below. 'Kack, need to go higher,' I urged myself, quickly climbing into the now blizzard-filled sky.

Looking over to my right, I saw the river Thames. The snow quickly melted on its surface, but the boats that were tied along its banks were covered, giving it a very eerie look.

'COME OUT, TARA,' I heard Rhea scream maniacally into the night. Her screech echoed over the quiet lapping of the Thames as the cold water soaked up the snow that gently fell upon its surface.

Twisting my head around, I searched for where the sound came from, but the winds confused me; tossing her voice like it was a single feather inside a tornado. There was no way I could pinpoint where it came from. Flapping hard against the frigid winds I flew up and over the Thames and that is when my vision became reality.

The tower, or as it's usually known as Big Ben, was suddenly growing in size as I flew towards it. The old buildings, the Houses of Parliament, quickly came into view and so did Tower Bridge. From what I had seen in my vision, Rhea would come from behind me, so I had to be vigilant.

Flying faster towards the huge clock tower, I saw the face reading half past midnight in the morning, damn I needed some sleep. As I approached it, I began to slow down. Any second now, I thought, any second. But nothing happened. Rhea didn't shoot from behind me. Quickly banking right, I went around the entire tower, searching in the silent whiteness of the London skies without success.

Flying right to the top of the tower, I clung to its metal spire and took a breather. 'Where is she?' I asked myself hearing the distant noise of the traffic below. Then I heard it. Her scream, high pitched, full of anguish and tension pierced my heart. Panic suddenly flooded through me like a burst dam. Diving off the tower, I hurtled towards Rhea's screams. Passing over the Thames like a peregrine falcon, I zoomed to the other side. I had to find her now; I had to stop her from changing.

My wing-joints burned on my back as I pushed on through the strong winds, racing across the snowy night sky. My mind spun as I tried to contemplate the consequences of Rhea's actions. The world will be plunged into chaos, into madness as myth and reality clash. The weird, strange and magical would obliterate the explained and scientific. Though I tried to think of a way to try and stop the war, I couldn't; the humans wouldn't stand a chance. The planes of the world were divided for a reason, that reason was annihilation of the human race.

Rhea's screams became loud and intense as I hastily flew over the snow-covered buildings.

Then suddenly, high above me, there was an explosion of red and blue light. The force of it threw me off course, making me smack painfully onto the glass roof a building. Breaking through it, the crossbow fell out of sight as, I fell onto concrete floor below, hearing it crack beneath me. Gasping from more painful bruises that I could feel form on me, I gingerly stood up, shaking the glass from my hair and wings and looked up.

The blast of red and blue light lingered in the air behind Big Ben in the distance and within it, a blinding light shone in a single beam onto the snowy ground below. Searching for the crossbow, I couldn't find it and cursing myself, I decided to leave it behind, knowing it may cost me dearly. Flying up through the hole in the glass roof I looked ahead and saw a small, brown, winged figure heading to the centre of the light. I knew what the beam was and it scared me. It was the Ancients. Though I had never met them, though I had only just found out who they were, they had opened their own portal to look down on us. And Rhea, who was pushing to become a full myth, was heading for it and once she hit that source of light, it was game over.

'RHEA, NO!' I yelled. Pushing my wings to the max, I flew directly towards the beam; the wind screaming in my ears. My heart palpitated in my chest; my mouth became dry through sheer terror of what would happen if Rhea got into that beam. Flying at least fifty miles an hour, I reached the other side in seconds, but Rhea was still far ahead of me, nearly reaching Big Ben.

'RHEANOSTOP,' I screamed, the words stringing into one. The urgency in my voice caused the idiot cow to turn around briefly to see how far I was behind her. 'RHEA STOP NOW,' I yelled into the winds, throwing all of my authority into my voice.

One of Rhea's wings suddenly froze. 'NO, NOT NOW,' she screeched. Unable to fly properly, she began to spiral out of control, hurtling towards the ground, at least sixty feet below. Reaching out she managed to grab onto the side of the tower and dug her hands in for purchase. Twisting round, she stared at me evilly.

The bright light from above pulsated violently, pushing out another bout of forceful energy; throwing me like a ragdoll through the air. I wrapped my wings around trying to protect myself as I was hurtled away from the light. Feeling as though there was a horrendous out of control hurricane pushing against me, the forceful energy died down just as I was about to fall into the freezing waters of the River Thames. Opening my wings, I rode the winds and headed back towards Rhea, quickly tilting to the right to avoid smashing into Big Ben.

Reaching the tower, I didn't see Rhea. She must have broken my command and that wasn't good. Hovering above the ground searching around for her, it didn't click until I heard a scraping from above me. Gasping in horror, I turned around just in time to see Rhea pointing her gun at me, just as my vision previously showed me.

Dodging quickly out of the way, by banking a hard left, the bullet ricocheted off the wall of the clock tower. Looking up, Rhea wasn't there, which confused me. Hovering and looking for her, the wind blew a strong gust of wind from behind me. Stupidly I was unable to counteract it and as my vision predicted, I ended up flying into Big Ben. Hitting my head on the cold brick, I was disorientated and my wing muscles went limp. I felt like a bird who smacked into a window and yet as I fell, I heard Rhea scream from above. Glancing up in that split second, I saw her dive toward me, her gun drawn, pointing at me once more.

Powerless to curl my wings around me for protection I suddenly hit the snowy ground, cracking the pavement on impact. Rhea then fell on top of me, with our bodies colliding at a great speed, she winded us both.

Rhea rolled off me as I clutched my stomach and chest, trying to breathe normally. I heard her panting as well as people screaming random things like, 'CALL AN AMBULANCE,' or, 'OH MY GOD THEY'RE MONSTERS!'

Panting, I rolled onto my side and saw Rhea struggling to breathe. It was a good luck for me that I couldn't die by hitting the pavement from such a height and speed. Rhea, on the other hand, looked worse for wear.

As the silent falling snow covered my wings, I carefully stood up and shook myself. I felt a bump on my head where I had hit the building. Touching my skin, I saw my fingers were covered with blood. 'Ah, damn it.' Testing my wings, I slowly opened them with some difficulty then yelped as Rhea's hand suddenly grabbed my right ankle.

'You are not going to take this from me.'

Looking behind me, I saw the strange lights in the air. They had now combined and had turned purple; the beam of light was still in the middle.

Pulling my leg away from her, I looked down on her, pitying her. It was over. 'Rhea, forget it. You cannot become a true Siren. I won't allow it.'

Glancing down at the floor, Rhea reached out for her gun, but as I bent down to take it from her, she lunged at me, grabbing my hair and pulling me down towards her. With a great thwack, she brought her right knee up and kneed me in the head. Bright lights burst into my vision and yelling in pain, I fell back onto the crunchy wet-ground. She pounced on me, wrapping her hands around my throat trying to strangle me, but she was weaker than me and I easily managed to prise one hand off and punched her in the face.

'Ow!' I shouted, feeling a throbbing in my hand and in my head. Gazing around, I noticed that there were some people watching from a distance. Their phones were out filming us. 'EVERYONE GET OUT OF HERE!' I bellowed. 'RUN AWAY!' With their legs shaking in fear, they turned and sped, slipping and sliding on the wet, icy ground.

Then without warning, the blinding purple light from above pulsated again but this time, the force was explosive. The buildings around shuddered as though there was an earthquake; glass from windows exploded outwards, shards raining down onto the streets and night-time walkers below. More people, who hadn't heard my commanding voice, ran screaming or shouting in fright. They didn't understand what was going on and I was glad of it.

My attention snapped onto Rhea, who had scrambled up as I was distracted and reached over for the gun once again. I was too far away from it and before I could think to command her to stop, she shot me in the chest.

Pain suddenly exploded, making me crease over and fall flat on the ground; clutching my chest as blood pooled out of it. I cried out from the sting of the bullet as it had lodged in between my ribcage. But as I tried to take it out with my fingers, a wave of nausea beat down onto my stomach, making me retch. The pain was intense. Over the pounding of blood in my sore head, I saw Rhea walk towards me out of my peripheral vision. She crunched softly through the snow and kicked me in the stomach, rolling me over onto my back. I screamed and heard her giggle gently.

'Welcome to the afterlife, Tara.'

Blocking out the light from a lamppost, Rhea walked a little way from me and shouted loudly to the heavens, 'CHANGE ME!' The snow-filled wind suddenly shifted direction and a vortex formed around her. Rhea yelled out in anguish, as I had done and I saw through streaming eyes, her form change before me. She grew taller, her hair became longer, her wings grew almost double in size. While she was changing, I gritted my teeth and dug my hand into my chest, pinching the bullet in my forefinger and thumb and yanked it out. Heaving deep breaths, I felt relieved that my skin was healing quickly, but as with my broken arm, I felt a large bruise ache where the bullet entered. Through blurry vision, I looked up at her. Rhea had now finally changed.

My heart sunk as I stood up on wobbly legs. The bullet was still in my right hand covered in blood. I twisted it around, trying to think of a plan...

'I saved the last one for you,' she smiled evilly as the vortex died down. 'Shame they aren't special bullets that your brother used. I see they can't kill you.' Rhea stretched her wings and began to admire herself. 'Wow, the power... it's tenfold.' She laughed. 'And I beat you down without changing. Wow Tara, you are pathetic just like Maynard said. Without your friends, you're useless.' That hurt me more than she could have possibly known. I knew sending the others had been a bad idea, but it was the only thing I could think of at the time to protect them. I guess my snap decisions sometimes weren't always a good idea.

Suddenly there was another massive explosion of light; shaking the buildings around us, threatening to make them crack at the foundations and fall on top of everyone. Rhea moved out of the way just as I saw the beams split and divide into dozens, positioning themselves over London, they looked like search lights, but what or who were they looking for. I heard police sirens in the distance coupled with people running and screaming in terror exclaiming it was the end of the world.

'The war has begun,' Rhea smiled happily. 'I just wish Lynn was here to see me and my accomplishment. I think she would have appreciated it.'

'Yeah, well why don't you ask her yourself?' I shouted and lunged at her, ignoring the pain throughout my body. Rhea lashed out at my face trying to scratch me. I dodged to the left but up came her knee again, hitting me in the side. Crying out in pain, I toppled over and rolled, my chest hitting the ground, a fresh burst of pain pounded where the bruise was. Rhea ran towards me, slipping and sliding as she went. As she neared, I flapped my wings will all my might and lifted off the floor.

'Come back here!' she ordered, but her words didn't affect me. I heard people scream out as they saw me take off from the ground, but as long as Rhea was following me, they would be safe from her. I didn't trust Rhea. She had the power to command people to do what they wanted and that was dangerous.

Flying around Big Ben, I had to get into one of the searchlights. They, the Ancients, were searching for someone. If I could just get into a light and plead my case to the Ancients, maybe they could help stop this once and for all.

I heard the sound of heavy wings beat against the winds from behind me. There was no need to turn around to see Rhea following me. But I wondered how good at flying she had become. 'Come and catch me then!' I shouted and sped off into the night. I flew up into the icy air, the wind screamed through my hair and feathers and then suddenly I felt a hand around my ankle.

'Got you,' she laughed, and stopped me, mid-flight and threw me to-wards the ground. Recovering quickly, I dove into the blackness and had her chase me close to street level, dodging and weaving through the alley-ways. Hearing the sound of a loud crash of a large industrial waste bin, Rhea swore loudly and turning briefly, I saw she had plunged headfirst into it. Laughing, I flew up and away from her, minding the people who saw me and headed straight towards one of the lights but as I reached it, Rhea screeched behind me.

'NOOO!' She had caught up with me in a heartbeat and I felt my left wing being yanked back. Then with a kick to my back, my right wing bent in at an angle; pain erupted in both my wings and I was unable to fly.

Rhea let go of me and I fell onto the roof of a building. As I glanced up, I saw Rhea heading into one of the lights. It fell upon her as though a wave had crashed into a rock and within seconds I felt the atmosphere around me tremble with electricity. The lights collided together and in brightest flash of light; I heard a piercing scream from Rhea and then she was gone.

'That is enough!' A deep booming, powerful voice roared over me, sounding as though it came from the light.

A great torrent of wind suddenly whipped around me, my long, black, hair flying with the upturned snow that was scattered along the frost-covered roof. I closed my eyes for the slightest moment and then next thing I knew, I was back outside the British Museum, staring at the remains of the damaged back entrance. I had been taken back to the T.A.T. headquarters.

Unable to fly, I fell through the hole and landed neatly on the ground. Standing in the middle of the computer room; the bodies were now laid out around the edges, white blood stained sheets covered their faces. With the realisation that it was over somehow, unsure of why or what happened, I fell to the floor and cried.

Nathaniel and Amjee came over to me as they saw me on the broken floor; Amjee fell beside me and hugged me, silently crying on my shoulder. Nathaniel put a bandaged hand on my shoulder. I was thankful the idiot was alive, but I remained quiet, unsure of how to begin.

After an hour or so, the crying and shaking had stopped, but not the sad-ness that still lingered in my heart. I had done a foolish thing. I had sent my friends away when I needed them the most. Was this the way it had to be? Was the war truly a war between myths and humans? Or was it between Rhea and me?

I didn't know and maybe, I will never know.

Amjee had called in some former T.A.T people to help clean up the mess at headquarters. Jeff was one of them. And while Nathaniel and I were in the cafeteria sitting at a table looking at the floor, we realised that neither of us wanted to speak to the other. There were so many things we wanted to ask each other- but the pain we both felt for what had happened kept our mouths shut tight. Every time I kept remembering Henry, a wet salty tear fell down my cheek. I had come to the realisation that my friends could no longer be in this plane. After all, they were all myths now. There was no chance of getting them back and with the Ancients taking Rhea and me, unable to fly, I wasn't posing a problem. The balance was fixed.

'What happened to... to Rhea?' Nathaniel asked in a raspy voice.

I had to ask him to repeat the question as my mind had wondered to a future that I could now no longer have with Henry.

'She was taken away,' I told him, wiping my tears away for the others. 'There was an explosion of light. A single beam surrounded her, she screamed then there was this blinding flash of light. This loud voice then said "That is enough" and then I found myself outside the back entrance.'

'Someone said, "That is enough"?'

I nodded. 'I don't know who it was, but it doesn't matter.' Sighing, I got off the table and glanced at my wings. There was no need for a Siren any-more. The T.A.T. was over, Rhea was gone and everything was normal, apart from me. I couldn't stay in this body anymore. My parents found a cure to turn myths into humans. Somehow, I had to find it. 'There is one more thing to do.'

'What's that?' Nathaniel asked as he slid off the table.

'I need to be human again,' I said sadly.

'Amjee,' I called, as I went up to her, Nathaniel trailing along behind. We entered the destroyed cathedral room. It seemed even more damaged than before.

'Everything is being taken care of,' she said looking troubled. 'But there is something you should listen to. Jeff,' she called over her shoulder.

Looking in her direction, Jeff was talking to a tall, fair haired man who looked tired and frazzled. I knew how he felt. After a few seconds Jeff came over to us, giving me a small smile.

'Let Tara listen,' she told him.

Frowning slightly, Jeff pulled out his phone, which was attached to an ear-piece and gave it to me.

Taking it gingerly, I placed it in my ear.

"...police are asking for any information on the whereabouts of two large winged-birds that destroyed part of Big Ben and the Houses of Parliament in the early hours of this morning, after a giant explosion in the sky. Police and the army have been trying to track these creatures, with reports from witnesses alleging that they were actually women with wings. Eyewitnesses have placed videos of these winged women on websites and information is pouring in from all over the world trying to explain what they are. If anyone has any information on who these winged women are or if they know their whereabouts, please contact the police on..." I took the ear-piece out and passed it back to him. My stomach twisted, I felt physically sick.

'What are we going to do?' I asked them.

'We were hoping you would know,' Jeff told me.

I came up blank. 'Ah, damn and here I was wanting things to go back to normal.' I softly laughed to myself. I sounded like Macie.

'Go back to normal?' Amjee asked me. 'Hunny, you won't ever be normal.'

'No, I can,' I told her confidently. 'My parents were working on a cure, they could change us back, well... they could change me back at least.'

'The others,' Amjee said softly, 'they cannot get back can they?'

Shaking my head, I pushed the thought aside. There was another problem to take care of. 'I need to think,' I said. 'I'll be back soon, I promise,' I added to Nathaniel as he gave me a quizzical look.

Heading down the sooty corridor towards the cafeteria, I stopped before the double doors and kicked down the door to my room. It looked exactly how I left it, completely untidy. Smiling to myself, I stooped under the doorframe and went to my bed. Flopping down on it, I tried to spread my wings out behind me, but they pained me too much. Inhaling my own scent, I became instantly unhappy. I tried to pretend that none of this had happened; that I was back home in my old house. My parents talking in the living room in those brief moments they were both in the house and my brother in his room playing awful music, but no matter how hard I tried, I couldn't imagine it clearly. That ship had sailed.

Suddenly I felt my bed depress, it felt like someone or something had sat on it. Turning my head around, my eyes grew wide in horror. Yelling out, I scrambled off the bed to head to the door but the broken door to my room had vanished. In fact, my whole room had disappeared. Without knowing how, I was back in that same strange white void where I found Macie.

Spinning around, the person who had sat on my bed was now standing looking at me in an odd way. Wearing a long white and green robe with a black sash around his middle, he stood complacently. His dark black hair fell past his shoulders; startling violet eyes piercing my blue ones, as though trying to see into my soul.

'Who are you? Where am I? What do you want?' I shouted flexing my wings to prepare to fight, but I gasped in pain.

Smiling slightly, he gestured around the void. 'This, as your friend Macie said, is the stepping stone to the magical plane. Its actual name is called The Null. It is the place in passing onto each plane. I have brought you here to tell you the consequences of what has happened on both planes.'

'You're, you're not a myth are you?' I asked him, realising that his voice sounded familiar. 'You're an Ancient.'

'That is correct,' he said inclining his head. 'Tara Young. You have faced dangers beyond your years, truths and falsehoods which have almost rendered you incapacitated on such an emotional level, yet here you are, alive and whole. I have watched you from the very beginning. I have seen you strive through the struggles of being thrust into a world which you yourself did not believe in. For this reason, I wish to help you.'

'Help me? How?' I asked, utterly confused.

'Your mother has taken the Phaistos Disc into our plane. My brethren and I wish to destroy the disc after a new Ancient came into our midst just recently. But first, we must take care of the problem in London. There is a Golden Rule, Tara. Myths cannot be seen by humans. Myths need to be believed, not to be seen, captured and experimented on. As a result, I will clean up this mess that you have caused, if... you become human.'

Scoffing at him, I rolled my eyes. 'I was already contemplating that. I just want my friends back.'

He eyes saddened. 'I cannot give them to you. They were sent there, on your orders and to not return,' he said sternly. 'Also they are myths, Tara, and they like being myths. You cannot force them, they must choose on their own. We are just happy that they have turned into a myth that is not a duplicate of a pure myth.'

'Look, I know I screwed up. But, they don't belong there. They were human too. If... if I can find my parents cure and it turns me human, will you let them go?'

The Ancient closed his eyes in thought. After a few seconds, he opened them and stared right at me. 'If your cure proves false, you will forever be hunted by the humans that you wish to become,' he told me, frowning.

'Also, if your friends do not wish to be human, you will never see them again. You cannot tell them this, do not sway them like that. Do you understand?'

'I understand,' I said.

'Then Tara Young, we are in an agreement. Become human, I shall return London as it was before and will give your friends back to you-.'

'Thank you,' I smiled.

'-if you can find them,' he laughed.

'No wait! I didn't agree to that!' I shouted, but suddenly I was shouting to no one in a dark room, that once belonged to me in the destroyed headquarters of the T.A.T.

Racing into the corridor, I burst out into the cathedral room. 'Nathaniel,' I shouted at him. 'Call the fairies; I need one more favour from them.'

'Why, what do you need?' he asked me looking anxious.

'I need the solution or whatever it is, to turn me human.'

Amjee and Jeff gasped in horror.

'What?' Amjee shook her head, butting in front of the others. 'But Tara, your mother is a Siren; you belong to the magical plane.'

'Won't you need your powers again?' Nathaniel asked, looking shocked and sad. 'The Mage said that you are meant to be a guardian. You can't be one if you're human.'

'Forget that, I can't be a guardian or need my powers if I have nothing or no one to guard,' I said, angrily. 'Rhea's gone, Lynn's dead along with the rest of the T.A.T.'

'Not everyone,' Jeff said darkly.

'Who?' I asked, my eyes glancing at the covered bodies.

'Maynard.' He said quietly, as though afraid to speak his name.

'His body isn't here,' Amjee told me. 'We checked every body. He's still out there with power, money and influence. If he wanted, he could potentially start this again.'

'I think Maynard became a God,' I told them forlornly. 'Rhea I think was a decoy, to distract me while Maynard went into the other plane. The big purple light was the portal the Ancients made. I saw there was just one beam, then after a burst of energy the light split into several as though search lights. In that one beam, I think Maynard went into the other plane. But even if he has become a God, the Ancients can control him in the other plane. He is no threat to us.' Sighing, I added. 'If I become human, I can get the others back one at a time- if I find them. Just… just call the fairies for me, please. I need to know where Mum and Dad put the anti-myth solution.'

Nathaniel bit his bottom lip. Exhaling a deep breath of air, he looked down at the floor. 'I'm not going to call the fairies for that.'

Getting suddenly angry I turned and glared at him, 'this isn't about you. Just please, do what I ask. Don't make me force you.'

'Tara, I won't do it, there's no need-.'

'I need to be human!' I shouted at him.

'FINE!' he shouted back. Suddenly, his hand delved into his left trouser pocket and he whipped out a small silver pocket-knife. Slitting his left palm, he reached out and sliced my palm in the same place. Yelling in pain with blood trickling onto the floor, he clasped his bloody palm with my own.

'What are you doing?' I asked feebly, as I quickly began to feel strange; almost light-headed and dizzy.

'Ever wondered why I'm not like you? Why both of our parents are myths and I'm not, why I need magical protection since I was young? Also wondered why I was never picked for the T.A.T.? Because I am a virus. I destroy myth's blood. No matter what it is.'

'If you give her too much, she'll die Nathaniel,' Amjee told him gently.

'Explain,' I gasped, my body felt as though I had just run a marathon. My legs felt as bendy as heated rubber and unable to keep my balance I pitched forwards. Nathaniel caught me and together we slid onto the floor. I could feel my arms, body and legs shrink back to my normal human size, my ears tingled and my eyes became blurry and human.

'I'm so sorry,' he whispered sorrowfully.

Then as though large, heavy, boulders were ripped out of my back, I felt my wings disintegrate for the final time. I sensed every feather leave my wings. Experienced the muscles on my back painfully withdraw into nothing; the cartilage dissipating; the blood draining and the ancient knowledge leaving me feeling ignorant and stupid. Then there was nothing but the freezing coldness of the Cathedral room and I knew I was human once more.

Scratching an itch on my back, my hand froze. I wondered if it had gone. Wearing baggy clothes, I turned my back on Nathaniel and pulled my top up. 'Is it there? Is my tattoo still there?'

'It's there,' Nathaniel told me, pulling my top down. 'But it's very faint as though it's been tattooed with grey ink or partly erased. But no matter what it looks like, it's still served a small reminder of what you had been through and done.'

'At the beginning I hated them, but I grew rather fond of flying with huge wings the colour of night itself. But now that I am human and the Ancients will know that, they'll let my friends go if I could find them. But hell, where do I even start?'

Nathaniel shrugged his shoulders and helped me up.

'I'll go and find you something to wear,' Amjee said with a small smile and looked at Jeff. 'I've just had a thought. You'll need to inform Garrick. He helped with the funding of this place and was quite close to Maynard.'

Jeff gave a quick nod. 'Excuse me you two,' he said then hurried off in a different direction.

Nathaniel and I headed into the cafeteria. There was no one there, but it was quiet, almost eerily calm. Last time I was in here there was a goodbye party for us. Grabbing a chair, I slumped onto it, hitting my head on the table. Everything had turned to crap.

'You need to think of the places you have been,' Nathaniel said trying to be logical.

I mumbled all of the placed we had gone to in one breath and Nathaniel was silent for a while. 'You have practically been all over the world within two weeks. That's mental.'

'That's my life… Or was my life. But how is it going to help me find them?' Turning my head to look at him, he frowned in puzzlement. 'Nothing of significance happened really apart from meeting our operators and changing.'

'Where did you meet your operators?' After I had told him, he frowned. 'Hmm, and where did each of you change, was it into full myths?'

I nodded and reeled off each person and where they transformed, then added. 'If it was when they first changed into their "first stage",' I air-quoted, 'then Darren would be in the swimming pool right about now and he's not. So I guess it's to the nuclear base first. Saskia, Henry and Sam changed there.'

Nathaniel hmmed in thought then digging into his black jeans pocket brought out a small packet of what looked like some sort of dried herbs. Pinching some in his fingers, he said, 'I call upon the fairy Mage by offering you this gift of sage.' Blowing on it, the sage fell onto the table then in a flash of light; the Mage appeared above it. She smiled up at us.

'Tara, it is nice to see you...' she glanced behind me where my wings used to be and smiled sadly. 'I am sorry it worked out the way it did.'

'I had to be human,' I told her feeling upset. 'It's to get my friends back.'

Nathaniel got the Mage's attention. 'I need a favour.'

She frowned. 'I'm not your errand fairy,' she said waspishly.

'It's for Tara's sake,' he said and she seemed a little happier. 'We need to know if there are any of her friends in the Welsh bunker you took me too.'

She frowned again. 'Why?'

After explaining she nodded in understanding. 'Ah, I see. Let me check.' In a flash of white she vanished then a few minutes later she came back looking glum. 'No, no one is there. Are there any other places?'

'There's an old Welsh farmhouse near the bunker that Macie changed in, thanks to Saskia.' I added bitterly as I remembered Macie's pained cries. 'But the majority of people transformed in Ha Long bay.'

The Mage laughed. 'Well then that's your first port of call, Tara. You need to go to Ha Long Bay.'

'Could you?' I began to ask, but she shook her head.

'Sorry Tara. But if they are humans, I cannot show myself to them. If truth be told, I shouldn't be showing myself to you. I'm only here because of your brother.' She nodded towards him. 'I'm sorry I cannot help you get there.'

I shrugged. 'Thank you for helping anyway.'

'I wish you the best my dear.' Fluttering up to my cheek, she kissed it gently then disappeared in a flash.

'We need to have a word with Amjee. Looks like we're going to Ha Long Bay.'

'Cool.'

★ ★ ★

'Okay, listen up,' Amjee called to everyone, silencing them from their small conversations. Along with Amjee, Jeff, Nathaniel and myself, the remaining members of the old T.A.T, which Jeff and Amjee assured me were trust-worthy, were in the cafeteria. It was late in the morning on the 23rd of November. I was grateful that Amjee had let me sleep for most of the morning though I wished I didn't have such terrible nightmares. I was beyond tired. 'As we've noticed, the Ancients have held up their end of the bargain and there is no news that related to this morning's incident between Rhea and Tara.' There was a grateful murmur around the group. 'I have had some information about Tara's need to get the others. The first stop, we believe, is in Vietnam. The plane leaves in an hour. It flies non-stop to Kolkata, India, to re-fuel. Do not get off the plane!' she shouted making me and Nathaniel. 'From there, it will take you to Hanoi, in Vietnam. There will be a helicopter waiting to take you directly to Ha Long bay where you will have to tell the pilot where to find the others. Get Hannah, Lottie, Darren and Lionel and then go back to the airport. There you will get a direct flight back to London.'

'Direct flight?' Nathaniel asked frowning. 'Don't flights usually stop off on the way?'

Amjee nodded. 'Yes, but I've had to call in a few favours. The flights you are going on are not commercial. They are private. We can thank Garrick for that,' she said eyeing Jeff.

'Who's Garrick?' I asked her, but Jeff answered.

'Garrick is a long term friend of Maynard's,' he explained. 'We had a lengthy discussion about the financial implications of the T.A.T. and what's to become of the base. There are still a lot of people who work for the T.A.T. the um… corrupt people passed away last night,' he said sadly. 'But the original work behind the T.A.T. will still continue.'

'And what was that?' Nathaniel asked sarcastically.

'To keep the Golden Rule,' Jeff told him in a matter-of-fact way. 'And we want to uphold that. The base will only have a few members and we'll work closely with the other bases around the world.'

'There's more?' Nathaniel and I asked, shocked.

Jeff and Amjee nodded. 'Oh course. Where do you think Maynard came from?' When neither of us answered, he said, 'Area 51. He was head of the department there for some time before he transferred over to us.'

'So, Area 51 is real?' I asked feeling as though I really didn't know anything about the T.A.T. and its affiliates.

'Oh yes,' Jeff said. 'I went over there some years ago. They have a lot of magical artefacts that's been found in the past several decades, but no one can top Germany.'

'Germany has a secret base?'

'The Nazi's scoured the world for precious artefacts, but after WW2, they laid forgotten. A rather precocious woman from Area 51 founded the German base but left shortly after. We haven't seen nor heard of Von Reed for a long time.' Jeff folded his arms and huffed. 'Besides, it doesn't concern you anymore.' He said with a frown. 'We best get you to the plane.'

An hour later, Nathaniel and I were in the air heading to India. The plane was relatively small, only equipped with twelve seats for comfortable legroom and a dance space to boot, but it was fast.

Nathaniel told me in was called a Cessna Citation TEN jet. One of the fastest private jets in the world but I didn't really care about the model or make. I was just upset that it could fly and I couldn't. As I stared out of the window, I looked down and smiled. 'I could have flown up this high once,' I told Nathaniel, as he looked straight ahead, clutching the armrests with white hands and looking absolutely petrified. Laughing softly, I rested my head on his shoulder and finally, drifted off to sleep.

I woke up as the plane bumped onto the tarmac of Hanoi Airport. The jet moved slowly away from the commercial flights that gathered to the right and one of the pilot's voice sounded above us. 'The helicopter will arrive shortly.' The plane's engine died down to a low growl and I unfastened my seatbelt. 'Please remain on the plane until it arrives.'

'Um,' Nathaniel began, forcing himself to look at me. 'Do you know where this place is?'

'Huh?' Not paying attention to him.

'The island where the others are. Do you know where it is?'

'I know what it looks like, from above anyway,' I said realising what he was getting at.

'Brilliant,' Nathaniel groaned. 'I hate heights.'

Scoffing, as I said the same thing only a few weeks ago. I responded with, 'Should have told me before I swept you up and threw you into that gas,' I grumbled, but Nathaniel just sighed and didn't reply.

When the helicopter arrived, the pilots helped escort us from the jet onto the tarmac and a little ways towards another chopper that was awaiting us, its blades swirling around noisily. Putting on our seatbelts and strapping ourselves in, it quickly ascended into the air and took off towards Ha Long Bay.

'Can you hear me?' The Vietnamese pilot, a woman, asked. I gave her the thumbs up.

'Yes I can hear you.'

'You have some people to pick up on an island, right? In the bay?'

I nodded then asked, 'Yes, but as its pitch black, won't it be difficult to find them?'

'Not to worry. I have heat sensors,' she pointed to some dials which I could barely see in the dark of the cockpit. 'We'll find them.' I saw that Nathaniel had taken a small orange box with him. He frowned as he touched its smooth plastic case then depressing the locks, the box flicked open. He stared at its contents for a few seconds, then closing it gently, placed the box beside him.

'They will all change,' I told him confidently, 'they'll accept them and we'll all lead normal lives.'

Nathaniel scoffed. 'So naive.'

'Why?'

'You may be human, Tara. But you will never lead a normal life now. None of you will.'

My stomach turned upside down as guilt enveloped me. Looking away from him, I worried how the others would react. I hope they would accept the Ancient's bargain with me and I hope they would understand.

The helicopter didn't take long to get to Ha Long Bay and upon arrival the pilot, Chi, told us we didn't have long to search the islands. 'Use these to search for your friends,' she said passing me some rather expensive looking binoculars. 'There are people living around the islands and they will show up on the sensors.' Thanking her, I took the binoculars and tried them on.

'Whoa cool.'

'So where is it?' Chi asked. 'The island.'

'I'm not sure where the island is from the mainland, but it looks like a Shark,' I said, motioning for her to go higher.

With a brief nod, she pulled the stick towards her and we went higher. Fifteen minutes later and with no luck, we descended towards the water. There was a handful of heat signatures on Chi's sensor, but there were too many to be the group. The two of them would be in the cave, the others in the water close by.

'I have found something,' Chi said happily nodding at the sensor and pointing out to the right. 'The island has four heat signatures. Two are on the island, two are...' she paused and frowned, 'the other two are in the water.'

'That's them!' I exclaimed.

Chi flew to the island easily. The trees were whipped up like cream in the downbursts from the rotors. Hovering twenty-five feet above the path that lead to the cave behind the waterfall she sent a rope ladder down. 'I'll give you twenty minutes.'

Nathaniel went down first taking the orange box and I quickly followed landing safely on the ground and waving. Chi left us in a flurry of rotor blades and with it the light. Nathaniel was about to walk off, when I reached my hand out and stopped him.

'No, stay here.'

'But you might need me,' he protested but ignoring him, I moved around him and headed towards the cave. I brought out the binoculars and saw that there were two heat signatures. One was dazzling which I gathered was Lottie, the other, was small, which was probably Lionel.

Stopping just outside of the cave, I heard the slightest movement from inside it. 'Lionel, Lottie,' I began unsure of what to say. 'I need to talk to you.' Pushing through the waterfall I came out into the cave and made out, the shapes of Lottie and Lionel in their myth forms.

Lottie screeched out in fright as she saw me while Lionel howled like a wolf baying at the moon. They came towards me and slumping to the floor I apologised profusely for sending them away. I couldn't help but shed a tear or two as they looked downcast and forlorn. Touching my hands I knew they were trying to communicate with me, but I couldn't hear them and it pained me even more. Wiping my tears, I asked them to listen to me and told them what happened after I had sent them to the other plane. About Nathaniel, Amada, Lynn, Rhea and Maynard. I explained about how I got here and also I explained the reason why I was here and about the Ancient and his bargain.

'I had to be human, there's no reason for me to stay as a Siren. Maynard can't hurt us in this plane and as a human. He's a God now and the Ancients will watch over him, they have more power than him. 'The cure, my parents' cure it works on me and...' I paused and realised what I was going to ask them. I took all my courage to ask them this. I was shaking with fear from their reaction, it worried me that much. 'If you want to be human, it will work for you as well.'

They immediately backed away from me. Lionel shook his head and Lottie's head dropped. I waited on the wet floor until they could, in their own way, give me an answer but after a few minutes of silence, I stood up. I wanted to tell them if they didn't become human then I would never see them again, but I promised the Ancient I wouldn't and I keep my promises.

'I'm sorry that this happened. I hope in time you'll forgive me.' Turning around, I walked out of the cave and met Nathaniel. In the light of the moon above us, he saw my saddened face. 'They aren't coming. They want to be myths.'

'After all you've done for them? You saved them and they...' he looked past me and shouted, 'YOU ARE COWARDS!'

'Nathaniel, leave it alone,' I yelled, grabbing his arm and pulling him away, but he was too strong for me.

'No!' yanking his arm from my grip. 'My sister sent you to the other plane to be safe. It was her own decision at the time because Rhea, Lynn... They would have killed you to get to her. And Tara gave up her wings to restore London and the mess that Rhea had caused. My sister is a hero and you're going to rot in the other plane having a dandy time while Tara is stuck here alone? Some friends you are!'

'Nathaniel, please let's go,' I pleaded. 'It's their choice.'

'Its cowardice!' he spat then stormed off.

'Tara?' someone called, it was faint, but I heard it from down below. 'Tara?'

'It's Hannah,' I gasped and ran down the path, skidding and sliding as I went. Nearing the edge of the waters, I saw two ghostly figures in the water. 'Hannah!' I called, waving at her.

Turning, she brought the water with her, pushing her up towards me. She gasped as she saw my small wingless form. 'You... you're human.'

With the sound of a splash, I saw Darren smack his tail angrily in the water. Ignoring him, I looked at Hannah. 'Yes, I am.'

'Why? What happened?'

As with Lottie and Lionel, I explained what happened and she understood immediately what I had to do. 'So, the cure works?'

'Tara? Where are you?' Nathaniel called from above. 'I need you!'

'I'm down here,' I shouted and Hannah backed away. 'No don't go, it's just my brother. He has been protected by fairies since he was a child. He knows about myths and about the T.A.T. for a long time.'

'Lottie and Lionel, they are in the cave?'

'Yes and though I can't hear their thoughts, I know Lottie misses you. It's your choice if you want to be human again. I won't force you and I won't sway you.'

'Tara, before I give you my decision, there is something I have to tell you.' I nodded, though I was human, the others still regarded me as their leader. It was nice and respectful, but it also made me sad. 'When Darren and I left for the other plane, we met a lot of water myths. We were escorted to a large palace made out of coral and oyster shells. It looked like the palace at Petra; it was carved so intricately. Poseidon, Amphitrite, The Lady of the Lake, Ahti, Nut, Hapi, Shinto, Neptune, Lir. Every God or Goddess attributed to water or lakes from around the world all resided in that huge palace. They explained to us that Darren and I had a destiny, one that would change the course of events on this planet forever. Neither of them revealed when it would occur, but I knew that in order for our destinies to happen, we have to be myths.' She looked so sad and reached out to smooth my face. 'I'm so sorry, Tara.'

Hearing Nathaniel come down to meet me, strangely topless, he came to my side and I introduced him to Hannah and told him that she and Darren were going remain as myths. 'Huh, well I think the others may want to have a word with you. Guys, down here!' He called behind him.

Through the cracks and rustling of trees and bushes, dressed in Nathaniel's coat and shirt, were the shivering human forms of Lottie and Lionel. Screaming in delight, I ran to them and hugged them both. 'I'm so sorry, I'm so, so sorry!' I repeated over and over again.

'We get it Tara, you can let go now,' Lionel gasped.

Lottie moved past me and went to talk to Hannah while I spoke to Lionel. 'What changed your minds?'

'Him,' Lionel thumbed to Nathaniel. 'He was right, annoyingly. But Lottie and I had a reason to become humans for Macie and for Sam. In the other plane, we weren't in a group; we were instantly separated into our own mythologies. Henry and I were together, Egyptian myths, Macie and Lottie I guess would have been together... We were all categorised. It didn't feel right.'

'Hannah, please!' we heard Lottie shout at her. 'Darren, we know you love Saskia,' she called down to him. 'Don't let her go like this!'

'Lottie, that's unfair on Darren, you know about his heart!' Hannah spat in a thunderous tone.

Lionel stepped forward, placing his hands on Lottie's shoulders. 'Hannah, it's over. You were told this when every myth was on tenterhooks with the Ancients. You'll make a big mistake if you remain like this and it turns out for nought. If you become human and you still have a destiny, magic has a funny way of keeping you bound to it. It'll find you again in another way.'

Hannah looked away from us and down towards Darren. There was a long pause between us then sighing heavily she nodded. 'I think you're right, Lionel. For the time being, we can be human, but I know that Darren and I are destined for something great… just maybe not right now.'

Chi gained an extra four shivering bodies and flying back to Hanoi airport, the others were given food and clothing on board the speeding jet. In the early hours of the night and with four injections of Nathaniel's cure taken from his orange box, we flew off back to the UK.

CHAPTER TWENTY-THREE

WHEN WE TOUCHED BACK ON ENGLISH SOIL, LONDON'S Heathrow was surrounded by the frenzy of holidaymakers, either trying to get out of the cold country before Christmas or attempting to get in to see families. It was pandemonium.

'Everyone, stay together,' I called, as we left the gate and headed towards the south terminal exit.

'God, it's like a rat maze,' Lottie said, as we were pushed and shoved in different directions. Bringing out some coins, I headed to a telephone booth and after waiting for one that was free, the seven of us crowded around it.

'Hi Amjee, we're by the South exit,' I said quickly as she picked up her disposable phone.

'Okay, we'll be there soon to take you to Wales. Go and get something to eat first, we'll meet you out front.'

'Alright, cheers,' I said putting the phone down. 'Amjee is going to meet us soon but let's get something to eat.'

Digging into a disgustingly good greasy chicken burger, we sat together at a table and devoured everything we bought.

'That was nice,' Nathaniel said burping loudly.

'Disgusting pig,' I said smirking.

'So Nathaniel,' Hannah said as she leant over the table to look at him, 'we didn't get to talk much, what do you do for a living?'

Suppressing a smile, I turned my attention away from them and had a lengthy chat with Lottie. She told me about all the magical creatures that were in the other plane and said she couldn't stop smiling that she had her body back. 'It's nice having front-facing eyes and a nose,' she laughed, 'the only thing I miss is, well, the flying.'

'You flew?' I asked, as the last time Lottie was with me. She was too small to fly properly.

'Yes. Well, when I got to the other plane, I became a normal sized phoenix and my powers had fully developed. It was fantastic, flying over the rivers and hills. It was a lovely place to be.'

A pang of pain hit my stomach again, that same yearning of wanting to be back in the sky, flying away from all the bad things, but there was none of that anymore. It was just us.

★ ★ ★

Amjee picked us up in a sleek black Toyota Rav4 and we drove non-stop to Wales. She was surprised to see the others, but I also noticed that she hid how sad she was to see them human. Nathaniel had strapped himself into the seat beside Amjee chatting away with her about going to Ha Long while the rest of us had small conversations about the other plane or about Rhea and Lynn.

'Head to the university,' I told Amjee as we turned off the M4 heading towards Pontypridd.

'So this is your university,' Amjee said as we passed it on the left.

'Yeah, but the farmhouse is over the hills to the south, the bunker to the north,' I pointed out towards them.

'Gotcha,' she nodded and we drove on.

Having to stop and ask for directions to the old abandoned farmhouse, we found a rough dirt road, which the Rav4 easily negotiated, and soon saw the silhouette of the dilapidated house close by. When Amjee stopped, I got outside. 'Lionel, I think you should come with me.' Nathaniel was about to get out, but I stopped him. 'No don't. Just Lionel.'

Surrounded by darkness, yet again, and also frigid, trudging on the crunchy snow covered-ground, Lionel and I used a torch to get to the farmhouse. Stopping just outside we heard something move inside and froze.

'Macie,' I called, 'Macie are you in there?'

Hearing a soft beat of wings and the sounds of clawed padding on tiled floor, Macie emerged from the house and screeched out, as Lottie had, when she saw Lionel and me in front of her. Human.

She flapped her wings in anger, I think, then raced towards me and pounced on me. I fell back and caught Lionel's terrified looking face. 'No, its okay,' I told him and stared at Macie's golden right eye. I wasn't scared of Macie, she was my best friend, but I was worried that Macie would take my words in the wrong way and would be majorly upset with me. She nuzzled her head against my hand, but I heard nothing but silence.

'I can't hear you Macie,' I said softly. 'I'm not a Siren anymore, I'm human.' She backed off and turned to look at Lionel and moved to him. Nuzzling his hand, he shook his head.

'No Macie, I'm human too.'

She cried out in anguish then clicked her beak angrily. Standing up on her hind legs, she flapped and screeched again. Lionel moved in front to protect me, but it was unnecessary. I moved forwards. 'She has to hear what I have to say,' I said to him. 'Macie, please calm down and listen.'

Settling down on her four sleek lion legs, she stopped flapping and folded her wings back to her body. Calmly, I told Macie as I had told the others. Lionel confirmed it and told her from his point of view why Macie should be human.

'But it's your choice,' I told her. 'You should want to be human for yourself and not for Lionel or the others and definitely not for me, no matter what my brother might say,' I mumbled crossly. Macie's wings dropped sadly by her sides and sighing she sat down and nodded her head.

'You want to be human?' I asked, 'Your own choice?'

Nodding again, Lionel went to hug Macie and stayed with her as I got Nathaniel. Taking out one of the needles that were full of his blood he administered it in her left shoulder. I took my jacket off, shivering from the cold and placed it around Macie as she turned back into a human. Then carrying her, bridal style, Lionel took her back to the car where she was warmly greeted by a heated car and happy faces.

As Amjee took us to the bunker, she parked up just outside the hill and Nathaniel and I got out. I told everyone to stay in the car, but they refused, apart from Lionel and Macie.

'We're coming with you,' Lottie smiled. 'We're all in this together. Even though the group's formation was based on a lie, I don't think I'd want you to face this alone.'

'Yeah Tara,' Darren piped up. 'Your annoying and all, but human or not, we're your friends and you are our leader, come what may.'

Nathaniel tapped me on the shoulder and smiled as the others headed up the hill towards the half destroyed bunker, each laughing and talking happily. 'You are a very lucky person, Tara. I'm proud of you and I think mum and dad would be proud of you too.'

Getting into the bunker was difficult as the stairs were completely obliterated. Ducking for cover, we managed to slide into the near caved-in entrance and took a right.

Lottie squealed as she saw a strange liquid in the form of a body on the floor. 'That was Amanda,' I told her. 'Don't look at it, just keep going.'

'So we are looking for Sam, Henry and Saskia?' Hannah asked me.

'Yes. Keep your eyes peeled, Sam's pretty quick,' I told them as we got closer to the house.

'That's moronic,' Darren snapped. 'If he's quick how can you keep your eyes peeled?'

Realising he was right, I ignored him and tried to see if there were any signs of him. 'Sam,' I called out, 'it's Tara, please show yourself, we want to talk to you-.' Suddenly something smacked into the back of my legs causing me to fall over, hitting my head on the ground. 'Jeez,' I yelled angrily as stars burst into my eyes. 'You little git!' I shouted. 'Sam, we only want to talk to you, stop being an arse.'

Then without warning the others starting shouting out in pain and began to fall over. Sam was attacking us.

'Sam, stop this!' Hannah shouted, 'Lottie is with us. She's human again. Please listen to us.'

A hissing sound suddenly came from behind me in the shadows of the tunnel, sending a chill down my spine. Scrambling out of the way, I held my sore head and headed to Nathaniel.

'You alright?' he asked as he checked my head. 'It's not bleeding, but I feel a bump,' he said rubbing it gently.

'Ta,' I said irritably, pushing his hand away as it was hurting me.

Blinking my pulsating eyes, I saw Sam's scary weird figure in the corner, he was on the defensive, his beak opening; making that hissing sound.

'Sam, you have a choice to be human again, we have,' I told him, but Hannah put her hand out to stop me.

'Don't. Let him take us in first. He's not himself,' she warned me. Feeling like a child being told off, I remained quiet and watched Hannah as she slowly made her way towards him, crouching down all the time, trying to show a non-threatening position. 'Sam, it's Hannah, do you remember me?' She asked quietly. Sam hissed loudly and backed himself further into the corner. Hannah abruptly stopped moving. 'Sam, we're human again,' she told him gently, 'you can be human too if you want. You can come back with us.'

'Sam,' Lottie came out from behind Hannah and Sam immediately relaxed. 'It's true, we are all human.' Walking towards him, she knelt down and opened her arms for him. Sam stopped hissing and clicked his beak, gazing intently at her. His eyes then flicked over to Darren and Nathaniel and he hissed again.

'He's my brother,' I said to him. 'He's here to help you if you want it.'

Sam took a tentative step towards Lottie and lowered his head. Creeping towards him, Lottie placed her hand softly on his head, 'It's okay,' she smiled.

Explaining to Sam what Nathaniel intended to do, the boys quickly brought out some extra clothes and covered Sam as he began to change back. Hannah, Lottie and I went around the corner to give him some privacy.

Darren and Lottie helped carry Sam and they headed back to the car while the rest of us carried on searching for Henry and Saskia. But a few moments later after Darren and Lottie left, Hannah stopped walking. 'Tara, I don't think I should go with you. You and Nathaniel can handle it by yourselves.'

'But-' she shook her head.

'Saskia is more than your annoying Scouser, she's your friend and Henry is your boyfriend.'

'You have a boyfriend?' Nathaniel piped up.

'You have to face these two on your own.' Reaching out, she squeezed my hand and smiled. 'Good luck.' Hannah she headed towards the exit and when she was out of sight, Nathaniel quickly rounded on me.

'You have a boyfriend and you neglected to tell me?'

I scoffed. 'You've never been interested in my life before, so why now?' Walking away from him I quickly stopped as I saw a particular form slink out from the darkness. A deep guttural growl issued from his mouth and I saw the pearly-white fangs glisten in the light from my torch.

'What the hell is that?' Nathaniel demanded, but I motioned for him to stay away. Putting the torch down, I walked into the darkness. Holding my hands out in front of me and after hearing the sounds of two padded steps, my hands felt the soft, warm fur of Henry's chest. I gasped as I touched it, then buried my face in his fur and inhaled deeply. He smelt warm and homely, and as his arms embraced me and he bent down to kiss his furry lips on top of my head, I couldn't help but laugh.

'What's so funny?' He asked his voice different from what I remember. Maybe it was my hearing had changed.

'You're taller than me now.' Smiling, I looked up at him.

'How,' he asked quietly, pressing his paw on my shoulder blades where my wings used to be.

'The Ancients asked me to and I obliged. There were too many people who saw Rhea and me fight in London. Nathaniel, my brother, long story short, he knew about myths and was protected by fairies and tried to find out what Maynard was up to. Anyway his blood kind of eradicates myth blood. It's how myself and the others are all human.'

He moved slightly from shock. 'You all are?'

'Yes. I even found Hannah and Darren.'

'I thought I'd never see you again,' he said softly and stroked my hair. 'If I have to become human to be with you, then I will.'

Pushing him from me, I stared up at him seeing his cat-eyes reflect in the pale beam of the torch from behind. 'No, Henry, become human if you want to be, not because of me.'

'Tara, wingless or not, I… I want to be with you because I love you. I love you for reasons that people would never understand, but only we do.'

Nathaniel came out from the darkness behind me and Henry growled warningly. 'It's alright Henry. Nathaniel, bring an injection, please.'

Nathaniel threw a jacket at Henry as the fur fell away from him like burnt pine needles from a spruce and shrinking back to his normal size, I ran over to him to give him some support. The transformation was painful for him, as it was the others, but panting he looked at me and smiled with his deep, blue eyes. 'No matter which form I'm still taller than you.'

Before Henry went with Nathaniel back to the surface, he used a torch and scooped up a brown disc that was on the floor. 'I… I met your mother in the other plane. She told me to give this to you.' Taking it, I ran my fingers over the bumps and grooves of the pictogram covered disc. I knew immediately what it was, but for Nathaniel's sake, he said, 'It's the Phaistos Disc, the real one.'

'Why did she want me to have this?'

Henry shrugged. 'A way to talk to you. She said you'd be able to understand the pictures or hieroglyphs.'

I laughed. 'Yes I do. They were on the walls of the cave in Ha Long. Everything comes full circle it seems.'

Giving me a fleeting kiss with full kissable lips, Henry was guided out of the tunnel by Nathaniel while I carried on searching for Saskia. She was my biggest worry. She had resented me for not being turned sooner. I had ordered her, caused her pain and I wasn't there to share the experience of being a true Siren with her.

Heading deeper into the gloomy debris-ridden bunker, I called and searched for Saskia, but there was no trace of her. 'Saskia,' I called out for the millionth time, 'come on, where are you!' Somehow I walked down a familiar corridor and seeing the open door on my left, I noticed it was the computer room. Shining the torch in front of me I was standing in the spot where I had ordered the others to go. I looked around the place and my heart sank. I did miss Saskia. Sure she was bad-tempered and annoying but Hannah was right. She was my friend.

'Oy Ancient,' I yelled out, feeling annoyed, 'I've done what you asked, give Saskia back.'

Right on cue, there was a brilliant bright light ahead of me; the figure of the Ancient stepped through the light and darkness enveloped the light greedily.

'Tara Young,' he spoke his voice just as powerful and booming as before. 'You have done what I asked, but alas, I cannot give you Saskia back.'

'Why the hell not?' I shouted at him. 'We are all human, we had a deal.'

Snorting, he closed his eyes, 'Just like your mother.'

'What's she got to do with it?' I snapped at him. 'Please, give me back Saskia.'

'What is she worth to you?' he asked.

'She's my friend. She's part of the group. Yeah, she's a pain in the arse, but she is needed,' I told him.

'What is she worth to you?' he repeated himself looking at my hands.

'The disc?' He nodded. 'But my mother gave this to me.'

'It is not your mother's to give,' he said bluntly. 'The disc now belongs to my plane, not in this.' Handing it to him, he gave a curt nod. 'Take Saskia March and live your mortal lives as best you can, but know this; the wheels have only just barely started turning for this world.'

'Wait,' I blurted out, stopping him. 'What happened to Rhea?' I quickly asked as he looked like the lecture was over.

Sighing, he shook his head. The look of irritation on his face. 'She has been taken care of by her own kind.' He said pursing his lips. 'But the purple light has sent a ripple effect through both planes. Myths and legends that have lived on the human plane peacefully and undetected for centuries on the planet are now in disarray.'

'The purple light wasn't you?' I asked him and he shook his head.

'No. As I said, we gained another Ancient that night,' he said a little impatiently.

'What about a God? Did Maynard become a god?'

He scrutinised me for a moment, then shook his head. 'No, he did not.'

I breathed out a sigh of relief. Maybe he never made it to the portal as Rhea had thought. Nodding, I thanked him and I saw him place the disc inside his robes. 'Goodbye, Tara.' Without uttering another word, in a bright light the Ancient suddenly vanished and in his place, Saskia was laid on the floor, human.

'Saskia!' I called as I ran towards her.

'Git! He said that it wouldn't hurt,' she mumbled, gingerly standing up. 'Oh, it's you,' she glared at me. 'You piss ant,' she said quickly punched me on the arm.

'Ow,' I cried, holding my throbbing shoulder. 'Okay, I deserved that,' I told her. 'It's nice to have you back,' I said giving her a small smile.

'If ya do tha' again, I swear I'm gonna kick ya arse all the way ta Scotland,' she said, smiling at me. 'It's nice ta be back,' she added. 'But er, who the hell is this?' she pointed behind me. Turning around I saw Nathaniel coming towards us with a bashful look on his face, trying hard not to look at Saskia's naked body.

'It's a long story,' I said, giving her a hug.

CHAPTER TWENTY-FOUR

'TARA,' HENRY SAID SOFTLY, AS WE CUDDLED TOGETHER ON the settee in the living room on Christmas Eve. The house was overly festive. Cinnamon scented candles, bunches of wild holly and mistletoe were strung around every room, doorway and lintel. Red, green, silver and gold streamers hung awkwardly on the plastic fir tree in the corner of the room, lit with coloured twinkling lights. And beside it on a table sat a Singing Santa who sung Slade whenever someone walked past it. Saskia became more and more agitated when people approached the tree, placing small gifts underneath it to which every time, Singing Santa would start up. Her eye was beginning to twitch.

With everyone making it back into the country a few days before Christmas Eve after they all visited their families, the group decided to stay at my house for Christmas. Even Macie, who we all knew, was desperate to stay with her family wanted to spend Christmas with us, her new family. I had noticed that Hannah and Macie were somewhat on icy terms with each other and I didn't want to press Hannah on why she let Macie go. Although, I hoped we could get to the bottom of that after Christmas. At the moment, I didn't want any arguments. After all the crap we had been through, I wanted a relaxing week with my new family.

Macie and Lionel were in a lip-lock on a chair to themselves, Sam and Lottie were staring avidly into each other's eyes. Darren on the other hand kept glancing towards Saskia trying very pathetically to grab her attention, but she purposefully ignored him.

'I have something to tell you,' Henry whispered, kissing my forehead gently.

'You've got me a pony for Christmas?' I giggled.

Laughing, he smiled warmly and shook his head, 'No it's-,' he said, stopping himself and looking at the others. 'Maybe, it can wait until next week.'

'Next week?' I scoffed, sitting up and staring at him. 'What if I don't want to wait until next week? What if I want to know now?'

'You're such a child,' Saskia spat, folding her arms and glowering at me.

Ignoring her, I grabbed Henry's hands and held them. 'Please tell me. I will find out sooner or later.'

Raising an eyebrow, he said, 'oh yeah? How? You don't have your-' he abruptly stopped as he saw my face falling; I dropped his hands and got up.

'I'm going to get a drink,' I said lamely, leaving everyone to stare at me as I left.

Heading into the kitchen, I closed the door, only to yell out in fright as I saw Nathaniel reading at the kitchen counter. 'Dear God you scared me,' I said, breathing heavily. 'You could have warned me.'

Not looking up he quipped, 'I'm here, Tara.'

Rolling my eyes, I went towards him and sat down, 'Why are you in here alone? It's warmer in the living room.'

'I'm perfectly fine reading here,' he said, looking down at his book, when I realised that there was a piece of white paper underneath it.

'What's that?' I pointed, but he snatched it away from me.

'None of your business,' he snapped. 'Just leave me alone alright?'

'What's wrong?'

'Forget, it doesn't concern you anymore.'

'What do you mean "anymore"?' Annoyed, I banged my fist on the counter. 'Why are people keeping secrets from me? Damn it, I'm your sister, tell me what's wrong!'

'No one can find Maynard!' he yelled, grabbing the piece of paper and shoving it under my face. I read the letter from a secret informant in Europe and felt both sad and annoyed. They explained that Maynard had vanished from the face of the planet. 'Since you told me that the Ancient said he hadn't turned into a god I assumed that he would surface at his old haunt but he hasn't. Jeff and Amjee, no one has seen or heard of him and that makes me anxious.'

I must admit, it was making me anxious as well, but as Nathaniel spitefully said, it wasn't my concern anymore. Handing him the letter I put my hand on his shoulder but he shrugged it off.

'Don't,' he snapped. 'Look, you and the others have a nice Christmas alright, just pretend everything is going fine and let the rest of us deal with this.' He made a move to leave. 'I have to get back to the T.A.T.'

'But Nathaniel, this is meant to be a happy time for family. It's Christmas Eve!'

'Yeah? But the thing is Tara, we don't have a family anymore.'

His words stung, but I was determined to try and find something positive in all the loss we had gone through. 'If you took the time to notice, you'd see that Hannah has a bit of a crush on you. As it happens, you are too cooped up in your own little world to care about anyone else but yourself.' Getting myself a drink I left Nathaniel to his thoughts and bumped into Henry in the hallway.

'Hey,' I began, but he didn't smile when he saw me. My stomach dropped to the floor, making me feel instantly sick. By the look of his face, this didn't look good.

'I think I have to tell you this now. I didn't want to say anything because I want you to have a wonderful Christmas. So,' he rubbed the back of his neck, expelling air and I saw this was difficult for him to tell me his worries. 'I'm sorry I'm telling you this on Christmas Eve, but I have to.'

We went and sat on the bottom of the stairs and I let him continue.

'When I went into the other plane, I went in search for your mother. Gabrielle, strangely enough, found me and I've got to say, you look so much like her, it's uncanny. I mean both your wings are black, your eyes, ears and your smile-.'

'Henry, I don't have wings anymore,' I said sadly, 'what did she tell you?'

'She gave me the disc for starters but also she told me that the Ancients don't want you or Saskia to be a Siren, you especially.'

'But why?'

'The Ancients fear the Sirens; they have done for a long time. Your mother said that if you were to be a Siren it would undermine the Ancients. Plus she also said that the Ancients didn't think they could trust you to keep the Golden Rule about showing magic to humans. Ergo-'

'We had to be human again. Damn these Ancients are annoying. I didn't mean to break the Golden Rule; I was trying to stop Rhea.' I said, and then pounded the stair with my fist. 'It was kill or be killed for Rhea. There was no other way.'

Henry smiled, his eyes twinkling with pride, 'Your mother said you weren't a killer, not of the innocent. By the sounds of it, you just beat the crap out of her.'

'Ha!' I shouted, making him jump. 'Rhea wasn't an innocent. She killed my Dad. There wasn't even a body to bury.' Nathaniel and I had had a funeral of my father several weeks ago. We placed a plaque in the T.A.T. in remembrance of his service and dedication to magic. Amjee and Jeff even said a few words in respect of him and my mother and their duty for the T.A.T. And no matter how many times people told me that my father was a hero, that he worked tirelessly to keep Nathaniel and me from harm, I only thought of Rhea and what she had done to him.

But Henry shook his head. 'Rhea is an innocent in all this. She's a pawn on a huge chess board.'

'Are we pawns?' I asked him, fearing his answer. If Rhea is a pawn in all of this, then surely so are we, which made us dispensable.

Seeing the pain on my face, Henry placed his hands on my shoulders and gently pulled me towards him, 'I'd like to think of us as Knights.'

'Knights without swords or shields,' I told him, biting my bottom lip. 'Maynard is still alive and we can't do anything about it.'

'I think Maynard is more involved with this than we initially believed,' Henry said with bitterness in his voice. 'Gabrielle told me the night that Rhea changed into a Siren, a new Ancient appeared.' He paused then placed his hands on my shoulders. 'I'm hoping that Maynard isn't an Ancient-.'

I vigorously shook my head. 'No, he wouldn't be. The Ancient I met would have told me.'

Henry shrugged, he didn't seem so sure. 'But we can do something about us,' he said, withdrawing a little to look into my eyes. 'Nathaniel's power, it isn't forever. If you already have myth blood in you, it's only nullified, it isn't gone forever. That's something she learnt from the other plane.'

Frowning in confusion I couldn't get my head around it. As far as I was concerned the Ancients had their own laws and rules that had to be adhered to. 'But, I don't get it. The Ancients word is law.'

'He's the law of the mythical plane, but not this one. Here we have our own laws that the Ancients must hold fast.'

Shaking my head from perplexity, Henry laughed and kissed me. 'Tara, the Ancients created myths from humans and their ideas. They took humans and turned them into myths. Myths are based on us. If we got enough people to create a whole new belief system, the Ancients would create it for us. That's how it all works.'

'So we can all become myths again,' I stated, but Henry shook his head.

'No, not like we used to. We need help from the Fates- the only problem, is that they live in the Underworld.'

'Is that our next task then? To get to the Fates?' Staring into his eyes Henry brushed my cheek.

'Only if you want to. No one is going to force this on us, we are going to choose this ourselves,' he said softly.

Pausing to think, I smiled. 'Let's have a normal life first; let Macie see more of her family. Try and sort things out with the house and our lives before we go gallivanting off into the Underworld.'

'I think, that's a very good idea,' he laughed, taking my hand and leading me back into the living room where everyone was happy, laughing and normal, but I stopped.

'I'm just going to my room, I'll be back in a minute,' I told him, having a fleeting thought and heading upstairs into my en suite. I took a deep breath and lifted up my top to look at my back in the mirror. The lines of the tattoo of the black angel-wings had become darker since the last time I saw them only a week ago. Staring at them in the mirror, I delighted in my reflection. My eyes were the slightest shade of the crystal blue and my ears looked a little pointier. Gazing at my back, I smiled.

The end...for now.

ABOUT THE AUTHOR

A E Kirk is a writer of sorts. Mostly she writes fantasy or science-fiction for young adults as well as horror. After travelling most of Asia in 2012, Abi now lives in Devon, UK and is constantly inspired by the views of the sloping idyllic landscapes around her.